# DEAD OF WINTER

**Also by Sherry Knowlton**

*DEAD of SPRING*
*DEAD of SUMMER*
*DEAD of AUTUMN*

## Praise for Sherry Knowlton's
### *DEAD of WINTER*

"With riveting suspense and vivid details, *Dead of Winter* by Sherry Knowlton brings the towns and forests of Southcentral Pennsylvania to vivid life as cultures and beliefs clash in a searing tale of murder, love, and communal fear. From flying drones to police investigations and legal wrangling, *Dead of Winter* will keep you guessing and glued raptly to your reading chair."

—*Gayle Lynds,* New York Times *best-selling author of* The Assassins

"Sherry Knowlton brilliantly weaves contemporary issues into a riveting mystery that will stick with you long after the last page is turned. In *Dead of Winter*, the reader can sense a fuse has been lit and is burning closer to a rural Pennsylvania town that is on the brink after a series of deaths appear to lead back to the normally tranquil setting. While addressing xenophobia, racism, and America's complicated history, *Dead of Winter* is the novel we need and the story we want."

—*J. J. Hensley, author of* Bolt Action Remedy *and* Record Scratch

"In *Dead of Winter*, Sherry Knowlton examines the explosive combination of ignorance and fear that results in hate and violence.

Knowlton uses her familiarity with both small town Southcentral Pennsylvania and the wilds of Africa to good advantage in her fourth Alexa Williams novel. Her use of drone technology to set up the discovery of the crime in which Alexa will find herself caught up is clever.

Knowlton skillfully weaves together two story lines. One involves the flight north of two Virginia slaves in the years leading up to the Civil War, with Pennsylvania representing the land of freedom and equality. One involves current-day racial tensions, where the same ground is the site of racially motivated intimidation tactics and terroristic threats.

A thought-provoking novel dealing with issues that are as important now as they were at the time of the Underground Railroad."

—*Matty Dalrymple, author of the* Lizzy Ballard Thrillers *and the* Ann Kinnear Suspense Novels and Shorts

"Ms. Knowlton is a fine writer, who writes beautiful prose as good as that of much of our finest fiction. . . . The book is an intriguing, suspenseful story which grabs the attention of the reader from the very first page . . . Alexa Williams again proves a formidable heroine in this suspenseful tale of international corruption and hatred."

—*Alma Bond,* Midwest Book Review

"An easy read that hooked me right away and I couldn't wait to finish it. There were plenty of twists and turns, including a former-now-current love interest, a relocated Middle Eastern family that naturally becomes implicated in the killings and Alexa's adjustment to returning to Carlisle after a successful career in NYC. Plenty of opportunity for guessing and nice surprises at the end. . . . this was one of the two best books I've read this year. Very enjoyable if you like Crime/Murder/Thrillers and an author worth following."

—*Reader Stan D., Goodreads*

### Praise for earlier books in the Alexa Williams suspense series

*DEAD of SPRING*

"A lawyer who yearns for the quiet life proves a magnet for murder." . . . in a "mystery/thriller/romance with a complex heroine."

—*Kirkus Reviews*

*DEAD of SUMMER*

"Alexa Williams is a sassy, alpha-female heroine. The plot is knotty, lots of will-she or won't-she, all woven into an intense battle of wits that heats up every page. While reading, I could almost see the credits rolling for the movie."

—*Steve Berry,* New York Times *and #1 international bestselling author*

*DEAD of AUTUMN*

"Sherry Knowlton's *Dead of Autumn* features a dead body harkening back to the crimes of an earlier era—there are conventions in genre writing that fans appreciate."

—*Library Journal*

# DEAD
## OF WINTER

**SHERRY KNOWLTON**

## MILFORD
## HOUSE

an imprint of Sunbury Press, Inc.
Mechanicsburg, PA USA

MILFORD
HOUSE

an imprint of Sunbury Press, Inc.
Mechanicsburg, PA USA

For information about special discounts for bulk purchases, please contact Sunbury Press Orders Dept. at (855) 338-8359 or orders@sunburypress.com.

To request one of our authors for speaking engagements or book signings, please contact Sunbury Press Publicity Dept. at publicity@sunburypress.com.

ISBN: 978-1-62006-071-1 (Trade paperback)

Library of Congress Control Number: 2018956862

FIRST MILFORD HOUSE PRESS EDITION: February 2019

Product of the United States of America
0 1 1 2 3 5 8 13 21 34 55

Set in Bookman Old Style
Designed by Crystal Devine
Cover by Riaan Wilmans
Edited by Jennifer Cappello

*Continue the Enlightenment!*

*Do not look for my heart anymore; the beasts have eaten it.*
—Charles Baudelaire, "Causerie," *Flowers of Evil*

*An eye for an eye leaves the whole world blind.*
—Attributed to M. K. Gandhi

*For the Knowlton/Kuehn clan;*
*thanks for being both family and wonderful friends.*

# CHAPTER ONE

AT FIRST, SHE smiled, thinking the splash of red was a stand of sumac in its rusty fall glory. Then, Alexa spotted the dark shape in the center of the crimson splotch, and her smile faded. She jumped from her seat on the couch. With ragged breath, she turned to ask, "Did you guys see that?" When she glanced back to the television, the image was gone.

"Umm, not really. I'm helping Scotty here fix the Enterprise." Reese glanced up from the small drone he was holding.

"Say what?" Tyrell mumbled. Typical of him to go all-in on this new drone just like he did with each new cause. Sometimes his obsessions drove Alexa crazy.

"No joke. Look at this video." Alexa dove forward, scattering papers as she searched her coffee table for the remote. She gritted her teeth. Get two grown men together and suddenly they start to act like teenagers. "We came back here for lunch so we could watch the video from this morning."

Attaching a miniature camera to the underside of the quad-copter in Reese's hand, Tyrell shrugged. "We got distracted. Had to fix the camera. No wonder it came loose. You were crashing the Land Rover through field and stream like a Mad Max movie." He patted the side of the drone, as if it could feel his encouragement.

"You said off the beaten track," Alexa muttered as she ran a hand over the seat of the couch, still searching.

"That was tame compared to northern Kenya." With a flourish, Reese placed the drone onto the table, camera attached. Alexa felt her heart skip a beat as she watched his strong, tan hands cradle the delicate drone.

1

"Found it." Tyrell lifted the remote from the arm of the couch and waved it at Alexa.

"Yes." She plopped onto the couch, tapping her foot.

Tyrell pointed the remote at the TV. "Just chill a sec. How far back?"

"Maybe three minutes? A field—right past an old farmhouse."

Tyrell's short dreadlocks bobbed as he saluted with the device. "You got it, Counselor."

Alexa felt tension build in the pit of her stomach. A voice in her head kept saying: It can't be. It can't be.

"Far enough?" Tyrell hit the play button.

The roof of an old farmhouse rolled onto the screen. "I think this is it." The picture blurred for a moment as the tin roof reflected scattered beams of sunlight. The edge of a silo slid into view.

"Now, watch as it flies over this field," she commanded. As if sensing her distress, Scout, Alexa's English mastiff, shuffled over and lay on her feet. Holding her breath, his mistress scowled as the scene zoomed out and everything on the screen shrank.

Tyrell commented. "I remember this. I caught sight of that silo and sent the drone up. A chance to play around with a higher altitude."

"Now. Look, now!" Alexa leaned forward to study the field that flowed into view.

"What the—? Pause it," Reese cried.

"Damn. I wish we had a closer shot." Tyrell's voice was subdued, his eyes glued to the image frozen on the monitor.

Alexa rose from her chair and strode to the TV for a closer look. The camera had captured a desolate field ringed by weathered fence posts and a thicket of dying weeds. The center section of the field was almost bare. Alexa's eyes went to the splash of red in the far end of the field. With the video stilled, it was clear that this was no stand of sumac. Dark crimson splattered the ground and a tall clump of weeds. Dead center, framed in a shaft of morning sunlight, lay a crumpled form.

"A deer?" Tyrell asked in a hopeful voice.

"Possible. Someone hunting out of season." Reese's doubtful tone belied his words.

Returning to her seat, Alexa nodded her head. "Could be a deer."

She paused to take in the somber looks on her companions' faces. "Yeah," she sighed. "It looks a lot like a body." Scout whined at her bleak tone and rested his head on Alexa's knee. Alexa's stomach fluttered. She couldn't believe she might have found another dead body. This had to be a deer or some other animal. Maybe a cow?

Tyrell jumped up and strode toward the phone. "I'll call 911."

"Wait." Alexa held up her hand. "Do either of you remember where this farmhouse was? We might have filmed this segment when we followed that long, bumpy lane; a few miles after we left Mt. Holly. But it could have been on that other road, closer to the mountain."

"Do you know how to get to both spots?" Reese asked. "I lost track of where we were. We stopped, what, five times to send the drone up?"

"Only four," Tyrell interjected, hand on the phone.

"Right now, I wouldn't know exactly where to send the police."

Reese snapped his fingers. "Wait, doesn't the drone have GPS?"

"Yeah, but I didn't get to that chapter in the instruction manual yet. I haven't figured out all the different functions." Tyrell's voice tightened. "I'm no fan of cops, but shouldn't we call them? Like, now?"

Alexa shook her head. "We don't even know that it's a person. What if it's just a dead animal? First, let's try to figure out which farm this was."

"But what if that is really a person and he's still alive?"

Alexa and Reese exchanged a quick glance before he replied. "I'm pretty sure whoever, whatever is dead. That's an awful lot of blood. But the drone was so high on this shot, the detail sucks. I agree with Alexa. We should try to pin down where we took this part of the video."

Alexa added, "Then drive there and check this out ourselves. That way, we can be sure of what we're seeing and tell the police the exact location. I could retrace our steps to where we stopped each time we sent the drone up." Alexa continued to fidget. She flashed to the other bodies she'd found in the past. Elizabeth Nelson in the woods. Cecily Townes in her home. The senator who'd crashed to his death in the Capitol Rotunda. Death seemed to seek her out.

Reese put a steadying hand on her arm. "Alexa, your instinct is always to jump right in. What if the people who did this are still around? Even if it is an animal and not a human corpse, poachers can be dangerous."

Alexa shook her head, frustrated by the men's hesitation. "We can check the video again, but I didn't see any people around. And we took that a few hours ago. What's the chance they'd still be there now?" She paused. "Look, the last thing I want to do is involve the cops and find out it's not a body at all." She remembered how foolish she'd felt a few years back when she'd reported some guys for harassment. Turned out they were students working on a college project. She wasn't anxious for a repeat of that embarrassing episode. She might develop a reputation around the courthouse as the attorney who cried wolf.

Running a hand through his hair, Reese gave Alexa a long look. With a wry smile, he said, "You're right. Let's see what we're dealing with before we call the police."

Tyrell shrugged his shoulders. "I defer to the experts. Reese, you've had police training, right? Girl, you're an attorney. You've been in situations like this before." With a sigh, he trudged to the couch and hit rewind.

Stunned by Tyrell's words, Alexa wondered what wrong turn her life had taken to qualify her as an expert in dealing with dead bodies.

Less than a half hour later, Alexa gripped the steering wheel tightly as her old Land Rover Defender barreled down the road. The bubble of anxiety in her chest felt like it might explode.

This was supposed to have been a fun, carefree day. Her old love, Reese, had been back from Africa for a few months, and she wanted him to meet her friend, Tyrell. That was it. Flying a drone and spending a few hours together. Now they were rocketing across the valley to check out—what? A corpse? She really didn't want this to be another dead body. The odds were against that, right?

She spied a road ahead to the left. "The terrain's pretty flat here. I think this might be it."

"Could be." Reese's tone was encouraging.

She downshifted and turned into a narrow dirt lane. "Let's try it." They drove past two ranch homes, both with pickups in the driveways. A green ATV sat in the first yard, a tattered For Sale sign on the windshield. The second yard featured a life-size Styrofoam deer, its body peppered with holes.

Reese gestured toward the deer. "Those things are designed for archery practice. Check out how big chunks of foam are missing. Looks like someone got drunk and decided to use a rifle instead. The type of jerk we used to haul in for hunting violations."

Alexa noted the word "we" and wondered if Reese missed his days as a state park ranger. When he decided to leave for Africa, his life had moved away from the law enforcement aspect of that job for a focus on animal conservation. He'd been a good ranger but was passionate about wild animals. The conservation project he worked for now focused on saving the big cats of Africa.

They left the ranch homes behind in a cloud of dust. But a few minutes later, Alexa had to slow the Rover as it lurched back and forth. The unpaved road was now rutted with bumps and potholes. Acres of bleak fields, their crops long since gone to harvest, stretched for miles on both sides of the lane.

Alexa glanced at Tyrell in the rearview mirror. He was gripping the seat, his eyes glued to the passing scene. With a scowl he said, "Now all we have to do is find the spot where we stopped."

Reese added, "And figure out how to follow the drone's path. We stood along the main road while you flew the quad-copter all over the place. I'm not sure I actually saw the farmhouse."

Alexa noticed a faint dirt track on the left and screeched to an abrupt stop. "I remember this place." She rolled down the window and pointed a short distance down the track. A rickety gate sagged wide open. "Didn't we park here?"

Reese opened the door and unfolded his lanky body from the SUV. He walked a few feet, peered at some scuffmarks in the dirt, then scanned the area. "Yeah. I remember that fenced-in field and the gate." He pointed to the northwest. "Tyrell, you sent the drone out that way."

"I guess." Tyrell cast a bewildered-looking glance out the window as Reese climbed back in the car. "All these fields look the same to me. But you're just like that dude Leo plays in the movie, the one about the trapper in the wilderness. The Oscar one. If you say we were here, we were here."

Alexa gave a half-hearted laugh and squinted at Reese, trying to ignore the queasiness in her stomach. "OK, trapper dude. Should we keep driving and look for a farm on the left? This morning we headed straight back to the main road after we stopped here. Ahead is virgin territory."

"Makes sense. We should be able to spot the silo even if it's set back in." Reese nodded, drumming his fingers on one knee.

Keeping the speed low, Alexa moved forward. They hadn't passed another vehicle or seen any signs of life since those first two houses. As they searched for evidence of a farm, Tyrell's uneven breathing rose above the crunch of gravel in an unsettling syncopation. Alexa swept her eyes in a rhythmic pattern to the left and back to the road as she drove.

After several minutes, Reese shifted in his seat and asked, "How far can it be? There's a limit on the distance the drone can fly, right?"

"What's that over there?" Tyrell interrupted.

"An old windmill. It could mean we're close." Reese leaned forward to peer through the windshield.

As she looked for the windmill, Alexa let her attention stray from the road, and the Land Rover's front tire drifted into the field on the right. A flock of starlings, their iridescent coats gleaming blue-black, shot up from the field and flew across the car's path. Startled, Alexa gasped and slammed on the brakes.

"Whoa." Alexa put a hand over her pounding heart. "I'll pay attention to the road. You two look for the farmhouse."

"This could be it." Reese's tone was clipped as he pointed to a mailbox just up the road. Beyond it, a red silo rose above a cluster of trees, their withered leaves a pallid yellow. Alexa recognized this Reese from when they'd first met during the investigation of a homicide on state forest land. Focused. Direct.

"You were right, trapper man," Tyrell muttered when they reached the gravel lane. Surprised that her usually smooth and confident friend seemed so shaken, Alexa worried if he was going to fall apart on them.

"This place has seen better days." With a melancholy smile, Alexa gestured toward a large galvanized steel box, tilted at a right angle to the post. She wondered about the farmer who'd taken the time to paint the now-faded mailbox green, attaching wheels and a wooden cab to suggest a tractor.

"Looks like it's been abandoned for years," Reese agreed. "Go slow. The video didn't show anyone in the area. But let's be cautious."

"Given my dislike for law enforcement, this day's going down in history. Dudes, I'm all for calling the cops. Now." Tyrell glanced at his phone. "I've got reception; four bars."

"Let's just make sure this is the place," Alexa said as she turned down the lane.

"What? There's the house, the silo, the barn." Tyrell pointed ahead.

"Yeah. But all these old farms have houses, silos, and barns. We're here. Let's be absolutely sure before we call this in."

When they neared the parking area in front of the ramshackle farmhouse, Reese said, "Let's stop here. Can you turn around before we go investigate?"

Alexa was surprised how quickly Reese had slipped back into law-enforcement mode. He hadn't been a park ranger for almost two years. She made a U-turn in a field thick with weeds and parked the Land Rover in the middle of the lane, facing toward the main road. Last out of the vehicle, she shivered as she joined Reese and Tyrell, who were studying the house.

"Looks deserted," Alexa whispered.

"Yeah, but let's take it slow," Reese replied, his voice pitched low.

Tyrell hissed, "All this whispering is creeping me out. I'm a social worker, not a cop. What if the killer's still around?"

"The Girl Scouts taught me to Be Prepared," Alexa muttered.

"So, you have a gun. Good."

Alexa shook her head.

Tyrell looked at Reese, who opened his empty hands.

At Tyrell's look of dismay, Alexa whispered, "On RESIST business, you go into some of the roughest districts of Mumbai, Bangkok, and who knows where. This can't be any scarier than that."

Reese raised an eyebrow. "Proceed? Or call it in?"

Tyrell sighed. "Proceed."

"Maybe someone should stay with the car?" Alexa looked at Tyrell.

"Not me." He shook his head.

"Then let's do this." Alexa squared her shoulders and walked toward the house. White paint curled in uneven strips from the wood siding. The front door hung outward on one hinge, and glass pooled beneath a gaping front window on the weathered front porch.

As they approached the house, Reese motioned for a stop. Alert to any sounds of human activity, Alexa heard only the rustle of the wind through the leafless branches of a lilac bush and the creak of a loose shutter on an upper window.

"Let me take a quick look in the house. It seems empty. No vehicles, although this driveway has been used recently." Reese pointed to overlapping tire tracks in the dust. "Can you two check the barn?"

"OK." Alexa swallowed hard. "I think the body—what we think is a body—is out past the silo." She grabbed Tyrell's arm and steered him toward the larger structure.

The decaying barn sat on a limestone foundation. A faint trace of red clung to a few boards, but years of sun, rain, and snow had stripped most to a weathered gray. As they made their way up a grassy incline toward the huge double doors, Alexa said, "I'm surprised someone hasn't torn this baby down and sold off the wood for furniture or something. Barn wood décor is all the rage these days."

"We might run into a murderer any minute, and you're talking interior design?" Tyrell flashed a strained smile.

"They used better paint on the silo than the barn. Looks strange that it's still bright red, and all this has faded to gray. Growing up, I loved to play in my grandmother's barn." Alexa continued to babble as they approached the entrance. The tall door on the left stood ajar. She stopped a few feet short of the opening. Beyond the door was inky darkness.

Tyrell's voice jarred Alexa from her thoughts. "Why don't I go in and you stay outside?"

"Let's just check it out from here first." The pair sidled up to the doorway together. Alexa stood on the threshold, waiting for her eyes to adjust to the gloom. She could sense Tyrell just behind, peering over her head into the interior. Murky daylight streamed into the dilapidated structure through a hole in the roof. The far wall was missing several boards in a random pattern. Several disintegrating bales of hay moldered in one corner.

Alexa wrinkled her nose at the dank, musty odor—a far cry from the pleasant smell of drying hay that she associated with her grandmother's barn. "Look." Alexa pointed to a yawning black hole a few feet into the barn. "The floor's shot to hell. We don't want to fall through and break a leg. Or worse."

"Ain't no one home here. Even the animals are long gone." Tyrell sniffed in disdain and turned away from the door. With a nod of agreement, Alexa took one last glance and followed him down the slope.

Reese emerged from the back of the house just as they reached level ground. "Anything?" he asked.

"It's been ages since anyone's used that barn. What about the house?"

"There's been some activity in the kitchen. Empty soda cans and dried mud on the floor. I stayed out of that room. The intruders used a back door that leads straight into the kitchen. There are clumps of dirt on the steps and the back porch. The rest of the place looks deserted."

"We're alone here now, right?" Alexa sighed in reluctance. "It's safe to search for that field?"

"Only way to find out if we're at the right place." Reese touched her shoulder.

"In for a penny, in for a pound, as my mama says," Tyrell said.

Three abreast, the friends trudged down a dirt track that edged past the towering crimson silo. The morning's bright sunshine had given way to roiling black clouds. As they walked in silence, Alexa couldn't shake a sense of impending doom about what they might find ahead. When they moved beyond the shelter of the farm buildings, she zipped up her jacket to ward off the sudden chill. Her lightweight down was no match for the unseasonable bite of the late-October wind.

Without exchanging a word, Reese and Tyrell slowed their pace as the track narrowed. A dense thicket of brambles and bare-limbed bushes, some higher than their heads, lined both sides of the passage. To Alexa, who had fallen behind, the narrow pathway felt like a living, breathing tunnel as it writhed and shuddered with each gust of wind. She jumped and bit back a scream when a coil of blackberry bush grabbed her sleeve. Using a glove from her pocket, she ripped the branch from her jacket. Despite her caution, a thorn pricked her finger. Alexa dabbed at the spurt of bright red blood with the glove, then looked up. Reese and Tyrell had stopped a few feet ahead. Her heart lurched into overdrive, pounding against her chest.

When Alexa neared, Reese held out his hand in the motion that movie marines use to indicate: Go slow. She tiptoed the last yard until she drew even with the two men, and then she stopped to study the scene before them.

With a final abrupt turn, the serpentine track spilled into acres of open fields. Rows of sheared stalks from a late-summer corn harvest climbed up a slope to the left. In the half-light of the gathering storm, the short, jagged leavings glinted like shards of smoked glass.

Ahead lay what could have been an animal pasture at one point. The fence on the near side had collapsed. On the other three, strands of rusty barbed wire stretched between tall wooden posts.

Straining to see through the gloom, Alexa wondered why the farmer had cut the posts so high. Then she caught the first flicker of movement. The next. And the next.

Perched on top of each weathered post sat a huge turkey vulture, the flock's eyes riveted on the center of the field. The dark birds were enormous—more than two feet tall—their scaly, bald heads too small for the bulk of their feathered bodies. The grotesque red color of their crowns and necks made Alexa think of blood. There had been so much blood in the video. She stuffed her throbbing hand into her jacket pocket as her heart sank.

"I think we're in the right place," she said.

Reese whispered, "Yeah. With the wind this direction, the vultures don't know we're here. But they're on alert."

Tyrell rose onto the balls of his feet to peer into the field. "Can you see in there?"

"No, the weeds are too high," Alexa replied. "We have to move closer."

"We need to be sure what we're dealing with. It could be a large animal."

"Well, you usually see those ugly mothers tearing apart dead groundhogs on the road. With the size of this crowd, word musta gone out that they hit the frigging jackpot." Tyrell bit his lip.

"We don't all have to walk over there." Reese shot Alexa and Tyrell a questioning look.

"Nah. We've come this far." Tyrell shrugged.

"Agree." Alexa nodded. She didn't want to see what was ahead but felt she had no choice. She'd pushed for them to come here. She was obliged to see it through.

As the three crept toward the fenced-in area, the vultures rose as one from their perches in a loud tumult of flapping feathers. The ungainly birds acquired increasing grace as they flew higher, spread their wings, and soared upward toward the thermal currents.

Just beyond the fallen length of fence, the pasture had been trampled to dirt; only a few tufts of vegetation remained in the near section of the field. But the far end was ankle-deep in brownish grass. Beyond, a swath of taller, dying weeds rustled in the wind.

Glancing around, Alexa checked to make sure they were still alone. Her heart pounded, and her breath came in gasps. Reese took her hand as they proceeded across the open area toward the figure lying on the grass.

"Oh, shit, shit, shit, shit, shit," Tyrell moaned as they approached the body.

Alexa stumbled and clutched Reese's hand tight as she took in the bloody corpse before them. The slight young man's body lay spread-eagled on the ground, his torso and thighs riddled by bullets. Splashes of gray camouflage pattern were visible on his lower arms and legs, but his jacket and pants had turned reddish brown and stiff with dried blood. A tight black skullcap and more dried blood covered most of his head and face, but Alexa could see one brown eye staring wide open. Then, it hit her. The second eye was missing. She jerked her gaze away from his face, only to shudder as she caught sight of his hands.

"Oh my God," she breathed, gorge rising.

"The vultures already started on the body." Reese shook his head. "I've seen hundreds of lion and leopard kills in Africa. And I've seen dead people on the ranger job. But damn, this is something else." His expression was bleak.

Alexa pulled the collar of her jacket up to cover her nose. She was still fighting nausea, made harder by the rank, coppery smell that rose from the body.

Between shallow breaths, Tyrell spoke in a choked voice. "This guy is a brother. The middle of a field in east bumfuck PA is a mighty strange place to find a dead brother. Looks like he pissed someone off real good."

"I hoped that we were letting our imaginations run away. That we'd all have a good laugh when we found a pile of red-stained rags or something." As Alexa spoke, she took in the clump of tall weeds about three feet behind the body. Dried blood splattered the plants at least three feet from the ground. "He was standing when he was shot."

Tyrell gestured toward the body. "Look at all those bullet holes. Could have been more than one person shooting."

"Like an execution." Alexa gulped, her voice rising toward hysteria. "What's going on here?"

Reese nodded. "It looks like a firing squad from one of those old movies. Unless the killers took it with them, this guy faced death without a blindfold. And look at the powder burns around the missing eye. That looks like a very close shot, possibly post-mortem."

Alexa forced another quick glance at his eye. "Post-mortem. You mean someone shot out his eye after he was dead?"

"Maybe. My training on things like gunshot wounds is pretty limited." Reese's expression was sober.

"Damn. What kind of sicko would shoot a guy after he was dead?"

"Or do any of this?" Alexa put a hand over her mouth, still fighting the smell.

Reese skirted the body and walked a few feet to the left. He drew a faded blue bandanna from his coat pocket and wrapped it around his hand before he bent to pick up a piece of white cardboard. It reminded Alexa of the poster board that her niece and nephew used for school projects. Scrawled across the front in a deep slash of black were some symbols.

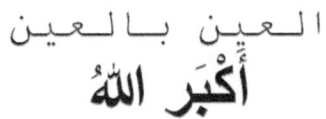

Tyrell whistled. "That could be Hindi, but it doesn't look quite like the signs in India."

"Clearly not one of the Romance languages. Maybe Thai? Arabic?" Alexa peered at the strange letters but stepped no closer.

"I'm betting Arabic. They included a handy translation." Reese's expression tightened as he turned the cardboard to show the back.

## An Eye for an Eye
# ALLAHU AKBAR

Alexa recoiled and took a step backward. Her entire body turned to ice. She darted a frantic look at Reese and Tyrell. Both men wore expressions of pure shock. A gust of wind whipped across the open field and snatched away Alexa's words as she moaned, "What the hell have we gotten into?"

Raising her head to the ominous black clouds scudding across the sky, Alexa reeled when she spotted the flock of vultures high above. Circling. Waiting.

# CHAPTER TWO

WHEN THE STATE police SUV turned down the farm lane, Alexa slid out of the Land Rover and stopped short. Already distraught from the encounter with that body in the field, her eyes teared as she saw Pennsylvania State Police logo on the SUV. Her last relationship had been with a state trooper, John Taylor, who had died last spring. Recovering her composure, Alexa walked toward the approaching vehicle.

Tyrell hesitated, then followed at a slower pace. A solo trooper switched off the siren and lights and eased out of the SUV, gun drawn. Alexa could hear additional sirens in the distance as she held her hands in front of her, palms forward.

"We're responding to a call about a dead body?" The driver spoke, still standing behind the car door. "Can you identify yourselves? We were told that three people had located a dead man?"

"We made the call. I'm Alexa Williams. I'm a local attorney. This is Tyrell Jenkins; he works with an advocacy organization called RESIST, Resolve to Stop Illegal Sex Trafficking. Our friend, Reese Michaels, stayed with the body." Alexa let her hands drift back to her sides.

"Yeah," Tyrell took a step forward. "He's trying to keep the vultures away." Alexa turned to take a quick look toward the field where Reese had remained with the dead man. They shouldn't have left him alone out there, but Reese had insisted. He was always the stand-up guy; the responsible one; the man who'd always take care of her. Until he stopped and left for Africa.

Still gazing toward the field, Alexa imagined she saw black specks circling against the gray sky. She jerked her attention back to the state trooper at his sharp command.

"Stop!" The policeman extended his hand like a crossing guard halting traffic. "Sir, I'd like you to stop right there. As soon as another trooper arrives, you can lead us to this body."

Tyrell halted abruptly but muttered under his breath, "It's always the black guy."

Alexa touched his elbow and whispered, "Cool it. For all this guy knows, we could be mass murderers intent on ambushing a bunch of cops."

"What's that about cops?" The uniformed trooper cast a suspicious look at Alexa then glanced over his shoulder as the wail of a siren neared.

She breathed a sigh of thanks when a second state police vehicle barreled down the farm lane and skidded to a stop behind the first SUV. Another solo trooper emerged from the car and called to his colleague, "What's the status here, Martin?"

"These two called in the report. They say the body of an unidentified male is in a field on the far side of that house. Another guy from their group is there with the body."

The new trooper took charge as he walked to face Alexa and Tyrell. "I'm Trooper Barnes. You've met Trooper Martin. We'd like to make sure you're not armed. Could you remove the sweatshirt, sir?"

Tyrell snorted. "Man, we the good guys in this story."

"I apologize, Mr. . . . ?"

"Jenkins, Tyrell Jenkins."

While Barnes played nice, Trooper Martin circled closer to the group. Although he'd holstered his weapon, he kept a hand at his waist. Tyrell continued, "Alexa and I already gave our names to the first trooper—the one who held a gun on us until you arrived." The last few words were muffled as Tyrell peeled off his sweatshirt and raised his hands.

Still standing a few paces away, Trooper Martin reported, "Ms. Williams says she's a lawyer and Mr. Jenkins is a social worker or something."

"A lawyer, huh? I guess we better go by the book on this one." Trooper Barnes flashed a brief smile. "I'm going to pat you down lightly, sir. Just a precaution." As he reached toward Tyrell, he stopped and looked at Alexa. "Alexa . . . Williams? Weren't you engaged to John Taylor?"

As always, at the mention of John's name, Alexa felt a pang of guilt. "We were never officially engaged, but yes, John and I were together before his death."

Barnes stepped back from Tyrell and gave a brief wave to Martin. "We're OK here. I didn't make the connection when I first heard Ms. Williams' name." He turned back to Alexa. "I believe I spoke to you at John's funeral, but that was a rough day. He was a good man and a fine trooper. I'm sorry for your loss."

Alexa forced a smile. "Thank you. I've been trying to move on with my life." She felt like a fraud whenever she accepted condolences on her old boyfriend's death. Few people knew that the relationship was floundering when John had been killed in the line of duty. Secretly, she'd concluded that she and John had never really had a chance because she was still pining for Reese.

The park ranger had been her savior when she'd killed a man, a fundamentalist minister, in self-defense. But, burdened by the trauma of taking a life, she'd turned inward and pushed Reese away. When he got a job offer on a conservation project, he'd returned to Africa—a place he loved. Only after he was gone did Alexa realize how much she loved him. That regret and yearning for Reese had doomed her attempt at a relationship with John.

To Alexa's relief, the whoop, whoop of an ambulance pulling in behind the police vehicles interrupted the conversation. A line of flashing blue lights and a fire truck followed a short distance behind.

Tyrell had slipped his sweatshirt back on during the exchange between Alexa and the now-friendly trooper. He looked at the ambulance and shook his head. "You ain't gonna need no ambulance for that brother out there in the field. The ride he's on is the permanent kind." In the presence of strangers, Tyrell had regained some of his lost bravado.

Trooper Barnes said, "Why don't you walk us out there? Then, we'll need to interview each of you about how you came to find the deceased." He called to Martin, who had walked a few paces toward the arriving vehicles. "Tell the fire police to stay out there. Maybe the blue lighters can set up a roadblock at the end of the drive. Doesn't look like that main road gets much traffic, if any. But the press or some lookie-loos could show up. They need to keep everyone out by the main road until we scope out the situation."

Squaring her shoulders, Alexa bit back her reluctance and turned to lead the trooper out to the pasture. Tyrell brought up the rear. Alexa set a slow pace as she pushed against the driving wind and a deep dread of revisiting the young man's bullet-ravaged body. She knew she'd be having nightmares for months over this. Why did she think she had to solve all the world's problems? Why hadn't she just agreed to calling the police in the first place?

Four hours later, Alexa, Reese, and Tyrell returned to Alexa's cabin. When Alexa opened the front door, Scout rushed past and headed for the trees, oblivious to the falling rain. She punched in the code to disarm the security system while Reese headed to the fridge.

"Beer?" he handed a bottle to Tyrell and took one for himself.

"I was thinking hot chocolate. I'm cold," Alexa said as she sailed into the kitchen, snickering at the disdain written all over the men's faces. "OK then. Hot chocolate for one." She reached into the cupboard for hot chocolate mix.

Reese and Tyrell plopped down on stools at the island and watched Alexa assemble her drink. "That was quite the afternoon." Reese's tone was dry, but he was pale beneath his tan—a lingering vestige of his time in Kenya.

"No shit, Sherlock." Tyrell shuddered. "I've seen some pretty rough things in my days with child welfare and RESIST. But this was my first murder. I'm hoping it's my last. I don't even look at the bodies at a viewing."

"What a way to die." Alexa grimaced, then leaned against the island and took a sip of the chocolate. The warm drink helped soothe her distress. Drained by the day's horrible experience, she was glad that Tyrell and Reese had been with her. That's right, she thought. So they can be miserable too. How selfish.

"Whoever killed the guy wanted to make really, really sure he was dead." Reese shook his head and ran a hand through his thick brown curls.

"Yeah. The word 'overkill' was invented for that poor dude."

Alexa set her cup on the counter. "That sign though. None of this could actually be related to terrorism, right? The killers must have used the Allahu Akbar thing just to throw the cops off. Although he was wearing one of those Muslim caps."

"What? You don't think the Cumberland County branch of ISIS was at work here," Tyrell scoffed.

"This is Southcentral Pennsylvania. That just doesn't compute." Reese frowned. "We know from experience that we've got right-wing militia activity in the area. I'd think there's more chance that they or some KKK offshoot killed that man than ISIS. Didn't you tell me there was a KKK march in the square a few months back?"

"KKK? Yeah." Alexa shuddered. "I couldn't stand to look at his face for too long. That eye." Alexa's voice trailed off before picking up strength. "He looked pretty young. Early twenties at most."

"Maybe even late teens." Tyrell nodded. "Young and way out of his element. I guess he could be foreign-born. Black and brown come in a lot of nationalities, not just U-S-of-A. A lot of Muslim men wear those skullcaps."

"The police were pretty pissed that we went out there on our own. I still think it was the best choice. But, from their perspective, an odd thing to do." Reese rubbed his temples. "Do you have any Tylenol? I have a splitting headache."

Alexa took a pill bottle from a cupboard and handed it to Reese, along with a glass of water. "If Trooper Cannon had caught the call, he wouldn't have been surprised to see me there. He knows I'm always getting into strange situations. In retrospect, maybe we should have called 911." She put her hand over Tyrell's for a moment.

"Spilt milk at this point," Reese sighed. "Although I'm sure they'll check us all out. We could get called in for another round of questioning." He picked up Tyrell's empty beer. "Another?"

"No. I'm heading home as soon as I pack up my drone. It may sound cold, but I'm really pissed that my first drone flight was such a disaster." Tyrell slid off the stool, shoulders slumped.

"At least this morning was great. A lot of fun." Alexa tried for a perky tone but fell short.

"That's only because we didn't know we were filming a dead body until we came back here for lunch." Tyrell sighed. "And the camera fell off. And I have to turn the video in to the cops tomorrow. Hard to believe, but I thought getting a drone would be cool."

"I'm glad you two got to meet, finally." Alexa dredged up another smile, which quickly faded. "It was a little more memorable than I'd planned."

"Hey, this was a freak, once-in-a-lifetime thing. Let me know when you want to send her up again. I'm in." Reese touched Tyrell's back in an awkward man-pat.

"Me too," Alexa chimed in as her friend walked out the front door. But the day had worn her down. She remembered the horror and sleepless nights after the first time she'd found a dead body; she'd also thought that would be a once-in-a-lifetime thing. "Great how that's working out," she muttered under her breath.

"What?" Reese asked.

"Nothing. Just talking to myself. Are you going to stay for dinner?"

Reese bent over the counter to kiss Alexa's forehead. "I need to get back to Harpers Ferry. I still have a lot to do for my Monday presentation. The Trust is banking on this first look at the Samburu lion study to bring in funding from several donors. It has to be perfect."

Alexa's heart dropped. She'd hoped that Reese would stay the night. But, she knew this presentation was important to his project. "You'll do well. I hope you raise a lot of money."

"Me too. Otherwise, I might not have a job." Reese shot her a concerned look. "Will you be OK here alone? We had a pretty brutal day."

"I'll be fine." Alexa heard Scout whining at the front door and walked over to let the damp mastiff inside. As she toweled off his muddy paws, she said, "This guy will keep me company." She grimaced. "Who would dream that three friends, out flying a drone for fun, would spot a corpse in a field? A sad, crazy stroke of bad luck. A terrible experience. But it has nothing to do with us, really."

A few minutes later, Reese slipped on his coat and patted Scout on the head. "See you, boy. Take care of this one." He tilted his head toward Alexa.

"I'll be fine," she protested once again.

Reese gathered Alexa in his arms for a swift hug. "I'll call you early in the week."

Alone, Alexa put a chicken breast in the oven and prepared a salad, although she wasn't really hungry. She couldn't shake the sick feeling in the pit of her stomach. Hoping to lift her spirits, Alexa grabbed a beach towel from the laundry room.

"Come on, Scout. Let's hit the hot tub before dinner." Alexa slipped off her clothes and wrapped the big towel around her torso. Bordered on one side by state forest land, Alexa's remote cabin was nestled in acres of woodlands, far from any prying eyes—except for one man, a sniper who'd once preyed on Alexa during a nighttime moment of Zen. She'd vowed to never let that incident deter her and still refused to wear a bathing suit in her hot tub.

The rain had stopped, but the deck was damp on her feet as she padded to the far side of the cabin. Slipping into the hot water, Alexa sighed with contentment and listened to Scout rummage at the edge of the woods. The light had faded over the deep stand of pines that stood several yards in front of the cabin. And the wind that had dogged their search for the body at the farm had vanished with the rainstorm.

This serenity was exactly why Alexa had returned home to Southcentral Pennsylvania after years in New York. Her fascination with the big city had lasted for more than a decade; through college, law school at Columbia, and a prestigious job as a junior attorney at a major law firm. But the higher she climbed on the ladder of success, the more she wanted off. So, she'd headed home for a berth in the family law firm, where she could connect with her clients— and this remote cabin in the forest, where she could rekindle her love for nature.

Scout came racing back to the deck and settled into his damp bed next to the hot tub. With a big harrumph, he nodded off. Quiet fell over the dark woods.

Alexa leaned back and closed her eyes, trying to merge with the stillness of the forest. But she kept seeing vultures and the bloody crater left by a missing eye. After a few minutes, she sat upright, tears streaming down her face. The death of this stranger had touched a well of emotion that Alexa thought she'd put behind her. But John's death was still too recent. And what Reese's return meant was still too uncertain. More troubling, finding this body only confirmed Alexa's fears that she had become a magnet for death.

# CHAPTER THREE

AFTER A RESTLESS night, Alexa tumbled out of bed at first light. She walked to close her bedroom window and faltered. The russet leaves dancing outside her second-story window brought back yesterday's experience with a rush. The murder of that young, nameless man seemed so savage. No accidental shooting or crime of passion, it looked like a cold-blooded, methodical execution. Alexa shivered at the thought and wondered who had done it.

Although the Arabic note had been shocking when they'd found it at the scene, Alexa didn't find the idea of terrorism very plausible. More like the killer or killers had watched too many movies or played too many video games and thought that they could throw the police off the trail by masquerading as ISIS. Especially since their victim had been a Muslim.

Absorbed in her musings, Alexa jumped when Scout pushed his cold nose into her hand and whined.

"I guess you want to go out? Right, buddy? We have plenty of time before we have to be at this brunch." Alexa threw a sweatshirt over her pajamas and headed downstairs, Scout lumbering behind.

"Can I help with anything?" Alexa asked when she and Scout slipped through the back door of her parents' home. Now retired, Norris and Susan Williams divided their time between Alexa's childhood home in Carlisle and a small villa in Umbria, Italy. After a brush with death two years earlier, Susan had convinced her husband to bow out of the family law practice and pursue their lifelong dream of living in Italy. Alexa was glad that cool weather had brought her parents back home for the fall and winter.

Alexa's mother looked up from the baguette she was slicing at the kitchen counter. "Hello, Lexie. Hey, Scout. I think I'm fine here. I decided to go more informal today with a buffet."

Alexa hung her jacket on the coat rack by the door and held out her arms. "Do I look OK? It's been a while since you've had one of these soirées. Not sure about the dress code."

Her mom, Susan Williams, smiled at her daughter's outfit, a black boho shift dress and cowboy boots. "You look lovely, dear. That's one of the New York designer purchases, right?"

"Right. I still have a closet full of city dresses but little chance to wear them here in Carlisle. They'll probably go out of style before I wear them out. You look nice." Susan wore a floor-length tailored skirt and a white blouse with the cuffs turned back. A lapis-blue scarf brought further polish to the look. Alexa's mom was one of those effortlessly chic women, tall and willowy with blunt-cut ash-blonde hair. She looked like a model, even in her late sixties.

Alexa wandered down the long island, studying the huge layout of food. "Mmm. Three kinds of quiche. Sliced turkey and beef. Hummus and crudités." She snagged a piece of pumpkin bread and pointed to a ceramic bowl. "What's this one?"

"Cranberry apple quinoa salad. Decided to try something new."

"Looks good. Where's Dad?" Alexa asked as she watched Scout wander out of the kitchen and down the hall. "TV room? I hope he has a biscuit for his favorite granddog."

"Of course." Susan glanced at the clock. "Everyone should be here in about ten minutes or so. Graham and Kate may be a few minutes late. They decided not to bring the kids. Said they'll be able to socialize better without having to worry about Jamie and Courtney."

"Remind me. This Army War College family is from Iraq?"

"Yes. And we also invited their friends from the Carlisle Barracks, a Colonel Dean Finley and his wife, Jill."

"I know that you like to support the community relationship with the War College, but didn't you give up hosting these International Fellows a while ago? How can you and Dad do this when you're at the villa in Italy for months at a time?"

"We took our name off the list about three years ago. But the War College has an unusually large class of International Fellows this year. We worked out an arrangement with Midge and Tom Crane. They spend their winters in Florida. We spend spring and summer in Umbria. So, the War College agreed that we could split the community sponsor duties this year. The Cranes were here to greet them in August. Now we've taken over the local host duties. Actually, it will give the Al-Badri family a chance to get to know more people here. Salim's a brigadier general."

Alexa heard the click of Scout's nails on the hardwood floor as he and her father approached the kitchen. "Hey, Dad." She laughed at Scout, who settled his hindquarters onto her father's foot. "That dog adores you. Sometimes, I think he'd rather live here."

Norris Williams stretched his tall frame over the dog to hug his daughter and kiss her on the forehead. "I don't think he'd like Umbria, though. Too hot in the summer. Did your mom tell you that all the attorneys from the firm are coming today?"

"That's great, but forgive me if I don't get too excited. Graham and I see them every day."

"Well, the guest list even includes our former partner. I managed to coax Pat O'Donnell off the golf course for a few hours."

"I hear he loves retirement. Isn't it getting a bit chilly for golf though?"

"Not until the first snowfall." Dad chuckled. "He's thrilled I convinced him to leave the firm when I retired. Oh, Frank and Alice Crowe are coming too."

"Wonderful. I never see Frank anymore since I stopped volunteering at the Family Planning Clinic. Wow. I didn't realize you were having so many people. I would have left Scout at home." Alexa fell silent and bit her lip. She'd avoided the subject of yesterday's discovery as long as she could. She'd considered the best way to break the news about the dead man but decided just to come out with it. Her parents were never happy when she stumbled into dangerous situations. And, unfortunately, there had been several.

"Um, before the crowd gets here, I want to fill you in on something."

Mom placed the bowl she was holding on the counter and frowned. "I know that tone. What's happened?"

Dad extricated his foot from the dog and sat on a stool at the counter. "Tell us, Lexie."

Alexa took a deep breath. "Well, yesterday, Reese, Tyrell, and I were flying Tyrell's new drone out in the country. We found a dead body."

"Another one?" Her mother's struggle for calm was apparent. "How does this keep happening to you?"

"If it wasn't so alarming, it would be ridiculous," her father spluttered. "Are you OK?"

Alexa noted how her dad's face had paled beneath his silver hair and outdoorsman tan. "I'm fine. We were never in any danger because—" she stopped at the peal of the front doorbell. "I'll fill you in later. It's really not that big a deal. Let me get the door." She took off down the hall feeling drained. Crazy how she forgot she was an accomplished lawyer and independent woman when she had these bad-news conversations with her parents. Instead, she felt as sheepish as she had in her teenage years when they'd caught her sneaking in after curfew.

After brunch, Alexa slipped out the back door to give Scout a chance to romp around the yard. She looked forward to a brief break from the nonstop socializing. Her heart sank when she saw that two of the guests of honor had also escaped the hubbub. The men turned to greet Alexa as she approached their spot on the patio.

"General. Colonel. Lovely afternoon, isn't it?"

General Al-Badri gestured toward the brilliant red sugar maple in the corner of the back yard. "We don't have seasons like this in my country. But I went to college in New Hampshire. At Dartmouth. Seeing this tree and the other fall colors here in Carlisle brings back the memory of my college days."

"Dartmouth explains your excellent English." Alexa smiled as she tried to envision this thickset, imposing man, who carried himself with such confidence, as an Ivy League frat boy. "As you might know, we Americans tend to expect everyone else to learn English but rarely speak other languages."

"Not entirely true, ma'am," Colonel Finley said. He struck Alexa as one of those guys who embraced fitness as a religion. Someone who got up at four in the morning to run twenty miles before he bicycled to class. Then worked out at lunch in the gym.

He ran a hand over his silver buzz cut. "Many of us in the military speak multiple languages. Like the Arabic I picked up during my two tours in Iraq." He turned toward the general. "*Sawf tuktashaf 'asdiqa'ak alhaqiqiiyn fi lahazat al'azamat.*"

"*Inshallah,*" Al-Badri replied, then looked at Alexa. "Forgive us. The colonel reminds me that you discover your true friends in moments of crisis. My country certainly has seen much crisis in the past decade or so."

Being her mother's daughter, Alexa remained polite in the face of the rising testosterone. "Are language courses part of the curriculum at the War College?"

Al-Badri answered. "All the classes are in English. One of the requirements for International Fellows is that we're fluent enough in English to do the coursework. The college offers an advance session for those who might need extra help before the official session begins."

"And, of course, most of the class are American officers," Finley added.

Colonel Finley's wife opened the back door and called out, "Dean, desserts are on the table. Come in and be sociable."

"On my way," the colonel announced as he strode toward the door.

Alone on the patio with Alexa, the general said, "Your parents and the Cranes have been so gracious to Noora and me. Not just today, but since we arrived in Carlisle. It has helped ease the transition to our temporary home, especially for my wife." Al-Badri gestured toward the door. "Are you coming inside?"

"In a moment. I need to round up my dog." Alexa waved toward Scout, who was meandering around some shrubs in the far corner of the yard.

"More like a small pony than a dog. I'll leave you for now. *Ma' Al-salāmah.*" The general smiled with a slight bow and marched inside.

Alexa assumed that his parting words meant good-bye. From her time in East Africa, she was familiar with a similar-sounding Swahili phrase used to bid someone good night. *Lala salama.* All the same, she shivered. How weird was it that yesterday she finds a man whose violent death was marked by a sign in Arabic, and today she encounters two Arabic-fluent men whose profession is violence? Surreal.

Alexa was helping her mother serve another round of coffee when her sister-in-law, Kate, dashed into the living room. Sidling up to Alexa, the petite strawberry-blonde whispered in her ear. "Your phone kept ringing. So, I answered. I think you might want to take the call."

"Sure. Who is it?" Alexa followed Kate out of the room, gripping the half-full coffeepot in her hand. For a minute, she gave a worried thought to Reese, over an hour away in Harpers Ferry. Had something happened?

When they reached the kitchen, Kate picked up the phone from the counter and handed it to Alexa with a question on her face. "The FBI."

Kate was still leaning on the counter when the brief conversation ended. Alexa shrugged her shoulders. "Hey, it's nothing to worry about. They just have some questions about something I saw yesterday. But I have to ask a favor. Can you take Scout home with you for a little bit? I need your husband to come with me. I'll pick up Scout when I bring Graham home."

"You need a lawyer, but there's nothing to worry about?" Kate's tone dripped with skepticism.

"Not from the FBI. But you know I'm right. If I don't ask my big brother to come along, I'll hear about it for the next six months." Alexa grinned and trotted off to find Graham.

# CHAPTER FOUR

"GOOD MORNING." MELINDA looked surprised when Alexa breezed into the office. "The early bird catches the worm and all that. But this is unusual."

"What? I often get here early."

The ample redhead giggled. "Sure you do, Boss. Especially on Mondays." She jumped up from her desk. "I'll get you some tea while you get settled. Your mother left a message. She said to call as soon as you got in."

"Thanks." Alexa walked into her office and tossed her briefcase onto a chair. She loved her current work schedule. In the New York City law firm, the work had been all-consuming; the days were long. Now, those grueling years and relentless caseloads seemed like a distant memory.

At her desk, Alexa scanned the local newspaper for an article about the young man's body. There was nothing in either the paper version or online.

Melinda arrived with a cup of tea in one hand and a printed schedule in the other. "Nothing on the calendar this morning, but you have a hearing on the Henninger divorce at two this afternoon. Then, a meeting with a potential new client—an adoption matter."

"Remind me to steer all future divorces to Stewart." Alexa grinned. "These people can't stand each other. Ron Garver and I thought we had worked out all the details of the settlement. Now, they're fighting over who takes possession of their Penn State football bobblehead collection. I can't believe I'm going to have to stand in front of the judge and argue that, as a Penn State alum, Rhonda's claim to the bobbleheads should take precedence even though Henry was the season ticket holder."

"Things aren't always what they seem, you know," Melinda said as she headed out the door. "Maybe they're both just having a hard time letting go. Did you call your mom?"

Thinking that Melinda could be right about the Henningers, Alexa pondered the possibility as she dialed her parents' number.

"Mom, you called?"

"The FBI? I know you didn't get a chance to tell your father and me the whole story before we were interrupted yesterday. But, Lexie, why in the world is the FBI questioning you?"

"Sorry I had to leave so abruptly and drag Graham out with me. I'm not in trouble or anything. Just a wrong-place-at-the-wrong-time sort of thing."

"Lexie, I'm on the line too," Dad said. "This sounds so familiar that I am now officially worried. Just spit it out."

"My God, Alexa. Were you in harm's way?" her mother asked.

"No. I'm fine. We're all fine. The person was dead long before we got there. We just reported it and spent a while answering questions. The police are clear that we had nothing to do with the death. Sorry, I've been asked not to discuss this. I can't really say much more."

Her father launched into lawyer-speak. "We understand that you're not at liberty to disclose the details, dear. It's apparent from what you're not saying that foul play was involved. Would that instruction have come from the FBI?"

"Yes."

"That means this is serious, right, Norris?"

"Perhaps." Dad replied. "Graham sat in on your interview with the bureau, correct?"

"Yes." Alexa sighed. "Look. I know you're concerned. And finding the corpse was pretty rough. But none of us knew the victim. The FBI wanted to talk to us directly rather than rely on the local police interviews. I don't expect to hear from them again during their investigation."

"OK. It's just that you have a knack for getting drawn into dangerous situations." Norris's voice caught. "I can't help thinking about that day in Umbria . . . Silas Gabler's body lying at the bottom of a cliff. None of us thought that would happen either."

"Let's not go there, Dad. That was a horrible day." Alexa winced that her father had dredged up the painful memory. "Your old college buddy had us all fooled. But I have no idea who this dead guy is. We can talk more about this later, although there's not much more I can discuss. For now, I have to start my workday."

Mom's calm voice replied, "We won't keep you further, Lexie. You know that we're here if something unexpected develops with this."

By mid-morning, Alexa had reviewed a series of documents prepared by Ted Freet, one of the Williams, Williams, and Stewart firm's junior associates. She had just turned to an adoption case when Melinda buzzed her.

"Tyrell Jenkins is out here with two boys and their parents. Says he needs your help, and it's urgent." Melinda lowered her voice. "I'm not sure if the family speaks English."

Alexa closed the document on her computer screen and sighed. "I wonder why Tyrell didn't mention this yesterday. Send them in."

She rose to greet the group. Tyrell led the pack, his usual cocky gait more tentative this morning. His hand rested lightly on the arm of a brown-skinned preteen with dark hair and eyes. The boy's torn and dirty T-shirt hung loosely over his blue jeans. His lip was swollen, and he cradled an arm in a sling.

Behind the boy, an adult couple shuffled through the door. The man, dressed in a worn windbreaker and khakis, walked with a slight limp. The petite woman's impeccable posture gave her a regal air. She wore a flowing, floor-length shift dress and a dark-green hijab. A wiry teenager in a bright-red soccer jersey paused at the threshold. He surveyed the room with an angry expression and stalked to the far corner.

Alexa dropped the hand that she had extended and gave the group a slight nod, remembering that many Muslim men never shook hands with women.

Tyrell said, "Alexa Williams, meet the Qassims. They're one of the families that RESIST's new refugee resettlement program is sponsoring here in the Carlisle area." He gestured to each member of the family. "This is Eshan. Zahraa. Their eldest son, Bassam. We're here today to ask you to help this guy, their son, Ali." He shot Alexa a look, eyes flashing. "Thanks for seeing us without an appointment. It was urgent."

Alexa knew Tyrell well enough to interpret the look. He was hot on the trail of a new cause. To right some injustice that he thought this young boy had suffered. "Lucky I had some free time this morning. Please sit. How are you, Tyrell?" She was still shaken from yesterday, but Tyrell looked fine.

"Hanging in," he replied with a shrug.

"Would anyone like tea or coffee?"

"Thank you, but no," the mother, Zahraa, replied for all in accented English.

Tyrell plunged right in. "The Qassims arrived here in June after a horrific escape from Syria. They got out of the country on a boat that took them to Greece. Spent two long years in a refugee camp in Central Greece before their request for asylum in the US was vetted and processed. RESIST got them set up here in Carlisle with a house. Eshan is a doctor. He has a job at a one of the warehouses while he's starting the coursework to get his license to practice here."

"Or perhaps a physician assistant; we'll see what I may be able to realistically obtain," Eshan said.

Tyrell smiled at the woman sitting on the couch. "Zahraa taught at the University of Damascus. I believe you're just taking some time to adjust to your new home before you decide next steps?"

Zahraa gave Alexa a rueful look. "Yes. First, I want to create a home here for my husband and sons. Soon, I will explore what jobs an unemployed Syrian instructor of English literature might find here in America."

"We have several colleges and universities in the area. One of them may be happy to give you an opportunity," Alexa replied, mentally noting that this woman might possibly speak better English than she did.

"Both Bassam and Ali have started classes. Even with the spotty schooling they got in the refugee camp, Bassam placed as a junior at Carlisle High. Ali is in his first year at Wilson Middle School." The boys sat silent as Tyrell spoke.

"How can I help?" Alexa asked, wondering how well the younger Qassims spoke English. "You referenced an issue with Ali?"

With a chop of his hand, Bassam cried, "You must help us punish those *humr* necks who hurt my brother."

"Bassam, enough." His father's stern voice shut down the teenager's angry answer. His mother grabbed Bassam's arm with a firm hold until he jerked it away and turned to the wall.

Although the kid's accent was pronounced, this young firecracker had answered Alexa's question about English skills. She aimed for a calming tone. "No problem. Emotions often run high around legal issues. Um, 'humr' necks?"

"I must apologize for my son, Ms. Williams. His anger has caused him to lose his English." Zahraa's voice was tight. "I think the American expression is redneck. 'Humr' is an Arabic word for red."

Tyrell said, "Bottom line here: Some kids at school have been bullying Ali. The Qassims and I alerted the school authorities. They promised to handle it. To speak to the kids and their parents. They did, but the bullying didn't stop. So, we went back again and got the same assurances. Then, first thing this morning, the school called Zahraa to notify her that they'd taken Ali to the emergency room. A group of these hellions jumped Ali on his walk to school and beat him up pretty bad. She rushed to the hospital. I rounded up Eshan when he got home from his night shift. Then, we picked up Bassam from his school.

"Turns out that it could have been much worse. But after the ER patched up Ali, and Eshan took a good look at him, we decided to head over here. This has to stop. And, clearly, the school needs some incentive to deal with it aggressively."

Alexa walked over to the young boy and crouched in front of his chair, happy she'd worn a pantsuit today. Her heart twisted at the haunted look in his eyes. "Ali. Can you tell me what happened?"

The boy looked at her, eyes dark and wide. "The mean ones, they jumped from behind *el-hait*." Ali made a rising gesture with his hand and looked to his father.

"A wall. The boys who attacked him were behind a wall," Eshan said.

"Yes. A wall," Ali rolled the word over his tongue. "They came from front and back. Pulled me down to ground and beat me with their fists. My arm, the pain came, when I fall. They kicked me and called me *Irhabi*."

"What did they call you?" Alexa asked.

"Towelhead. Rag head. Terrorist. Dirty Arab. And more." A tear slid down Ali's face. "What they call me every day."

"I'm sorry, Ali. These kids are probably just spouting off things they've heard on TV or at home." Alexa scowled. Kids could be so cruel. Sad thing was, cruel kids all too often grew into cruel adults.

She rose and went back to her seat, turning her remarks to the adults. "But that makes it no less inexcusable. How many kids were involved in this attack?"

"We think five. The same four who have been bullying Ali since day one. And an older kid. Ali doesn't know his name," Tyrell answered. He looked at the Qassims. "There aren't any problems with the rest of the class, are there?"

"No. But one of the teachers has made some unkind remarks. A Mr. Wallace, the art teacher. Correct, Ali?"

"Yes, *Ya-umma*."

"The one who coaches soccer?" Bassam asked as if this were news to him. "What a pig of a man." Then, he sank back in his seat at another glare from his father.

Tyrell turned to Alexa. "What are our options?"

"It depends. I usually try to avoid legal action in disputes between children. The first line of action on anything school-related should come from the school administration or the school district. That being said, it appears that the school hasn't been effective in stopping this. And now the bullying has escalated to include assault with physical injury. That can't continue. And the kids involved should be punished. What makes this more complicated is that it may not have happened on school grounds. And this bigoted comment from a teacher is quite concerning."

Alexa looked at Ali's parents. "What course of action would you like to pursue? I don't practice criminal law, but I do deal with protection from abuse orders. I would be happy to attend a meeting with the school—and even involve the Carlisle Police if you want to press charges. These kids can't get away unscathed."

Eshan replied. "We are new here and don't want—what's the American expression? Ah, to rock the boat. Still, we cannot sit by and let our child be harmed, even by other students. Ms. Williams, the Qassim family has endured much. We escaped our homeland with very little, knowing that the Secret Police were on their way to arrest me. We survived a very perilous voyage in high seas. And we experienced hunger, heat, and many more hardships in the refugee camp. But we had our sights on America. Land of the free. We knew there would be an adjustment to the language, a new culture, different customs. We had so many stars in our eyes." His expression soured. "Perhaps we should have expected that not everyone in your wonderful country would welcome us with open arms."

When he paused and looked down at this lap, Zahraa patted her husband's arm. "We'd prefer that these misguided children not get in trouble with the police. Although, I understand that your police operate under many rules; that arrest is not the nightmare that it can become in our country. Over time, Ali must grow a thicker skin and learn to deal with bullies. There is an Arab proverb that says, 'Stars cannot shine without darkness.' But he is a child in what is still a foreign land to him. We need our son to feel safe. Tyrell recommended we take your advice."

Alexa leaned back in her chair. She deferred to her clients' wishes, but if it were up to her, these kids would be suspended for a few days, and the school district would step up and take responsibility for the whole mess. "Ali should be safe, especially at school. Why don't you folks set up a formal meeting with the school, and I'll come with you. Sometimes, just having a lawyer present in such a meeting lets the school know that you mean business. We ask them to deal with this art teacher. And I suggest we ask them to identify and punish all five children to the fullest extent. A suspension from school comes to mind as one option. And that they present you with a plan to make sure that Ali is protected. You may also want me to meet with the parents after that, or communicate with them in some other way. I could make it clear that, if their children's behavior continues, you will consider pressing charges." She looked at the elder Qassims and Tyrell for affirmation.

The parents nodded, and Tyrell said, "Sounds like a plan." From his chair in the corner, Bassam continued to glower. Ali closed his eyes and held his arm as if in pain.

Alexa moved to her computer. "I have some time tomorrow if you can schedule with the school. Work with Melinda on a time. And one more thing." She frowned at Ali's sling and bruised mouth. Kids often picked on anyone who didn't fit the mold, but Ali's injuries were serious. If his attackers had been adults, the charge would be assault. She tried to keep the anger from her voice as she said, "I'd like to get some photographs of Ali's injuries before you leave."

# CHAPTER FIVE

BEMOANING THE EARLY hour, Alexa tried to appreciate the last gasps of autumn scenery as she drove down the mountain. The Land Rover plunged through pockets of fog that swirled up from the ground, while above, a few trees still blazed crimson and orange in the early morning sun. Alexa cranked on the heat and cried aloud, "Why did I schedule a class at this godforsaken hour?" She'd begun taking a self-defense class a few months ago. Developed by the Israeli Army and Mossad for hand-to-hand combat, Krav Maga seemed to offer the best focus on real-life situations. Since she couldn't make her regular evening class this week, she'd signed up for an early-morning session.

She rushed into the studio on the outskirts of Carlisle with just a few minutes to spare. Jamming her work clothes into a locker, Alexa hurried toward the classroom. The instructors, Lev and KC, stood in front of the group of nine women as she slid into the room.

"Nice to see you, Williams. Even numbers always make it easier," KC barked.

Alexa didn't reply. This woman was all business in a black tank top and loose black pants. A retired colonel, KC held a black belt in Krav Maga and seemed steely enough to have used the hand-to-hand skills in a combat situation. Every time Alexa looked at the instructor's wiry muscles, she wished she'd worn a long-sleeve tee.

In contrast, Lev came across as a warm, fuzzy teddy bear. Quick to smile, he was a very patient teacher. But when he and KC demonstrated new techniques, his prowess left no doubt that he had mastered this intense art of self-defense. Another student had told Alexa that Lev had learned Krav Maga at its source in Israel.

The hour flew by. As always, KC and Lev began with a series of individual exercises to improve fitness, then turned to self-defense techniques. Tired from squats, push-ups, kicking, and grappling, Alexa lost her concentration during one of the final blocking exercises. Alexa's blocking glove wobbled, and Barb's hand chop glanced off the blocker and rammed into Alexa's chest, delivering a stinging blow to her sternum.

"I'm sorry. I didn't mean to whack you so hard." Barb bit her lip and hovered over Alexa, who was gasping for breath on the floor.

"Never apologize, Franklin," KC ordered as she approached. "Any hesitation could cost you your life." She looked down at Alexa. "And losing focus could be even more dangerous, Williams. That's your take-away from today."

Just as Alexa recovered enough to take two normal breaths, Lev clapped his hands. "That's it for today, ladies. Stay fierce."

Most of the class ran into the locker rooms for their jackets and left in their gym clothes. Barb made a detour to Alexa's locker on her way to the door.

"Hey. I'm sorry." She looked at the mark on Alexa's breastbone, a red splotch above her tank top. "Looks like it hurts." She lowered her voice. "KC can be a bitch sometimes."

"It does hurt." Alexa gave a rueful laugh. "But this is a tough discipline we're learning. I really want to improve my self-defense skills." She hesitated before she continued. "I've been in some difficult situations where I've felt vulnerable. And I don't want to feel that way if I'm ever in danger again." She grinned. "Still, I'm not sure I'm cut out for Krav Maga. Some of our classmates seem to have no problem with sustained aggression in the attack exercises."

Barb nodded. "Yeah. That woman, Nikki. She's a beast."

"Exactly. And I'm more a yoga type of girl."

"Well, my ex beat the shit out of me one too many times." Barb bristled at the memory. "That's why he's an ex and I'm here. Never again. Don't get discouraged. Anything we learn is going to make it harder for the next bastard to hurt us." She smiled. "You seem to be doing OK in class. Today was just a temporary setback."

Alexa pondered Barb's advice as she showered and dressed in the empty locker room. After two months of classes, Alexa wasn't picking up the moves as fast as she'd like. She was in good shape, and the training had only improved her fitness, but she wasn't sure she had that killer instinct that seemed fundamental to this aggressive self-defense training. "Stop whining, Williams," she muttered. She'd nearly been killed by a much larger man—more than once. Although she survived, Alexa felt she needed training on how to fight back with skill and determination. To be prepared. "You can do this. You need to do this." Gathering up her gym bag, she headed toward the exit.

She softened her steps, not wanting to disturb the class in session. Believing the studio to be closed for several hours after the early morning classes, she had assumed that she and a few staff were the only people left in the building.

A quick glance into the classroom brought Alexa to a complete halt. To avoid distracting the students, she stayed back from the doorway, just out of sight.

Not that they were paying attention to anything outside the room. Four pairs of combatants were locked in a knife training exercise. Alexa knew the knives must be made of rubber, but the students' intensity made everything look very real. One partner approached the other with knife raised. The other delivered a huge defensive kick to the knife-wielder's midsection. The attacks were swift and aggressive. Although the knife-holders had blocks for their stomachs, their partners delivered hard, swift kicks that made Alexa wince just looking at them.

They switched to another exercise. This time, the objective was to deflect, and possibly control, the attacker's knife hand. Alexa's breath caught in her throat as a black man with ripped muscles lunged his blade toward his partner's eye. His opponent parried the attack with an elbow and twisted from his grasp. It wasn't until she heard the partner shout a command that Alexa realized, with a start, the student who had bested the muscled man was a woman.

"Break and reassemble, please." The lithe woman, tall as a runway model, strode to the front of the class. "Good contact on the thrust and block. Any rough spots?"

Seven young men stood before her, a mix of skin tones and heights. Their one unifying feature: All appeared to be experts at Krav Maga. Alexa had seen a few instructor demonstrations during her time in training. She had no doubt that this group was all advanced level, maybe even black belts.

"My left hand ain't worth crap when we're in close." With a shake of his wrist, a thin student, who looked little more than a teenager, responded to the woman's question. Alexa strained to catch the hint of a Hispanic accent before she felt a rush of embarrassment. Why was she standing here in the shadows watching these people like some sort of spy? Even though she was impressed with their skill level, admiration didn't give her license to lurk out here and snoop on their session.

Rubbing her sore chest, Alexa backed away from the door and padded down the long hall to the exit. A glance at her watch kicked her into high gear. She'd gotten so distracted by the expert class, she'd lost track of time. The Qassim meeting with the school district started in just ten minutes.

"I think the meeting went well. They heard your concerns. It's clear that they don't want Ali—or any other child in the school— to be harmed or bullied." Alexa stopped when they reached the parking lot. Although Tyrell hovered in the background, Alexa addressed her question to Eshan and Zahraa Qassim. "What was your impression?"

Eshan wrinkled his brow. "The superintendent and the principal seem to be honorable people. I agree that they are concerned about Ali and want to help. I'm just not—what's the word—convinced. I'm not convinced that talking again to the boys' parents will solve the problem."

"They tried that once, and those kids still attacked Ali. A vicious attack." Zahraa shuddered.

Tyrell shrugged. "They both talked the talk. Let's see if they can walk the walk. I got a better vibe from the superintendent than the principal. She jumped every time I spoke. That's one twitchy woman to be in charge of hundreds of rampaging adolescents."

"Maybe that's why she's twitchy." Alexa grinned. "I think she's terrified we'll sue the school district, and she'll be in the crosshairs."

"No. No. We don't want a lawsuit or anyone to get fired. She seems like a good woman." Zahraa raised a hand in protest.

Eshan nodded. "We just want Ali to be safe."

"Me too," Alexa said. "Why don't we give them a chance to follow through? We showed them that we mean business and that we are holding the school district responsible."

Tyrell nodded. "Sounds reasonable."

Alexa looked at the parents. "Meanwhile, we watch things closely. Talk to Ali about today's meeting. Ask him to tell you if he's bullied or taunted again. If it doesn't stop, we'll figure out the next step."

"What else can we do?" Eshan asked.

"I can talk to the Carlisle Police and ask them to put the fear of God into these kids and their families. We could even press charges. Like it or not, sometimes the threat of a lawsuit spurs people and organizations to take decisive action." Alexa touched Zahraa's shoulder. "Try not to worry. We can't guarantee that Ali will never have to deal with racism or bullies. People in America, whether native-born or immigrants or refugees deal with both every day. We're a far from perfect nation. But we are going to make sure this little pack of budding bigots stops harassing your child. I guarantee you that."

Alexa rubbed her sore sternum, a reminder that she was learning Krav Maga because she didn't feel safe. She'd found out the hard way that a five-foot, four-inch female, no matter how fit, was at a disadvantage if attacked by a larger man. But this kid deserved a peaceful childhood. She was going to do her part to guarantee he got it.

Alexa and Tyrell were to first to arrive at the Om Café after yoga that evening.

"The regular for me, Ariel. Chai. And maybe one of those." Alexa pointed at a tier of mini-cupcakes on the counter.

Ariel looked at Tyrell. "Cappuccino, right?"

"Of course." He flashed his aw-shucks grin. "No cupcakes for me though."

"Just you two tonight?"

"No. Melissa and Haley are on their way. They had something to discuss with Isabella."

Claiming a large round table in the corner, they picked up on the conversation from their earlier meeting at the school. Tyrell sprawled back in his chair and steepled his fingers. "So, level. Do you really think the school is going to put a stop to the bullying?"

"I think they're going to try. They have a lot to lose if they don't. School officials don't want to be in a public brouhaha about this. A kid flees a violent civil war and the threat of death. Then, gets beat up by his classmates. Doubt that would play too well in the local media."

"But he's a Muslim. And this is a pretty conservative area."

"We'll see. The school's in the business of educating kids, not condoning bigotry and violence."

"I hope you're right." Tyrell's tone remained skeptical.

The door chime tinkled as Alexa's best friends, Melissa and Haley, swooped into the café with another woman from class. This had been her first night at yoga, but Alexa was sure she'd seen the tall woman somewhere before. After a brief conversation with Ariel, the group came to the table.

"Have a seat." Haley pulled out a chair and gestured to the new woman.

"Success," Melissa pronounced, tossing her long auburn hair. "I knew Isabella would agree to run the yoga demonstration."

"I'm psyched. I'm sure I can get the Chamber to pony up some money for food. And we'll put it on the community calendar." Haley turned to accept her chai from Ariel. "Thanks."

"And Sloane is going to participate too." Melissa nodded toward the newcomer, who was now sipping coffee. "Oh, sorry. Do you two know Sloane Chapin? She's joining our yoga class."

Alexa shot a welcoming smile in the woman's direction. Before she or Tyrell could respond, Haley interjected, "I know Sloane from the Chamber. As a small business owner, she attends the monthly luncheons."

Sloane smiled. "Do you come here after every yoga class? I hear from Haley that you're old friends."

"It's become a routine since I moved back here a few years ago from New York City. Melissa, Haley, and I have been friends since grade school. Yoga gives us a good excuse to get together at least once a week."

"And an excuse for me to get out of the house on my own for an evening. Blair is wonderful with Charlotte, but new mommies need some me-time too." Haley patted her perfectly coiffed dark hair as if it needed attention.

"And then there's our buddy, Tyrell." Melissa flashed him a wicked grin. "Somehow, he showed up one night and never left."

"Don't believe them for a single moment," Tyrell leaned across the table toward Sloane. "They begged me to join them. I mean, who wouldn't?"

Alexa giggled. For a moment, Tyrell had slipped into his alpha male persona, the one she'd been so put off by when they'd first met. Now, she knew it was just a front he used to hold people at arm's length.

Melissa interjected, "Tyrell runs RESIST, the anti-sex-trafficking advocacy organization. It's recently branched out into refugee services too. I do some volunteer work there."

"You own a small business. Here in Carlisle?" Alexa asked.

Haley interrupted before Sloane could answer. "Wait." She looked at Alexa. "You must have met Sloane at Krav Maga. She owns the studio."

Sloane smiled. "You take one of our classes? Great. Have you been coming to Courage for long?"

"Courage is the name of your martial arts studio?" Tyrell grinned. "Great branding."

Alexa flashed on why Sloane looked familiar. This was the woman she'd seen that morning, teaching the class of young men. She flushed at the thought of the way she'd spied on the group, hoping that Sloane wouldn't notice her red face. "I started taking the Women's Self-Defense Class a few months ago. I'm getting better, but the whole concept of Krav Maga is a little outside my comfort zone." Alexa laughed. "Which is probably why I need to stick with it. KC and Lev are great instructors."

"Ah, I didn't think we'd met. I'm rarely around the studio in the evenings."

Tyrell turned to Melissa. "Girl, go back to this conversation with Isabella. I have no clue what you're talking about with yoga and Krav Maga and art and the Chamber."

"Me either," Alexa added.

"Really? I thought I filled you both in. I found this new photographer who studies the human form in action. The way she photographs people doing yoga, martial arts, basketball, and so much more—it's lyrical. When I exhibit her work, I want to combine it with some actual demonstrations of the activities she's capturing in her art. Just for opening night of the exhibit."

Haley said, "Now that I'm back to work part time, I pitched this as a project for the Chamber to sponsor. We're working on a date. Probably in the spring."

While Alexa listened to her two childhood friends chatter away about the exhibit, she studied Sloane Chapin. The woman was beautiful, with an elegant air. Maybe it was the aristocratic name. She was tall and lithe with high cheekbones and stunning blue eyes. Owning a Krav Maga studio seemed at odds with the image she projected. At its heart, Krav Maga was a discipline for people who expected to encounter violence, or, at its worst, people who wanted to do violence to others. There had to be a story there. Like Alexa, could this woman have been assaulted at some point in her past?

As if he could hear Alexa's thoughts, Tyrell redirected the conversation. "And what about you, Sloane. Are you a Carlisle native?"

"No. I've been here just a few years. Long story short, I grew up all over the globe because my father was in the State Department. I married a guy I met during college, but he was killed in the Iraq

War." Sloane's voice wavered for a moment before she continued. "I kicked around overseas after that, working a series of low-level embassy jobs. Finally, I decided it was time to put down some roots. Krav Maga is one of my passions. So, I came here and opened up the studio."

"I'm sorry about your husband," Alexa replied. "I lost someone close to me last year. It's tough."

"Why Carlisle?" Tyrell asked.

"My husband came from an army family. He spoke often of Carlisle and the Army War College. The town sounded like the perfect place to start over." Sloane smiled. "And I like it a lot. I'm happy with my decision."

"You're welcome to join us here anytime." Alexa looked at the clock on the wall and pushed back from the table. "Sorry to leave you, but I have to get home to Scout—my English mastiff," Alexa directed the last part to the newcomer. "Talk to you guys later. Nice to meet you, Sloane."

On the drive home, Alexa thought about the strange patterns of life. She'd seen Sloane for the first time that morning at Courage. Then, she showed up at yoga that night. Admirable how the young woman seemed to have faced life head on. After losing her husband in tragic circumstances, she'd built a new business and a new life.

Alexa spoke aloud to the empty Land Rover. "Maybe you could learn something about moving on from this stranger. John's death threw you for a loop . . . but you never really loved him. And now you're holding Reese at arm's length. Maybe you need your own version of Courage, Williams." She touched her bruised sternum before she downshifted and turned into her lane.

# CHAPTER SIX

*June 27, 1859*

Steal away. Steal away, sweet Jesus. I ain't got long to stay.
—*"Steal Away," a Negro spiritual*

"Boy. I need your help outside, to tend the chickens. You can finish cleaning out those coals later." Susannah tilted her head toward the door.

"Why are you doin' chickens, Mama? That's Pompey's job." Elijah set the half-full bucket of ash on the hearth and slid the fire screen into place. Then, he followed his mother out of the big house and through the garden, glad to be outdoors in the morning breeze.

When he caught up on the kitchen garden path, Elijah asked, "Mama, what if the mistress sees I'm not done with the ashes?"

"Mistress is getting dressed for lunch at Albemarle House. She won't be downstairs for hours." Susannah set the basket she'd been carrying on the ground before she opened the door to a small shed. Filling two bowls with grain from a burlap sack, she handed one to her son.

Elijah scattered the grain to the flock of brown and white chickens. On the other side of the yard, his mama did the same. He turned the bowl upside down to empty every piece of meal then unlatched the door to the chicken coop. Master had designed the coop to look like a smaller version of the plantation house. The coop was bigger than the little house where he lived with his mama and two sisters. And had nicer walls, lined with rows of wooden roosts for the hens to lay their eggs.

*Mama walked up and down the aisles, checking the nests and placing each smooth, brown egg into the basket on her arm. Using a big ladle, Elijah filled a pan with water from a crock in the corner. The sound of clucking hens welled through the small building and made him smile. He found the hens' noisy chatter soothing and often stole away from the big house to visit Pompey out here.*

*"Finished? Come and hold the basket for me, please."*

*Elijah started down the aisle toward Mama, noticing the sad expression on her face.*

*She passed him the basket and spoke in a low voice. "Tomorrow is the day. Coleman got passes for the two of you to visit Twelve Oaks. George and a new girl be jumping the broom, and the pass gives you leave to go to the wedding. But once you on the road, head north."*

*Elijah gulped in fear, his heart pounding. "Mama, I don't want to leave." Although they had talked about him running, he never believed the day would actually come.*

*"You have to. Mistress be after the master to sell you. Says you getting too old to help in the house. But that ain't the real reason. Now that you're rising up to a man, you're the spitting image of your daddy. Every time Mistress looks at your green eyes, she sees the master. She's fretting on it and will make him put you on the auction block or sell you off to a house far away."*

*"Master likes me well enough. He jokes with me all the time."*

*"That be true. But remember Rex. Master dearly loved that coonhound. Took that fool dog everywhere. But when Mistress complained about the dirt and the smell, Master sold Rex lickety-split. Besides, the man looks in a mirror every day. When he sees your face, he knows the truth is plain as day to his wife and the children. The whole neighborhood. That man can be a force to reckon with, but he bends like grass in the wind when that wife of his gets her dander up."*

*Elijah blinked away tears. "I don't know how to get north. I never been anywhere past Twelve Oaks." He set the basket on the floor and wiped at his eyes.*

*"Honey-child, I know this is a frightful journey. But I want you to become a free man. Coleman has been talking to the peddlers who come by and learned a lot about the way to go. And Wabee is traveling with you; he'll meet you on the road. He's big and strong. He knows some of what's out there."*

*"He knows because he got caught both times he ran, Mama." Elijah shuddered. "I'm scared."*

"I knows you are. So am I. But if you stay here, you'll be sold, and it could be to the fields. You get far enough north, with those green eyes and high yellow skin, you will blend right in as a free man. Coleman says there are people along the way, white people, who help runaways to get north."

Elijah bit his lip. "All right, Mama. I'm worried what they will do to you when I'm gone. And the girls? You could get the whip!"

"Maybe. But I'll tell them I know nothing. That Coleman filled your head with wild notions and convinced you to run. I don't think Master will let them scar me."

Susannah's matter-of-fact tone made Elijah angry. He knew what happened behind closed doors with Mama and the master. Although it was rarely spoken, he knew that his own existence stemmed from one of those encounters fourteen years ago. And his sisters sprang from the ongoing infatuation that their owner had with his beautiful house slave. Mama accepted the situation. As the man's property, she had no choice. But the mistress, who was a harsh woman, delighted in finding small ways to punish Mama and her children. Things the Master never noticed. Elijah worried that Mama's lot would get much worse if he ran.

"I'll finish up here. You get back to cleaning the fireplace. You must go about your normal day. Just do your chores. Tomorrow, wear your jacket. I'll have some food for your pockets." Susannah touched her son's cheek with a gentle hand. "Be brave, Elijah. The Lord will protect you. Now, go."

Elijah hurried down the aisle. At the door of the elaborate chicken coop, he paused and looked back at his mother. She reached into the top row and plucked an egg from a nest. Her arm a graceful arc, she held the egg aloft, examining it for cracks. Framed in a shaft of sunlight that filtered through an upper window, his mama looked beautiful and serene. The halo of light softened her coarse blue dress and headscarf and highlighted her bronze cheekbones. Elijah wished he could make a painting of her, like the ones they had in the drawing room in the big house. But even if slaves had been allowed to have paints, he didn't have that talent.

Instead, he took one last look and painted Mama's picture in his heart.

Coleman arrived at the cabin door just after sun-up on Sunday morning. Mama was at the big house, serving breakfast. Even though the workers got Sundays to rest, the house slaves had to tend to the family meals.

*Elijah choked back a sob as he thought about hugging his Mama goodbye this morning in the dark. He could barely make out her beloved features in the half-light of the smoldering fireplace. "Everything must seem normal, Elijah. Don't alarm the girls; they're too young to keep a secret."*

*"Mama, I'm scared."*

*"You are going to be on your own, Elijah. You're a man now. And you must find the strength that God has given you to take the journey north. Keep away from the dogs. Watch for the patrollers, the bounty men. If they bring you back, you know the driver will whip you to the bone.*

*"If you're clever and strong, you'll become a free man. I'll keep you in my prayers every night until the day I die, son." Susannah kissed Elijah on the forehead and walked out the door, dry-eyed, with shoulders squared. She didn't look back.*

*At Coleman's second light tap on the door, Elijah slipped into his loose jacket. His sisters were still fast asleep in the corner bed, but he resisted an urge to kiss them goodbye. He felt bad that he hadn't told them he was leaving. But, this way, they wouldn't get in trouble when the driver found Elijah missing.*

*"Morning." Elijah nodded to Coleman, closing the worn door behind him.*

*"Nice day for a broom party," Coleman said.*

*"Sure enough is." Although the dim morning was still cool, Elijah could feel a line of sweat trailing down the middle of his back. The more he thought about acting normal, the more nervous he felt.*

*"Settle down, boy," Coleman whispered. "We just going to a wedding. Having a visit with my sister over at Twelve Oaks. Ain't Sundays something special?"*

*Coleman's tone soothed Elijah, and the fluttering in his abdomen stilled. When they reached a turn in the carriage lane, he looked back at the big house. A bank of azaleas bloomed along the fence. Behind it, a weeping willow, bright with the green of spring, rustled against the white sideboards of the house. He swallowed and bit his lip. This plantation was the only home he'd ever known. Mama had been whispering the words "free man" in his ear for years. For so many years that he could no longer remember when the longing for freedom had become his own dream.*

*"Come on, boy. We got miles to travel."*

*Coleman's raspy voice spurred Elijah to action. He hurried to catch up to the older man with a sudden burst of enthusiasm for the adventure that awaited.*

Elijah looked around to make sure that he and Coleman were alone. "Tell me about your plan so I knows what's ahead. Mama said that we're going to meet up with Wabee somewhere?"

"He plans to slip away this morning and take his own path to our meeting point. You and I will stick to the main road until we get close to Twelve Oaks. Then, we's going to head into the deep woods and go west."

Elijah gave Coleman a look of dismay. "West? But north is where they makes Negroes into free men. I want to be free."

"Boy, we are going to be walking for weeks. By tomorrow, the driver and the Master will find that we's gone. They'll be coming after us with the hounds. And the first place they'll take them demon dogs is north toward Nottaway Courthouse. That's the way slaves always run. Even ones who almost got clear away like Wabee."

"I been talking to the peddlers for years. Especially the one that used to come maybe three, four years ago. Name of Brandt. He traveled regular from Pennsylvania down to the Carolinas."

"I remember him. He had the blue cart. Mistress bought those silver candlesticks from him; she makes me polish them every fourth Tuesday."

"Well, that man, Brandt, seemed partial to the abolitionists. Talked a lot about some northern man named Garrison and a free Negro, Frederick Douglass. Not in front of the family, of course. Only when we were alone. He often asked me to shoe his mare or patch up a wagon wheel. He talked about some big hills to the west of here, called them the Blue Ridge Mountains. Said a man could get so deep in those mountains that no one would find him. That they're so steep and rocky, it would be hard for a tracker to follow. Even those bounty men. That's when I got the idea that would be a good route north. Hard going, but safer."

"How far is them mountains?" Elijah had never seen a mountain, but he hummed a few bars of a song that Mama sang, "Go Tell It on the Mountain."

"At least two days walking. Maybe more. Depends on how much we can walk during the day."

"What then?" Elijah tensed at the sight of a man on horseback approaching.

"We head north until we come to a place called Waynesboro. Still in Virginny. Word is there's a man living outside that town who helps runaways on the journey north. We'll go to him for help." Coleman stopped speaking as the rider drew near.

*Elijah recognized him as a neighbor, Mr. Shepherd. Master often invited him and his young wife to dinner. Elijah bobbed his head in acknowledgement but kept his eyes cast down.*

*"Where you boys off to this fine morning?" Mr. Shepherd's tone was mild. "Your master knows you're out here on the road?"*

*Coleman swept his hat from his head and nodded. "Yes, sir. We be having a pass to go to Twelve Oaks for the day." He drew the passes out of his pocket and took a step toward the mounted man.*

*Shepherd waved him away and gathered up the reins. "Your master is a kind man, letting y'all go on a visit. Just make sure you leave for home well before sunset. No one likes to see bucks out on the road after dark."*

*"Yes, sir." Coleman backed away, bowing.*

*"Yes, sir," Elijah mumbled.*

*Shepherd urged the horse forward a few steps, then pulled up again. "One more thing. If you see ladies on the road, whether in a carriage or walking, you boys give way to your betters. Hear me? You get to the side of the road and stand until they pass you by." Without waiting for a reply, Shepherd spurred his horse into a canter and continued down the road.*

*"Yes, sir." Coleman's words were lost in the noise and dust of the man's departure.*

*Elijah let out a shaky breath. He was sweaty again. "Do you think he suspected that we're running?"*

*"Nah." Coleman shook his head. "We have a pass. We ain't doing nothing wrong. Most of the masters take every chance to let us know they in charge. Even when we're clean-dressed like you and me. Anyone can see we ain't no field hands. But that don't make no difference to white men. They treat us all the same."*

*After almost an hour of walking, traffic picked up on the road. Several plantation families passed, the carriages filled with women in bright dresses. The men followed on horseback.*

*Each time one approached, the pair scrambled to the edge of the road. The first time, Coleman told Elijah, "They families be going to church. Master and Mistress do they worship at home in the chapel. Most families around here go to out to church on Sundays, though."*

*They also encountered a number of Negroes on the road. Several tried to engage Coleman and Elijah in conversation. But after a few pleasantries, Coleman would steer Elijah to the side of the road, saying he had a stone is his shoe or he had to use the bushes.*

*After the third time Coleman avoided a question about where they were headed, Elijah understood. "You don't want them to be looking for us at Twelve Oaks, do you?"*

"No. We don't want anyone raising the alarm by asking if we got lost on the way. In fact, it's time for us to leave the road. See them woods up there? That's where we going." Coleman looked in both directions and then stepped back onto the road. He nodded toward the two men they'd been talking with earlier. "Just let those two get a-ways ahead."

Elijah and Coleman ambled up the road toward the forest. By the time they reached the trees, the men in front had moved so far ahead that Elijah could no longer see them.

"This is it, boy. We go into that woods, we're done for if we get caught. They'll take us back and whip us raw," Coleman said.

"Only if they catch us," Elijah declared. "And I ain't fixing to get caught." He glanced up and down the empty road.

"All right then, boy. Let's skedaddle," Coleman replied and stepped through a stand of redbuds, blazing pink in their early-summer glory.

Elijah followed on Coleman's heels, gasping in a mix of terror and elation as they raced away from the road and deeper into the murky shade of the unknown.

# CHAPTER SEVEN

SCOUT CAME BOUNDING through the door when Alexa arrived home early on Wednesday. "Hey, buddy. Surprised? I didn't have any more meetings, and I needed a break. I thought we'd go for a hike."

The big mastiff's entire body shook with joy as he pursed his lips in a smile.

"Let me change. I'll be back down soon." Scout ran to the edge of the woods and snuffled the ground as Alexa entered the house.

A few minutes later, the two set off on a favorite trail to Weaver's Pond. When they entered the cathedral of towering, old-growth pines, Alexa breathed in the crisp smell of evergreens with a contented sigh. She loved hiking in the woods, and this grove of huge trees was one of her favorite places. The carpet of brown needles beneath their feet muffled Alexa and Scout's steps as they ambled along. She smiled at the loud burst of insistent drumming in the distance—a pileated woodpecker. A few minutes later, the big black-and-white bird with the red crest flew overhead. A rare treat.

At the far edge of the pine grove, Scout dashed ahead on the path, kicking up a flurry of fading crimson leaves as he ran. Sharp bursts of the tannin aroma that Alexa associated with fall marked the dog's progress down the trail.

When they reached the pond, Alexa sat on a fallen log while Scout snooted along the edge of the water. Although she had tried to put it out of her mind, Alexa knew that she had to confront the horror of finding that dead man in the field. She seemed to have a knack for finding trouble. For finding dead bodies.

And although she knew there were risks, Alexa couldn't walk away from an injustice or a puzzle. Her crusading nature had put her in several life-or-death situations. But, did she ever learn? Not really.

Alexa often wondered: If she'd gone into criminal law, would that have fulfilled her need to do good? She loved her job and helped people with a range of problems in her civil law practice, but the cases were more low key. She'd been searching for more serenity in her life. That's why she'd fled New York City for the family law practice and this cabin in the woods.

But, Saturday, she'd been the one to leap in and say, "Let's go check this out ourselves." Like some sort of danger junkie. And look what she'd stumbled into this time. Each encounter with a violent death had shaken her to the core, but something about this man's end seemed particularly horrible. Maybe it was the calculated nature of the execution. Maybe it was the sign in Arabic, likely a deliberate attempt at diversion. It was such a cold and terrifying way to die.

Scout returned to Alexa and rolled onto his back, pumping his legs into the air in a frenzy of delight.

"Got an itch, buddy?" She laughed. "Come on. Time to head back home. It gets dark pretty early these days." Alexa rose from the log and headed back down the trail. With an oomph, the mastiff jumped to his feet and followed.

As Alexa walked up the steps to the deck, she heard the faint ring of the telephone inside the house. She ran to the door, unlocked it, and managed to reach the phone just before the answering machine kicked in.

"Hello."

"Hey. I tried you at the office, but Melinda said you ducked out early."

Alexa smiled to hear Reese's warm voice. She hadn't spoken to him since Saturday.

"Glad you tracked me down. How was the big meeting? Did you convince any billionaire donors to cough up funds for big cat conservation?"

"We won't know for a while. Two family mega-foundations asked all the right questions, said good things. One of the environmental organizations seemed interested in partnering. The rest—who knows? Let's say we got positive vibes, but no commitments."

"Don't these outfits usually need to take decisions like this to their boards?"

"Yeah. I'm impatient though. I've put a lot into this study, and these preliminary results are alarming. If we're going to save lions in Africa, we need to act now."

Alexa opened the door to let Scout into the house as she grinned. One of the things that appealed most to her about Reese was his enthusiasm for his job. He'd thrown himself wholeheartedly into his job as a park ranger here in Pennsylvania. His love of Africa and its animals was even stronger. He'd joined a field conservation project in Africa after his college years at Middlebury and had loved his stints in Kenya and Tanzania. He'd gone back about a year and a half ago to study big cats for the Animals of Africa Trust and now worked for them here in the States.

She replied, "It sounds like some of these foundations might come through. In the meantime, you still need to finish the report, right? Just keep plugging away." Alexa perched on a stool at her kitchen counter.

"I will, I will." Reese paused. "Sorry I didn't call before this. How are you dealing with Saturday? I'm glad I've been so busy, because I keep seeing his body. And all the friggin' blood. My God. It was worse than a lion kill."

"I've been trying to put it out of my mind. But the whole thing dredged up some bad old memories. Elizabeth Nelson, Cecily Townes, Reverend Browne." Alexa's voice broke. She was able to be honest with Reese. "The way this guy died. It was so cold and heartless."

"Definitely not spur of the moment. I've been thinking about the sign. They had to bring the ISIS sign along. There was nothing in that farmhouse to write on."

"I agree. They planned the execution. And they brought the sign along to throw the police off. Send them down some terrorism rabbit hole. But who does something like that?"

Reese switched to a careful tone. "Has the FBI contacted you?"

"I talked to them on Sunday. Had to leave Mom and Dad's soirée. The interview was pretty much a repeat of the one with the state police."

"Yeah. Two agents interviewed me on Sunday. And again just a while ago at the Trust office. I'm glad they didn't show up until after the donors left."

Alexa frowned. Reese seemed to be holding something back. "Why the second FBI interview? I mean, we found the body. That's it."

"Not quite." Reese paused again. "Turns out, this isn't the first dead body. In August, just after I came home from Africa, they found another dead guy like this—in a remote area a few miles outside of Harpers Ferry."

"No!" Alexa said in disbelief. "He was executed too?"

"With the Allahu Akbar sign and everything." Reese replied with a catch in his voice.

"What a strange coincidence." As she spoke the words, the lawyer in Alexa grasped the implication. Her tone became flat. "Law enforcement doesn't believe much in coincidence."

"You're right." Reese's voice dropped. "They were nowhere near as cordial on this second interview."

"Do you know any criminal lawyers down there in West Virginia?"

"There's a guy from the gym who practices law." Reese stopped. "Wait. You think this is serious?"

"I don't know for sure, but I suggest that you have a lawyer with you next time the FBI wants to talk. I'll track someone down for you tomorrow. The firm has contacts throughout the mid-Atlantic."

"Now I'm really bummed," Reese fretted. "We didn't really think it through before we rushed out to that farm. We were Good Samaritans, and now it might bite me in the ass. Same thing that happened all those years ago with that young girl. It took me years to put that false rape charge behind me."

"I'm sorry. I pushed you, and especially Tyrell. You know I tend to leap before I look. I hate that this is dredging up that whole mess with the false rape charge. In the end, you were exonerated. Same thing here. The FBI guys have to do their job. But we know that you had nothing to do with any murders. Innocence is the best defense."

"If you say so. But how many times have you read about some innocent guy being released from jail after serving thirty years on a bad rap?" Reese asked in a brittle tone. Then, his voice lifted. "Are we still on for this weekend?"

Alexa was thrown off balance by Reese's abrupt change of topics. "What? Oh, yes. I'll be down on Friday evening, but late. I have to drop Scout with the parents before I hit the road."

"I'm looking forward to it."

"Me too. I'll see you then." Alexa walked the phone receiver back to its base with a faint smile on her lips. She and Reese had agreed to take it slow this time. And they had both been walking a careful path, afraid of getting hurt again. But, there was no denying it: This man still took her breath away.

Alexa ate a salad at the kitchen island, jotting down names of attorney friends she could contact about possible representation for Reese. As she put her plate in the dishwasher, Scout lifted his head and became still. A second later, the bell chimed to indicate a car approaching down the lane. Alexa felt a frisson of alarm but pushed it away. Walking to the far wall, she switched on the deck lights, the mastiff right on her heels.

Alexa peered out the big dining room window at the two men climbing out of a nondescript sedan. She recognized Agent Carter; the other was a stranger. "The FBI? Guess I should have expected this."

Scout barked once when the pair knocked on the door. A male voice said, "Ms. Williams. This is Agent Carter from the FBI. May we come in?"

Alexa ran her fingers through her loose halo of honey curls and tugged at her sweatshirt before she opened the door. "Hello. This is Scout; he's big but harmless."

As the agents entered the cabin, Alexa told the dog, "Sit."

"Big is an understatement. His head is huge." Carter held out the back of his hand to the dog, and after a moment the agent scratched the mastiff's head. The other man nodded but remained silent. Despite the late hour, both men wore blue suits with white shirts and subdued gray ties in almost interchangeable patterns.

Carter looked at Alexa. "We have some follow-up questions about the incident this past weekend. Sorry to show up so late. And unannounced."

Annoyed at having her evening interrupted, Alexa suspected that the agents weren't sorry at all. Showing up here late and unannounced was intended to throw her off balance. She bit her lip and wondered why they thought such an approach was necessary. Of course, she would be polite and cooperative. Maybe she could find out why they were leaning on Reese.

"No problem. I just finished dinner. Would you like something to drink? A Coke? Coffee or tea? We can talk in the living room."

"No thanks." Carter refused for both men and headed through the arched entrance to the adjacent room.

The agents each took a leather armchair. Alexa sat on the deep couch, curling her bare feet beneath her, and gazed at the two men in expectant silence.

After a long pause, Carter spoke. "Alexa, this is Agent Fox from our Counterterrorism Unit in DC."

He turned to Fox. "As I mentioned, Ms. Williams and I first met when she helped expose an international sex-trafficking ring operating out of Cumberland County. Without her, we might never have broken it open. We spoke again on Sunday about this latest incident."

Alexa smiled at Carter. She liked the guy. He'd been a straight shooter when she'd dealt with him in the past. Earnest and by the book. Good-looking in that bland, blend-into-the-crowd way typical of the FBI.

Fox finally spoke in a reedy voice. "Trouble seems to find you, Ms. Williams. Do you consider it a blessing or a curse?"

"Excuse me?" Alexa frowned at the man's critical tone.

Carter glared at his companion but softened his expression when he turned to Alexa. "Agent Fox wanted to walk through some of the same territory that we covered on Sunday. Plus, we have a few additional questions. I'd like to tape this, OK?"

Alexa nodded. "OK with me."

Fox sniffed and wrinkled his nose before he began. "Ms. Williams, can you tell me exactly how you came to find this body on Saturday—afternoon, wasn't it?"

"Yes. Saturday afternoon." Slipping into her lawyer mode, Alexa walked them through the drone flight, the trip to the farm, and the distressing moments when she, Reese, and Tyrell found the body and the Allahu Akbar sign.

Both agents took reams of notes. Fox interrupted Alexa from time to time with a clarifying question. As she reached the end of her narrative, Fox asked, "Who chose the places where you flew the drone?"

"Me, I guess. Tyrell wanted field and mountain shots, so we piled into my Land Rover and drove around. I took back roads, somewhat at random. Neither Reese nor Tyrell know the area as well as I do."

"And did either Mr. Michaels or Mr. Jenkins offer any input about the route?"

"Input?"

"Advice on where to turn, which road to take? Or objections about a decision that you made?"

"Not really. They were looking for the best spots to pull over and send the drone up. Both Reese and Tyrell suggested places to park."

When Fox sniffed and twitched his nose at her response, it hit Alexa that he actually looked like a fox. His thinning hair even had a reddish cast. A pop song from a few years back popped into her head: "What Does the Fox Say?" She struggled to suppress a chuckle.

"You say the image on the video concerned you. Why didn't you call the police? Why did you and your friends decide to play detective on your own?"

Alexa tried to concentrate on Fox's questions but kept getting distracted by the silly tune running through her mind. What did the Fox say?

She shook her head to clear away the song. "Play detective? I guess you could call it that. But we didn't know exactly where the drone had captured the photo. We flew it for several hours that morning. I wasn't sure where that particular farm was, and I thought it would make more sense to track it down. Also to make sure that we weren't overreacting; it could have been a dead deer or something."

"Did anyone object to your approach, to driving around until you found the right place?"

At the derision in Fox's tone, the tune in Alexa's head shut down cold. This guy was an ass. Feeling warm, she pushed up the sleeves of her sweatshirt. "Tyrell wanted to call the police, but Reese and I convinced him that finding the place first was the right way to go."

"I thought you said it was your idea, not Mr. Michaels'?"

"It was, but he agreed with my suggestion. He was a forest ranger in Michaux State Forest at one time. He has a good appreciation for how many places in this area can look very similar."

"You are aware that Mr. Jenkins' drone's telemetry includes GPS coordinates?"

"I know next to nothing about drones."

"Would it surprise you to know that the GPS coordinates could have been retrieved?"

Alexa shrugged. "Like I said, I don't know anything about drones. And, frankly, Tyrell doesn't know a whole lot either. This was his first flight with the thing—and he was reading the directions most of the time." She paused and sat up straight, tired of being on the defensive. "Is that extraction process something that could be done immediately, or would it have taken time? Because the way that those buzzards were attacking the body, it might have been gone if we got there much later."

Scout must have sensed some tension in Alexa's voice because he rose from his bed in the corner and plopped onto her feet.

Agent Carter, who had been silent during Fox's extended questioning, said, "We're almost finished, Alexa. But could I trouble you for that cup of tea you offered earlier?"

"Sure. I have Constant Comment, Zen, black?" Alexa rose. "Would you like a cup too, Agent Fox?"

"Just some water for me, please."

"I'll have Zen tea. Thanks." Carter smiled.

Alexa could hear the two men murmuring in low voices as she heated water and assembled cups and sugar on a tray. Carter didn't sound very happy with Fox. She suspected that his sudden thirst for tea was a ruse to get her out of the room for this intra-agency discussion. So far, this interview had been a B.S. repeat of everything she'd told the FBI on Sunday. She expected that they'd get to the point now. And that the point, for some reason, was Reese.

Back in the living room, Alexa inhaled the soothing wintergreen scent of her tea and again imagined Fox prancing around the forest like the creature in the silly "What Does the Fox Say?" video. The image lightened her mood, and she leaned forward, repressing a smile. "You said that you have more questions?"

Fox responded, "Yes. Can you tell us where you were on August twenty-eighth and twenty-ninth?"

Alexa had expected them to bring up the other body. Even so, being asked her whereabouts like a murder suspect was disconcerting. "Not off the top of my head. Let me look at my calendar. Is this about the body found near Harpers Ferry?"

At Fox's sharp look, Alexa said, "You must have expected that Reese would mention this to me. It's freaky that not just one but two guys would be killed in this horrific way. Not that far from each other." She lifted her iPhone from the coffee table and checked her calendar.

"Oh, August twenty-eighth and twenty-ninth were a Friday and Saturday. I spent that weekend at the Outer Banks in North Carolina. A family thing at my brother's vacation home. You can check with Graham or his wife, Kate. And if you need further verification from someone outside the family, they had some friends to a barbeque on Saturday night. I don't have their names, but I can get them from Graham tomorrow."

"Have you ever been to the Harpers Ferry area?" Carter asked.

"A few times over the years. I've visited Reese once since he moved there. Beautiful little town."

"And tell us about Reese Michaels. How long have you known him? What is your relationship?"

Alexa figured that this was where they'd been heading all along. "Reese is a great guy. I met him a few years ago when I found a dead girl in the Michaux State Forest. Reese was a forest ranger who acted as a liaison to the state police on the investigation. We became involved. In fact, we lived together for a while. Here." Alexa waved her hand with a sad smile.

"Reese got an offer to work on a wildlife conservation project in Africa. That was his dream job." Alexa bit her lip as she remembered the role her emotional state at the time had played in Reese's decision to leave. She couldn't get past her guilt from killing Reverend Browne, and she had pushed away Reese's support. She'd made it easy for him to leave.

"He went to Africa?" Fox prodded.

"Kenya. Reese contracted malaria. After he got back on his feet, his doctor suggested he leave the continent and take some time to recuperate. The organization he works for assigned him to their headquarters outside Washington, DC. Now that he's back, we've been spending time together."

"So, you and Mr. Michaels broke up?" With an expression of distaste, Fox looked at Carter. "Didn't you mention a relationship with a state cop?"

Alexa bristled. "I'm not sure why my personal life is relevant here. But, yes, Reese and I broke up. I went on with my life, got involved with another guy, a state policeman."

Carter leaned forward. "We're just trying to get the full picture."

Alexa took a deep breath. "Well, John Taylor is hardly relevant. He died in the line of duty this past spring." She shot a scornful look at Fox but tried to calm down. Getting pissed off wasn't going to help.

"I understand that Mr. Michaels lived in northern Kenya. There's quite a lot of terrorist activity along that Somali-Kenya border and now in Kenya. Al Shabaab."

"Reese, a terrorist? You can't be serious?" Alexa's mouth dropped open in shock. "I visited him in Samburu once. He and his team were all about lion and leopard conservation, twenty-four/seven. He doesn't have a terrorist bone in his body."

Fox wielded the next question like a knife. "Wasn't he accused of rape? That speaks to violent tendencies."

Alexa was fed up. It was clear that Fox had expected this incident would be a surprise to her. "It was a false accusation. The girl retracted her story; she'd been trying to cover up her own misconduct. Reese was never even arrested. Quite a leap from a false charge by a hysterical teenager to terrorism and murder."

Alexa's voice rose in anger. "You are way off track, Agent. Reese Michaels is a good man. He'd never be involved in anything like these murders."

Alexa looked at Carter and said, "You have to do your job. But I've answered all your questions. I believe we're done here." She rose and walked to the door.

A few seconds later, Carter and Fox joined her at the threshold.

"Thank you, Alexa." Carter kept his tone neutral. "If we have any more questions, we'll be in touch."

"Yes. Thank you, Ms. Williams." Fox gave a final twitch of his nose, but Alexa had moved well past finding any humor in the gesture.

She looked at Carter, ignoring Fox. "I have some questions for you. Have you identified that young man in the field? Or the one in Harpers Ferry? Is this really related to Islamic terrorism? Are my friends and I in any danger because we found this dead guy?"

Carter glanced at Fox before he responded. "Because it's an ongoing investigation, there's little we can share. Neither of the men is local. One's last-known address was Philadelphia; the other was from Washington, DC. We are withholding names pending notification of any family that we can track down. Both men were known to have been homeless at one point."

Fox chimed in, "I can add only that we have not established any definitive links to Islamic terrorism. I would advise that you and your friends be vigilant and aware of your surroundings; pay attention to any anomalies in your lives in terms of events or people that don't seem quite right. But the FBI and local law enforcement have protected your role in discovering the body. It's unlikely that the perpetrators, regardless of motivation, have any idea that you've been involved."

Alexa seethed at the agent's matter-of-fact tone as he brushed by her and out into the night.

At the edge of the deck, Carter turned back and said, "Goodnight, Alexa. Thanks again for your time."

Fox walked straight ahead and slid into the passenger side of the car.

Alexa plucked a jacket from the hook by the door. "Come, Scout. Let's take you outside and then head to bed. It's late."

Standing on the deck, Alexa watched the dark forest swallow the glow of the FBI car's taillights and shivered. The autumn night was cool, but fears for Reese caused her chill. This Fox guy seemed to have decided Reese could be a terrorist who honed his skills in Kenya and had returned home to, what? Extract homeless men from major cities and transport them to the countryside for execution? It didn't make sense, even as a theory.

But Fox had acted like a dog with a bone. No way was Reese a terrorist or a killer. Still, if the FBI had him in their sights, he could be in big trouble.

# CHAPTER EIGHT

"Traffic bad?" Reese asked as he kissed Alexa's cheek. Plucking the small suitcase from her hand, he smiled. "Hope burgers on the grill are OK. I bought some other stuff at the deli to go with them."

Alexa grabbed her purse from the seat of the Land Rover and followed Reese up the sidewalk. She smiled as he ducked to clear the doorframe. Builders from the early nineteenth century had not envisioned men as tall as Reese.

"I'll run this upstairs to your room. There are drinks in the fridge." Reese disappeared into a narrow stairwell.

Slipping off her jacket, Alexa looked around the living room trying to pinpoint what seemed off. Then, she identified the change from last time she'd visited. Most of the furniture that had come with the leased house had a chintzy, faux-Colonial feel. Now, a huge leather recliner and big-screen TV dominated one corner of the room, hulking like a rugby fullback among a troupe of ballet dancers.

"Nice chair," she remarked in a dry tone as Reese hit the bottom stair. "Looks comfortable."

"It is so sweet. I couldn't take it anymore. Try to sit for a whole hockey game on that couch from hell—or one of those little frou-frou chairs."

Alexa's tone was teasing. "Frou-frou chairs? They look like valuable antiques to me; maybe Chippendale."

Reese hooked an arm around Alexa's shoulders. "I'm starving. Let's start the burgers. We can discuss antiques over dinner. Chippendale? I thought that was the show with male strippers."

Alexa laughed at his lame joke. She loved Reese's goofy sense of humor.

Over dinner at the butcher-block island in the tiny kitchen, Alexa asked, "Did you get in touch with the lawyer I recommended?"

"Luke Grandin? Yeah. I met with him yesterday. He told me to sit tight. That the FBI might just be casting a wide net, and I'm one of the fish that got swept up. That they might take a closer look at me and my background, then throw me back into the sea."

"That sounds encouraging?" Alexa tried to gauge Reese's reaction.

"I guess. And he seems like a good guy to have your back if the FBI comes calling again." Reese grinned. "Or should I say, if the FBI scoops me up with a smaller net." He pantomimed fins with his hands and moved his mouth into a fishlike O.

Alexa giggled. "At least you can laugh about it." Her voice became serious. "It's so unfair. We are the good citizens in all of this. And now you've come under suspicion."

"You're right. It sucks. Especially if I have to shell out money to hire this lawyer, Grandin. He don't come cheap. But, Hakuna Matata."

Alexa shook her head in bemusement. "You know you've been in Africa too long when you start channeling *The Lion King*."

"Have some respect, woman," Reese joked as he snagged another beer from the fridge. "All the safari guides say it. I'm not sure if it was always a common expression in Kenya, or if they picked it up from the movie to entertain their clients. But everyone on our lion project used the phrase. All. The. Time.

"Boss, the computer crashed, and we lost yesterday's data. Hakuna Matata. Sorry, we drove all afternoon but couldn't find the Ewaso pride. Hakuna Matata. We're out of fruit for lunch. Hakuna Matata."

"OK. I get it. I get it. Stop." Alexa laughed.

"You finished with that?" Reese pointed to her empty plate.

At Alexa's nod, he said, "Why don't you hang over there on the sofa? Unlike the one in the living room, it's comfortable. I'll put this stuff away."

"I might fall asleep in front of this fire." Alexa sighed as she settled into the deep couch facing a limestone fireplace that had to be original to the old house. She studied Reese across the room as he scraped dishes and tidied the kitchen. Every small movement the big man made touched her heart. She was so glad that he was home. They'd had a brief reunion in Kenya after Reese had left for his dream job in Africa, and it had been glorious to see him again.

The sex was wonderful. But, she had to go home. And their history, combined with the barriers of geography, had made them decide to go their own ways.

When they'd parted in Samburu, Reese had quoted an African proverb: Love never gets lost; it's only kept. Alexa had kept him in her heart ever since. And she felt that she had remained important to him as well. Otherwise, would she be sitting here tonight? Would they have spent these few months dancing around their relationship? She yearned for a day that they'd find their way back to each other. To find a bridge over the chasm that had opened between them. But a cold, logical part of her brain warned: Alexa, he'll leave again.

When Reese joined Alexa, she snuggled into the crook of his arm. "Are you settling in here? The house doesn't really seem to suit you."

"I can't complain about the price. I only pay utilities." Reese fondled a strand of Alexa's hair. "Harpers Ferry is just over an hour to the Trust offices. Not much farther to you and Carlisle. That being said, it's a little cramped. I'm always afraid I'm going to knock over one of these precious antiques by mistake."

"I get it. Tough to say no to a free place to live. How many houses does this Trust board member own, exactly?"

"He mostly lives in DC. This is one of three weekend places. One in Aspen, or somewhere out west. One in the Caribbean. But his teenage kids don't like to come here anymore. It's too boring."

"Tough life."

As a silence fell, Alexa wished she hadn't brought up the topic of Reese's living arrangements. He'd decided to move in here before he landed back in the States. Although she would have been wary about having him move back into her cabin, Alexa was still hurt that he hadn't at least floated the idea.

Reese whispered, "Are you asleep?"

Alexa shook her head. "No, but I'm beat. It was a long day."

He eased his arm from behind her back and sat up straight. "If you want to go on up to bed, I'll tamp down the fire. Our plans for tomorrow include a lot of walking."

"Then I definitely need a good night's rest." Alexa smiled.

Reese stood and pulled Alexa to her feet. Her heart raced as he leaned forward to brush his lips across hers in a fleeting kiss.

Alexa still lay awake, tasting that brief kiss, when she heard Reese make his way up the stairs and into the bedroom across the hall. She sighed. Africa, another man, more than a year spent apart—none of this had diminished her love for Reese. But how did he feel about her?

# CHAPTER NINE

"WHAT A QUAINT town. Too bad we didn't have time to explore the last time I was here," Alexa said, inhaling the crisp autumn air. "Of course, the trees wouldn't have been as spectacular. Look at all those reds and oranges. They're fading already at home." Cool and clear, this was one of those perfect fall days that were Alexa's favorite. Or maybe she was just thrilled with the chance to spend time with Reese.

"Last visit, you barely made it here for the Trust event in Washington. Just pretend this is your first time in Harpers Ferry." Reese smiled and grabbed her hand. "Stop. Close your eyes. Turn three times." He guided her through a slow spin. "Now, open your eyes. Voila! Your first sight of Harpers Ferry. It's magic."

Alexa laughed in delight as Reese brought her to a halt. "I'm not sure it's that easy. I was here as a kid. But I don't remember a whole lot. John Brown and a really pretty view. That's about it."

"Well, those are the main highlights, but there's a lot more history. There's a rock up there," Reese pointed up the hill, "named for Thomas Jefferson. He and Washington hung out here. That rock and the John Brown raid of pre-Civil War fame are why most of the town is a national park."

"Is your house part of the park?"

"No, the lower part of town is in the park. My neighborhood's called the Historic District."

"Oh, look at this shop." Alexa darted into a bookstore that had a poster for Harpers Ferry Ghost Tours in the main window, just above an assortment of books and soaps. "I'll bet the ghost tour is booked full. When better to see ghosts than Halloween week?"

She giggled as Reese rolled his eyes with an indulgent smile and followed her into the store.

They spent the rest of the morning shopping and wandering through the Lower Town before taking a break for lunch in a charming house-turned-restaurant that Reese had been wanting to try. When she looked at the menu, Alexa teased, "Let me guess, the beef sandwich au jus?"

"Exactly," he smiled. "And the Asian salad for you?"

"Of course." Alexa settled into the cozy booth. She and Reese were so comfortable together that she sometimes forgot they'd ever been apart.

After lunch, Reese led Alexa to John Brown's fort. "Quiz time. What do you remember about John Brown?"

"He was an abolitionist, but a real zealot? Didn't he and his sons terrorize Kansas with raids to free slaves? Then, he came here and tried to seize federal weapons. He was going to lead a slave uprising or something like that." They stopped in front of a small red brick building, much like a barn with several large doors.

"You get a gold star, Ms. Williams." Reese hugged her in congratulations, and Alexa drew a deep breath, forgetting about the history lesson.

But, Reese released her and continued his train of thought. "Brown fell on the extreme action end of the abolitionist scale. He wasn't content with writing earnest tracts about the evils of slavery. He thought the sword was mightier than the pen." He pointed to the building. "This is the Federal Armory they raided. Like you say, they wanted to arm a slave rebellion. But, it didn't go as planned. When townspeople tried to stop the raid, Brown's group took most of the town hostage. They battened down in this Armory building.

"General Robert E. Lee and J. E. B. Stuart led federal troops to the rescue. The army overpowered Brown's gang of rowdies. Killed several of them. Wounded Brown, himself. Freed the hostages."

"Robert E. Lee and J. E. B. Stuart. I thought this was before the Civil War."

"It was. Lee and Stuart were still in the US Army when all this happened. They both joined the Confederacy at the start of the Civil War. Must have been surreal to turn around and fight the army you'd served for years."

"What happened to John Brown? Isn't there a song about him dying?" Alexa searched her memory banks and hummed a few bars of a melody, still thinking about the warmth of that quick hug.

"No, that's the 'Battle Hymn of the Republic.'" They walked into the building, empty inside except for a few old cannons.

"Same tune, but different words. The one you're thinking of is called 'John Brown's Body.'"

"That's right. The one where his body molders in the grave. When I was a kid, I thought that part was soooo creepy."

Reese flashed a smile. "Right. 'Molder' is such an expressive word." He slid an arm around Alexa's shoulders and guided her to one of the cannons. "West Virginia didn't exist in the 1850s. Harpers Ferry was in Virginia. The good citizens of that slave state didn't take too kindly to the idea of a slave rebellion. So, they put John Brown on trial over in Charles Town. He was found guilty and hanged by the neck until dead."

Alexa tried to focus, but her pulse was racing with Reese so near. She wrinkled her brow. "It's coming back to me. We studied this in middle school. Wasn't Brown credited with putting the country on track to the Civil War?"

Reese cleared his throat. "That's a controversial question. Some people say that Brown's raid and the speech he gave at his trial crystallized the argument for ending slavery and ignited the Civil War. Others say that he was just a small piece of the puzzle and that the nation was headed to conflict anyway over economics, slavery, and more."

In front of the fort, Alexa regained her composure and grinned at Reese. "Thanks for the history lesson, professor. You could moonlight as a tour guide." Typical of him to become an expert about Harpers Ferry when he'd only lived here a few months. Reese had a boundless curiosity that she admired.

"I think I'd rather do the ghost tours. Very scary from what I hear. Bwahahaha." Reese did his best Boris Karloff impression and grabbed Alexa's shoulders in a pretend-monster move.

Alexa stumbled, then steadied, caught in his grip. As she looked up at Reese, the mood shifted in an instant. Alexa met the intensity of his kiss as Reese brought his mouth down hard on hers. The surroundings disappeared as she gave herself to the moment.

Then, a group of teenagers walked by, snickering. One of them yelled, "Get a room," and the mood was broken.

Reese twisted his mouth into a soft smile. "Who knew history could be so inspiring?"

In a burst of sudden happiness, Alexa grabbed Reese's hand. "Yeah. Who knew?"

Reese looked at his watch. "Wow. We don't have much time. I want to be up at the Point for sunset. We better get a move on."

"The Point?"

"You were probably there on your trip as a kid. The place with the view? It's off the Appalachian Trail and overlooks the point where three states meet: West Virginia, Virginia, and Maryland. You can see the confluence of the Potomac and the Shenandoah Rivers; and the way the rivers cut through the Blue Ridge Mountains."

As Reese turned up the incline toward the overlook, Alexa lagged behind. She wanted to take a look at the walking bridge that continued over the Potomac River. A steady stream of people crossed the bridge in both directions.

"What's across the river?" Alexa asked, then saw that Reese was too far ahead to have heard her question. She turned back for one last look and stopped cold. Two men were leaning on the railing of the bridge and looking her way. Although at a distance, Alexa thought she recognized one of the men from her first interview with the FBI. In his twenties or early thirties, very fit. Dressed in dark pants and a windbreaker. Her heart dropped. Was the FBI following Reese?

# CHAPTER TEN

*June 28, 1859*

Wade in the water. God's gonna trouble the water.
> —*"Wade in the Water," a Negro spiritual*

*Coleman picked up the pace the minute he led them into the forest. When they left the road, a burst of adrenalin and fright powered Elijah; he had no trouble keeping up with the older man. But, after a half hour of walking through the underbrush at a breakneck speed, he was tiring.*

*He had also lost any sense of direction. Elijah had lived his life in the big house and its surrounding fields. The plantation had some small woodlands, but a forest this large was new to him. Earlier on the road, Coleman had pointed straight ahead when he spoke of the mountains they were aiming to reach. But now it seemed they were headed another direction.*

*Elijah touched Coleman's shoulder. "Can we walk a little slower? I'm tuckered out."*

*"Soon as we reach the stream, we can rest." Coleman slowed long enough to make sure the boy had heard, then marched forward.*

*The underbrush thinned out as they traveled farther, and Elijah settled into the brisk pace. The ground was flat but littered with fallen debris. Tripping over several branches cut short his attempts to study their surroundings and forced Elijah to concentrate on the ground beneath his feet. Although it had to be coming on noon, the thick green canopy overhead filtered out any sunlight and pressed* down with a dark, watchful silence. The only sound Elijah had heard for hours was the shallow rasp of his own breath and the occasional scrape of Coleman's boot against a fallen log.

Just as he heard the burble of water in the distance, Elijah noticed the forest brighten ahead. He smiled at the prospect of a break. This must be the stream that Coleman had mentioned.

"Let's be careful," Coleman whispered. He moved toward the noise with caution, stopping behind trees as he inched forward. Elijah imitated the blacksmith and darted from tree to tree as they approached the stream.

When the water came into sight, Coleman took a long look around, then said, "She be clear." He walked up to the mossy bank of the stream and sat.

Elijah scampered toward a small waterfall, the source of the burbling in the otherwise placid little stream. As he approached, a deer burst from a thicket of bushes near the water, sending his pulse racing.

"Come here. Let's rest and take a bite to eat. Your mama packed food for you, didn't she?"

Elijah dropped to the ground next to Coleman. "That deer scared me half to death." He took a piece of johnnycake wrapped in cloth from his coat pocket. "I brought some food with me, but only enough for a day or two. If we could have brought a sack, I would have packed more."

"Yes. But we couldn't give any sign that we were planning to run. We're going to have to find food along the way. Make what you brought last as long as you can. Now, let's talk about the plan." Coleman pointed to the water, "Upstream is west, toward the mountains. That's the way we're heading. But first, we need to make a false path to fool them dogs that the master will send after us. Your mama and I figured that he'll start them north first to Nottaway. But when they don't catch a scent, he'll probably bring them down the road to Twelve Oaks. Especially if he hears from that Shepherd man or someone else who saw us on the road. The dogs be sure to catch our scent on the road."

Elijah shivered at the thought of the coonhounds and bloodhounds that Master kept to chase down runaways and keep the field hands in line. He'd seen them run a slave down once when he'd bolted from the tobacco field, frightened by a snake. Then, panicked by what he'd done, the man had continued to run. The overseer had sent for the hounds and run the man down. In his terror, the field hand hadn't gotten far. Elijah had been walking the master's sons home from school when they came across the scene. He would never forget the baying and snarling dogs, lunging at the fallen man. If their handler hadn't had a firm grip, Elijah was convinced that they would have killed the field hand; maybe eaten him alive. Instead, the overseer had the man dragged back to the plantation and had the driver give him fifty lashes with a horsewhip. Elijah was used to seeing slaves whipped. Although it was horrible to watch, whipping was a weekly occurrence. But those dogs. He'd had nightmares about the hounds for months afterward.

"You listening, boy? This important." Coleman tapped Elijah's arm.

"I'm listening."

"I heared that this woods ends at a road. It ain't used as much as the one we just left, but it gets some traffic. On the other side are the fields for Macon. We is going to walk onto that road, then retrace our footsteps back to here. Then, we'll wade up that stream for a good piece. We'll meet up with Wabee there. Near the big bridge."

"What's the big bridge?"

"I don't rightly know. But the peddler said that there's a big bridge that crosses this stream at a deep gully. I told Wabee what to look for."

Elijah wondered about the reliability of this plan of Coleman's. It seemed pieced together, based on fragments of conversations he'd had with different people. But he admired the blacksmith for the work he'd put into planning this journey to freedom. If Elijah had been on his own, he would have had no idea which way to run. Those hounds would make short work of tracking his skinny body. But, even with all the thought, Coleman's plan had a lot of holes.

As if Coleman read Elijah's mind, he said, "I been studying to run for years. My life ain't been as bad as some. I got a nice cabin and special privileges because of my skills. Lord knows what they's going to do without a blacksmith. But, ever since I was your age, I been plagued by how unfair it is. That just because I was born in a black body, I be spending my days as property. Even a high yellow like you, who could pass as white, is doomed to be property. Master ain't as bad as most. But I been aching to be a free man.

"Your mama has been good to me. I was happy to bring you along, Elijah. But you have to pull your weight for us to make it north. It ain't going to be a cakewalk."

"Yes sir, Mr. Coleman. I want to be free just as much as you. And some day come back and get my mama and sisters."

"Lord willing, boy. But first, we must get ourselves far away from Nottaway County."

Elijah's feet were so numb he could no longer feel them. "Coleman. Can we step out of this stream for a while? I'm going to trip and break my ankle; it's like walking with two blocks of ice." Wistful, he remembered the ice Mistress had brought in for a big party one summer.

Coleman turned around, a weary look on his face. "I could use a rest too. But we can't step out on the bank. Those devil dogs can't follow a man's tracks in the water. We step out, they could catch our scent on the ground." He looked upstream. "There. Those rocks in the middle of the stream. We'll sit a spell there."

Climbing onto one of the flat rocks, Elijah made sure to keep his bundled-up coat and the food in its pockets from dipping into the water. He sat with his legs extended and studied his bare calves and feet. They had a bluish undertone from the hours walking in the cold woodland stream. Minutes later, his relief at being out of the cold disappeared as needles of pain pricked his lower extremities.

"Way to get rid of the pain is to rub your feet and legs, warm them up. The hurt comes from the ice inside thawing," Coleman advised. "Let's move back into those branches. Maybe even close our eyes for a few minutes. We can take turns."

After a painful few moments of trying to walk on thawing feet, the two fugitives hid in a web of branches from a tree that had fallen onto the flat rocks. Coleman said he'd take lookout duty first.

"How far to this big bridge where we're meeting Wabee?" Elijah yawned. As the pain in his feet subsided, he felt very sleepy.

"I don't rightly know. The peddler said it was about a day's walk or half-day's ride. I hope we get there by dark." He looked at the slice of sky above them. "It be past noon now. Let's rest a short spell before we push on. I aim for us to make that bridge and meet Wabee by dusk."

Elijah still struggled on the next leg of the journey. The stream widened as they'd moved on, but with the change came new challenges. Although trees still hugged both banks of the water, fields of tobacco sprawled out just beyond the narrow band of oaks and willows. Run-off from the farmland had deposited a thick layer of silt beneath the water's slow-moving surface. Elijah fought against the pull of thick mud with each step, all the while watching and listening for human activity. Coleman insisted that they keep close to the right *bank of the stream. Twice they had to sink into the cattails to avoid horsemen cantering nearby. During the last incident, the riders had pulled up just yards away from their hiding place. Elijah thought his arms would collapse as he held his coat with its precious food just above the water's surface. After what felt like hours, the riders exchanged a few words and rode away.*

*The blood had been pounding so hard in Elijah's ears that he couldn't make out the white men's conversation. But Coleman chuckled as they again walked upstream. "That one young gentleman has courting on his mind. They was talking about a Miss Amelia. I believe that's the eldest Buckner girl. If that's where those gentlemen be headed, we must be close to Buckner Meadows. That's the plantation near the big bridge. We be getting close."*

*Despite Coleman's optimism, the pair walked for quite a spell longer. Elijah's weariness turned to alarm when the speed of the current increased and the water level rose. Mama had insisted he learn how to swim in the pond back beyond the tobacco curing barns, but that had been in placid water. Elijah wasn't sure he'd be able to swim in a current like this.*

*Fretting with each step, Elijah wondered if he was up to the task of walking north. Coleman had said it could take weeks, and here he was, struggling on the first afternoon, exhausted, afraid of drowning, and jumping at each sound. When he lifted his gaze, Elijah stopped dead in his tracks, frightened by the scene ahead. He'd never seen terrain quite like this: steep banks on both sides of the stream and water tumbling over big rocks. A curve to the left kept him from seeing too much farther. But the hairs on the back of his neck stood up when he figured out that the water sweeping around the curve was making that roaring sound.*

*Coleman had stopped too. "We have to get out of the stream. We can't walk through fast water like that." He looked to their immediate right where the bank was still low enough to climb. "At least we're back in deep woods again. We're not far from the bridge. The peddler said that it was built to go over a stretch of rapids so long and fast that travelers couldn't ford the stream."*

*By the time they had scrambled out of the stream and found a sheltered place to hide, the sun was sinking low. Elijah leaned back against a tree trunk and breathed a deep sigh. It felt good to rest. Feeling a cool breeze, he leaned over and rolled down his pant legs.*

*"Leeches. Oh no, leeches." Elijah swatted at a big one near his knee.*

*"Quiet down, boy. No one can know we're here. Let me get those bloodsuckers off you." Coleman slid a thumbnail under the first*

leech's mouth and flipped the detached blob into the bushes. Calm and steady, he did the same to five other leeches on Elijah's legs. "Now, stand up and drop your drawers. We have to make sure there are no more."

Blood trickling down his leg, Elijah submitted to Coleman's inspection. He wanted to blubber like a baby over the bloodsuckers, but he bit his lip and stayed silent.

"No more. That's good. The blood should dry up soon. They something in those demons' spit that makes the blood flow." For the first time, Coleman looked at his own legs. "They got me too." He used his fingernail trick to detach the insect then doffed his pants and stood. "Any more?"

Elijah inspected the older man's legs in the dying light. "Nope. Just the one."

"Good. Those demons must just like the taste of young fresh blood better than old tough meat like me." Coleman gave a muted cackle.

The two travelers sat in silence for a few minutes. As they watched the sun set and dusk fall over the forest, they munched on Mama's cornbread. When the first frogs started to croak, Coleman said it was time to push on toward the bridge.

In the gathering dark, Elijah almost stepped out into the road by mistake. But he sensed a smoother texture underfoot and stopped. "Is this it? The road to the bridge?" he whispered into Coleman's ear. The roar from the rapids to their left filled the forest with thunder.

Coleman nodded and took a few steps back into the trees, then worked his way toward the noise. Moisture in the air muffled their footsteps as they approached the bridge.

Elijah listened for sounds of traffic on the road—the creak of a carriage wheel; the clip-clop of horses' hooves; the careless conversation of travelers confident in their right to be about at night. But he could hear nothing but the roar of swift water.

Coleman stopped in sight of the bridge and hooted like an owl. On the other side of the roadway, an owl replied. With a quick glance in both directions, the older man scurried across the gravel. Elijah followed, heart once again pounding. What if this was a trick and it was the patrollers out, hoping to catch a runaway slave?

This side of the road seemed darker; the ground under Elijah's feet felt springy and soft. The air was aromatic with a pleasant scent that he couldn't identify. Coleman led the way deeper into the trees, pushing away low-hanging branches that slid back into place silently as they passed. Still traveling parallel to the river, they came to a gap in the trees and stopped. Coleman looked around and hooted again.

*Elijah gasped as Wabee emerged from the trees, so close that, even in the darkness, he could see the tribal scars that marked the huge man's face.*

*"I wait. We go now. Must walk," he said.*

*Coleman nodded. "Yes. Let's try to walk through most of the night and find a place to hide before dawn. The peddler said to follow the river west for two days until we see the mountain. After the bridge there are farming villages and plantations, so we must be careful."*

*Energized, despite the daylong slog in the cold stream, Elijah felt the excitement build. He flashed a joyous smile. "The road to freedom."*

# CHAPTER ELEVEN

AT BREAKFAST ON Monday, Alexa couldn't get her mind off the weekend with Reese. She pushed away a half-eaten bowl of oatmeal and slammed her mug down so hard that it splashed tea onto the counter. She couldn't figure out if she was upset with Reese or herself.

That burning kiss in front of John Brown's Fort had been the romantic highlight of her trip to Harpers Ferry. During a lovely dinner at one of the town's best restaurants, the Bistro, Reese had been natural, charming, and sexy. But he made no attempt to build on that passionate kiss they'd shared. She'd spent another night alone in the narrow spindle bed.

Alexa addressed Scout. "How can I fault him when I didn't try to push it either? Hell, I don't even know if I want to take it further." As she spoke those words to the dog, Alexa knew she was lying. She was ready to plunge back into a relationship with Reese, consequences be damned.

"I just wish I knew where he's coming from, buddy." When had Reese become so timid? Or was she sending mixed signals? Reese had waited to declare himself when they first met because Alexa had been involved with another guy. Maybe he thought she was still grieving for John? Shaking her head, Alexa scratched the mastiff's big ears, planted a kiss on his nose, then jumped up. "Enough with the angst. I have to get ready for work."

"I'm leaving in a few minutes. It's PTA night." Melinda stood at the threshold of Alexa's office. "Do you need anything before I go?"

Alexa swung her chair around to look at her computer screen. "No. Looks like my calendar's pretty clear tomorrow morning.

Maybe we can talk about our upcoming court filings then. I want to loop Ted and Vanessa in on that discussion. They'll be doing most of the research."

"I'll schedule something tomorrow."

"Oh. That's right," Alexa remembered. "Thank you for your guidance on the Henninger divorce."

Melinda gave her a puzzled look.

"When I told you about the ridiculous fight over the bobblehead doll collection, you said that things aren't always what they seem. Turns out, you were right. When Ron Garver and I met with the Henningers on Friday afternoon, we floated the idea of a reconciliation. Both Rhonda and Henry jumped on it. Turns out, the divorce process has made both of them question whether they really wanted to end things. They're going to remain separated but try to see if, just maybe, they can find their way back together."

Melinda smiled. "I'm happy to hear it. You know what they say: Love makes the world go 'round. Hey, if they reunite, they might give you one of the Penn State bobbleheads."

Alexa raised an eyebrow and laughed. "I can only hope. But who knows? She could be back here in a few months to restart the divorce. But the thanks go to you. Your comment reminded me to be more sensitive to what's going on beneath the surface."

"Glad I could help on this one. But, other times, what you see is what you get, Boss. Gotta run. I'm in charge of refreshments for the meeting tonight."

At home, Alexa popped a chicken breast into the oven and ran upstairs to change into jeans. When she let Scout into the house from his romp, the dog was clingy, hugging Alexa's leg with every step. What a baby, she thought. She felt a twinge of guilt for abandoning him over the weekend, but he was much too large for Reese's tiny little dollhouse. "Did you miss me this weekend? I thought you loved staying at Grandma and Grandpa's. And you got to play with Courtney and Jamie on Friday night. You always like playing with the kids."

She sat at the kitchen counter and sorted through some bills, then checked her email. Reese had sent a brief note, telling her that he'd had a great weekend. It went on to say, "That guy you saw on Saturday? Not sure that he's who you thought. I've seen no further sign."

Alexa read the oblique message to mean that Reese didn't think the FBI was following him. She had to acknowledge that he could be right. The guy on the bridge looked familiar, but she couldn't say for certain he was FBI. It might be more that he fit the clean-cut, young-guy-with-a-windbreaker image of an FBI agent. Or someone she'd met somewhere else.

She typed, "I had a great time too. Will I see you this weekend? Let me know if you get any calls that require legal advice." After she hit send, Alexa laughed and looked at Scout. "I'm losing it, buddy. Writing these cryptic sentences like I've got the NSA intercepting my e-mails."

Fixing a salad to go with her chicken, Alexa wandered into the living room with her meal and turned on the news. Another terrorist attack, this one in France, was the main focus of the day. A lone man had set off a suicide bomb near the Eiffel Tower, killing scores of tourists. After the anchor had cycled through the high points twice, Alexa reached for the remote to change the channel. But she paused at a question the newscaster posed to a tough-looking man billed as a terrorism expert.

"What causes someone like this to embrace terrorism, to blow himself up? According to people who knew Raoul Sebert, he had no ties to a mosque, no strong religious beliefs. Family and friends had no idea he'd been radicalized."

The expert adjusted his glasses and frowned. "If we had all the answers, we might be able to prevent incidents like these. Authorities say Sebert had a criminal record, mostly burglaries and petty drug offenses. He was a loner, with few close friends. He struggled economically. Maybe he was radicalized online. Maybe he was drawn in by an acquaintance. I'm sure the police will put together a complete profile. But we may never really know what predisposes a person to identify so strongly with a cause that he's willing to commit suicide."

As Alexa switched to another channel, the phone rang. Scout followed as she leapt to pick it up.

Tyrell began speaking before Alexa could say hello. "Alexa. I need your help. It's the Qassims. Some assholes attacked their home tonight. No one's hurt, but the place is swarming with police, and crowds are forming. It could get ugly."

"Give me the address. I'll be there as soon as I can."

Flashing police lights and clusters of people spilled into the streets as Alexa neared the neighborhood not far from the center of Carlisle. She found a place to park and walked the final few blocks to the Qassim home. Yellow crime-scene tape blocked off the sidewalk, but a Carlisle police officer let her through when she identified herself as the family lawyer.

Alexa gasped at the words spray-painted across the clapboards facing the street: ISIS GO HOME. The big front window had a ragged hole through the center. Smashed pumpkins and glass shards littered the postage-stamp yard. She kept to the left as she climbed the few steps, trying to avoid the mess. Before she could knock, another policeman opened the door and directed her to the back of the house.

Tyrell, who had been leaning against the wall, gave Alexa a quick hug when she entered the dining room. "Thanks for coming."

"No problem. What's happening here?" She gestured toward the table where all four of the Qassims were huddling with two plainclothes policemen. A fifth man, perhaps another refugee, stood near the family.

"Counselor, it's been a while." The older plainclothes policeman nodded to Alexa.

"Detective Miller. I'm surprised to see you here. Isn't homicide your specialty?"

"We're short-staffed this evening."

Alexa looked at Eshan and Zahraa. "Are you OK? Was anyone hurt?"

Zahraa answered, "We are fine. Eshan and I were sitting here, having coffee. We jumped up at the crash when the glass broke in the big window. We got to the front room in time to hear several more pumpkins hit outside. Like mortars hitting the front of the house. I dropped to the floor, but Eshan ran and opened the door, shouting."

"Two pickup trucks squealed their tires and drove away down the street."

"Did you see the people who did this?"

Bassam said in a strained voice, "Ali and I were upstairs doing homework. When I heard the glass break, I looked out the window of my room. Four men in army clothes were in the back of each truck, throwing something at our house. They looked like Assad's soldiers, but they wore baseball caps."

Miller looked at Alexa. "We've already gone through these details. I believe they were wearing camouflage. That's what Bassam means by army clothes."

Alexa shook her head. "Pickup trucks. Camouflage. That narrows it down to about sixty percent of the Cumberland County population. What a frightening experience." Alexa's stomach had clenched at Zahraa's matter-of-fact statement that she'd mistaken the sound of smashing pumpkins for mortar rounds and Bassam's reference to the army of the brutal dictator they'd fled. It was hard to imagine the life they'd left in Syria.

Tyrell grimaced. "You saw the ISIS thing on the wall? They must have painted that before they let loose with the barrage of pumpkins. Nobody heard the graffiti artist at work. What idiots, though. ISIS? If they bothered to learn the Qassims' history, they'd find out that their home in Syria was destroyed by a rebel group associated with ISIS."

Eshan nodded. "Yes. Yes. That was a year before the Assad government started questioning my activities. I volunteered at a Médecins Sans Frontières medical facility. That raised suspicions that I was a spy for the West."

"Ah, Doctors without Borders. They do a lot of good in the world," Alexa smiled.

The other policeman, who'd been introduced as Officer Kramer, said, "These days, most people think of ISIS when they think of terrorism. And a lot of people tend to confuse the Muslim religion with terrorism."

"Ignorance is no excuse for this behavior. What if someone had been in that front room? They could have been cut by flying glass or worse." Alexa's spoke each word as if dipped in ice.

Detective Miller stepped in. "I don't think that Officer Kramer meant to excuse the vandalism or minimize the danger. We're lucky that no one was hurt."

The skinny man hovering behind Eshan scowled but remained silent. Instead, he rocked back and forth on his heels in a disquieting manner, reminding Alexa of a mountain lion preparing to pounce.

With a weary look, Eshan said, "We are Muslims, but we are not terrorists. We have come to America to escape violence and terror."

"It's ridiculous to think that we are part of DAESH," echoed Zahraa. "Here you call them ISIS. They are nothing but brutes. Savages. They want to take everything they touch back to medieval times."

Alexa leaned on the table and looked the detective in the eye. "Three questions. Have you caught the perpetrators yet? How will you protect my clients against future incidents like this? And do you plan to call in the FBI? Tonight's assault could be viewed as a hate crime."

Tyrell stepped next to her. "I'm sure RESIST volunteers will help clean up the damage and repair the window. But part of the refugee resettlement process involves a safe and secure setting for the people we sponsor. How can I guarantee that safety when the community acts out against one of our families?"

Officer Kramer spluttered, "Just a minute—"

Miller cut off his subordinate. "We are already looking for the vandals, and we'll bring the appropriate charges when we catch them. I'll ask for patrol cars to run by the house. At this point, Mr. Jenkins, I don't see evidence that the community is unsafe for Mr. and Mrs. Qassim and their sons. This looks to me like the work of a small, isolated group of people. Could be rowdy kids taking a post-Halloween trick too far. Could be adults with an agenda. If we're lucky, a neighbor taped the whole thing on their phone."

Rising, Miller tucked his notebook inside his jacket pocket. "I think we have enough for now. We'll have a patrol car cruise by every hour tonight. A team will be back tomorrow to process the scene. If any of you remember a new detail, give me or Officer Kramer a call." The detective handed a card to Eshan and another to Tyrell. "You still have my number, right?" he asked Alexa as Kramer headed out of the room.

She nodded. "Can I have a word?"

"Sure." Miller shrugged.

"Back in a moment," Alexa assured Tyrell. She followed the policemen out onto the street. The other cops were gone. The crowd had dwindled to just a group of teenagers, who seemed less interested in the Qassim home than their cell phones.

Out on the sidewalk, Detective Miller touched Alexa's elbow in a comforting gesture. "Sorry I never reached out after John Taylor's death. He was a good cop."

"He was a good cop. That's what got him killed." Alexa sighed.

Miller frowned. "What's up?" he asked, crossing his arms and resuming an official-business air.

"Maybe I'm overreacting here, but I want to prevent another tragedy with this family. They fled their home just steps ahead of arrest, spent years in the living hell of a refugee camp, before traveling thousands of miles to find refuge here in Carlisle. I can't imagine the hardships they've endured. And it's a damn shame that they keep running into jerks who are tarnishing America's good name."

"Have there been other incidents?"

"The youngest boy, Ali. A group of kids at the middle school have been bullying him. Last week, they jumped the boy and beat him up. Broke his arm. The parents didn't want to involve the police, so we dealt with school authorities. They suspended the brats for a few days. You might want to look at their parents for tonight's incident."

"Thanks. We'll check out that lead for sure. Some of these parents think Junior can do no wrong, and then get mighty annoyed when their little darling is disciplined. Worse if it's a family who taught their child to hate Muslims. Definite possibility. Or could just be some good ol' boys out to have some Halloween fun lobbing pumpkins at the newest Carlisle residents. All the more fun if they worship Allah."

"At least they used pumpkins and not cherry bombs or grenades."

"Thank God for small blessings." Miller rubbed a hand across his brow.

Alexa flashed a sympathetic smile. "Looks like it's been a long day. But imagine that this was your house. I know I'd be both angry and frightened at the same time. Just one more thing on the hate crime angle. No one was hurt tonight. The damage can be repaired. It's likely too small potatoes for the FBI. But there's no doubt that this was about religion and, thus, ethnic intimidation under the Pennsylvania statute." She pointed at the spray-painted words.

Officer Kramer, who stood just out of earshot, saw Alexa point at the house. He pulled a phone from his pocket and snapped some photos of the graffiti. Alexa hoped that they weren't the first of the night.

"Let's catch the guys first. Ethnic intimidation charges are usually secondary to a primary charge like vandalism or whatever. If the investigation warrants the secondary charges, we wouldn't hesitate to recommend them to the DA."

"Fair enough. I'm going back inside. Will you call me with an update tomorrow?"

"I can do that," Miller agreed. "Did I miss something? Have you switched to criminal law?"

"No way." Alexa shook her head. "I'm just helping out RESIST, and by extension, the Qassims. Who, in this case, are the victims not the defendants." She curled her lip into a sardonic smile. "A civil lawsuit wouldn't be out of the question though."

"More than half of the people we arrest don't have two nickels to rub together, so good luck there." Miller nodded to Kramer and headed toward the police cruiser. He opened the door, then glanced back. "Nice to see you again, Counselor."

# CHAPTER TWELVE

WHEN ALEXA WALKED back into the house, Bassam and Eshan were arguing, their faces dark with anger. She hesitated to intrude on the family row but took a deep breath and joined the group in the dining room.

"We should leave this country and go home. We don't belong here," Bassam wailed.

"But you have made friends. You like your classes." Eshan's sad tone undermined his encouragement. "Going home is not an option."

"They destroyed our house. They've made Ali's life so miserable that he cries in the night." Bassam's tone continued to rise, and his knuckles turned white from gripping the chair in front of him. "It's all true; they are infidels. No one wants us here." The teen looked to the thin man in the leather jacket. "Tell him, Uncle. You know it's true."

"Bassam. I will not have words like this in my home. You are a child. What do you know of extremist words like 'infidel'?" Zahraa's tone was sharp. "Apologize to Mr. Jenkins and Ms. Williams, who have shown our family nothing but respect and friendship." She threw a steely glance at the man Bassam had called Uncle.

With a questioning look, Alexa glanced at Tyrell, but he seemed unfazed by this volatile family dynamic. Of course, he'd spent years as a Children and Youth social worker. Dysfunctional and shattered families were all in a day's work to him.

The angry teen dipped his head. "I am sorry."

"It has been a disturbing night." Eshan's calm tone became stern. "But it is time for you to go to your room and finish your homework. We will discuss your rude behavior tomorrow."

As Bassam stormed from the room, Alexa focused on Ali, who had shrunk into his chair, cradling the arm in a soft cast. "Is your arm better, Ali?" she asked. "I see that you're not wearing your sling anymore."

"A little, Miss." A tear spilled from the boy's eye, leaving a dark splotch on the fabric of the cast. "Ya-umma. I only cried the one night because my arm hurt. I am not a baby. And I don't want to go home or back to the camp."

"As your father said, *habibi*, we are staying here. This is our new home. And your brother knows it. It's his way to become excited and angry when he is frightened. He did that even when he was a small child." Zahraa hugged her son. "Now, go upstairs and get ready for sleep."

Ali followed his brother up the stairs.

Alexa asked, "Do you need help in cleaning up this mess?"

Tyrell, who had been quiet during the family drama, replied, "No, I called a few folks from RESIST. They're bringing a board for the window. We'll put that up and help clean up the living room." He looked at Eshan. "We can order glass and paint tomorrow. I know the best place for both."

Eshan gestured to the thin man. "Brother, you can help with the work while you're here."

Alexa turned to the silent man. "I'm Alexa Williams. I don't believe we've met."

The man looked at Alexa with a stony expression but did not reply.

"Our apologies." Zahraa rose from the chair. "This is Nabil Qassim, Eshan's brother."

"Nice to meet you," Alexa replied.

The man remained silent and unresponsive.

Eshan spoke in a stern voice that brooked no dissent. "Miss Williams is our lawyer and has been a friend to our family. Please make her welcome in our home, Nabil."

Alexa gave this surprise brother a tentative smile, trying to remain pleasant despite the hostile vibe radiating from the guy.

With clear reluctance, the brother muttered, "Hello." Then, he lurched forward and seized Alexa's hand in a quick, firm handshake.

Alexa felt an intense energy from the brief contact, almost like the unpleasant zap from a shorted electrical wire. Shaken, she dropped her hand and took a small step backward.

Only then did Nabil allow a fleeting smile to play across his lips. "*As-salaam'alaykum*. Peace be upon you, Miss Williams. I am grateful for the help you've provided to my nephew and with the police this evening." His almost unaccented English seemed rote. "Excuse me. I must see how my nephews are getting on." With a nod, the man darted from the room.

"Apologies for my brother." Eshan fluttered his hands. "He is a man of strong temperament. Also, very religious. Although he has lived in America for quite a while, he holds fast to many of the old customs."

Zahraa coughed to cover a derisive snort.

"No problem." Alexa's words were more casual than she felt as she tried to regain her balance from the weird interaction with Nabil Qassim. The crackling tension in the room had disappeared the moment he left. "I didn't know you had a brother in Carlisle."

Tyrell said, "He's been living in Detroit but wasn't in a position to sponsor these folks at the point that their refugee status was approved."

"Yes. Layoffs at the automobile factory. He is staying with us and may relocate to Carlisle if he can find work. It has been many years since we've seen Nabil. It is such a joy to reunite." Eshan beamed.

"Yes. Such a joy." Zahraa rolled her eyes.

With a sudden chill, a sense of foreboding about this sinister brother settled between Alexa's shoulder blades, weighing her down. "Well then. I'm going to head home. I'd like to touch base with you about the kids at Ali's school; how that's going. But you've had enough to deal with tonight. I'll stay on top of Detective Miller and let you know if there's any news about the jerks who vandalized your home." She touched Zahraa's shoulder and smiled at Eshan. "Carlisle is a good place to live. But even the best trees have bad apples. Don't be discouraged."

Tyrell walked Alexa to the front door. "Want me to escort you to your car?"

"Nah. It's just down the street. I'll call you tomorrow. But thanks, Sir Galahad. Who says chivalry is dead?" She dropped to a whisper. "You need to fill me in on the charming brother." Then, she made a mock curtsey and descended the steps.

Alexa was surprised to find the street deserted. The teenagers had vanished. The only sign of the earlier tumult was a heap of shattered pumpkins ringed by two strands of yellow crime-scene tape on makeshift posts. The plastic ribbon fluttered in the soft breeze, but Alexa could have sworn that it was shuddering at the waves of pungent odor rising from the mashed squash.

She wrinkled her nose and hurried down the block. Although Detective Miller had promised periodic safety-checks of the Qassim house, neither police nor any other traffic cruised the deserted street. Parked vehicles lined the far side of the road; the near side was empty. As Alexa walked the few blocks back to her car, she thought how terrible the Qassims must feel. They risk everything to end up in Carlisle, and some idiots graffiti their house with anti-Muslim drivel. Her platitudes about bad apples had sounded lame, even to Alexa's own ears; especially since this vandalism fell hard on the heels of Ali's injury.

Then her thoughts returned to the surprise brother. Nabil Qassim. What a piece of work. Churlish. Rude.

Alexa looked down the last block and stopped short in dismay. What had happened to her car? Then, she saw that the big pickup ahead was parked right behind the Land Rover. One of those monster-sized trucks with a double wheel-well, like a farm vehicle; it was big enough to dwarf the Rover in its shadow from this angle. She plucked her keys from her pocket as she drew even with the jacked-up truck's high running board. The enormous vehicle looked empty, but the windows were too dark to tell.

Creeped out by the dark windows, Alexa stepped into the slim opening between the truck's grille and the back of the Land Rover. She'd taken two strides at street level when the monster truck roared to life, headlights blazing. Alexa froze against the Land Rover, yelling, "Hey! Watch out."

She wasn't sure the driver could see her or hear her shouts. But when the engine rumbled with a series of deep vroom-vroom-vrooms and the truck bucked in place, Alexa realized that the driver was trying to scare her.

It was working.

The huge engine revved into a high-pitched whine, and Alexa leapt forward into street. Stumbling, she grasped the Land Rover's back fender to keep from hitting the asphalt. The neighborhood was still empty and seemed darker despite the relentless glare of the truck's headlights.

Reaching the driver's-side door, she fumbled to get the key into the lock; this vehicle had been made long before anyone dreamed of automatic keys. Just as she felt the lock click, the monster truck backed up a few yards, screeched to a halt, then shot out onto the street. It passed so close that Alexa could feel her hair whip in the maelstrom of the truck's wake as it blew by.

Alexa jumped into the front seat, heart pounding. "Asshole!" she yelled at the truck's receding taillights, already a few blocks down the street. Too far to see a license plate. She locked her door and sat for a few minutes, dropping her head to the steering wheel until she felt calmer. Then she fastened her seat belt and pulled away from the curb. Taking a quick left turn at the first cross street, Alexa fumed.

What kind of jerk tries to scare a random stranger half to death just for kicks? She was lost in nasty thoughts about men who overcompensated for certain shortcomings with the size of their vehicles when it hit her.

Pickup truck. Bassam said that the vandals had driven a pickup truck. Had someone from that group come back to gloat over the spectacle that ensued after their pumpkin assault? And watched her enter the Qassim home? Alexa blanched at her next question. And waited for over an hour until she emerged from the house?

This new theory seemed pretty implausible. Most run-of-the-mill vandals, or "pranksters," as Detective Miller had suggested, would immediately get as far away as possible. Even if it were one of the vandals, how would he know her car? Implausible or not, the sick feeling in Alexa's stomach didn't dissipate until she'd arrived home at the cabin. Door locked behind her. Security system on.

# CHAPTER THIRTEEN

"BREATHE IN, ONE, two, three, four. Out, one, two, three, four." Isabella's serene voice filled the darkened yoga studio and soothed Alexa's nerves, still frayed from her encounter with the monster truck.

Alexa sat near the back of the class, legs crossed in Half-Lotus position, eyes closed. Her hands, resting on her knees, were curled into a Gyana Mudra, index finger touching thumb. As she sank deeper into the meditation, Isabella's voice seemed to float from far away.

"At your own pace, lengthen the exhale to five. Then, six."

Alexa drifted toward that still place in her mind, counting ever-deeper breaths. Just as she approached a peaceful state, a jarring flash of red pierced the calm. A scaly neck and savage beak pecking at a sightless eye. She shook her head but couldn't erase the vision of the bird perched on the dead body.

Isabella instructed, "Shorten your breath, back to a count of four."

Tranquility destroyed, Alexa clenched her hands into fists, digging fingernails into palms. Her stomach was in knots.

"Now, lie back in Shavasana," Isabella murmured.

Alexa stretched back onto the floor into the relaxation pose known in English as Corpse Pose, but she could not unwind. Instead, she stared at the ceiling, dismayed at the irony. She was too preoccupied with a real corpse to relax. She kept thinking that she'd coped with the shock of finding that young man, dead on the abandoned farm. But the moment her mind roamed free, it fled to the gruesome scene. Maybe the fright she'd received from that trucker last night had put her on edge.

When Isabella rang the bell to signal the end of class, Alexa considered heading straight home. But, Melissa motioned to her across the room, and she brushed away any disquiet. Maybe hanging out with her friends would help.

"Namaste." Alexa brought her hands together and nodded to Isabella, the yogini, on her way out the door. She loved the traditional Hindi greeting used in yoga, which means "the divine in me bows to the divine in you."

Outside the studio, her friends waited on the steps. The Krav Maga woman, Sloane, was there too, chatting with Haley.

Melissa grabbed Alexa's arm. "Has your mom talked to you?"

"About?"

"This event for the RESIST refugee program? Your mom has this idea to work with volunteers, mostly wives of the officers, to put on a big fundraising gala." Melissa turned to Tyrell, who was trailing behind. "Are you going to be part of the planning committee?"

"Me? No, no, no." Tyrell held his hands up, palms forward, as if to ward away bad vibes. "We'll put Maria on that."

The group breezed into the Om Café, calling out their coffee and tea orders to Ariel, and made their way to the big round table in the corner.

Haley leaned toward Alexa, "Come on. It will be fun to work together on this. A winter ball." She curled her mouth into a slow smile. "Seems like I haven't worn a beautiful dress for a year. First, the pregnancy. Now, between work and Charlotte, Blair and I don't have time for parties."

"You're on the planning committee too?" Alexa asked.

"Yes. The Chamber appointed me. Well, I sort of volunteered. And I drafted Sloane too."

The martial arts instructor looked at Alexa with a slight shrug. "Why not? It's a good way to get know people and give back to my adopted community."

"Let me talk to Mom," Alexa said, Ariel's arrival with a tray of hot drinks saving her from making an immediate commitment. Busy with work and this long-distance relationship with Reese, Alexa wasn't sure she wanted anything to do with planning a winter ball.

Tyrell took a sip of cappuccino before he leaned back in his chair with a frown. "Do you think there will be a lot of community support for an event to benefit refugees? After last night, I'm not convinced."

"Last night?" Melissa pushed a strand of auburn hair from her face. "Did something happen?"

"Yeah. Some yahoos vandalized the home of one of our refugee families."

"No!" Melissa clanked her cup against the table as she leaned forward.

"Was anyone hurt?" Haley wrung her hands.

Tyrell recounted the entire incident at the Qassims from the prior night. As he drew to a close, he asked Alexa, "Did you hear anything from the police?"

Alexa frowned. "I spoke to Detective Miller today. No arrests. They're still interviewing the neighbors. They were going to go back tonight after people got home from work and do another round. He'll contact me tomorrow with an update."

"I spoke to Zahraa about the repairs. Tough family. They made the kids go to school today." Tyrell shook his head. "I worry about Bassam. That kid has a short fuse. He reminds me of some of the foster kids I supervised when I was a social worker. It's a fine line between troubled and trouble."

"Just think what he's been through. Civil war, living in a refugee camp." Alexa addressed the three women. "He's seventeen. Zahraa and Eshan seem like good parents. But think what he's experienced at such a young age. The other boy seems a little less volatile. And he's probably too young to fully remember everything the family has had to cope with."

Sloane furrowed her brow with a look of concern. "Maybe the teenager needs an outside activity. Something to channel his energy." She looked at Tyrell. "Why don't you bring him around to the studio one day after school. We have an Intro Krav Maga class. Or maybe Taekwondo would be better for him; it's more structured. I'd waive any fees. And I speak Arabic, so there should be no communication issues."

"What a great idea. His English is pretty good, but I take it you've lived in Arabic-speaking countries and know the culture. That would be a plus."

"I've spent years in the Arab world. My last job was in Tunisia."

Tyrell smiled. "Can I text you to arrange a time? I have to make sure that Bassam will go for this. And that the parents approve. But I think he'll jump on it."

Sloane handed Tyrell a business card. "Here's my phone and email. Just let me know if he's interested." She dropped her voice. "The Krav Maga discipline helped me get through a rough time in my life. Maybe martial arts will do the same with this boy."

Haley looked at her phone. "Oh no. I'm late. I promised Blair that I'd be home early to put Charlotte to bed. He has a conference call with Toronto. No, Tokyo. It's morning there."

"Give that sweet darling a kiss from me," Alexa called as Haley sprinted for the door.

Melissa spluttered a mouthful of chai. "Did you just tell her to give Blair a kiss?"

"You are sooo twisted," Alexa groaned. "Charlotte. Not her husband."

"Speaking of kisses, will Reese be visiting this weekend?"

Tyrell mock-whispered to Sloane. "The boyfriend."

Wistful, Alexa wished she could be certain that 'boyfriend' was the correct term for Reese. But, she nodded. "Yes. If Jim's not working, do you want to get together on Saturday?"

"Sure. I think this is his free weekend." Melissa looked at Sloane. "Sorry, I keep forgetting that you don't know the full cast of characters here. Jim's my fiancé. He's a forest ranger at Pine Grove Furnace State Park. He and Reese shared a house at one point."

Sloane smiled, but her pale blue eyes clouded. "No problem. My dad was in the Foreign Service, and I moved around a lot growing up. I'm used to meeting new friends and filling in the pieces of their puzzles over time."

"That must have been an exciting childhood," Tyrell said. "I travel now on RESIST business, mostly to India and Thailand. But when I was a kid, travel meant driving from Carlisle to Harrisburg. And that was a major event."

"Sometimes exciting. Sometimes lonely, especially after my mother died. My father was away a lot but didn't believe in sending kids to boarding school. So, I stayed with him as he traveled from post to post, but I was raised by a series of amahs and nannies." Sloane stared into her empty cup for a long moment, then looked up with a smile. "But, there's a saying: Not all who wander are lost. Until my husband was killed, I enjoyed the journey. My life is very different now. This is the first time in years that I've lived in the States."

Melissa asked, "How's that working out?"

"My business is fulfilling. This area is lovely. Now I'm exploring yoga, and I've met you all." Sloane flashed a restrained smile. "I'd say so far, so good."

"Sweet!" Melissa grinned. "We'll see you in class again next week then." She jumped to her feet and wound a shawl around her shoulders. "I'm off. I have a ton of photos I want to go through tonight."

"I need to get home too," Alexa said.

With a shuffling of chairs, all four rose from the table and headed out the door.

"I'll call about this weekend," Melissa said over her shoulder as she hurried to her car.

As Tyrell and Sloane headed in the opposite direction, Alexa walked up the street to the Land Rover. A pickup truck approached, its engine rumbling, and she tensed, remembering the previous evening. But the truck drove on by without slowing, and she laughed. "Always looking for trouble." It made her feel a little better that she'd mentioned the truck incident to Detective Miller when they'd spoken today. Of course, without a license plate number, he had little to go on.

Driving home over dark roads, Alexa's mind kept returning to the previous night. What was wrong with people that they'd terrorize others for the hell of it? The guy who scared her half to death playing Transformers with his truck. The jerks who vandalized a refugee family's safe haven. Even the Qassim brother, Nabil, had seemed to enjoy making her uncomfortable.

Her thoughts flickered to the ultimate terror: the young man who had been gunned down in an empty field and left to the scavengers. The scene that had interrupted her meditation at yoga class came flooding back. The vulture. The ravaged face.

As Alexa tried to push away the disturbing images, a vision of camouflage, thick with dried blood, stopped her. "Wait," she said aloud. "The vandals last night wore camouflage too." Could the bigots who attacked the Qassim home be the same people who killed the young man in the field—and the one in Harpers Ferry? Maybe a hate group that left Allahu Akbar signs as a way to provoke anti-Muslim sentiment?

Alexa's skin crawled at the thought that a militia group could be responsible for a spate of anti-Muslim violence. Her run-in with the Army of Judah flashed through her mind. The night she'd fled from her cabin in terror to escape the soldiers they'd sent to kill her. Her shoulder still bore a faint scar from the bullet that had grazed it as they'd hunted her through the dark forest.

Although most of the Army of Judah had gone to jail, they weren't alone in their cause. Pennsylvania had something like sixty right-wing militia groups; more than any other state in the country. Reese had been part of a task force to investigate them when he'd worked in the state parks.

Knowing that she could be leaping to a convenient conclusion, Alexa kept turning the idea over in her head. The militia idea was a little farfetched but not entirely outrageous. Alexa vowed to contact Agent Carter first thing tomorrow. She could tell the FBI about the incident at the Qassim home. Maybe it would get them to consider someone other than Reese as a suspect.

# CHAPTER FOURTEEN

"MOM AND DAD are thrilled that you're coming to pizza night," Alexa told Reese as she downshifted at a stop sign. Scout started to rise but settled back down when the Land Rover moved forward.

Reese laughed. "It's been a while. I always enjoyed spending Friday nights with the Williams clan. How old are the kids now?"

"Jamie is almost eleven. And Courtney is nine. Seems like I don't spend as much time with them anymore. Of course, they were away the entire summer at their beach house."

"Graham took the summer off from the law firm? That doesn't sound like your brother."

"Kate and the kids stayed down at the Outer Banks. Her parents live near there now. Graham joined them for several long weekends." Alexa snickered. "No way he'd leave the new partners to run the law firm for three months."

Pulling to the curb in front of her childhood home, Alexa turned to Reese. "One more thing. Mom and Dad are doing this War College host thing where they sponsor a foreign officer who's attending this year's session. They've invited their guy and his wife tonight. He's a brigadier general in the Iraqi Army. Pretty imposing. Last time, they also invited a colonel who's a professor at the War College. He knew the general in Iraq. I expect the colonel and his wife will be here too."

"Wow. They sound like two no-nonsense dudes." Reese scratched Scout's head, which was now draped over his shoulder. He cracked a sardonic smile. "So, better to not bring up the fact that the FBI thinks I'm a serial killer with an ISIS complex?"

Alexa shook her head with an indulgent grin. "How can you joke about it? But, yeah. Some things are best left unsaid." She looked at all the cars in the driveway and realized that she was a little nervous. Mom and Dad hadn't seen Reese since their breakup. "We better get inside. I think we're the last ones here."

After a hectic round of greetings and introductions, the group gathered around the big dining room table. Scout settled down on the floor between Jamie and Courtney. Alexa nibbled on a piece of pepperoni pizza, waiting for her mother to start cross-examining Reese. Although Susan Williams had never practiced, she'd honed the skills she'd picked up in law school while working in the rough-and-tumble world of politics, first as a legislative staffer then as a county commissioner. Poor Reese didn't stand a chance.

"It's good to see you again, Reese. You're working with the Animals of Africa Trust on a study about lion populations?"

"Yes." Reese laid the slice of pizza he was holding back on his plate. "It's related to the fieldwork that I was doing in Kenya. In Samburu, we were tracking all the big cats in that region. Animals of Africa has sponsored similar projects throughout the African continent. We've compiled that information with other existing data and are using the report to enlist donors for further conservation efforts."

Norris poured a can of soda into his glass. "The safari that Susan, Lexie, and I took last year was just amazing. I'd love to go back someday."

"I can imagine the great memories." Reese shot a look at Alexa that made her blush. For a moment, she was back in that tent at Archer's Camp, beneath the mosquito netting, tangled in the sheets with him.

The colonel asked Reese in clipped tones, like he was one of the troops to report, "How long were you in Samburu? That's northern Kenya, right?"

"North-central." Reese's face lit up. "About a year and a half. Then, I came down with a case of malaria. After a hospital stay in Nairobi, the doctors suggested I come back home for a while to fully recover."

"Malaria's tough. I was stationed in Kenya for a few months. During a break, we went out to the Masai Mara. Never got to Samburu, though."

"Camp Simba?"

With a look of surprise, the colonel replied, "Yes. Can't tell you about my mission though."

Reese smiled. "It's a pretty open secret that it's a drone base, but I won't press for confirmation. I took a trip to Lamu and Manda Island about a year ago. Beautiful place. Didn't realize quite how close it was to Somalia until I got there. I didn't actually see Camp Simba, but I heard a lot about it while I was in the area."

Jill Finley laughed. "The kids and I remained Stateside during the Camp Simba deployment. At first, I was a little miffed because I'd heard that all the beautiful people visit Lamu. But then I heard about the Frenchwoman who was killed by Somali pirates. And I decided it was OK to miss the famous beaches this time."

Placing his half-eaten slice of pizza on his plate, General Al-Badri looked down the table. "Mr. Michaels."

"Reese, please."

"Reese. I admire your work on preserving endangered species. In my country, we once had lions, tigers, cheetah, and many other magnificent animals. But they were killed off by the beginning of the last century. Years of war have decimated many other species. A country with few wild animals is a desolate place."

"Yes. That's why the world community hopes to preserve the big cats and elephants of Africa." Reese flashed a smile. "The Trust welcomes all contributions, large and small."

"Mom, can I be excused to watch TV?" Courtney scrooched in her seat.

"Me too. Me too." Jamie raised his hand as if in school.

Kate nodded. "Sure, kiddos. Carry your dishes to the kitchen first." The two kids slid from their chairs and marched from the room, plates in hand. Scout trailed hard on their heels.

Alexa eyed their departure with envy. This was turning out to be an awkward gathering, even though most of the group had met before. Sort of like one of those bar association sessions full of strangers who had three minutes each to introduce themselves to the group.

Norris turned to Colonel Finley. "Sounds like you've been posted all over the world. A wonderful opportunity."

The colonel gave his wife a wry look. "Not always wonderful. Jill and the family could be with me in the European postings and in the Far East. But they had to stay Stateside during the stint in Kenya. And I did three tours in Iraq."

His wife grimaced. "That was one tough stretch. Two of the tours were extended, so it was almost three and half years until he was home full time. Shortly after he returned home, the kids flew the nest. But we love Carlisle. And the kids visit often."

General Al-Badri patted the colonel's arm and said, "I, for one, am glad that Finley and I crossed paths in my country. Without the brave action of the colonel and the soldiers in his company, I would likely not be enjoying this wonderful pizza with you today."

"Now you have our attention." Susan leaned forward and rested her clasped hands on the table. "You have to finish the rest of this story."

Alexa raised her eyebrow as she caught Reese's sardonic glance. She'd warned him that that there would be a lot of military talk at this dinner.

Caught up in his story, the general continued, "I was part of a contingent accompanying several high-government officials to a meeting with US diplomats at a remote site. Men under Finley's command were assigned to escort us. It was kept small and intended to be secret. On the way, we were attacked by a large force of Al-Qaeda. Somehow, they had gotten details of the meeting and our route. The terrorists outnumbered us. Many died. Reinforcements arrived, and Colonel Finley prevailed." He spread his hands with a flourish as he finished his tale.

Noora Al-Badri gave a shy smile. "I am so grateful for the colonel's heroism. And now to renew our acquaintance during our year here at the War College."

Graham said, "That's impressive."

Alexa put a hand over her mouth to cover her smile. Strange to see her usually talkative brother reduced to the role of Greek chorus. But, he was right. Finley did seem like an impressive guy. Stiff, but impressive.

General Al-Badri nodded. "Our prime minister cited Finley for heroism in the face of overwhelming odds."

Norris asked, "Isn't it unusual for an officer of your level to be directly involved in something like that?"

Finley grinned and ducked his head. "Chance. I was with another part of the company, en route to another mission. When the call came in for reinforcements, we diverted to help. Little heroism was involved. Only reason anyone even noticed is because we saved this guy's ass—along with some other top Iraqi brass."

Al-Badri laughed a little too loudly. "Or, perhaps, because you killed one of the top Al-Qaeda chiefs in the region. A man they called the Poet. It took them months to recover from Kaamil El Sayed's death."

"No wonder they singled you out for recognition, Colonel." Susan's tone contained the appropriate amount of admiration but stopped short of fawning.

A wail came from the television room. "Bad dog, Scout. Mom, he ate my last cookie."

Just as Alexa pushed back her chair, Kate leapt to her feet. "I've got this."

Amid chuckles from most of the adults, Alexa said, "Why don't I clear the plates? Mom, should I bring in the dessert?"

"I'll help you, dear." Susan reached for an empty plate.

"Well, that was a bit different than the Williams pizza nights I remember." Reese spoke from the passenger seat as Alexa stopped for a red light at the Carlisle square. "But it was great to see your family again. Boy, the kids have grown."

"I wish it had been just family. But, Mom and Dad are taking this War College hosting thing to heart. Especially since they're only doing part of the year before they head to their home in Italy next spring."

Reese laughed. "I've never met an Iraqi general before. You can tell he's used to being the main man. At home, I'm betting enlisted guys quake in their boots when he speaks."

"Yeah. He's a nice guy, but no stranger to being the center of attention. I wonder if it's cultural or just their relationship, but his wife barely speaks."

"Finley's an impressive guy. I think he's the real deal. Something about the way he carries himself."

Alexa nodded as she continued down Hanover Street. "Yeah. Did you notice how uncomfortable he seemed when the general talked about his heroism? The colonel went along with it, but I don't think he's ever the one to tell his own story."

Reese nodded off on the last stretch of the drive home, waking when Alexa turned onto the slate lane. Inside the cabin, she said, "You look beat. Go up to bed. I'll take Scout out for a few minutes."

He yawned. "What time are we meeting Jim and Melissa tomorrow?"

"Not until noon. You can sleep in as long as you want." Alexa was exhausted too. The dinner had been strangely tiring. She grinned. Probably all the strain of being polite and interested for three hours. She'd escaped unscathed, but Reese had sure had his time in the witness stand. No wonder he was tired.

"All right then. I'll see you in the morning." Reese kissed Alexa's forehead and headed toward the stairs.

"Scout, come on, boy." The mastiff dashed out to the tree line the minute they stepped outside.

Alexa leaned on the railing of the deck and looked at the night sky with a sigh. It was one of those nights that seemed to come only in autumn, when the stars pulsed brilliant as diamonds in a clear obsidian sky. For months, even when she was dating John, she'd gazed at the Big Dipper and imagined Reese watching the same constellations in Kenya. Now he was here, upstairs in this very cabin, and she was still watching the stars alone. Something had to change soon, but when was the right time? She was reluctant to push Reese until he was ready to talk about their relationship. What if she lost him altogether?

Scout moseyed up the deck steps and nudged Alexa for a pet. She scratched his ears. "You're tired from playing with Courtney and Jamie, aren't you? But stealing a cookie? That's not very nice." Alexa walked back inside and up to her bedroom, babbling to the huge dog the whole way. Even the nonsensical talk couldn't drive away her acute awareness that Reese lay behind the closed guestroom door.

# CHAPTER FIFTEEN

"WHAT A GREAT day. I'd forgotten how much fun we've always had hanging out." Melissa picked up Ansel and plopped the French bulldog in her lap. "And what a long hike for you, little one."

Her fiancé, Jim, grinned. "Now that Reese is back, maybe he can help me figure out what's wrong with the Corvette."

The four friends were sprawled in Alexa's living room, tired from a day of hiking in the late-autumn air. Scout snored in his corner bed. The smell of bubbling lasagna filled the house.

"You still have that pathetic excuse for a sports car?" Reese grinned. "The one that was always blocking the driveway at our old house? I thought Melissa might make you leave it there when you two moved into your new place."

Reese shot Alexa a warm look, like they were in on the joke together. Jim's Corvette obsession had been a running source of good-natured amusement throughout their relationship.

"Of course I kept the 'Vette. She's my pride and joy. But she's running pretty rough right now." Jim scowled. "Maybe you can help me work on it some weekend."

Reese shook his head. "I know nothing about Corvette engines."

"How could I forget?" Jim ribbed. "Is that your hybrid SUV parked out there? You could still help. Pass me the tools."

Alexa shook her head at the two friends' banter. Just like old times. She headed toward the kitchen, Melissa on her heels.

Opening the oven, Alexa asked, "What do you think?"

Melissa looked at the bubbling lasagna and said, "Another fifteen, twenty minutes?"

Alexa pulled salad ingredients out of the refrigerator and began shredding lettuce. "Hey. As you predicted, my mom hit me up about this Winter Ball. It's going to be at the Army Heritage Center, right?"

"Oh, I'm so glad you're helping." Melissa looked up from slicing tomatoes.

"Clearly, you're more excited about this event than me. I'm willing to do my part. But can you give me a job that won't take too much time? I have a lot going on these days." Alexa added Melissa's tomatoes to the salad bowl and shook croutons on top.

"I'm just glad you're going to be part of the planning committee. I'm doing the decorating. Sloane's helping. I came up with a great winter theme: big snow scene panels and hanging crystals. Sloane's going to recruit some folks from Courage to help with the actual grunt work and hang all the decorations. Your mom, Kate, and some of their friends are doing the refreshments. I think they already signed a band. Haley and the Chamber will manage the ticket sales. Maybe you could think about an emcee for the night and whether we should have any speeches. Being a lawyer and all, the talking part seems right up your alley." Melissa grinned.

"OK. I'll come up with a few ideas." Alexa looked at the clock. "The lasagna should be done." She called to Reese and Jim, "Dinner's ready. Come grab a plate."

Not long after dinner, Jim and Melissa left, carrying their exhausted pup. Alone, Alexa asked Reese, "Want to watch a movie?"

He smiled. "Maybe later, but what I'd really like to do is try out your new hot tub. How about it?"

"Sure. There are big towels hanging in the pantry. I'll run upstairs and change."

When Alexa came back downstairs, wearing a swimsuit, Reese was leaning against the dining table in a pair of gym shorts.

"Do you have a favorite?" he picked up two towels from the table, holding one in each hand.

Alexa laughed. "The blue. You take the green."

When Reese handed her the towel, his hand brushed Alexa's and she felt a sudden shyness. Flustered, she twined the towel around her torso and slipped outside. The cool air felt good on her warm face. Scout bolted past her into the forest.

"Be careful. There's no light past this point. I like to sit out here in the dark and watch the stars." Alexa held out her hand to lead Reese on the path that had become so familiar to her. They walked across a narrow section of deck that fronted the living room and emerged onto a large deck on the far side of the house. Alexa dropped Reese's hand and opened the hot tub lid against the cabin wall.

She asked, "Have your eyes adjusted to the dark yet? There are two steps on the outside. Here." She tapped them with her foot. "There are seats along the side, so step inside carefully. Maybe I should have brought a flashlight."

"No, I'm good. You get in first. I'll follow."

Alexa slid over the edge and sank into the water. This was the point at which her usual reaction was complete contentment as she luxuriated in the warmth. But Reese's presence unsettled her. She was nervous, not knowing where this might lead. At the same time, she was breathless at having the man she longed for so near.

Reese eased into the hot tub and found a seat facing Alexa. "Wow. This is great. I haven't spent that much time hiking lately. The warm water is perfect for my tired calves."

Silence fell between them. Above the rustle of branches blowing in the steady breeze, Alexa could hear Scout wandering around in the front yard. Moments later, he returned to the deck and settled into his pillow next to the hot tub.

The dog's appearance seemed to rouse Reese. "This is a great addition to the cabin." He sat up in a swirl of waves.

"I can turn on the jets. They work wonders on sore muscles."

"Nah. I like hearing the night sounds." He tilted his head and looked up. "Wow. Great sky."

"One of my favorite things about coming out here at night." Alexa smiled into the darkness. "You should come over here beside me. On that side, the house cuts off the best view of the sky."

"OK." Still submerged to his chest, Reese slid across the few feet that separated them. She tried to stop his momentum with a hand to the shoulder, but with a soft bump Reese's chest skidded into Alexa's left breast.

"Sorry for the body check. My depth perception is shot to hell in the dark." Reese breathed into her ear.

Rapt with the feel of his soft laughter on her cheek, Alexa looked up at this man she craved. Her hand tingled where it still rested on his wet chest, and she drew a sharp breath as his knee grazed the inside of her thigh. Her heart felt like it was turning in slow loops as she anticipated a kiss. In an involuntary motion, she moved her damp palm to draw him closer. But with an abrupt splash, Reese swung his body away and sat beside her. Bereft, she was left clutching only droplets of water.

Closing her eyes, Alexa tried to swallow her disappointment. Next to her, Reese slouched low in the water, his breathing ragged. Then, he spoke, his tone careful.

"You're right. The view of the stars is much better over here. Is that the Milky Way?"

"Yep. And you recognize the Big Dipper over to the right. In early winter, I have a great view of it in early evening." Alexa couldn't believe she and Reese were prattling on about the cosmos when this unresolved issue about their tiny piece of the universe, about their lives, loomed so large. The uncertainty was sucking everything out of their relationship. Like a black hole. Alexa giggled in disgust. And in that instant, she decided that she had to know.

"When you were in Kenya, I would sit out here and remember the falling star we saw together one night in Samburu. Somehow, knowing that we could see some of the same stars at night made you seem closer. Even though we'd called it quits. Even though we were thousands of miles apart. You were always in my heart. That's one of the reasons that I wouldn't commit to John. And he knew."

Reese, his voice rough, turned to look at Alexa. "I'm not—"

"Let me finish, please." A tear trickled down Alexa's cheek and merged with the water. "You've been home for months now. And I can't do it any longer. I can't dance around the 'Will he or won't he.' I can't take it slow. I want you back. All of you."

"Me too. Why do you think I lured you to the hot tub?" Reese sounded relieved. Happy.

"Seriously?"

"Yes. I'm not great at expressing these things." Reese touched her shoulder. "We've been working our way back to each other, step by step. I thought we needed to take it slow. But, I know what I want. I wasn't sure you were ready to, to . . . this." Reese swept his hand through the water, then continued. "I remember that falling star; rekindling things on safari. And, like we promised, I've always carried you in my heart. I never got over you.

"Even with the malaria, I could have stayed in Africa." His voiced lowered. "You must realize that I came home because I missed you."

Before Alexa could catch her breath, Reese pulled her onto his lap and drew her into a long, smoldering kiss. She melted into his body with rising passion. With an impatient splash, he lifted Alexa to her feet and peeled her swimsuit off in one fluid motion. Exposed above the waist to the crisp night air, she shivered, a delicious mix of reaction to the cold and her mounting anticipation. Below her waist, the warmth of the water mingled with the heat between her legs.

Tearing off his shorts, Reese looked at Alexa and ran his thumb across her mouth in a gentle caress. Then, wrapping his hands around her waist, he swept her back onto his lap and his surging erection.

"Oh, yes," Alexa cried.

Then, she lost herself in a world of liquid warmth and wet flesh as she and Reese reached their peak together.

Alexa snuggled against Reese beneath the water until she saw Scout standing on the hot tub steps. "Did we disturb you?" Alexa leaned across the water to scratch the mastiff under the chin.

Reese ran his hand through Alexa's curls. "It's time to relocate anyway, don't you think? How about we take this inside for a second act?"

Alexa giggled. "Excellent idea."

When she woke the next morning to find Reese beside her, Alexa smiled with contentment. Having this man sleeping in her bed again felt right. She lay on her side for a few minutes just watching him breathe, studying each tousled brown curl. Then, Scout interrupted her dreamy musings by bumping his chin on the mattress.

Sighing, she edged from beneath the covers and threw on sweats. After letting the giant mastiff out for his morning romp, she made a cup of tea and settled into a corner of the couch. Wrapped in a faux-fur throw, Alexa studied the motes of dust flickering in the sunlight that streamed through the rear window. Their whirling dance mirrored the joy bubbling in her heart. She thought about last night's lovemaking. After the fierce urgency of their reunion in the hot tub, their second coming together had been slow and exquisite. She'd felt like a traveler rediscovering beloved territory. Being with Reese was like coming home.

The beep of an incoming message interrupted her dreamy thoughts. She absently picked up her iPhone from the coffee table to check it out.

"Need to schedule an interview ASAP. Want to further discuss Yusuf Said Gufu. Please call FBI office . . ."

The rest of the message was cut off. Alexa frowned as she entered her password to get the rest of the text. Since when did the FBI send text messages instead of calling? And she had no clue who Yusuf Said Gufu was.

The phone didn't unlock, so she slowed her typing as she punched in the code a second time. I really need to do the fingerprint thing, Alexa resolved for the umpteenth time. The password failed again.

"Duh," Alexa said aloud as she saw another iPhone sitting on the far corner of the coffee table. She held Reese's phone in her hand. Hers was still on the table. She hadn't even noticed the different screensaver. Hers was the stock photo of dewy grass. This screen showed a photo of a green African plain, maybe the Masai Mara.

At the sound of footsteps on the stairs, Alexa laid down the phone and rose to greet Reese. Her heart stopped when she saw his tousled hair and ragged T-shirt over old jeans, the same indigo as his eyes. This is how she remembered their months together here at the cabin. Lazy Sundays in old clothes, wrapped up in each other. With a twinge, she conceded that it hadn't always been idyllic toward the end. But Alexa pushed that thought aside when Reese swept her into a long, searing kiss.

"How'd you sleep?" he asked with a knowing smile.

Alexa blushed. "Great. I was exhausted."

Reese gave an appreciative grin. "With good reason." He looked around. "Where's Scout?"

"Still outside. I got sidetracked from letting him back in." Alexa walked to the door and opened it to a waiting mastiff, who ran past her, tail wagging, to greet Reese. The dog loved this man.

"Hey, boy. Nice to see you too." Reese ruffled the big dog's ears then turned to Alexa. "Sidetracked? You're not working this morning, I hope?"

"No. Actually, I have to apologize. A message came in on your phone. I thought it was my phone, and I tried to open it up to read."

"No problem. Did you see who the message is from?"

"The FBI, I think. Who's Yusuf Said Gufu?"

A cloud passed over Reese's face. "Did the message mention him? I thought you couldn't read it."

Alexa paused at the hint of anger in Reese's voice. "That part was right on the screen. Since I thought the message was for me, I was really confused. I don't know anyone by that name. Do you?"

"Yes. A guy who worked for a while at the Samburu project."

Reese opened the message and read it as Alexa talked. "Did the FBI ask about him before? Why are they interested in this Yusef guy?"

"His name came up in the second FBI interview. From their questions, I think Yusef might be on a terror watch list. And, apparently, they think he's in the United States now." Reese stuck his hands in his back pockets and looked at the floor.

"What?" Alexa cried. "How well did you know this man?"

"Not very well. He seemed like a nice enough guy. When John Thomas and a few of us went to Lamu, he tagged along. We hung out in the bars. But later, some equipment went missing. And we were pretty sure he was the one who stole it. I won't go into the details, but there was little doubt. So, we fired him. That was . . ." Reese scrunched his face as he counted. "A good six months before I left Kenya. Long before I came down with malaria."

"You haven't seen him since? He hasn't contacted you in Harpers Ferry?"

"Alexa. That's ridiculous. How would he even know I'm back in the States or where I live? No, I haven't seen the guy. The FBI just picked up on the coincidence. That I'd worked with this guy at one time and he's possibly of interest to them. I just wish they'd leave me alone."

Reese sat on the couch and pulled Alexa down next to him. He wound her hands in his and softened his voice. "I don't want to talk about this anymore. We have a lot to celebrate. Let's ignore this whole dead body thing for a day."

Alexa ran her hand over his cheek. "Fine with me." She raised her lips to his. "Very fine," she sighed. She pulled herself away and stood. "Just one more thing. Please make sure your attorney is involved with this. In fact, let him return the FBI call."

Reese stood. "That's who the text is from. Grandin, not the FBI."

Relieved by that small fact, Alexa wrapped her arm around Reese's waist. "Enough drama for the morning. What do you want to eat? Eggs?" Alexa wrinkled her nose. "Or pizza? Mom sent leftover pepperoni home. I can't stand cold pizza for breakfast, but I know it's one of your favorites."

Later that afternoon, after Reese had left for Harpers Ferry, Alexa walked toward the pine grove with Scout. The wind was gusting and moaning through the trees. A fine mist hung in the air. The weather forecast called for heavy rain later in the day.

Inside the tall trees, it was calm and dry. Alexa wiped the mist from her face and wandered through the giant conifers. With a laugh of pure delight, Alexa extended her arms and spun in a series of circles, like a whirling dervish, savoring the joy that she felt about reuniting with Reese. Although it seemed like they'd wasted valuable time by not resolving their relationship earlier, Alexa knew that she'd not been ready to move forward until very recently. She suspected that it had taken just as long for Reese to be sure that he wanted to give it another try. But now she was dizzy with thoughts of Reese's indigo eyes; tall, lanky body; and familiar touch.

Excited by Alexa's silly behavior, Scout started barking and turning three-sixties in the air. Breathless and dizzy, Alexa collapsed to the soft forest floor. The dog lay down next to her on the cushion of pine needles and licked her cheek. Laughing, Alexa sat up. "Admit it, buddy. You're glad he's back too. You moped for months after he left for Africa." She scratched the mastiff's huge head, still smiling.

"I'm getting cold. Let's go back to the cabin." When they emerged from the pine grove, ground fog enveloped the meadow and swallowed up the cabin. The thick fog dampened Alexa's good spirits as she crossed the murky field. Caught up in her happiness, she'd avoided thinking of Reese's text about the FBI all day. But, she couldn't ignore it any longer. Why hadn't he mentioned this Yusuf guy, a suspected terrorist? Why had he been evasive when discussing the issue? Alexa finally confronted the question that bothered her the most: Did Reese have something to hide?

# CHAPTER SIXTEEN

*July 8, 1859*

The old man's awaiting for to carry you to freedom. Follow
the drinking gourd.
> —*"Follow the Drinking Gourd," a Negro spiritual*

*Lulled by the whisper of wind through the trees, Elijah closed
his eyes in exhaustion. He'd never imagined how tiring this trip
would be. Or that the flight to freedom would be more of a long,
backbreaking trudge. The last ten days had been a blur. Walking
day and night, stopping just long enough to catch a few hours of fitful
sleep. They'd bedded down in damp gullies, deserted tobacco curing
barns, an abandoned lean-to, and a rank cave that smelled like its
rightful owner might return any moment. For the most part, the three
fugitives had avoided anywhere they might encounter people by
day: farms, plantations, villages, and roads.*

*However, out in the flatlands during those first days, the
runaways made a necessary nighttime raid on a lone farmstead to
gather food. They'd made off with a ham from the smokehouse and
some vegetables from a cart that looked ready for the next day's
market. Hanging on the clothesline, Wabee had also found a shirt
that fit over his broad chest. Elijah felt bad for the family they'd
robbed. From the looks of their property, these people lived hand to
mouth like many of the poor whites.*

*"Don't be too sorry, boy," Coleman admonished. "These crackers
be like all the rest, looking down on the colored, both free and slave,*

because they black. No doubt that they'll tell the patrollers that they food is missing and pray that we is caught and whipped until we bleed."

As they trekked onward, Elijah's feet ached like the blazes, and fear was a constant. But, every day he was excited see new territory. He'd never traveled more than a half-day's walk from the plantation of his birth. So, he marveled at the changing terrain. The day that Elijah had first set eyes on the Blue Ridge Mountains was magic. He couldn't believe that such a tall hill existed. And the trees. A profusion of hardwoods gave way to stands of the fresh-smelling evergreens that they'd encountered the first night of their flight. Coleman said they were called pines. Elijah rolled that word over his tongue for most of a morning as they climbed upward through grove after grove of the strange-looking trees.

Their trek toward the mountains had been nerve-wracking. They'd had a few close calls. Scrambling through a loose board in a deserted tobacco curing barn just as two white men rode up to the front entrance. Waking up at dawn to find that the gully where they'd chosen to sleep was next to the route an overseer was using to drive his slaves to field.

The day of the dogs had been the most terrifying. Elijah shook his head at the memory and stopped in his tracks to listen. The mountain ridge they were traveling was quiet. But that afternoon in the field at the foot of the mountain, he hadn't heard the dogs until they were almost upon the group.

Wabee was the first to react. "Dogs," he warned with a frightened look on his face.

Coleman kept on walking. Wabee imagined he heard the bay of hounds at least once a day. Coleman had explained the big African's preoccupation with tracking dogs to Elijah. "Wabee hears them tracking dogs in his sleep. Sometimes, even when he's wide awake.

"Both times he escaped before, the hounds tracked him down. And the slavers used dogs to march him to the ship over there in Mandinka territory. Those scars on his arm are from a dog mauling. I probably wouldn't be too partial to hounds either if I'd of run up against them that many times."

So, both Coleman and Elijah had ignored Wabee's first warning. But then Elijah heard a deep baying in the distance. "Wabee's right. There's a pack of dogs over yonder." Searching for a place to hide, the boy cocked an ear toward the barking. It was still far off.

Coleman pointed to a tall outcropping of rock ahead. "Up there," he yelled. The three ran for the boulders, scrambled over an outer ring of rocks, then shimmied up an eight-foot crevice to the top of the largest rock. It was so big that a tree grew from a jagged crack in its surface.

Elijah lay prone, trying to melt into the granite, as the yelping dog pack drew closer. He was afraid to lift his head to look at Coleman or Wabee but hoped they were staying low.

The noise drew closer and closer. Elijah could hear several men encourage the dogs with hoots and laughter. He shuddered at the sound. To his left, Wabee stifled a whimper. With one voice, the dogs' yelps turned into a high-pitched baying. Elijah thought of his mama and how devastated she would be to see him dragged back to the plantation in chains. Then, he noticed that the baying dogs and shouting men were crashing up the mountain slope, away from their hiding place. Yes. They were heading away.

When the sounds of the tracking party faded into the distance, the three fugitives sat up and spoke in whispers.

"I thought we were goners." Coleman's laugh was shaky with relief.

"Devil dogs." Wabee imitated the hounds' high-pitched baying and rubbed his arm. "Hurt. Bad."

"Do you think they smelled some other runaways? They was on to something for sure," Elijah said.

"Maybe. But they could have been hunting squirrels. Too early in the day for raccoons. They sounded like they was having a mighty good time." He sighed. "Whatever they're after, we don't want them dogs to catch a whiff of us. Let's just stay up here until dusk; get some sleep. Then, we'll start walking uphill."

Elijah pried his thoughts away from last week's brush with the dogs and thought about how much he liked these Blue Ridge Mountains. He'd never seen a place this wild and green. As he fell asleep, he thought, These mountains would be a fine place to live.

The three fugitives were up at dawn. A morning mist had settled over their campsite as it had most mornings on their journey. Elijah knew from experience that it would burn off by midday. As they ate handfuls of the wild raspberries that they'd picked the day before, Coleman cleared his throat.

"I think we be coming up on a big change in our route. We been making good time up here in the mountains."

"Yeah," Elijah smiled. "After we climbed up the side so steep we near fell off."

*Wabee cackled. Elijah had learned that the big man understood English better than he could speak it.*

"You're right about that, boy. Who knew God made land pitched as high as the roof on a house? But once we made it to the top, it's been easy traveling. Especially since white folks don't seem to be crazy enough to climb up this high. But we still need to stay alert. We don't really know if men come up here to hunt the deer and bear. We've sure seen enough of them creatures."

"Why don't people live up here?" Elijah asked. "There's plenty of water. And they could live on squirrels like we been."

*Wabee pulled a crude slingshot out of his pocket and tapped it on his knee with a smile.*

*Elijah nodded. Wabee had kept them supplied with a steady diet of squirrel meat and even a few rabbits. As a blacksmith, Coleman was an expert in starting fires with a pile of dry leaves and material from his tinderbox. That meant they'd had cooked meals each night, without fear of detection in the uninhabited expanse of forest.*

"We don't know for sure that people don't live up here somewhere. Or they could be passing through. I think we been getting a little lazy; we need to stay more alert."

*Elijah reminded the older man,* "You said we change our route?"

"The peddler said to head north for five or six days until we come to a gap in the mountains. Of course, we need to keep looking to the drinking gourd and following that star north."

"A gap?" *Elijah asked in a puzzled tone.*

"A space between two mountains. We have to go down into that Rockfish Gap and cross up into another stretch of mountains. We're coming up on that gap. And since that's the way through the high country, they'll be lots of folks around. He said they just put a railroad tunnel in there too."

"We'll be careful. Maybe we should go through at night," *Elijah suggested.*

*Wabee nodded.*

"Let's take it as it comes. But be careful," *Coleman cautioned.*

*As they continued that afternoon, the land began a gradual slope downward. At one point, the three runaways edged out on a big rock that gave them a clear view over the gap and on to the next mountain. A road cut through the woods below. In the distance, Elijah spied a small village surrounded by fields.*

"Is that a train whistle?" *Elijah asked as he heard a faint melodic note on the wind.*

*Wabee nodded. "Train from ship."*

*Elijah stifled his excitement at hearing a train for the first time, feeling bad for the big African. How terrible must it be to have experienced Wabee's fate. A free man, a warrior, from another place over the ocean, where black men roamed free and white men were the strangers in their land. Only to be captured by a rival tribe and shipped to Virginia and sold into a life of bondage. No wonder Wabee had tried to escape many times.*

*As darkness fell, a heavy mist settled into the gap. The damp muffled the three runaways' footsteps but prevented them from seeing more than a few feet ahead. They had planned to slip into the town and try to steal some food but abandoned that idea as they lost a clear sense of direction.*

*"Didn't we pass that fence before?" Elijah whispered to Coleman. They'd been walking on level ground for a while, and he thought that they would have crossed the road by now.*

*"I don't rightly know. They seem partial to these split-rail fences up here. But I'm all turned around in this mist," Coleman replied.*

*Wabee held his hand up for silence. Straining to hear, Elijah caught the jingle of reins ahead. The three runaways sank to the ground.*

*Only a few yards away, a man's voice said, "Here's the sign. Waynesboro is just ahead."*

*Another voice responded, "I hope they have hot food and a cold mug at that inn. This blasted fog has been a trial."*

*When the sound of horses' hooves had moved far away, the fugitives rushed toward the road ahead.*

*"Praise the Lord," Coleman said. "When we cross this road, the mountain should be straight ahead."*

*Elijah walked up to the signpost and strained to see the words in the dark. "The riders went toward Waynesboro, to the left. From what we saw this morning from up on the ridge, we want to go forward and a bit to the right for the next mountain."*

*They stepped off the road and continued to walk through the fog. Coleman followed Elijah's suggestion and curved their path a few degrees toward the right. After several hours of cautious walking through fields and forest, Elijah felt the ground beneath them rise. Soon, they were walking up a steep slope. When they came to an outcropping of rocks, Coleman called a halt.*

*"I think we be out of the gap now. Let's get some rest and wait until daylight to climb this mountain." He pointed to a trickle of water falling over the rocks. "Water."*

Elijah pulled from his pocket leftovers of the squirrel they'd cooked last night. Unwrapping it from its cloth, he gnawed the tough meat with relish. He was always hungry these days. He dreamed about his mama's cooking and the delicacies that she slipped him from the big house. Biscuits. Bacon.

The other two men dined on leftover squirrel as well. When Wabee finished his portion, he said, "Hunt. With sun." Then, he rolled over and went to sleep.

Coleman raised an eyebrow as he looked at Elijah. "Boy, did you read that sign back there?"

"I did."

"Where'd you learn reading?"

"I walked the master's sons to the schoolhouse every day when they was just little ones; before they went away to boarding school. Teacher let me sit in the back of the room during lessons to stay warm in the winter. I paid attention and learned. And around the house, I snuck books or newspapers to read." Elijah looked concerned. "No one knows."

"Well, that's a fine thing. Frederick Douglass was a slave, and he not only reads but writes books. Book learning may go to waste in a slave, but it be a powerful tool in a free man."

After another week's walk along the ridge of the new mountain range, Elijah worried about the danger ahead. Patrollers were rumored to be thick along the border with Pennsylvania. That forced them to rely on help for the next stage of the journey and to trust people they knew only through word of mouth.

"See those two lanterns hanging side by side on the barn? That be the signal the peddler told me about. You sure that road sign said Port Royal?" Coleman asked Elijah.

"Yes. This road goes toward Berryville."

"This must be right. Walk ten minutes past the crossroads to Port Royal. Look for a lane on the left that leads to a white farmhouse. If it's safe, there should be a quilt on the clothesline and two lanterns on the barn at night."

Coleman mumbled the instructions from the peddler under his breath, but they were just as familiar to Elijah and Wabee. They'd heard the older man recite the words like a talisman for weeks. They had hidden in the brush for most of the day, waiting for dark. Now, it was time to take the leap and hope that this white house was still a station on the way to freedom. That a kind person who would help them lived inside.

Elijah swallowed hard before he spoke in a brave voice. "The night ain't getting any longer. Time to knock on that door."

"Bless us, Jesus," Coleman said and led the way toward the house. He directed, "Wabee, stay in the back. Them scars might terrify whoever opens that door."

Stealing across the tidy front yard, they stopped in the shadow of the house. Coleman took a deep breath and walked to the door and rapped, chanting, "Knock. Pause. Knock, knock. Pause. Knock." He had been instructed to use this special knock as a signal.

Elijah could see a band of light hit the yard as someone inside opened the door.

"Yes?" the man inside inquired.

Coleman stuttered, "Th-the geese fly north."

"Come inside, quickly. Are you alone?"

At the wave of Coleman's hand, Elijah and Wabee shuffled toward the door.

"Welcome, friends." The tiny white man opened the door wide and stepped aside. His kind face made Elijah want to burst into tears, but he clenched his hands as a distraction.

"You can tell me your story later. You all look like you could use a good meal. My wife always keeps a pot of stew on the hearth. You can call me James. This is Ruth." The man led them into a warm room and motioned for them to take a seat at the table.

Elijah was seized with sudden embarrassment about his dirty clothes. He and the others must smell pretty rank. They'd taken some dips in ponds and streams along the way, but they'd been sleeping rough for almost three weeks. His embarrassment disappeared when the round, tidy woman placed a heaping bowl of stew in front of him.

"Mr. James, sir. Can you help us get north?" Elijah asked when the bowl was empty.

"You'll spend the night here in the barn. There's a hiding place. You're the only travelers here tonight. In the next day or two, we'll take you up the road toward Harpers Ferry. There'll be a couple of other stops along the way. At each stop, the people there will move you along and tell you where to go next. They're all believers in the abolitionist cause.

"From Harpers Ferry, the folks will send you on across the Mason-Dixon Line to Pennsylvania; a town called Chambersburg. And then farther north."

"Will we be safe when we get to Pennsylvania?" Coleman asked, speaking the name of the state with reverence.

"Safer. But this Fugitive Slave Act Congress passed a few years back means patrollers can come into the free states and take runaways back down south. But it's harder that far north. And the network and the free Negro communities can help hide you."

Wabee looked up from his bowl. "Canaan? Go, Canaan?"

"He's Mandinka. His English ain't so good," Coleman explained.

"We're all God's children," James observed, studying the tribal scars on Wabee's face. "Yes, my man. The abolitionists up north can get you to Canada, ahem, Canaan. That might be best for you, with those scars. Not impossible, but certainly more difficult to pass as a free man in the States with the markings."

Wabee smiled in delight and mumbled, "Canaan."

James asked, "How long have you been traveling?"

Coleman took the lead in telling their hosts about the long walk from the plantation. He thanked them again for their help.

"Let's get you bedded down in the barn. Tomorrow, we'll see if we can find you some new clothes or get those washed. Don't come out unless I signal, using the same knock. Get a good night's sleep. You're on your way to freedom."

# CHAPTER SEVENTEEN

"You won't friggin' believe how beautiful these photos are. I'm thrilled with the entire show." Melissa grabbed Alexa by the arm and swept her into the main room of her art gallery. Half of the room was filled with pictures of women, young and old, black and brown. The other walls were empty.

Alexa walked around the perimeter, studying each photo in silence. The unifying thread among the photos was the feeling they conveyed. These women looked vulnerable and afraid. "Wow. You are a wonderful photographer, Melissa. How did you capture all this fear? It makes me sad to look at these poor women. It's a little overwhelming."

"That's what I'm calling it. *Faces of Fear*. They all live in frightening environments. I only got to photograph some of them because RESIST had taken them in." Melissa pointed to several photos to illustrate her point. "Girls from Nepal who've been trafficked; they were on their way to brothels in India. Refugee women from Somalia, living in a Kenyan refugee camp where rape is a nightly occurrence. Thai children who are sold by their parents and put on the block to be sold again by traffickers to vile oligarchs in Russia or one of the inbred Saudi royals." Her tone was contemptuous.

"Heartbreaking." Alexa paused. "But, congratulations. You raised a ton of money for RESIST the last time you did a show like this."

"Now that RESIST is branching out to help refugees, they really need the cash. I hope the donor well hasn't run dry."

"I predict that this exhibit will do even better than the first." Alexa smiled.

"Of course, the Winter Ball will help too."

"Melissa, where do you want the lunch?" a young voice called from the back of the gallery. A few seconds later, a college-age girl dressed in pink camouflage pants, Timberland boots, and a red T-shirt bopped into the room, swinging a bulging plastic bag from each arm.

Melissa shrugged at Alexa. "I forgot to tell you, we're eating in."

"OK." Alexa sighed with regret. Goodbye wood-fired margherita pizza from her favorite Italian place.

"Deidre and I have a meeting with the printer at one. Sorry. We got Chinese."

Alexa's expression brightened. "Emperor's Chicken?"

"Of course."

Then, Alexa took a closer look at the petite girl with Asian features and made the connection. She broke into a big smile. "Deidre? Deidre Townes? I heard you were coming to intern with RESIST for a couple of months. I didn't realize that you'd started. Your hair." Alexa scrunched her own curls. "It's different."

The girl broke into peals of laughter. "I'm so over the spiky purple look. I've been rocking this platinum pixie for a few months." She did a pirouette to provide the full effect. "Nice to see you, Alexa. The RESIST internship program assigned me to help Melissa with the fundraising part of her exhibit."

"Your aunt Cecily would be proud that you're continuing the family tradition by working at RESIST." Alexa smiled.

"She abso-friggin-loutely would be proud." Melissa looked at her watch. "Yikes. We've got less than an hour. Let's go to the conference room and eat."

Alexa stabbed a piece of Emperor's Chicken with her fork. "Why did you hang this show so early in the week? The official opening is Saturday, right?"

"Correct. But we have the entire RESIST board coming into town Wednesday, and Tyrell wanted them to see the exhibit. They're having a cocktail reception here that night," Melissa said. "Stop by if you can."

"I might be able to make it," Alexa replied.

"Don't you go to Krav Maga some Monday nights? Are you going tonight?" Melissa asked with an expectant look.

"Yes?" Alexa had no idea where the irrepressible redhead was going with this one.

"You could do me a big favor. I told Sloane that I'd bring her prints of winter scenes and crystal samples to look at. You know, for the Winter Ball. If you're going to Courage tonight, could you drop them off? That way, Deidre and I can finish hanging the exhibit today."

"Crystal samples are a thing?" Alexa asked in a droll voice, then relented. "Of course, I'll take them to Sloane."

Deidre jumped up. "I think they're on the table in your office. I'll get them."

The minute the intern left, Melissa turned to Alexa. "So, tell me."

"Tell you what?"

"Reese."

"What about Reese?" Alexa dissembled. She was still relishing the change in their relationship. She wasn't ready to share the news, even with her best friend.

"Lexie, I've known you since you were five years old and know about every boy you ever kissed. Except for New York; you were on your own then. And by all accounts, screwed things up royally with that jerk Troy, Terry, whatever."

"Trent."

"That should have been your first clue to steer clear. What kind of name is Trent? It's as bad as Skip or Buffy. Spill. You have that moony, preoccupied look that you get when you've fallen in love."

"I don't think I ever fell out of love with Reese," Alexa whispered.

"I know. That's why John never really stood a chance; God rest his soul."

Alexa smiled and relented. "You're right, of course. We're back together, and it's absolutely glorious." She bit her lip. "A little part of me worries that he'll leave again. Go back to Africa. But I can't destroy this second chance with a bunch of what-ifs."

Melissa put her hand on Alexa's arm. "The man is clearly head over heels for you. He always has been. Things will work out."

"I hope so. You're always pointing out my pathetic track record with men, but Reese is one of the good ones. He's smart, funny, kind, and brave."

"My God, Lexie, you sound like you're describing Scout."

"Well, I love Scout too." Alexa giggled. "But, Reese is so much more. There's this bond between us that I've never felt with another guy. We both love the outdoors. We're both using our educations to make a difference instead of chasing a glamorous career." With a twinge of guilt, Alexa shifted in her seat. "Granted, I was attracted to other guys while he was away."

Melissa's sympathetic smile vanished as she raised an eyebrow. "You mean poor John. And that married legislator, the environmentalist."

"We were just friends." Alexa flashed a quick grin. "You know he was happily married. But, I like Walt a lot. He reminds me of Reese—a real straight arrow."

"Hey, no judgement here, sister. You had no idea if Reese would ever tear himself away from the wilds of Africa and come home. But, he's back now. My mom would say, 'Why are you borrowing trouble?' Just enjoy it and go with the flow." Melissa paused, "Do you want me to toss you more clichés?"

Alexa sighed. "I'm happy when Reese is around."

"Well, there you have it."

Deidre called from out in the corridor, "Here's the stuff to take to Krav Maga."

Alexa looked at her watch. "OK. I have to get going. I have a meeting too. Thanks for lunch." She jumped up from the table and headed toward the hall, thinking about her friend's words of encouragement. Melissa had always been her best sounding board. Talking to her helped Alexa clarify things in her own mind.

Melissa was right: Life is short. Why waste time worrying about what could happen? The man she loved had walked back into her life. She was going all in.

As she opened the vehicle door, Alexa cracked up. A few minutes of advice from Melissa, and now she was talking in clichés too.

After work, Alexa threw herself into Krav Maga. Lev and KC worked the class hard.

Chest heaving, Alexa looked up from the floor at Barb, her partner for a series of exercises, and gasped. "Good job. I couldn't break through your defensive move on that last one. Guess that's why I'm down here." She laughed and jumped up.

Barb grinned. "I think you're getting better too. Must have been my pep talk from a few weeks ago."

KC walked by in time to overhear Barb's remarks. "I have to agree, Williams. Looks like you've finally gotten your head out of your ass. I liked the controlled aggression on that last exercise. Remember, there are no victims here."

"Wow," Alexa whispered to Barb. "A compliment from the drillmaster. Hard to believe."

Lev shouted, "OK. Last exercise. Back in position. We're going to practice how to escape from a rear choke hold. It's a four-step move. Start with ducking your chin. Let me demonstrate first with KC."

As the class ended, Alexa was surprised to see Tyrell and Bassam Qassim come through the studio door. Nabil Qassim followed on their heels.

"Hello. What are you folks doing here?" Alexa asked.

Tyrell answered. "Sloane arranged for Bassam to try an introductory Taekwondo class. To see if he likes it."

Bassam gave an uncharacteristic smile. "I can be like Jackie Chan. Ah yah!" the boy shouted and kicked his foot forward.

Nabil had been scowling at KC, who was dressed in a tight tank top and fatigues. At Bassam's cry, he refocused his scowl on the teenager. Then, he turned to Alexa, whom he'd ignored up to that point. "Is that woman the teacher?"

"KC? She teaches my class, Krav Maga. Not sure who teaches Taekwondo."

"Krav Maga? The Israeli tactic?" Nabil spat the words with disgust.

"Yes. It's a self-defense class." Alexa kept her voice neutral, glad to disengage from the tense exchange when four young boys burst into the room. A very toned young man followed them through the door and strode to the front. Alexa thought this twenty-something looked familiar; he could have been a student in Sloane's early-morning class—the one she'd spied on a few weeks ago.

Lev nodded to the young man, then called to the boys. "Take your places. Class will start in a few minutes." KC left the room, and Lev walked toward Bassam with a welcoming expression on his face.

"Looks like this class is Lev's," Alexa commented. "He's a good teacher." She gave Tyrell a quick hug, then looked at Bassam. "I'm out of here. Have a good class."

When she entered the locker room, KC was changing.

"Who's your friend with the kufi, Williams? He was really giving me the evil eye. Felt like I was back in Fallujah again."

"Nabil Qassim. He's related to one of my clients. You're right. The guy seems wound pretty tight. I don't think he liked the idea of his nephew being taught by a woman." Alexa tried to keep her instinctive dislike of Nabil out of her tone.

"Well, I guess he'll really freak when he sees the two girls who are in that Taekwondo class. Guys like that chap my ass. There're more of them than grains of sand in the Middle East."

"Nabil's a Syrian refugee. He seems a lot more conservative than his brother's family. They strike me as quite secular and anxious to assimilate. Odd thing. This guy's been in the country for years. My clients just arrived here a few months ago. You'd think it would be the other way around." Alexa buttoned her coat and folded her work clothes into her gym bag.

"You never know. He has a glimmer of that wild-eyed look you see in the jihadis. But, he might just be one of these conservative Muslims who think a woman's place is two steps behind her man." KC chuckled. "Hell, I've got two uncles who think the same thing—and they're Baptists."

Alexa winced. "I see a lot of that type of guy in my work. They're often the ones my clients are taking out Protection from Abuse orders against. Far too many of them." She headed toward the door. "Take care."

"Watch your back out there, Williams. Remember: No victims."

# CHAPTER EIGHTEEN

PING. PING.

Alexa groaned as the sound of an incoming text woke her before the alarm. She rolled over to grab her phone from the nightstand. She'd been so tired that she'd forgotten to switch off the volume the night before.

"Where are photos and crystal samples for Sloane?" the text from Melissa read. "I texted her. Says they're not at studio."

"Oh, shit. I forgot," Alexa said aloud. Oblivious, Scout snored from his bed in the corner.

She texted back, "Sorry. Forgot to drop off at Courage Monday night."

"Drop them at gallery. I'll deliver."

Alexa could tell that Melissa was pissed. When her texts got terse, she was unhappy.

"No. No. I'll take them to Courage or her house today," Alexa replied.

"OK. It's important that she gets them ASAP."

Seriously, Melissa? Sometimes her exuberant best friend could be a bit of a prima donna. Alexa doubted that a day or two would make a difference in ordering crystals. The Winter Ball wasn't until January. But, she had screwed up, so she'd add crystal delivery to her to-do list for the day.

Alexa slid out of bed and slipped a sweatshirt over her pajamas. Shutting off the bedside alarm, she called, "Scout. It's time to get up and go outside. I have to get ready for work."

Alexa had just sat down to tea and a bowl of oatmeal when the phone rang. "Mom, what's up? This is early for you to call."

"Lexie. Have you seen the news? The national news?"

"Not yet. I was just about to take a look over breakfast. Why?" A vague sense of anxiety seized Alexa. Her mom sounded stressed.

"ISIS. There have been two men killed by ISIS. One somewhere in this area. The other in Harpers Ferry. Although it makes absolutely no sense that terrorists would be operating here in the MidAtlantic, the FBI hasn't denied it."

At this point, Alexa had Googled the news on her iPad and was scrolling through the *New York Times* story. She wasn't surprised that something this big had leaked. It was probably more surprising that they'd kept it under wraps since August, when the first body had been discovered.

"When I saw FBI, I knew. Lexie, is this why the FBI wanted to interview you? This is the body that you found? Someone killed by ISIS? Oh my God, Lexie. ISIS?" Susan's voice rose until it bubbled with hysteria.

"Calm down, Mom. I'm not really involved. And I don't think the FBI knows for sure that ISIS has anything to do with this. But yes. This is the body that we found. The one here; not the one in Harpers Ferry. The guy was long dead. We were in no danger then. We're in no danger now."

"Harpers Ferry. Where Reese lives?"

"Weird, huh?" Alexa decided that now was not the time to mention that the FBI had zeroed in on Reese as a possible suspect. She was still angry that the FBI hadn't given him the all clear. The more she'd thought about it, the idea that he had some connection to Somali terrorists was just absurd.

"Is Dad home?"

"No, he went to breakfast with friends."

"Well, you can tell him about this when he returns home, of course. And Graham already knows. He was with me at the Sunday interview. But the FBI did ask me to keep this quiet. And I don't want my role in this to get out to the press. I'd bet Tyrell and Reese will say the same thing. Please don't tell anyone else about it, Mom."

"Fine, dear. We don't want ISIS to know anything about you."

"Mom, I really don't think ISIS has anything to do with this. The killers want it to look like ISIS, or simply to fuel an anti-Muslim sentiment, but that doesn't mean that they are terrorists."

After she got her mother off the line, Alexa shook her head. Her mom was not a woman who rattled easily.

I guess there's something about the idea of terrorism close to home that can shake the strongest of women, Alexa concluded. Especially when your daughter is involved.

By the time Alexa had finished reading three articles about the alleged terrorist executions on her iPad, her mood was glum. None of the ramifications of this story becoming public struck her as positive. The articles all cited "sources aware of the investigation," which sounded like a leak. If the FBI had been caught off guard with this news story, they would now be reacting to public pressure to resolve this case. Two local congressman and a West Virginia senator were railing against law enforcement for keeping these murders under wraps for so long, citing concerns with public safety.

Her immediate worry was for Reese. Agent Fox might come down harder on any suspects in the case, and they still hadn't ruled Reese out. He and his lawyer were scheduled to be interviewed by the FBI again tomorrow.

She also dreaded the news outlets learning that she, Reese, and Tyrell had found the last body. She'd had an earlier experience at the center of a media maelstrom, and it was no picnic.

Alexa glanced at the time. "I have to get out of here, Scout. One quick run outside before I leave."

On the way to work, Alexa called Reese. They'd had a brief and deliciously awkward phone call on Monday, in which they both tried to adjust to their new status as reunited lovers. Alexa grinned, recalling the conversation, while she waited for him to pick up. Instead, she got his voicemail.

"I imagine you've seen the news. This sure raises the stakes for your interview. Is it scheduled? Call me when you get a chance."

# CHAPTER NINETEEN

IN LATE AFTERNOON, Melinda hurried into Alexa's office. "Tyrell Jenkins is on the phone. He says it's urgent. But everything is urgent with that man. Do you want to take it?"

"Yes." Alexa put down her editing pen. She suspected he was calling about today's news articles.

"Alexa, the Qassims need your help again." Tyrell's voice seemed tense.

"The Qassims?" Alexa remembered that Detective Miller owed her another call about the vandalism at the refugee family's home. She had spoken to him several times about the lack of police progress in finding the perpetrators.

"This time it's Bassam." Tyrell paused. "You saw the news today, right?"

"Yeah, I planned to call you tonight about all of that. Today has just been too hectic. But what does that have to do with Bassam?"

"After school, Bassam and a friend went to a pizza shop. It's a big after-school hangout, apparently. A news story came on the TV while they were waiting for their slices. You know, one of the stations has tagged it 'Terror in the MidAtlantic.' Another is going with 'A Battle with ISIS on the Mason-Dixon Line.' Anyway, people are all riled up. Many are afraid; they think Osama Bin Laden's risen from his grave and is going to stroll down High Street to strike them down in their beds."

"He was Al-Qaeda, not ISIS," Alexa murmured.

"You really think most of the Cumberland County population knows the difference? Bottom line, people are freaking out."

"I've been wrapped up in meetings all day. A few people mentioned the terrorist story and said how terrible it was. But I had no idea—" she sighed, "or maybe I was hoping it wasn't a big thing."

"Well, it's big enough to get our boy Bassam in trouble. When the news story came on TV at the pizza shop, a group of boys started calling Bassam a terrorist and worse. They started slapping him and his friend around and telling them to 'go back to where you belong.' Interesting side note that the friend, Tony Biondi, was born and raised in Carlisle. His very Catholic, Italian-American family has been here for generations. Naturally, he has no foreign accent. He speaks pure Carlisle teenager.

"Anyway, from all accounts, the owner tried to break it up. He told the punks to leave. Before he could get around the counter to kick them out of the shop, Bassam threw a punch, and it all went south from there. The police came and dragged the whole lot down to the station."

Alexa frowned. "I feel sorry for this kid. But he walks around like a powder keg waiting to blow. Of course, living in a refugee camp probably conditioned him to fight back. I hear that they're pretty rough places. But what's my role here? You know I don't—"

"Do criminal law," Tyrell interrupted. "But your presence would be helpful. You could remind the Carlisle Police that they still haven't caught the jerk-offs who vandalized this kid's house, and that here's yet another instance where he's the victim. Cops watch TV, too, Alexa. Now is not the best day for an Arab kid to get arrested twenty miles from where they found a dead body with a sign praising Allah."

"OK. I'd think leniency would be called for here. The kid was the victim; he just resisted the harassment. And he's never been in trouble before, right?"

"Right."

Alexa sighed. "I'll meet you at the police station. We want to get there before they involve Juvenile Probation. Have Eshan and Zahraa gone over to the station yet?"

"They're leaving soon. They needed to make arrangements for Ali. He had some event after school."

"Maybe you should call and recommend that they leave him home with Uncle Nabil. This works better without having Nabil in the mix."

Sipping on her Coke, Alexa glanced around the Hamilton. "Empty for a Tuesday night."

Tyrell shrugged. "It's almost eight. The dinner rush is long over. Sorry I made you miss yoga."

"It's OK. I just hate to leave Scout alone this long. Although I have the neighborhood kid come in after school to take care of him, I'd usually be home by now."

Tyrell responded in social worker mode, "You have to eat. The dog will be fine for another hour." Then he gave her a broad smile. "This dinner is on me, by the way. I knew you could work your magic for Bassam. No charges. And I'm glad they decided to let all the other kids off with a warning too. God knows, Tony was just in the wrong place at the wrong time; and Bassam needs a friend. I hope the other punks learned a lesson. I recognized two of the kids from my old foster care caseload, though. I suspect at least one of them will be back in trouble with the law soon."

"I'm glad Detective Miller was there. He's a lot more tolerant than some of his fellow officers. Maybe working homicide gives you a clearer perspective on what's important and what's just bullshit. Anyway, he's knee-deep in the vandalism investigation and saw how it affected Bassam and Ali. And the fact that they've made no headway on solving that case . . . in an odd way, it worked in our favor too. He feels he owes the Qassims."

"Good call on Nabil, by the way. I know justice should be blind, but having the uncle who looks exactly like everyone's idea of a terrorist sail into the police station wouldn't have helped the situation."

"Not to mention his sunny personality. What's the story with that guy?"

Tyrell shook his head. "I don't really know. Eshan and Zahraa had mentioned him as their only relative in the United States. He'd lost his job. Wasn't in a position to sponsor them. Although we expected they'd get in touch and visit, we were a little surprised when he showed up one day without warning. And hasn't left. There are a lot of jobs in this area. In many ways, it makes sense he'd join his only brother. But he's been here for months and still hasn't gotten a job. I don't know if he intends to relocate here or go back to Detroit. And it's not my business unless he affects the Qassim family's ability to fulfill their part of the resettlement bargain." He scowled. "But the guy's such a surly bastard. I worry about his influence on Bassam."

"He gives me the creeps." Alexa shivered, then saw the waiter coming down the aisle. "Ah, here's our food."

As he finished his first hotchee dog, Tyrell said, "No question that the terrorism news stories had an impact on Bassam, but we haven't talked about what this all means to us." Reaching for the second hot dog smothered in chili, cheese, and onions, he lowered his voice. "I haven't told anyone about finding that guy at the farm; not even my mama. She would be pulling her hair out with worry."

"Well, Graham knows. He and I were at my parents' house when the FBI called for that first meeting. This morning my mom put two and two together. She's freaking out. So, it's probably best your mama doesn't know."

"Also, it would be the last thing our new refugee project needs—a news story about RESIST's executive director being mixed up with terrorism. You know how that would play. The news reveals the name of a black guy—*moi*—who found the body of a stranger who may or may not have been killed by terrorists. Two days later, in most people's minds, it's, 'Oh, yeah. Isn't that the black guy who's the terrorist? And isn't he bringing more terrorists in through that refugee program?'"

Alexa gave a rueful laugh. "I hope it wouldn't be that bad. But I'm with you. The last thing I want to see is our names go public. The media circus would be crazy."

"What's Reese say? I hear you two have finally stopped dancing around the issue and are—" Tyrell broke into song—"Reunited, does it feel so good?" He ended his mangled serenade with his hand to his heart. "Ah, Peaches and Herb; remember that classic?"

"My mom and dad had it in their Motown tape collection." Alexa giggled.

"You know, the minute Reese came back from Africa, I knew I'd lost my chance with you." Tyrell gave an extravagant sigh.

Alexa choked on a last sip of her drink. "Lost your chance? That train left the station a long time ago. And you were driving it in the opposite direction." She laughed, then thought aloud, "When we first met, all that manly beauty tempted me. I admit it. But at that point in your life, hitting on women was like breathing to you, Jenkins. I knew you weren't really interested. We were always better suited as friends." With a devilish smile, Alexa said, "I could try to hook you up with someone, though. What about Sloane? She's single, far as I can tell."

Tyrell grew pensive. "She may be single, but that one's heart is still in the grave with the dead husband. When she smiles, you can sense the chill of death, hidden just below that warm, charming surface. I don't think she's ready for casual dating yet." He smiled. "Besides, I'm working on something, or should I say someone, of my own. I'll let you know how it turns out after my next trip to India."

"Tell me more," Alexa prodded. "What's her name? Does she work for RESIST?"

"Nope. I only told you about her to keep you and your girl gang from throwing women at me for the next few months. I know how you all get when you take on a new project. I'm not in the mood to be your next one."

"OK. OK." Alexa laughed then became sober. "About the news stories. I haven't spoken to Reese. I hope I can reach him tonight. Find out how this is playing in Harpers Ferry."

"Yeah. The site of the first body. That must make Reese feel really special. Bodies following him wherever he goes."

"The FBI's giving him a hard time."

"A hard time?" Realization spread across Tyrell's face. "You mean like a suspect?"

"He had to retain a lawyer."

Tyrell curled his lip in disdain. "Now I get why that dude, Fox, was asking me some of those questions."

"So, they talked to you again?"

"I thought it was just routine. Until now. Suspecting Reese is friggin' ridiculous. The man's a walking Dudley Do-Right. And I mean that in the nicest possible way. He was a forest ranger, and now he's saving the planet."

"Don't tell anyone. If he wants Jim and Melissa or anyone else to know, it's up to him. But the three of us are in this together in a way. Especially if our names get leaked to the news." She looked at the time on her phone. "I have to get home. Thanks for dinner. It's been ages since I had a hot turkey sandwich."

As they walked to the exit, Alexa said, "One other thing worries me a little. What if these killers, ISIS or whoever, find out we discovered that guy's body? We could be in danger. They may think we saw something that would help the police. Probably a remote possibility that they'd target us in any way, but you never know."

"The same thought has crossed my mind. I've seen that movie a thousand times. The trusty black friend is the one who's always killed first." Tyrell looked glum as he stopped at the cash register to pay the bill.

"Thanks again for dinner. And stay safe," Alexa called as she left the restaurant.

# CHAPTER TWENTY

TEARING DOWN THE sidewalk to the courthouse in the pouring rain, Alexa skidded on a slick patch of pavement. She managed to keep her balance by flailing her hands but dropped both briefcase and umbrella onto the soggy grass next to the old courthouse. "Oh, great," she complained as she raised the hood on her raincoat.

"Here, let me." A man leaned over to pluck the umbrella and briefcase off the ground.

"Thank you." Alexa pushed her hood out of her eyes before she accepted the items, then drew a sharp breath as she recognized her Good Samaritan. "Agent Carter. What a surprise."

"I called your office, and your assistant said you were on your way to a meeting in chambers with the judge."

"Yes. An adoption case."

"Can I walk with you? I just need a few minutes of your time."

"Sure." Like I have any choice, she thought.

They crossed the street in silence. Shaking off her raincoat and umbrella, Alexa went through screening at the courthouse. She had to wait for Agent Carter while he went through the special procedures for law enforcement carrying guns. Then, she led him to a quiet bench. "I only have about five minutes," Alexa said. "This judge is a stickler."

"That's fine. I'm sure that you've seen all the press coverage on the body you found? And the one near Harpers Ferry?" Carter wrinkled his nose in disgust at the word, 'press.'

"A little hard to miss." Alexa raised an eyebrow.

"The bureau didn't authorize release of the information. We don't know who leaked the details, but the case has involved local law from two states, National Park Service, and more. It's hard to keep a lid on an investigation like this. But, I'm here today to assure you that we have not released your name or those of Mr. Jenkins or Mr. Michaels. And we have no intention of doing so."

Alexa's tone was bitter. "But there's no guarantee, right? Our names could leak as easily as the other stuff. Level with me. Do you think we're in danger?"

"I don't know. We are still exploring leads but haven't made as much progress as we'd like."

"Is Reese Michaels still one of those leads? I hear he has another interview. You are way off base. Wasting your time."

"You know how this works, Alexa. We follow all leads until we can definitively close them. That's what we're doing." He paused. "And the Counterterrorism Unit has point on this."

Alexa understood that this was the closest she or Reese would get to an apology from Carter. But, if Agent Fox was leading this investigation, he would push until satisfied that Reese was no longer a suspect. "Anything else?"

"Yes. I wanted to show you these. We tracked down a high school picture of the man killed in Harpers Ferry. And this." He gave her two photos.

Alexa looked at the high school photo of a white kid with unkempt brown hair and a shirt that looked a size too small. He stared into the camera with an uneasy look. The second photo showed three men in army fatigues. Carter pointed to the one on the right. "Do you recognize him? At the time of his death, he was twenty-five, several years older than in either picture."

Alexa shook her head. The young soldier had lost the hair to a buzz-cut but still looked uneasy, standing a few paces away from his companions. "No. Nothing about him seems familiar. He was in the army?"

"That's the last information we have on Wayne Perdue. He was discharged from the army after a few months with a general discharge."

"Is that dishonorable?"

"I can't go into the details of Perdue's case, but 'general' basically means that the soldier was just not a good fit for military service. At some point after the discharge, Perdue drifted to the streets. We haven't been able to put together much more than bits and pieces about his life after that.

"Same with the guy you found. He was another homeless vet, but he served his full four years. There's something wrong with a veteran's system that allowed him to end up on the streets too.

He was well-known in Philly's homeless shelters for a while, then disappeared. We don't have a good photo of him yet. The army ID photo is crap."

Alexa grew angry as she listened. "This makes your focus on Reese Michaels even more egregious. Sounds to me like you've got some psycho who came home from the Middle East and started taking out homeless vets. How in the world does that relate to Reese's time in Africa and Al-Shabaab?"

Carter looked down at his feet for a moment. "Like I said. We have to pursue all leads."

Alexa jumped up and yanked her briefcase off the bench. "Look. I have to get going. I'm expected in chambers in a few minutes." She took a pointed glance at her watch.

"Just one more thing. Be careful. We may not know yet who's responsible for these murders, but it's clear that it's a dangerous individual or group of individuals. If you see anything suspicious—if you feel threatened in any way—give me a call, day or night."

Alexa shook the agent's hand. "Thanks for coming to speak with me in person. I hope you catch these guys soon. People around here are on edge; they're seeing terrorists behind every bush. That's not a good situation."

"No, it's not. These murderers may or may not be ISIS, but they've appeared to follow one rule in the terrorist playbook: Use random acts of violence to create fear within the civilian population. It's our job to figure out if they are truly random. And if they're some sort of terrorists or just garden-variety killers with a twisted sense of humor."

Back in the office a few hours later, Alexa wiped a damp strand of hair from her eyes and noticed the yellow sticky note in the center of her desk: CRYSTALS TO SLOANE. "Damn, I'm losing it. Glad I wrote myself this reminder."

She called toward the door. "Melinda, can you do something for me?"

Her assistant appeared at the door. "I live to serve, Boss. Whaddaya need?"

"I need you track down a cell phone number for Sloane Chapin. Melissa or Haley might have it. Plus, ask them for a home address." Alexa grimaced. "Melissa gave me some decorating samples to drop off at her martial arts studio. I forgot. I'll run by the studio tonight, but I want to have a backup plan in case Sloane's office is locked. Melissa's going to kill me."

Dusk had fallen by the time Alexa made it out of the office, but at least the rain had stopped. Her phone pinged as she drove across town to Courage. "Give it a break, Melissa," she groaned aloud. At a stoplight, Alexa confirmed that this was yet another reminder text from her best friend. For someone who floated through life as a free spirit, Melissa's behavior on this issue bordered on obsessive. Alexa had been considering stopping by Melissa's gallery for the RESIST board reception, but now she wasn't really in the mood to socialize. By the fourth text this afternoon, Alexa's remorse at not delivering this damned package had turned to annoyance.

Alexa pulled into Courage and skidded to a halt. The parking lot was empty, the building dark. "No!" Alexa slammed the steering wheel in frustration. She slipped out of the Land Rover and walked to the front door. The headlights provided just enough light for her to read the sign that listed the studio hours. Wednesdays they closed at noon. Alexa grumbled at herself for not checking online for the hours of operation. Although she'd never been here on a Wednesday, she just assumed the studio was open every evening.

"OK. Plan B," Alexa said. Back in the vehicle, she found the slip of paper from Melinda with Sloane's cell number.

She texted, "I'd like to drop off these samples from Melissa tonight. Can I bring them to your house on way home? Am leaving now." Then, Alexa looked at the address, hoping it actually was on her way home. Or at least in the general direction.

"Hemlock Road. Hemlock Road?" Alexa tried to place the address. The vintage Land Rover was much too old for a navigation system, so she plugged it into Google Maps on her cell. Alexa got a general sense of where she was heading and checked her messages. No reply from Sloane. Cringing at the thought of another round of disappointed texts from Melissa, Alexa decided to deliver the damn crystals and be done with it. If Sloane wasn't home, she'd just leave them on the porch. Feeling better, Alexa drove to the exit and hit the navigation button.

"Turn left," the phone woman's dulcet voice directed.

After ten minutes on a series of country roads, the navigation system led Alexa into uncharted territory. She believed she'd been on most of Cumberland County's many back roads at one point or another in her life, but she didn't remember ever traveling these last few. Finally, the voice told her to turn left onto Hemlock Road.

The twisting Hemlock Road was also new to her. Just as Alexa slowed to approach a one-lane bridge, a huge owl flew across the road ahead in a blur of brown feathers. Startled, Alexa jammed on the brakes. With a muttered curse, she continued across the narrow bridge and inched along as the road curved and looped back over the creek. Then, it took a sharp turn to the left.

A few minutes later, Alexa drove right past the entrance to Sloane's property, just as the nav lady announced, "You have reached your destination." She'd been looking for a house, not two tall columns of limestone masonry. Alexa backed up on the deserted road until the headlights illuminated the set of gateposts. Then, she saw the number 1248 inset into one of the stones. Pulling through the open iron gates, Alexa drove down a winding gravel lane.

It took several more minutes of driving before Alexa spied the gray limestone farmhouse ahead, lights blazing inside. It appeared that Sloane was home. And it looked like she might have company. Alexa pulled the Land Rover into a paved parking area amid an array of pickup trucks and nondescript sedans. She found an empty spot in the far corner.

As she headed to the front door, toting the case full of crystals and photo samples, Alexa felt a twinge of remorse for barging in. But she had no intention of staying. She was still beat from last night's exercise with Bassam at the police station and wanted to get home.

Although light streamed through the windows, the small front porch was dark. Enveloped by deep shadows, Alexa rang the doorbell and waited. And waited. She knocked a few times. Nothing.

She turned and looked around, noticing the quiet. All those cars in the lot, but Alexa could hear nothing but the sound of her own breathing. A loud screech split the night and she jumped, heart thumping. The owl. The screech owl had flown into one of the big old trees on the front lawn.

Maybe they're in the back and can't hear, she considered. Could be watching TV or something. Alexa trudged back down the sidewalk and walked toward another small porch that jutted out from the back corner of the house. Seeing no buzzer by this door, Alexa gave a loud knock. Still no answer. Exasperated, she sighed and plopped the case down next to the door. Despite all the cars and the lights, it appeared Sloane wasn't home. Or didn't want to be disturbed. Next time, Melissa could deliver her own decorating samples.

Alexa snugged the case next to the door, where it would be easily found. The porch roof would protect it from any rain. She turned to leave but paused at the top of the steps. Boy, she thought. I'd like to see this place in the daylight.

Small solar lights illuminated a huge stone patio and a stone pathway that led to a few outbuildings. The windows of one long rectangular building were lit. Sloane might be there, but Alexa wasn't going to wander around the woman's property uninvited.

Another outbuilding was an old limestone barn, likely centuries old. Historic barns and houses like Sloane's were quintessential Cumberland County and highly prized. Alexa grinned. And highly priced. She'd thought that Sloane looked like she came from money. If this layout was any indication, it must be true. Good for her.

Alexa dug her phone from a pocket and dashed off another text to Sloane. Still no reply to her earlier messages. "Dropped off case of items that Melissa wanted u to have by your back door. Sorry I missed u."

She sensed the light around her dim and jerked her eyes away from the phone to do an uneasy scan of the area. The lone light from the outbuilding had gone out. The resulting darkness swallowed up all the remaining light. The house and path lights that had seemed so bright before now only cast an anemic afterglow—like the ebbing flicker of a firefly just before it died on a moonless summer night.

Alexa laughed at her overactive imagination. But, a part of her was still spooked. Where was everybody?

She dashed down the steps and headed toward the car.

Voices. Alexa stopped short. Maybe this was Sloane. Or someone she could tell about the case she'd left on the porch.

Peering in the direction of the voices, Alexa shrank back. A large, eerie shadow bobbed down the walkway from the barn, casting a shifting, inky shape onto the wet stones. As the dark, amorphous form neared, it resolved into several human shapes; from their voices, a group of young men. She felt both relieved and wary. They didn't appear to notice her, standing just beyond of the pool of dim light from the house.

She took a step toward them, then hesitated. She had no idea who these guys were. Or if they would take her for an intruder.

Come on, Alexa, she chastised. You're getting way too jumpy. Whoever they are, they're Sloane's friends. So, they must be OK. And they're going to see you standing here anyway.

She shrugged off her misgivings and moved toward them, calling out. "Hello. Would you guys happen to know if Sloane Chapin's home?"

The group fell silent and came to an abrupt halt.

"Hi. I'm Alexa Williams, a friend of Sloane's. Is she here?" Alexa tried again.

"Alexa. What a surprise to see you here." Alexa heard Sloane before she saw her emerge from the pack of men.

She turned back to the group and said in a low voice, "Give me a few minutes, and I'll be back out to the barn. I'll bring water." Then the tall woman strode toward Alexa.

"I apologize for disturbing you at home. Melissa has been relentless ever since I forgot to drop off those crystal samples at Courage for you. I went there tonight, not knowing it was closed. Then, tracked down your home address. I did send you a text to let you know I was . . ." Wondering why she was babbling, Alexa bit off her last words.

"No problem." Sloane took Alexa's arm. "Do you want to come in for a few minutes?"

"No. I can see you're busy."

Sloane laughed. "One of my advanced Krav Maga classes. I built a studio in the barn for my own practice. Turns out it's convenient for small group sessions, and I don't have to drive into town."

"Well, I'm out of here. Sorry to crash your session. I left the sample case by the back door."

"I didn't realize that looking at the décor samples was a rush. I could have picked them up from either Melissa or you."

"Talk to Melissa about the timing. When a project captures her, everything becomes a priority. Right now, she's in high gear on the Winter Ball."

Despite the offer to go inside her home, Sloane had been edging Alexa toward the parking area while they talked. She stopped at the end of the walkway. "Drive safe. These back roads can be dark and slippery on a night like this. Thanks again."

"See you at yoga next week." Alexa walked toward her car, then turned back. "You have a beautiful home here. I love these old limestone farmhouses."

"I don't entertain much, but you'll have to come back out in the daylight. It's lovely in the spring. We can do lunch."

Sloane stood and waited until Alexa got into the Land Rover and turned the ignition. Then, she hurried toward the house.

When Alexa switched on the headlights, she caught the figures of two men in the glare. Both men quickly stepped behind a small outbuilding. It appeared they'd been watching Sloane and Alexa while they spoke.

"Well, that's a little creepy," Alexa muttered. "Could be the guys were bored, waiting for their instructor to return. Could be they were nosy. Or maybe they're pervs who like to spy on women."

Alexa backed out of her space, then rolled forward toward the lane. The last vehicle she passed was a pickup. A monster pickup with a double wheel well. Alexa braked and inched by the truck, trying to determine if it was the same one that had harassed her outside the Qassim's home. A Pennsylvania license plate, but the numbers were obscured by mud. She considered jumping out of the car and wiping off the plate. Then common sense and her uneasiness about the men watching took hold. Alexa kept on driving.

She debated the significance of seeing the truck as she followed the long driveway. These double-wheeled trucks weren't as common as regular pickups. But there were a lot of farmers and campers who drove them. Yeah. It was possible that the jerk who played truck games with her took classes from Sloane. Odds were pretty slim though.

Easing through the limestone gate posts, Alexa headed home. As she followed the twisting road around the sharp bends and across the creek, she wondered about Sloane's choice of residence. It was a beautiful old place. Although Alexa suspected that family money had given her a leg up on being able to afford such a pricey property, she admired the way Sloane was trying to remake her life—and if that included a country estate, more power to her. But the house was almost as remote as Alexa's own cabin. While Alexa craved alone time, not everyone enjoyed solitude. She wondered whether Sloane held classes at her house so she'd have some company to help fill that aching grief that Tyrell had sensed in her life. Otherwise, this was a heck of a drive to ask students to make at night.

# CHAPTER TWENTY-ONE

*July 25, 1859*

Sometimes I feel like a motherless child a long way from home.
                    —*"Motherless Child," a Negro spiritual*

*When he slid out of the secret compartment in the big lumber wagon, Elijah's legs buckled. Yes, his legs had gone a little numb from the long ride, but the thrill of stepping on northern soil for the first time made his knees weak. He choked back a sob of joy. Then, he felt Coleman's hand on his arm.*

*"Easy, boy. Easy," Coleman murmured in a thick voice.*

*When Elijah looked at the old man, his face was wet with tears.*

*A tidy-looking white man in a business suit and slouch hat grabbed Elijah's other elbow. "Steady there, son. Welcome to Chambersburg. You must be thirsty. It's a dusty ride from Harpers Ferry." He pointed toward a well-padded woman with an angelic face, who held out a dipper of water.*

*After quenching his thirst, Elijah looked around. Several men were unloading lumber from the wagon into a long shed, which was piled high with a supply of boards and construction supplies. A big house made from a soft gray stone stood at the other end of the open courtyard. And what looked like a barn sat at the opposite end beside a small, tumbling creek.*

*The tidy man gathered together the group: Elijah, Coleman, Wabee, and the other runaways who had traveled with them—two* men and a young woman. "Please follow me to the barn. I'll show you where to stay; where to hide. We'll have some food for you soon."

Inside, he motioned for the runaways to sit on the hay bales scattered around the interior. "I'm Deacon McClure. I work with a group of people here in Chambersburg who will help send you on your way north. Generally, our goal is to move travelers out quick as we can, but there have been a lot of patrollers on the road this week. We'll move you when it's safe. Could be a few days; and we'll send you out in smaller groups. In the meantime, we'll work on papers for you; there's a fellow here who can make papers that will say you're free Negroes. We have quite a few free Negroes here in town, so travelers like you don't stand out as much as below the Mason-Dixon. But I ask that you stay close for now. Patrollers are good at picking out runaways because of the way you talk, and even your clothes." He nodded at Elijah, Coleman, and Wabee. "Although those duds should pass fine."

Coleman said, "Thanks to some kind people who helped us along the way in Virginny."

The deacon's gaze stopped on Wabee's face. "Your scars. Those from Africa?"

Wabee nodded.

"The quicker we can get you north, the better," McClure said. He looked at the six fugitives. "Get some rest. You are in God's hands, brothers and sisters. And God wants all men to be free. We'll be back soon with some food."

Elijah nestled his blanket in some loose hay and listened to the sad cooing of some birds in the rafters. He tried to nap, but his mind was racing. They had made it to the North. He wished he could send word to his mama that they'd made it to Pennsylvania. He'd pushed her out of his mind on the journey through the mountains. But now, he imagined her beautiful face and how happy she'd be. A tear slid down his cheek as he remembered he'd likely never see Mama again.

"Boy, it be time for praising the Lord, not crying. We made it to the Promised Land." Coleman stifled a cough before he sat down next to Elijah. "I know that Wabee has his heart set on Canaan, but I thought I'd ask Deacon McClure if he can send us to Massachusetts."

"Will he be all right on his own? His English . . ."

"We talked about it, and he be fine. These abolitionists, that's what they call themselves, will help him north. The deacon said there's more Mandinka in Canada, and he could find a home there."

"Then that would be good for him. His own people." Elijah nodded at the idea, then panicked at the idea of losing Coleman. "But we'll travel together?"

"Of course, boy. I promised your mama that I'd look after you until we found a new home." Coleman coughed again. "I be so proud of you, Elijah. It was a long, hard journey. Took longer than that peddler said. But then, a man with a horse and wagon don't rightly know how long it might take to walk them mountains on foot. One of them gentlemen told me it be the end of July. At home, the tobaccy be coming on shoulder high."

"I miss Mama and my sisters." Elijah's lip trembled again.

"That's only natural, boy. But your mama dreamed that you'd be a free man. Remember that when you think of her." Coleman coughed and rubbed his head. "My head hurts from bouncing in that wagon. I'm going to sleep a while."

Elijah wiped away sweat on his brow as he crossed the street to the square. Mrs. McClure had sent him out to the pharmacy for some medicine for Coleman. He was recovering, and this would be the last bottle of tonic that the blacksmith would need for his lungs. In these three weeks in Chambersburg, Elijah had experienced a freedom he'd never known. Deacon McClure said that such a light-skinned boy wouldn't get a second glance on the street if he did nothing to attract attention. With his forged papers in his pocket, Elijah walked around cautious but free. And Mrs. McClure allowed him to read her books after he finished his chores.

Elijah felt bad sometimes because he was so happy while Coleman was feeling poorly. But now that Coleman was on the mend, Elijah spent hours chattering to the older man about all the wonders out in the streets of the town. Wabee and the others had moved on north. Several other waves of fugitives had come and gone as well. But Deacon McClure wanted Coleman to rest up a few more weeks before he and Elijah left for Massachusetts.

Stopping by the barn when he returned, Elijah told Coleman, "Mrs. McClure said I should bring you inside the house when I got back."

"I don't need no more medicine. I'm feeling better. No more cough. No more sweats. We been a burden long enough on this family," Coleman muttered. Still, he rose to follow the boy into the big limestone house.

"Thank you, Elijah." Mrs. McClure took the tonic and poured some into a spoon for Coleman.

"I know the worst has passed, but you had quite a congestion in your lungs. I want to make sure you're fully recovered before we send you north. We'll wait until you finish this bottle of tonic. Then, the deacon will see to your travel." Mrs. McClure wiped her hands on her white apron and went back to filling a piecrust with sliced peaches. "I don't often get a chance to get to know our travelers; I daresay I'll miss you both.

"It's fortunate that you're still here in Chambersburg. We are having important company tonight, and the deacon wanted me to invite you both to dinner."

Coleman looked thunderstruck. "Dinner, ma'am?"

"Yes, a well-known abolitionist is staying in town for a few months. He's using the name Dr. Isaac Smith while he's here. The deacon and I attended his sermon at our church, Falling Spring Presbyterian. My husband also went to hear him preach at Emmanuel Chapel. Dr. Smith is a powerful speaker with a passion for the cause. He's widely known for some bold action that he and his sons took against slaveholders out west in Kansas." She blushed and wiped her hands on her apron. "We are honored to have him in our home."

"We'd be pleased to meet Dr. Smith, ma'am. But we can eat in the barn like usual. We don't want to be causing no trouble," Coleman said.

Elijah nodded, stunned into shyness by the very idea of dining with the McClure family and their guest.

Mrs. McClure seemed to sense the fugitives' discomfort. "I won't lie to you. Not all people in the North are as welcoming to the Negro, free man or slave, as the deacon and I are. But our faith tells us to help our common man. Like Paul said in his Epistle to the Hebrews: 'Remember them that are in bonds, as bound with them, and them which suffer adversity, as being yourselves also in the body.' You are welcome in our home and welcome at our table. And Mr. Bro—I mean Dr. Smith will be interested to hear your history on the plantation."

Several hours later, Elijah and Coleman filed into the house with tentative steps. Deacon McClure looked up from his chair and smiled. "Come in; come in. As you can see, Dr. Smith, his son, Oliver, and two business associates, Mr. Kagi and Mr. Leary, have just arrived.

"Gentlemen, these are two of our travelers, Coleman and Elijah, who have stayed on several weeks due to Coleman's illness. While he recovered, Elijah has been helping with chores and improving his reading and arithmetic skills."

A tall man with flowing white hair and beard fixed his piercing eyes on Elijah. "Unusual to find a slaveholder who permits reading in those bound to him."

After a pause, Elijah stuttered, "Y-yes, sir. I learned it when I took the young masters to school. No one knew." He was so nervous that he could barely speak. He'd never socialized with white people, let alone an imposing stranger like this tall abolitionist. He was terrified he'd do something wrong.

The handsome younger man slapped his knee. "Well, if that don't beat the Dutch. And then you made it the whole way North."

"Yes, sir. Me and Coleman here, and Wabee. But Wabee headed out to Canaan." As Elijah spoke, his gaze kept sliding toward the guest introduced as Mr. Leary. He was a Negro, dressed in fine clothes with a cravat; in similar style to Dr. Smith and his son. A colored man invited as a guest!

The man noticed his apparent bedazzlement and gave the boy a kind smile before he spoke to Coleman. "And have you recovered from your illness and the journey? How long was your path north?"

Elijah relaxed as the evening progressed. Mrs. McClure served a delicious dinner of roast chicken, mashed potatoes, and something she called corn pudding. He stayed quiet for most of the meal, content to savor the good food and listen to the older gentlemen talk. He followed their conversation carefully, trying to piece together the meaning. Some of the discussion was about the national news. All the men railed against a man they called President Buchanan, who hailed from Pennsylvania. Elijah gathered that the abolitionists in this room were disappointed in their fellow Northerner.

At one point, Deacon McClure called Buchannan "that damned doughface," only to receive a mild admonishment from his wife.

"Language, dear."

"I apologize." The deacon frowned.

The men also spoke of some lumber orders that Deacon McClure had in process at Dr. Smith's sawmill. But as the plates cleared and Mrs. McClure brought a pot of coffee, the conversation turned to something the group called "the plan." Elijah gathered that Dr. Smith had a group of people working with him on this plan, which had something to do with Harpers Ferry and a slave rebellion. Deacon McClure was raising money to help Dr. Smith but apologized that he hadn't collected the full amount needed.

Dr. Smith raised his hand to stop the apology. "Brother McClure. You are doing God's work. The Lord will provide because our cause is righteous. We have several months before we've gathered all the soldiers and arms we need for the assault. Brother Douglass is on his way to Chambersburg to discuss the plan. I hope that he will back us with his influence. Frederick has a strong voice among those who embrace our cause." Smith's eyes blazed. "He may calm the fears of those who criticize my zeal."

"Frederick Douglass is coming here? To this town?" With an expression of amazement, Coleman spoke for the first time in an hour. "We know that name even on the plantations. He was one of us who beat his master to a pulp before he ran north. Now he speaks and writes books against slavery. That be the man you talking about?" Coleman folded his shaking hands in his lap.

"It is. Although it is supposed to be a secret. As is our entire plan. So, I expect that you men will keep this conversation to yourselves."

Elijah had no one tell about the plan, but he was so intimidated by this zealous Dr. Smith that he nodded in obedience.

"Yes, sir. I swear," Coleman answered.

"If Douglass signs on, that would help with raising more money. Is there anything else you need right now?" the deacon asked.

"More recruits. We're going to start training soon at the farm over in Sharpsburg. And a blacksmith. We need some repairs to those wagons we bought. Is there a good smithy here in town?"

"I'm a blacksmith. Best in Nottaway County, Virginia," Coleman said. "I could help you out. This plan you been talking about ain't completely clear to me, but the cause sounds pure. And Mrs. McClure doesn't want me to travel for at least a week. To tell you the truth, it would feel right to put an anvil in the fire; that's my calling."

Dr. Smith looked at the deacon, as if for permission.

"Splendid! Would you bring the wagons here?"

"Papa, I can drive them up here when we deliver lumber," Oliver said.

"God does provide." Dr. Smith smiled.

When the guests had gone, Elijah helped Mrs. McClure wash up. Coleman and Deacon McClure sat in front of the fire and talked about using the forge by the barn.

"Then it's settled." The deacon paused for a beat. "I trust you men to keep all of this secret. I believe in my heart that, someday, slavery will no longer be allowed in the United States—in any of the states. But, change comes like spring: slow at first then all at once. We're still in the early bud stage with a long way to go until the trees are green. That means we could get into a lot of trouble if anything about this plan comes out."

"Deacon, you done so much for us. We'd never do anything to hurt you or the missus."

Their host rubbed a hand across his forehead. "You may as well know about Dr. Smith. His real name is John Brown. He's well known in the Abolitionist movement, but not everyone agrees with his approach. You may have heard of him down in Virginia."

Elijah shook his head. The name John Brown meant nothing to him. But the man himself was the most riveting person he'd ever met. A righteous fervor, both impressive and a little scary, seemed to burn through this Brown.

Coleman let out a long breath. "I heard about this man, John Brown. Ain't he the one who killed all them people out west somewhere?"

"Kansas. He fought to make Kansas a free state, not a slave state. One of his sons was killed in the fighting."

Coleman coughed, then rose to his feet, standing tall. "Mr. Brown carries hisself like a man who's bound for glory. I'd be proud to help with his plan."

# CHAPTER TWENTY-TWO

REESE HAD ARRIVED at the cabin by the time Alexa made it home on Friday afternoon. As she pulled next to his Toyota Highlander, Scout and Reese came tumbling out the front door. Alexa's spirits lifted as her lanky boyfriend swept her into his arms.

"I'm glad to see you," he murmured into her hair.

She melted into his chest, breathing in his familiar woodsy scent. Then she looked up with an impish smile. "Me too. Especially since you can help carry all these groceries." She walked to the rear of the Land Rover and opened the door, shooing Scout away.

"Are we having company? There is enough here for a small army."

"Mostly bread and milk. And Chinese food. You know they're calling for a big snowstorm tonight?"

"Big? I heard two to four inches."

"Well, it's unusual to even get snow this early in November. Be prepared and all that."

"Right. Did you get Cashew Chicken?"

Over containers of Cashew Chicken, Emperor's Chicken, and fried rice, Reese said, "I'm sorry I didn't call this week. It's been really rough, but I think everything has been sorted out. You got my texts?"

"I did. But I was a little freaked when you didn't return my calls." Alexa hesitated but decided to share her fears. "I was afraid you were having second thoughts about last weekend."

Reese looked confused then contrite. "Second thoughts? No, no, no. Last weekend was the best thing that's happened in a long time."

He squeezed Alexa's hand. "And thinking about you got me through this whole fuck-up with the FBI."

"They questioned you again?" Alexa asked with apprehension.

"Yes. It seems like I spent all week either in an interview with Agent Fox and his crew or prepping with my lawyer. Thanks for insisting I get an attorney. Grandin has been worth his weight in gold. Lucky I do most of my work from home, so the Trust has no idea that I was a person of interest in a terrorism investigation. I know that they asked my boss some questions, but he thinks it was just pro forma because I was a witness in a case. He knows none of the details."

"You said *was* a person of interest."

"Yes. After the second session with Fox, he let Grandin know that I had satisfied all their concerns 'for the moment,' and they didn't expect to speak to me again. But I'd have to make myself available if they changed their minds."

"That's a relief." Alexa curled her hand over Reese's, and he loosened his tight grip on the table.

"Fox strikes me as the overzealous, by-the-book type of cop. They never had anything on you that was more than peripherally circumstantial. Agent Carter tracked me down at the courthouse this week. I got the impression that he thought Fox was off base in pursuing you but could do little since the counterterrorism folks are in charge. He actually seemed to be delivering an under-the-radar warning. He said that you, Tyrell, and I need to be careful. That our names could leak."

"Damn. Just when the FBI clears me, they turn around and tell you that the terrorists—or whatever, the murderers—could be after us?"

"That's about the long and short of it." Alexa grimaced. "Unlikely that our names will leak. Unlikely that the killers would regard us as a threat. But not outside the realm of possibility."

"Hey, we're in this together. We'll get through it." Reese nodded. "We're a team again." Scout padded to the table and bumped Reese's elbow with his huge head. He laughed and scratched the dog's ears.

Alexa's heart melted as Reese told the mastiff, "You're part of the team, too, buddy. I think you're actually the one in charge."

As they cleaned up the meal, Alexa said, "My week can't match yours for drama, but Tyrell dragged me into a new problem with this refugee family, the Qassims. Pretty soon, Williams, Williams, and Stewart are going to have to add criminal law to our list of services."

Reese took a clean dishtowel from a drawer. "This is the kid that was beat up at school? I forget his name."

"Ali. No, that's taken care of. The school district dealt with the little thugs who had been bullying him. And it seems to be working. As long as the bullies leave the kid alone, everyone's considering that situation resolved.

"The second Qassim incident was vandalism. Some jerks threw pumpkins, broke a window, and spray-painted graffiti on their house."

"I don't think I realized this was the same family. Some anti-Muslim crap?"

"'ISIS go home.'"

Reese shook his head. "Given my recent go-round with the FBI, I can't find much humor in the fact that ISIS is popping up all over the midstate."

"I know. It occurred to me that our incident and the vandalism at the Qassims could be connected. That maybe one of those militia groups you were tracking during your time in Michaux is drumming up fear of ISIS as a recruitment tool or something."

"Maybe. But I'm not sure that any of those boys are smart enough to try to pin their bullshit on Muslim terrorists. They have an entire catalog of burning hatreds—the government, blacks, Jews, liberals—you name it. I'm sure they hate Muslims too. But those militia groups are pretty proud of whatever mayhem they create; I doubt they'd want some foreigners taking credit for it."

"You could be right. The Carlisle Police have made no progress in tracking down the vandals. Do you remember Detective Miller?"

Reese nodded. "From the Family Planning Clinic investigation."

"Right. He's made a sincere effort to solve the Qassim case. I think the rest of the department has written it off as high school kids getting carried away at Halloween."

"You said Tyrell roped you into something new this week? What now?"

"This week's Qassim incident involved the older son, Bassam. He and a friend got into a scuffle with some kids who taunted him at a local pizza place. They called him towelhead and an assortment of other insults. He lost it and attacked them. Luckily, the shop owner intervened. I helped Tyrell deal with the fallout on Tuesday night. The police decided not to charge any of them. They all got a stern warning. Next time, Bassam won't get off easy."

"Sounds like a family with a lot of problems."

"Or a quiet little town that's not as tolerant as I thought. Tyrell didn't expect a Syrian refugee family to run into this amount of pushback from the community."

"What was it that James Carville said about Pennsylvania: Philadelphia and Pittsburgh with Alabama in between?"

"Something like that. But you've lived here long enough to know that's an oversimplification. We have Dickinson College and Dickinson School of Law, Harrisburg, the West Shore—all very liberal pockets in a sea of conservatives. And labels like liberal and conservative don't always apply to individuals. This area welcomed the Indochinese refugee migration with open arms. They've taken in Bosnians and Central Americans. We're much more diverse here than we used to be."

"There are just as many, if not more, Rush Limbaugh-Fox News aficionados; some of whom have never even been outside the area." Reese smiled and circled Alexa with his arms. "But I like that you look for the best in people."

Alexa gave a rueful laugh. "Until it hits me in the face that I'm dealing with the worst. I'm a cynical optimist."

"Are you OK with spending all this time on this family's problems? I'm betting that Tyrell hasn't offered to pay you."

"He did offer, but RESIST operates on a shoestring. I told him that my time would be pro bono." Alexa grew pensive. "The Qassims are worth the effort. They've gone through some unimaginable hardships. The parents are both professionals, floundering a bit here in their new home. And I feel sorry for the boys. The teenage years are rough for any kid. Imagine going through it in a foreign language in an unfamiliar place—then finding that a lot of your new classmates don't like you just because you're Syrian or Muslim or an outsider.

"The only Qassim who makes me uneasy is the uncle. He's been in the US for years and now seems to have cozied up to his extended family. Something seems off about the guy. He's very religious; on edge. Not real warm and fuzzy. But then, I wonder if my discomfort with Nabil is just an indication of my own prejudices?"

"Your instincts are usually good," Reese replied. "But, when I first went to Kenya, it took me a while to learn all the cultural nuances. Could be something like that with Nabil. I'd give it some time."

Alexa awoke to snow falling outside the bedroom window. The space next to her was empty. Scout was gone too. With a groan, she rolled over and clutched Reese's pillow to her chest. Then, smelling the scent of bacon wafting up from downstairs, she sat up to face the day.

After a romp in the snow with Scout, Alexa threw together a stew in the slow cooker. Then, she and Reese curled up on the couch to watch old movies for the rest of the afternoon.

Over dinner, Alexa sighed with happiness. "A perfect snow day. It's great to take time every once in a while to just chill and do nothing. I'm glad Melissa postponed her exhibit opening."

Reese grinned. "Agreed. I was worried you would suggest snowshoeing or something that involved spending hours outdoors. But lounging around with you, watching mindless TV—that was exactly what I needed. Running into Carlisle this evening would have ruined everything."

"We can do a repeat tomorrow." Alexa grinned.

"I have to head back to Harpers Ferry in the afternoon. I have a meeting at the Trust office on Monday morning. But, I'm all for another laid-back morning."

"Can you stay again next weekend? It's short notice, but I was thinking of inviting Mom and Dad's War College adoptees out for dinner on Saturday. Give them a different view of Cumberland County."

"The forest view?"

"Something like that. I thought I'd include Melissa and Jim; Haley and Blair; Tyrell; and maybe this new woman from yoga, Sloane. Have I mentioned her?"

"Don't think so." Reese sounded uncertain.

"Turns out she owns the Krav Maga studio where I take classes. She's a war widow. Seems a little lost but determined to set her life on a new course. I like her."

"Sounds good to me." Reese arched an eyebrow and walked his fingers across the table until he touched her hand. "Assuming it's OK with you, I'd hoped to spend all our weekends together—either here or at my place—for the foreseeable future."

Alexa couldn't restrain the glow in her chest at Reese's declaration. "Fine with me," she whispered. So, he'd decided to go all in too. Hallelujah!

"Are you going to invite your refugees?"

"What? Oh, the dinner? I did consider inviting the Qassims. But I'm no expert on Mideast tensions. Sunnis. Shia. Various sects and political affiliations. I didn't want to create an awkward situation by asking Syrian refugees to sit down for a meal with an Iraqi general. I'd need to do more research before I went there."

"Especially if this Qassim uncle is a little wonky."

"I doubt that he would even accept the invitation. But yes. There's Nabil. I just can't see him and General Al-Badri in the same room."

"This uncle. When did he show up in Carlisle?"

"Tyrell said July; not long after the family resettled here. He'd been living in Detroit. The story is that he lost his job right before the family arrived. It's not clear if he's staying on permanently in Carlisle or is just thrilled to see his brother and taking advantage of their time together."

Reese's tone was pensive. "Would you say he strikes you as a jihadi type?"

Alexa shook her head. "All I know about jihadis is what I've seen on TV and in the movies. This guy's certainly wound tight and ultra-traditional, at least in his approach to women. But I don't know."

Reese frowned. "It's notable that this long-lost brother shows up in July, not long before the first terrorist killing in West Virginia. Then he remains in this area, where the second murder took place."

"Believe me. Nabil as a suspect has crossed my mind. But aren't we as bad as those kids who taunted Bassam? If there's a terrorist-related murder, it has to be the Muslim? Heck, by those standards, General Al-Badri could be undercover Al-Qaeda or ISIS. He arrived in July, and he's Muslim."

Reese shook his head. "Somehow, I don't see the general getting his hands dirty with two executions. This War College gig must be a big honor. I doubt he'd endanger his position by engaging in terrorist activity—or whatever these murders involve—on American soil.

"I get your point about prejudice driving suspicion of this Nabil. But give me some credit for my law enforcement background. Sometimes a coincidence is a clue to be explored, at a minimum."

"Says the guy who landed in the FBI's crosshairs as a result of coincidences."

Reese grimaced. "The experience wasn't pleasant. But I can't fault them for investigating me."

"I imagine the FBI has an extensive list of Muslims in this area; and they've probably looked at the entire Qassim family by now. Who knows? Maybe they've looked at the general too."

"Maybe. Talk about profiling. Just keep an eye on this Nabil guy when you're around the family. Even if he has no connection to terrorism, he sounds a little off to me."

Alexa saluted. "Yes, sir." She sighed. "The police have reached a dead end on the vandalism. The kids' issues seem to be wrapped up. Going forward, I don't expect to see much of the Qassims. Especially Nabil."

# CHAPTER TWENTY-THREE

AFTER A WEEK of rain and icy weather, Alexa was thrilled that Saturday's temperatures rose to a balmy sixty degrees; warm for November in Pennsylvania. Her entire guest list had accepted the dinner invitation. Plus, she'd added Deidre Townes to the group, suggesting that the intern also bring a friend closer to her own age.

Melissa and Jim arrived early to help Alexa and Reese set up for the event. The friends paired off. Reese and Jim set up chairs on the deck while Melissa helped Alexa organize the buffet.

"You've had large groups in the summer, when people can hang out on the deck. Not sure you thought this one through." Melissa laughed and gestured toward the guys, who were now extending the dining room table through the archway into the living room.

"I knew we could do it. Mom hosted huge crowds out here for Thanksgivings when I was a kid. She liked the idea of a harvest feast in the forest. At some point, she realized how much easier it was to do at home. But we have the space. Cocktails and hors d'oeuvres in the living room and on the deck if anyone wants to drift out there. Dinner here. It'll work."

"We'll see. I'm looking forward to meeting an Iraqi general." Melissa said with a sardonic grin. "I met his wife, Noora, when we did that Winter Ball walk-through at the Army Heritage Center. She seems sort of shy."

Alexa nodded. "A nice woman, but she really fades into the background when the husband's around." Lining up wineglasses on the counter, Alexa tried to dredge up some enthusiasm for this Winter Ball. She'd developed an allergy toward social affairs like this from her time in New York City, when attending charity events had been a law firm requirement. But, her mother, Melissa and half the people coming today were knocking themselves out for this big RESIST event. She vowed to get with the program. "Do you and Sloane have the decorating scheme pinned down? I hope you're using the crystals that I carted all over Cumberland County."

"Sloane couldn't make the walk-through, but she and I scoped out the Heritage Center later in the week. We're going with the winter scenes, screen-printed on long hanging banners, plus tons and tons of crystals hanging in strands from the ceiling. Sloane had this great idea to add crystal-studded boxes, like giant gift boxes, that we'll place in the corners. She knows a set designer who will lend them to us. The place will look like a crystal fairyland."

Alexa laughed at her friend's exuberance. "Sounds fantastic. I have the program together. Tyrell snagged the chairman of RESIST's board for the keynote. She's been on the board since Cecily organized RESIST. Senator Tyler from Connecticut."

"A politician? Hrumph." Melissa snorted.

"Hey, Mom was a politician."

"A county commissioner is different."

"Senator Tyler is pretty well known, so she might draw in attendance. Her keynote will be short and sweet. Mom and Tyrell are working on getting all the local RESIST refugees there; the adults, I mean. One of them might give a few remarks too."

"More speeches?" Melissa rolled her eyes.

Alexa ignored her. "One more thing. General Al-Badri is going to present a medal to Colonel Finley on behalf of Iraq. Have you heard the story about the colonel's unit fighting off an Al-Qaeda attack on the general and a number of other Iraqi bigwigs? The general had been thinking about a special ceremony at the War College but decided that this Winter Ball would be a better venue. Most of the War College will be there anyway."

Reese walked into the kitchen, rolling down his sleeves, as Alexa shared this last item. With a broad smile, he placed his index finger against his lips and said, "Shhh. That's a surprise, right?"

Joining them, Jim clapped his hands and said in a high voice, "Oh, I just love surprises."

Melissa batted her fiancé's arm. "You goof."

"And you want to marry this guy?" Reese laughed, shaking his head.

"A surprise." Alexa directed a stern glare at the trio. "The planning committee and War College brass know about the medal.

But we need to keep it a secret from Colonel Finley and his wife. Mum's the word. We're even going to mask that part on the printed program; call it 'Special Award Recognition' or something like that."

Melissa groaned. "All those speakers. What about dinner and dancing? Isn't that the whole point?"

Jim said, "I thought raising money for RESIST was the whole point."

Alexa sighed. "Absolutely, Jim. The speakers are going to encourage people to dig deep into their pockets and participate in the silent auction." She turned to Melissa. "It'll be a good time. The whole event is, what, four hours? All these speeches will take no longer than twenty minutes." She smiled. "If people get bored, they can admire the fantastic decorations."

"Hey. It's up to your mom and her steering committee. Whatever they approve is fine with me."

The security bell rang, announcing that a car was headed down the lane.

Reese grabbed his jacket. "Someone's here. Jim, can you help me direct the parking?"

The guests arrived in waves. Tyrell brought Deidre and the handsome young man she had in tow. Graham and Kate came with Alexa's parents, followed closely by the War College contingent. Haley and Blair, citing babysitter problems, hurried in the door about ten minutes late. Sloane, who drove on her own, arrived last.

"I thought *I* lived in the middle of nowhere." Sloane laughed as Alexa welcomed her to a crowded deck. Almost everyone had grabbed a drink and migrated outdoors to enjoy the warmer weather.

"I like being out of town," Alexa acknowledged. "But that night I drove to your house, it seemed that you're pretty far out too."

"Lifestyle choice." Sloane smiled.

"Exactly. Come in and get something to drink; something to nibble on. Then, I'll introduce you around. It's an eclectic group. A lot of the crowd is involved in the Winter Ball."

As she'd done with the other guests, Alexa ushered Sloane into the cabin for a drink and some food. Spying her mom and dad by the hors d'oeuvres, Alexa said, "Sloane, have you met my mother, Susan Williams? And this is my dad, Norris."

When her parents began a get-to-know-you conversation with Sloane, Alexa backed away with a nod to her friend. "It's a small crowd. Just introduce yourself to everyone. Excuse me for a moment. I need to check on dinner."

Melissa and Haley surfaced in the kitchen a few minutes later as Alexa was pulling the salad from the fridge. Haley asked, "What can we do? I'm so happy to have another adult evening. Charlotte's a treasure, but two nights in a row without her," Haley pantomimed a silent cheer before she chattered on. "Melissa, the exhibit's fantastic."

Alexa nodded. "The crowd at the opening last night was certainly larger than if you'd had it during the snow last weekend."

"I agree," Melissa said. "We had a nice turnout. Good sales."

Haley looked around the kitchen. "I could have brought a dessert or something."

"Thanks, but you're working full time and have a baby to take care of. No way." Alexa shook her head. "I took the easy route. Went with a caterer. But there are few last-minute things. Can you take the rolls out of the oven and put them in this basket? And, Melissa, can you arrange these cupcakes on platters so dessert is ready to go?"

"Oh, you got cupcakes from Sweeties? They're so wonderful," Melissa squealed.

"Thanks, ladies. I'll go outside and announce that dinner is served." Alexa first called to the folks in the living room, "Dinner, everyone. Please start through the buffet and find a seat." She grabbed her sister-in-law, Kate, and asked, "Can you get this crowd moving? It will take a while for everyone to make it through the line."

"No problem." Kate smiled. "You forget I spend most of my time with kids. This will be a snap."

Chuckling, Alexa walked out to the deck and caught Reese's eye. He was standing on the steps with Jim, Graham, and Sloane. "Dinner," she mouthed and made a motion to ask for his help in rounding up her guests. Then, she called, "The buffet is open. Time to come inside."

Alexa was glad to see a group of four start toward the door. Jill Finley and Noora Al-Badri had seemed to hit it off with Deidre Townes and her boyfriend, Chad, despite the clear difference in styles. Jill wore a suburban mom uniform of dress slacks and a classic sweater. Noora wore flowing pants and an ornate tunic that peeked out from beneath a Burberry trench. Deidre's jeans were rent with a series of artful rips and tears. She sported a bright scarf over a military jacket that looked like army surplus. Chad had complemented his oversized dark hoodie and jeans with an assortment of piercings on his ears and eyebrows. Amused by the contrast, Alexa walked past them to the far side of the deck where Colonel Finley was deep in conversation with General Al-Badri.

"Gentlemen. I hate to interrupt, but it's time for dinner. It'll be freezing out here when we lose the sun."

"Of course, my dear." The general switched on his ready charm. "You have such a lovely, rustic home here. Reminds me of the White Mountains in my college days."

"That's right. Dartmouth is your alma mater, correct?" Alexa began steering the military men toward the door. As they slowed to allow Reese and Sloane to pass, her new friend stumbled and stopped short.

Reese grabbed Sloane's elbow. "Steady. This deck can be uneven."

"Thanks," Sloane murmured to Reese, but her eyes were fastened on Alexa's companions.

Noticing that Sloane seemed pale, Alexa tried to smooth over her guest's apparent embarrassment. She was a bit surprised; Sloane's composure always made Alexa imagine that the phrase "*sang froid*" had been invented just for her. "Colonel, General; have you met my friend, Sloane Chapin?"

"We haven't yet had the pleasure," Al-Badri purred.

"Sloane, this is General Salim Al-Badri—he's with the Iraqi Central Command. And Colonel Dean Finley, an instructor at the Army War College. General Al-Badri is an International Fellow with this year's War College class." As Alexa spoke, she winced inwardly at her lack of foresight. This woman's husband had been killed in combat. Wasn't it in Iraq? And Alexa had not once considered the emotional turmoil meeting an Iraqi general might cause her new friend. She should have at least alerted Sloane when she'd extended the invitation to dinner.

But, Sloane seemed to have recovered her equilibrium as she smiled. "General, *tacharafna bemahreftak*. I apologize for my clumsiness. Colonel, to you as well."

"Ah, the young lady speaks Arabic," Al-Badri nodded in approval. "No need to apologize. A loose floorboard."

"My father was in the diplomatic service, so I spent most of my childhood overseas."

"So, you've lived in the Middle East?" Al-Badri continued his charm offensive.

"College at American University in Cairo. And I worked in Tunisia and Morocco for several years."

The colonel asked in a polite tone, "What kind of work?"

"State Department." At his questioning expression, Sloane waved her hand. "Administrative jobs, nothing very exotic."

Alexa, who was still trying to move her guests into the cabin, threw Reese a beseeching look.

He came to her rescue with a wink and a guiding hand on Sloane's back. "Shall we go in? Dinner smells great."

Last to step through the cabin door, Alexa turned to Scout. "You stay. The last thing we need in that packed room is a mastiff." Ruffling his ears, she closed the door.

Alexa sighed in relief as she took the last seat at the mega-table Reese and Jim had created for the occasion. Everyone had full plates. Her guests were talking to each other and seemed to be having a good time. No small feat, given the wild mix of people in the room.

When his daughter settled, Norris raised a wineglass and called, "Here's to Alexa for hosting a wonderful dinner party. It's always a pleasure to spend time out here at the cabin. And tonight is an especially joyous occasion as friends, old and new, gather to celebrate a good cause."

Tyrell, who had been a bit subdued, rose. "That's my cue. I have something to say, too. Most of you have been working quite hard, especially the ladies, to organize this Winter Ball. On behalf of RESIST, thank you for your time and your enthusiasm. We're grateful that you chose our new refugee program as the focus of your fundraising effort. I can't say enough about Mrs. Williams' organization skills."

"Susan, please," Alexa's mother insisted.

"Susan's organization skills. And thanks to all the rest of you as well. I'm looking forward to the event." Tyrell sat down.

"Enough with the speeches." Alexa laughed. "The food's getting cold."

Alexa exhaled a long breath when the only sign remaining from the dinner party was the long table extending into the living room.

Reese pulled off the tablecloth and extracted a leaf from the main table.

"No, no. Leave it until tomorrow." Alexa grabbed Reese's hand and tugged him toward the couch.

"Another glass of wine?" he asked.

"Just sparkling water." She smiled.

"Relax. I'll get it."

When Reese emerged from the kitchen with Alexa's water and a beer, she curled her legs up and patted the couch. "Thank you."

Reese kissed Alexa on the forehead and sank into the couch beside her. "Well, that was quite the social event."

"Remind me next time I come up with an idea like this to just say no," she groaned. "Who knew having a good time could be so exhausting."

"And remind me that I have some conflicting event in Harpers Ferry or DC or somewhere." Reese grinned.

"Was it terrible?" Alexa asked in mock concern. "I did work you pretty hard."

"No. I'm joking. It was fun. You sure threw together a hodgepodge of people."

"I'd like to think of it as an eclectic mix."

"That's another spin. I loved that the general ended up next to Deidre."

"She was quite self-assured in a roomful of adults."

"The boyfriend, not so much."

"Yeah. I nearly spit out my wine when he called the colonel, 'dude.' To be fair, the kid probably had no idea what he was getting into when a pretty girl asked him to go to a party. I think he's just a flirtation for Deidre. Her internship only lasts until February."

"Young romance."

"Hey, we're not that much older than they are," Alexa protested.

"Eight to ten years is a lot. But the kid loved Scout."

At the sound of his name, the exhausted dog rose from his corner bed and staggered over to the couch."

"Chad adored you, Scout," Alexa said as she scratched the mastiff's ears. "And why wouldn't he? You're such a good dog."

Reese patted the dog's back. "I noticed that you and Tyrell went on high alert when the conversation drifted to the 'Terrorist Murders.'"

"I should have known Haley would go there. She sees the whole world through the narrow lens of PR for the Chamber of Commerce. And Blair talks like he's thirty-five going on sixty-five. He's such a numbers guy."

"You mean the part where things come in threes so he's waiting for the police to find the next body?"

"That sounded more like some superstition he learned when he was fourteen. Lucky for us, Mom lives in fear of our role in finding Body Number Two going public. She and Dad were pretty smooth in steering the conversation in another direction."

"Did you notice, though? The two people in the room who have had the most experience with actual terrorism, the military guys—neither of them really bought the idea of Islamic terrorism having anything to do with these murders."

"Al-Badri said as much, didn't he?" Alexa winced. "Speaking of the military guys, did you notice how Sloane kept staring at both the general and Colonel Finley? What was I thinking, inviting a war widow to a dinner with another soldier and an Iraqi bigwig? Truth is, I wasn't thinking at all. I know she's proud of her husband's service. But, to be confronted with officers who were involved in the war that killed him—who knows what kind of emotions that would trigger?"

"Don't be so hard on yourself. She chose to live in Carlisle, home of the Army War College. And she's volunteering on this committee for an event at the Army Heritage Center. She must run into military personnel all the time."

"Maybe I am overreacting. Both of my Krav Maga instructors are former military. But, did you notice the way she stumbled when she saw Dean and Salim on the deck? You should see this woman in the Krav Maga studio; she's a powerhouse with amazing grace and balance. That trip. It was like she sensed they were military, even in plainclothes. And that triggered some sort of emotional reaction."

"I don't remember. Did she mention that she's a war widow?" Reese said.

"No. I waited for her to bring it up. When she didn't, I figured I shouldn't broadcast her personal information. You can understand why she doesn't shout it from the rooftops. I can't imagine the painful memories."

"Not entirely true, Alexa." Reese's voice was gentle. "You have a better understanding than many. With John, you lost someone to violence."

"True." Alexa thought about the way she'd fallen apart when John was killed. "But, Sloane was just out of college. They were newlyweds. Then, he's killed a few months later."

"She said she went to college in Egypt. Wonder how they met?"

"She hasn't shared many details. Melissa told me they met in Egypt. Maybe he was stationed at the embassy or something."

"Enough about Sloane Chapin; I think she'll survive her brush with the military. We didn't have to carry her out on a stretcher or anything."

"Don't even joke about something like that. My homeowner's policy has taken a beating over the last few years." Alexa groaned.

"OK." Reese smiled. "But, were you pleased with the party?"

Alexa smiled. "A lot of work, but I know Mom and Dad appreciated the effort to entertain the War College entourage. Plus, it gave Tyrell a chance to thank the core group working on the Winter Ball." She laughed. "Did you see him rolling out the charm for Jill, Kate, and Noora? The man can't help himself when he meets new women."

"While I only have eyes for you." Reese pulled Alexa into the crook of his arm. "Want to call it a night?"

"Soon. Let's go upstairs and decide. Remember, we'll be apart over Thanksgiving." Alexa gave Reese a devilish smile and drew him toward the stairs.

# CHAPTER TWENTY-FOUR

*Late August 1859*

Oppressed so hard they could not stand. Let my people go.
                         *—"Go Down, Moses," a Negro spiritual*

*Their journey north took a detour the night Elijah and Coleman dined with John Brown. Coleman's initial work as a blacksmith for the compelling abolitionist drew the old runaway further and further into Brown's plan. The man Elijah had known became a new person, gripped with passion for Brown's cause.*

*"Son, you may not understand because you still have a lot of growing to do. But, all my life, I lived under the thumb of a master. First, in the South Carolina lowlands, where my owner was meaner than a snake. When that demon sold me off to our master, I be glad. Master was kinder; not as coarse. Some days he even seemed to care about his slaves, especially us in the trades and the house who he got to know more direct. But, in the end, he'd have Driver whup anyone who disobeyed. He let Mistress play cruel games.*

*"After forty years of living as the property of one white man or another, it crush your spirit. The Bible and the preachers talk about the Promised Land but don't say why the Negro have to die to see that Promised Land. That's why I been planning to run for nigh onto ten years."*

*"Ten years?" Elijah said in surprise. "I only been alive four more years than that."*

"Yes, ten years. What a righteous feeling to step onto the soil of a state that says owning another man be against the law. But Mr. Brown made me see the light—that I have the chance to help other slaves, maybe end slavery in this United States. I am joining Mr. Brown on his raid."

"A raid?" Elijah didn't know much about Brown's plan.

"We going to go back to Virginia, to Harpers Ferry, and attack the Federal Armory, a place the army keeps guns. Mr. Brown be organizing a slave rebellion using those guns."

"Like Nat Turner's rebellion?" Elijah had heard chatter about this failed slave uprising from the slave quarters, where they spoke about Turner in admiration, and in the big house, where Master and his friends cursed Turner's name. He trembled at the idea of Coleman returning to Virginia and risking capture. Even worse, his friend could get killed.

"Don't be afraid, boy. Brown has a good plan. More people coming to take part in the raid. We're gathering guns and ammunition at the farmhouse in Maryland. And imagine slaves across Virginia and Maryland rising up against they masters. The rebellion could spread across the South."

"What about Massachusetts?" Elijah asked. He had no idea why that far-north state would be any better than this wonderful town in Pennsylvania, but Massachusetts had always been part of Coleman's dream.

"You be happy here for now, right? Deacon McClure told me that you doing good work in the lumberyard. Says you have a real knack for counting and arithmetic."

Elijah smiled in pleasure. "I like doing sums in the deacon's books. And my room in the barn; well, I never had my own room before."

"So, it won't bother you if we stay here a while longer; until after I help Mr. Brown see the plan through? Then, we'll go north to Massachusetts or maybe to New York. Mr. Brown told me about a village of free Negroes up in those parts."

"Can I help with the—" Elijah hesitated until he remembered the word—"raid?"

"No. You do your part by helping the deacon and Mrs. McClure."

Toward the end of August, Deacon McClure hurried into the house with a look of barely suppressed excitement. "Tomorrow afternoon. Cancel any plans you have. What an outstanding opportunity."

Mrs. McClure smiled. "My dear, what is this opportunity?"

"*Frederick Douglass. The great man is here in Chambersburg, as Mr. Brown had predicted. The townsmen have convinced Mr. Douglass to speak tomorrow to the general public. We must all go.*"

"*Frederick Douglass,*" Coleman repeated with awe in his voice. "*Never in my life . . .*"

When Coleman broke off mid-sentence, Elijah was shocked to see tears in the old man's eyes.

"*Well then. Let's declare tomorrow a holiday and go to hear the man speak,*" Mrs. McClure exclaimed.

"*Absolutely, my dear.*" The deacon turned toward Coleman and Elijah. "*You know, the words of Mr. Douglass convinced me to throw in with Mr. Brown. He said, 'It is not light that we need, but fire; it is not the gentle shower, but thunder. We need the storm, the whirlwind, and the earthquake.'*"

"*Them's mighty fine words,*" Coleman commented, his eyes shining.

"*That they are.*"

Two days later, Elijah's head was still spinning from Frederick Douglass' speech. He had to admit that he hadn't understood every word of oratory from the famous abolitionist, but he had understood enough. That a Negro, who had started life as a slave, could speak with such eloquence and education about the evils of slavery was astounding. At first, Elijah had kept looking around for the patrollers or some other white officials to come and arrest Douglass. But nothing had interrupted his fiery rant to a large group of Negro and white townspeople except loud clapping and an occasional boo. Not all the listeners agreed with Douglass, but they seemed to be in the minority.

Elijah had expected Douglass to rail against slavery but had been shocked to hear the man say that black men should be treated as equal to white men and be permitted to "sit in the same church pew, eat at the same table and vote at the ballot box." Even Elijah had never thought of freedom for Negroes in those expansive terms.

Elijah continued to mull over Douglass' words as he hurried down the street toward Mr. Brown's lodgings.

"*Remember. Ask for Dr. Smith when you get there,*" the deacon had instructed and handed him a folded note. "*Give this direct to the man. Not his sons or any of the others.*"

When Elijah reached the white clapboard house on East King Street, he climbed the steps to the second floor.

"*Wait here.*" One of Brown's group pointed to a chair on the landing.

*Elijah sat on the chair and watched a desultory fly buzz across the panes of a sealed window. As sweat streamed down his face in the close quarters, he imagined that the listless fly must feel as hot as he did. Then, raised voices on the other side of the door caught his attention. He recognized the unmistakable timbre of John Brown; the others he didn't know.*

*"Douglass brought money from our friends in New York and elsewhere. But I sensed a reluctance to fulfill his commitment. He kept referring to Harpers Ferry as a steel trap that could close on our band of raiders and thwart our success. What say you, Shields Green? You have traveled with the man for years. Will Douglass come through with the men he promised?"*

*Elijah had to strain to hear the broken reply. "Don't rightly know, sir. I believe he has lost faith in the plan."*

*"Damnation," Brown roared. "I told him that I needed him to help hive the bees once they begin to swarm. When the slaves rise up from the Virginia plantations, Douglass can organize and guide them. Even the most downtrodden soul on the plantation knows the name of Frederick Douglass."*

*"Should we postpone the raid?" a voice asked.*

*"No. Perhaps our friend Douglass will reconsider. Either way, it's time to proceed and ignite the fires that shall burn slavery to the ground."*

*When the door popped open, Elijah flinched, then let his expression go slack, as if he hadn't heard the conversation within.*

*Brown came to the door and boomed, "You have a note for me, boy?"*

*"Yes, sir." Elijah thrust the paper into the looming man's hand. "From Deacon McClure."*

*"Tell the deacon I will reply in due time." Brown fixed an intense eye on Elijah. "'Ye are my witnesses, sayeth the Lord, and my servant whom I have chosen.' Isaiah 43:10. Be prepared, boy. We might have a job for you at Harpers Ferry. Will you answer the Lord's call?"*

*Elijah's legs went weak as he felt Brown's burning eyes drawing him into their fire. "Yes, sir," he heard himself reply. "I'll answer."*

# CHAPTER TWENTY-FIVE

GRAHAM AND ALEXA were alone for the partners' meeting on the Tuesday after Thanksgiving since Brian Stewart had extended his holiday visit with his wife's family. After they'd run through the agenda, Graham asked, "Are things OK with you, Lexie? I thought you seemed a little glum at Thanksgiving."

Alexa looked out the window at the gloomy, late-November day. "No, everything's good. Better than good, really."

"I thought you might be bummed because Reese couldn't make it for dinner?"

Alexa shook her head. "No, he should spend time with his family. He hasn't seen enough of them since he's been back from Kenya. And like I said, we're good. Probably even better than before he left for Africa."

"OK. Save the details for Kate and your girlfriends. I'm your big brother, not Ann Landers."

"No kidding. When have I ever come to you for romantic advice? That would be like asking a polar bear for advice on palm trees."

"That's harsh. I must have done something right with Kate."

"You lucked out there, bro."

Becoming serious, Alexa lowered her voice as if someone might hear. "I did enjoy Thanksgiving. I know it sounds terrible, but I was glad it was just the family. I had visions of Mom inviting half the War College."

"Well, that's not very charitable." Graham pursed his lips.

Sometimes Alexa wondered where the carefree brother of her youth had gone. "Admit it. Wasn't it great to just concentrate on Courtney and Jamie and the family? With Mom and Dad in Italy half the year and you guys at the Outer Banks in the summer, we

get less family time now. It will only get worse as the kids get older."
She laughed. "Fess up. I'm not going to tell anyone."

Graham shrugged. "You're right. I breathed a sigh of relief when
I heard that the Finley kids were coming home for Thanksgiving,
and they'd invited the Al-Badris to dinner with their family. The
wives are both fine, but—"

"'The wives,' Graham? They have names: Jill and Noora."

"All right. Jill and Noora are both quite nice, but sometimes the
brothers-in-arms thing becomes a little too much with Dean and
Salim."

"At last," Alexa whooped. "The truth comes out."

"Be prepared for Christmas, though," Graham cautioned. "Kate
tells me Mom is talking mega-open house. The guest list has already
topped fifty."

"Let Mom do her thing." Alexa cracked in her best Bogie
imitation, "We'll always have Thanksgiving."

"Everything else is fine?" Graham returned to his original
concern.

"Yes, Graham. I love the work. Tyrell hasn't dragged me into any
new crises with the Qassims or any of his other refugee families.
Although, I have to admit, I sort of enjoy the challenge of working
with refugee issues."

"And the terrorism investigation?"

"As far as I know, it's gone quiet. I haven't heard from the FBI.
Don't know if that means the trail is cold or if they are about to
arrest a suspect. But the local panic about an imminent ISIS attack
on Carlisle seems to have died down."

"Probably why none of the refugee families have been hassled."

"Could be." Alexa paused. "There's nothing to worry about,
Graham. I'm not glum. I'm happy that my life is on an even keel.
Remember, I was seeking serenity when I left the New York rat
race."

"OK. Just doing my duty as a big brother. You have to admit,
Lexie, you've had some turmoil since you came back home."

Alexa gave him an impish grin, "Rest assured, Counselor, I have
no turmoil in my life at this point in time." She hesitated, "Well, I
am wrestling with a pretty big decision right now."

Graham looked at his sister with a resigned expression.

"I'm trying to decide whether to drop my Krav Maga classes."

He sputtered, "Krav Maga?"

"Yes. I've learned a lot, but I've decided I'm just not a hand-
to-hand combat type of girl. Some of my fellow students must be

reincarnated Greek warriors or something. They have no problem channeling some serious aggression. But me? Every time I'm in class, I feel like a Lara Croft wannabe."

"So, drop the class."

"Well, I've become friends with Sloane Chapin, who owns Courage, the studio. You met her out at the cabin. I don't want to offend her."

Graham shook his head and pointed to the door. "OK. Enough. That's a problem beyond my ability to help you solve."

As Alexa scooted to the door, laughing, she heard her brother mumble behind her, "Women. I'll never understand how their minds work."

Leaving her class that evening, Alexa ran into Bassam and Nabil Qassim in the corridor of Courage.

"Miss Alexa, how are you?" Bassam gave her a broad smile.

Surprised to find the usually surly teen in high spirits, Alexa returned his smile. "Fine, Bassam. Are you enjoying Taekwondo?"

"Yes. I take a night class and an early class before school another morning. Tonight, we learned to side-kick." Without warning, Bassam twirled and raised his leg to demonstrate, his gym bag swinging from his shoulder.

"Bassam. This move is for the class; not the hallway." Nabil put a warning hand on the teen's arm. He raised his eyes to meet Alexa's. "Good evening, Miss Williams." Nabil gestured to his nephew. "We must be going, Bassam. You have homework." Then he nodded to Alexa. "Inshallah."

"Nice to see you both," Alexa said and continued toward the locker room.

Heading home, Alexa took a shortcut that she'd been using after Krav Maga. Thinking about her encounter with the two Qassims, she marveled at Bassam's good spirits and Nabil's greeting, which, while terse, was at least polite. A big change from her other dealings with the two, even when she had rushed into the Carlisle Police Station to help the teen after his pizza-shop scuffle. Alexa conceded that her past encounters with both had been at stressful times. And she'd always been willing to give the boy a break. Maybe she needed to extend that same latitude to his uncle, who, despite his longer stay in the United States, was still a refugee in an unfamiliar country.

Alexa brought her attention back to the winding road as she approached a one-lane bridge. Immediately past the bridge, the road dipped then snaked to the left beneath a narrow overpass for the freight railroad. Last week, the bridge had been dry but the dip icy. She slowed just as a herd of deer dashed across the road. Alexa braked, pulse racing, as she watched a spray of white tails fade into the dark woods.

# CHAPTER TWENTY-SIX

TWO DAYS LATER, Alexa had to kiss her serenity goodbye. It started with the morning news.

When Alexa walked into the office, Melinda jumped up from her desk to take her boss' coat. "Did you hear about the new terrorist killing? Just awful."

For a moment, Alexa thought her assistant was talking about an overseas attack or a school shooting.

Melinda continued. "I can't believe that there was another murder. This one wasn't that far from my house. I'm afraid to let my kids outside to play when they get home from school. They haven't released many details, but everyone's saying it's another one of those ISIS killings. ISIS, here in Carlisle!"

"I didn't listen to the radio on the way to work. I don't know anything about this." Alexa didn't want to believe what Melinda was telling her.

"Pull up the news online while I get you a cup of tea. You don't have any meetings until ten."

As Alexa rushed to her computer, her cell phone rang. She ignored it and logged in, going directly to the local news. Melinda's brief recap had hit most of the high points of the police statement. The authorities were saying nothing about terrorism or anything that linked this murder to the other two bodies. The article mentioned only that there were some similarities to the other incidents, an observation that Alexa took as that of the reporter, not the authorities. Reasonable to point out since the victim was a male, probably in his mid-twenties, and there were multiple gunshot wounds. A pair of hunters had found the body in an abandoned quarry in the countryside.

"Scary. Right, Boss?" Melinda bustled into the office with a cup of tea.

"It is. But I doubt that you have to worry about your kids. This is miles away from your house. Whoever's doing this doesn't seem to return to the same site twice. And they don't seem to be shooting children."

Melinda shook her head. "An ounce of prevention is worth a pound of cure. I already called George and asked him to pick up some videos at one of those Redboxes for the kids. We never let them watch movies or even much TV on school nights, but I'm going to keep them inside for the next few days and let them watch a movie after they finish their homework. At least until the police put out some more information." Tears came to Melinda's eyes as she spoke.

"You should keep your kids safe, Melinda. Absolutely. They'll be thrilled to get some extra movie time." Alexa's cell phone rang again.

"You go ahead and get that. I need to go calm down." Melinda dashed out the door, dabbing her eyes with a tissue.

Alexa ignored this call too and returned to scanning the news. The story had hit the national wires, but their information added nothing to the basics she'd read from the local sources.

Pulling her cell phone from her pocket, Alexa listened to the messages. As expected, the first was from her mother; the second from Reese.

"You saw the news," Alexa stated when Reese answered.

"Yeah. Another one. This whole thing is bizarre."

"It doesn't look like they have many clues. But, you know that the cops always hold something back."

"Like was there an Allahu Akbar, Eye for an Eye sign? That's one detail that hasn't slipped out about any of the murders. Just that ISIS claimed responsibility."

"Which isn't really true. Whoever leaked that either doesn't have all the information or decided to embellish things for effect."

Reese sighed. "I expect we'll be getting visits from the FBI." Then his voice brightened. "One good thing, depending upon time of death. This latest murder might clear me."

"Right." Alexa replied. "You were in Denver at the Wildlife Preservation conference, then at your parents' for Thanksgiving."

"I have a phone meeting in a few minutes. Let's talk tonight, OK? Maybe there'll be more information out by then."

"I'll call you when I get home."

Alexa looked at the time. She had another half hour before her first appointment, so she returned her parents' call. They put her on speaker. She had just finished reassuring them that she was in no way affected by this latest murder when Graham opened the door and slipped in.

"Graham's here. I have to go. I'll let you know if I hear anything new. But I expect I'll be getting my updates from the news, just like you." Alexa hung up the phone.

Her brother closed the door behind him. "Sorry, I guess Melinda didn't realize you were on your cell. Mom and Dad?"

"Mom and Dad. You heard some of it. I know nothing more than what I've read in the news. I have to admit that it's frightening to have somebody out there, killing people in our own backyard. I'm making an assumption that this one's connected to the others, but it might not be. Could be a hunting accident."

"I doubt it. Do you expect a call from the FBI?"

"That would be standard protocol. Loop back and question all the key players or witnesses or whatever you'd call me, Reese, and Tyrell. I imagine it will be pro forma. If it goes any further, I'll send out a cry for help." Alexa's expression became more solemn. "Melinda's a mess. Not sure about the rest of the staff."

Graham nodded. "People all over town were freaking out when news came out about the first two murders and a possible link to terrorism. This third one might send people over the edge." He looked at his watch. "I have to get back to my office. Client appointment."

"Me too."

As Graham disappeared out the door, Alexa's cell chimed to indicate a text message. Tyrell, about the latest murder.

She texted back. "Can't talk now. I'll call this afternoon when I get a chance." She'd just hit Send when Melinda knocked on the door with her client.

By mid-afternoon, Alexa's stream of back-to-back meetings had ended. She was running through her to-do list and organizing the rest of her day when her intercom buzzed.

"Hey, Boss. Tyrell Jenkins is on the line. Guess what—it's urgent," Melinda deadpanned.

"Put him through. I was going to call him anyway." Alexa sighed and picked up the phone.

"Tyrell, sorry I didn't get back to you. I was tied up until just a few minutes ago."

"What? Oh, no problem. I'm dealing with a disaster here, and I really need your help once again. The cops arrested Bassam."

"Another fight? They might not let him walk this time. I thought the kid was getting his act together."

"I wish he'd gotten into a fight." Tyrell's tone was bitter. "This makes a teenage scuffle look like peanuts. They arrested him for gun possession."

Alexa couldn't speak for a moment. "He had a gun? Where?"

"A loaded gun. They found it in school. It fell out of his gym bag while he was changing after phys ed."

"What an idiot. First, to have a gun. Second, to take it to school."

"According to Eshan, Bassam swears that it isn't his. That he had no idea it was in his bag."

Alexa raised an eyebrow. "Possible, I guess. But the police have heard that line many times. And Bassam just had a run-in with them. I doubt they're inclined to give him the benefit of the doubt."

"I know."

"Juvenile Probation will get involved this time. Have the Qassims arranged a public defender yet?"

"Not yet. I was hoping you could go down to the station with me and work with whoever they appoint to represent him." Tyrell paused. "I know, I know. You don't do criminal law. But you know this family, and I think Bassam trusts you. This is a horrific experience for Eshan and Zahraa. Having you there will help them deal with this."

"Is he at the Carlisle Police Station, or have they put him in detention?"

"He's still being held at the station. Can you come now?"

"Yes. I'm on my way." With a long sigh, Alexa pushed back her chair and went to tell Melinda that she was leaving the office, probably for the rest of the day.

Tyrell was sitting, hunched over with his head in his hands, when Alexa walked through the door of the waiting area. Eshan and Zahraa were pacing the small room.

"What's happening?" she asked. "Eshan, Zahraa, I'm so sorry that this has happened. Did you know anything about this gun?"

"Of course not. We would never allow guns in our home. We have seen too much violence and bloodshed in our lives. Our sons both know that guns are forbidden." Eshan's reply was forceful.

Zahraa sobbed. "I believe the police must have made a mistake. Or some other boy put this gun in Bassam's bag to save himself from arrest."

"We'll see. Have the police or Juvenile Probation spoken to you?"

Eshan answered, "The school called us to tell us Bassam had been arrested. And they let us speak to him by phone for just a moment. Then, an officer talked to us when we arrived. But the police haven't let us see our son."

Tyrell said, "Can you find out what's happening?"

Alexa went to the main window. "I'm Alexa Williams; I'm representing the family of Bassam Qassim at this point in time. I'd like to speak to the arresting officer on his case."

"Just a moment, ma'am." The clerk spoke into a phone, then motioned Alexa through the door. "Detective Miller will meet you."

"Detective Miller?" As Alexa walked into the inner offices, she had a bad feeling. Miller was in homicide. Maybe he'd been assigned to Bassam since he'd dealt with the other incidents involving the teenager and the Qassim family? But the look in the desk clerk's eye had conveyed something more concerning.

The detective met her in the center of the room and extended his hand. "Alexa. Are you here about Bassam Qassim? Debra Winslow is on her way over from the public defender's office when she's finished in court. Juvenile Probation will be here soon as well. The district attorney has also been notified."

Alexa tried to evaluate this information. The juvenile justice process was different than the criminal system for adults. Juvenile Probation played a pivotal role in recommending how a child's case would be handled. The very fact that the police had lined up a public defender and notified the district attorney before Juvenile Probation had a chance to even meet Bassam was not good.

She voiced none of those thoughts aloud but instead stated, "The family's outside. Needless to say, they are quite upset. Can his parents talk to Bassam?"

"Not now. Let's sort that out when Juvenile Probation arrives. You know a Juvenile Probation officer will step in to work with the kid and family. They look at whether there's probable cause to prepare a delinquency petition and whether to recommend detention until a hearing."

"I take it you haven't questioned him yet?"

Miller avoided her eyes. "We read him his rights and asked a few basic questions right after we brought him in." He sighed. "Possession of a loaded gun is a felony. I'm pretty sure Juvenile Probation will set up a probable cause hearing and detain him. But, I'm not the one to decide that."

"Detective, this kid doesn't know the US justice system. He comes from a country where the secret police engage in torture and people are disappeared. It's possible that he would admit to something out of fear."

"He said nothing except, 'That is not my gun.' Over and over again."

"How long before you expect Winslow or Juvenile Probation here?"

Miller looked at the clock above Alexa's head. "Maybe another hour."

"An hour." Alexa pursed her lips. "In that case, I'd like to speak to my client—to Bassam. He may choose to change his representation to Debra Winslow, but he needs an attorney now to advise him on his rights and check on his well-being. Detective, this is a seventeen-year-old who just arrived in this country. English is not his first language. I'd suggest that the Carlisle Police would want to go over and above in protecting this kid's rights."

Alexa expected Miller to either agree or invite her to his office to discuss the issue further. Instead, he shot a nervous look over his shoulder. As she followed the detective's gaze, Alexa recoiled at the sight of Special Agent Carter standing in Miller's office. That bad feeling got worse.

When he turned back to face her, the detective's face reflected internal debate. "OK, you can talk to the suspect. I'll give you ten minutes to explain the process and give him whatever interim legal advice you believe appropriate on this gun possession charge. When the kid was here for that fighting incident, that was a much less-serious situation. We resolved that without bringing in Juvenile Probation. It's reasonable that you explain how this works to him."

Miller moved a step closer. "But you won't be able to represent Bassam going forward. It's probable that there will be additional charges brought against him. Those charges would create a conflict of interest situation for you."

Alexa paled as Miller's meaning sunk in. "That's why the FBI is here. You're telling me that Bassam is a suspect in these murders? How can that be?" Alexa's mind was spinning. "The gun. Does the gun link to one or more of those murders?"

The detective's answer was careful. "Any gun involved in a potential crime goes through certain types of analysis. I can't really say more."

"My God. Bassam is just a kid. Since you're talking conflict of interest, you must know I saw that second body. That man looked like he'd been shot with assault rifles or something really high-powered. Wasn't this a pistol that was found in Bassam's gym bag? I don't get it." Alexa's anxiety rose. What had this kid gotten into?

Agent Carter strode across the room to join them. "Alexa. I didn't expect to see you here."

"I've represented the Qassim family a few times when they were harassed by people in the community."

Miller turned to the FBI agent. "I gave her the OK to have a brief conversation with the boy on the local gun possession charge. Just because both Juvenile Probation and the PD are delayed. Then, she'll bow out."

Carter looked at Alexa. "I only shared your role as a witness when we heard you were asking to see the Qassim boy. You understand the potential conflict?"

Alexa nodded. "I've traced the dots and understand that you're talking about the so-called terrorist murders. I can't imagine Bassam is involved in those. And this arrest involves a pistol. I'm not an expert, but Reese is. He said the wounds had come from something like an AR-15."

"The FBI has done a complete analysis of the wounds in all three of the bodies that were found. Most were the result of semi-automatic gunfire. But we have not made public the full details of the wounds," Carter replied.

Alexa said, "I'm sure this will all become clear at some point if you bring additional charges against Bassam. I hadn't planned to represent the boy on an ongoing basis anyway. He needs a criminal attorney, which you've arranged. And if any additional charges proceed, I'll seek advice on what continuing contact, if any, I can have with the Qassim family. For now, just give me those few minutes with Bassam." She looked at Miller. "It's definite that the current charge will be brought in the juvenile system?"

Miller replied, "After Juvenile Probation's session with the youth, the attorney, and the family, a probable cause determination in front of a juvenile court judge has to take place within seventy-two hours. Ultimately, the case goes back to the judge for adjudication and disposition. The juvenile system is set up to work fast; adjudication is usually within ten days unless the defense lawyer makes a compelling argument for a brief delay."

Alexa said, "I'm worried about placing this boy in the general detention population. I'm not sure how a Syrian refugee would fare in that environment."

"Make sure the parents mention that concern to Juvenile Probation," Miller replied.

Agent Carter took an exasperated tone. "I know we're dealing with a single charge right now. Even that's a felony. But, Alexa. If this goes into federal charges, detention placement will be a minor aspect of this kid's troubles. The bigger issue will be whether he'll be charged as a juvenile or an adult. And his immigration status will play into this as well. Bassam Qassim is going to be in a world of hurt."

# CHAPTER TWENTY-SEVEN

THE DETECTIVE LED Alexa to a small room where Bassam sat alone at a table, slumped in a straight chair. The boy looked young and scared. Gone was the confident, joking teen she'd last seen in the corridor of Courage.

The minute Miller closed the door, Bassam jumped up and ran to her. "Miss Alexa, I am so scared. That was not my gun. Papa does not allow us to touch guns. I told my teacher that it was not mine. I told the police it was not mine."

"I'm glad to hear that, Bassam. Your papa and ya-umma are outside waiting to speak to you. And there will be an attorney who comes soon to represent you. She is a good woman named Debra Winslow. She is an expert in handling cases with the police."

The teen looked confused. "I thought you are my attorney."

"Yes, I've helped you and your family in legal issues. But I'm not the right kind of attorney for people accused of crimes like this. You need a lawyer who knows all the rules; she will be the best attorney to help you with this gun issue."

"But it is not my gun. I am framed."

Despite the seriousness of the situation, Alexa had to stifle a smile at Bassam's protestation. "Where did you learn that word, 'framed'? Let's sit down for a moment."

As Bassam trudged back to his seat, he replied with a small smile, "On TV. *Law and Order*."

"You can talk about that with your new lawyer, Bassam. But it may not be enough to say that the gun isn't yours. Your teacher found it in your gym bag. And that looks bad. There will be a Juvenile Probation officer who talks to you and makes recommendations to the juvenile court about this situation—you having the gun. Then, you'll see a judge, who may decide to hold you in a place called detention; a place to live that's specifically for kids and teens. About two weeks later, there's a hearing, where the juvenile court judge looks at the facts and decides whether to adjudicate you as a juvenile delinquent."

A tear rolled down Bassam's cheek. "What is this: 'adjudicate'?"

"Like on *Law and Order*, when the judge says guilty or not guilty. Your attorney, Ms. Winslow, will explain all of this in more detail."

"Will the police beat me?"

Alexa's heart went out to the boy. "No. There are laws in America to protect arrested people from something like that. But, Bassam, do not answer questions from the police or Juvenile Probation unless Ms. Winslow tells you that it is OK. Remember that your attorney, Ms. Winslow, is your friend. Your papa and ya-umma are always your best friends who want to help you. Other than that, don't talk about the gun to anyone."

"Are you my friend, Miss Alexa?"

"Yes, I am, Bassam. But I can't stay any longer or help Ms. Winslow. The police only let me in here to explain to you what would be happening. Ms. Winslow will give you a lot more information. And your parents will be allowed to see you soon." Alexa rose from her chair. She wanted to ask Bassam about the so-called terrorist murders but resolved not to cross that ethical line.

"Thank you, Miss Alexa." Bassam stood and shook her hand.

She left him standing in the middle of the room, his expression forlorn. Alexa had a difficult time envisioning this lost boy having a role in three brutal murders. But then she remembered the surly teen she'd first encountered. And the fact that he'd just been in possession of a loaded handgun. She'd misjudged capacity to commit a crime before—in someone quite close to her at the time. She could be wrong about Bassam Qassim too.

Back in the waiting room, Alexa told Eshan, Zahraa, and Tyrell that Debra Winslow had been assigned to represent Bassam and that she should arrive soon. "You both should be permitted to sit in on her discussions with Bassam and also with the Juvenile Probation officer who will be preparing recommendations to the court.

"They let me speak to Bassam for a few minutes. He is quite upset and scared. He insists that the gun is not his. He doesn't know how it got into his bag. However, the fact that it was found in his bag is a problem. It's his word against the evidence. Ms.

Winslow will know more about the legal aspects. You should ask her about that."

"Will Bassam be able to go home soon?" Eshan asked.

"I don't know for sure, but Detective Miller said that he might go to the detention center, a place where they hold kids who are accused of crimes. Having a loaded gun is serious."

"A jail; help me, Allah. My son in a jail," Zahraa wailed and broke into sobs.

Eshan drew his wife into his arms and whispered, "We must be strong for Bassam. Shush, shush."

Alexa exchanged a pained glance with Tyrell. This family deserved peace after the turmoil of their life in Syria and the refugee camps. Now, they had to deal with this new blow. She steeled herself before delivering the worst part of the news.

"I also need to tell you one more thing. Ms. Winslow should be able to get all the details. But the police implied that this gun that was found in Bassam's bag may have been involved in another, more serious crime. I don't think they have all the information they need to confirm this. But it's something they are looking into. That could mean more trouble for Bassam."

"I don't believe it. Bassam's a good boy." Zahraa sank onto the bench, her face in her hands.

Eshan looked stunned. "How can this be?"

Tyrell patted the distraught man on the back and shot Alexa a questioning look.

Just then, a woman with a briefcase bustled through the front door. Alexa had never met Debra Winslow, but she recognized her from the courthouse.

"Ms. Winslow." Alexa stepped forward to flag the woman down. "I'm Alexa Williams. These are Bassam Qassim's parents, Eshan and Zahraa. And Tyrell Jenkins' organization, RESIST, sponsors the Qassims through their refugee program."

"Nice to meet you all." Winslow looked at the parents. "Sorry about the circumstances. The court has appointed me to represent your son. I want to see Bassam as soon as possible, but what can you tell me about all of this?"

Alexa interrupted. "I have represented the Qassims on several issues. I know you need to talk to Bassam's parents, but can I have a few words first?"

"Sure, don't you practice Family Law?"

"Excuse us for just a moment," Alexa said to the parents and drew Winslow to a far corner. "I didn't want to jump on your case, but I was quite concerned about Bassam's lack of knowledge about the justice system. The police allowed me a few minutes with him before you arrived."

Alexa filled the public defender in on Bassam's earlier brush with the law and her conversation with Bassam and Detective Miller. As she had done with the Qassim parents, Alexa mentioned that there might be a link to another crime but stopped at sharing any details that would reveal her role as a witness.

"This family has only been in the country for a few months. They don't know our legal system at all, so please keep that in mind. I'll bow out now and leave you to your work. Good luck."

Alexa walked back to Eshan and Zahraa, with Winslow by her side. "Bassam will be in good hands with Ms. Winslow."

She asked Winslow, "Do you have any problem if I attend the probable cause hearing?"

"Not at all. I think the Qassims could use the support."

"I'll be there." Alexa looked at Tyrell. "Let's give Ms. Winslow some time with Eshan and Zahraa." She led him outside to the parking lot.

"What's up?" Tyrell demanded. "I could tell from your face that something is seriously wrong. Good that the Qassims can't read you the way I can."

"I still can't believe it. My conversation was with Detective Miller and Special Agent Carter."

"Carter? What was the FBI doing there? Isn't that overkill for a kid caught in school with a handgun? It's bad, but that shit happens all the time."

"I'm reading between the lines here. But I think the problem is the specific handgun that they found on Bassam. It has some connection to the terrorist murders."

Tyrell squawked, "Impossible."

"That was my first reaction. And I don't think they have definitive proof. Yet. Pure speculation on my part, but I think the gun matches the caliber of one that was used in one or more of the three murders. I suspect they sent it for ballistics testing. For some reason, Carter seemed pretty confident that it was going to come back as a match."

"That doesn't sound like the FBI. Aren't they super-cautious about making leaps of faith?"

"Yeah. I can't figure out. Is it a really unique make and model of handgun? That's the other thing. Bassam had a pistol. You saw that body. Something more than a pistol caused all that damage."

"But the eye." Tyrell grabbed Alexa's arm. "Don't you remember the eye?"

Alexa shuddered as she remembered the gaping hole where the man's eye had been. "Yes. Reese said he thought it looked like powder burns, like the eye had been shot out—up close and maybe after the guy was dead."

"The killer could have used a pistol for that," Tyrell observed.

"What kind of rage would that take? To shoot out a guy's eye after he's already dead? After you killed him with so many bullets he could have died ten or more times? What a sicko." Alexa curled her lip in disgust.

"Or that was part of the execution; the eye for an eye. The victim did something to seriously piss the killer off. And the bullet through the eye was the coup de grâce. The final message."

"I wonder if all the bodies had the eye shot out?"

"And if the signs all included the bit about an eye for an eye?" Tyrell winced.

"The FBI never mentioned that when they questioned me about the second body. They haven't contacted me about the third one yet."

"Me neither. But why would they mention the eye? Even though it leaked that there was some terrorist twist to the murders, they managed to keep the details of the signs in their back pocket." Tyrell stopped with a look of complete devastation. He looked around to make sure they were alone.

"If our theory here is correct, that would mean they suspect Bassam of participating in an execution and shooting a guy's eye out after he was dead."

"Or shooting three guys."

"My God. I still don't think the kid has the capacity for murder. But he's in a boatload of trouble."

Alexa put her hand on Tyrell's arm. "I can't help him in any direct way if he's charged. Not sure you can either. But, as an officer of the court, I have to toe the line to avoid any ethical violation."

"I don't get it. I know you can't represent him, but why can't we help?"

As Alexa explained the conflict posed by them both being witnesses in the FBI's case for the second murder, Tyrell became angry. "How can I not support the Qassims? RESIST is sponsoring them, and I can't think of a situation worse than having your kid face criminal charges."

"As long as we're dealing with just the gun possession in juvenile court, it's no problem. But, if they haul him into adult court on homicide or terrorism charges that involve the body we found, the FBI's going to want us to steer clear. They need evidence to charge Bassam for the more serious offense. A prosecutor may agree that possession of a weapon that matches the ballistics is enough. I don't know.

"By the way, Bassam insists the gun isn't his. That he's being framed."

"Who would frame him? Another high school kid who happens to be both a terrorist and take gym at the same time as Bassam? I want to believe the kid, but that's a stretch."

"What about Nabil? Not sure why he'd frame his own nephew, but I can picture him involved in some terrorist plot."

Tyrell shook his head. "You've had it in for old Uncle Nabil since the first night you met. I don't think he'd set Bassam up. But, maybe he slipped the gun in the kid's bag not knowing he would take it to school."

"Where is Nabil anyway?"

"Home, taking care of Ali." Tyrell's shoulders slumped. "We could sit out here and speculate for the rest of the evening, but I have to get back to Eshan and Zahraa."

Alexa looked at her watch. "Too late to go back to work. I'm heading home. Call me when you learn the details of the arraignment." She gave Tyrell a hug and headed toward the Land Rover.

When Alexa spoke to Reese later that evening, she told him about Bassam's arrest. "Your theory about the man we found; that he'd been shot close range in the eye? Good chance you were right."

Alexa explained the conversation that she'd had with Detective Miller and Agent Carter. And her talk with Tyrell.

"So, the cops gave you little that was concrete? Then, you and Tyrell made assumptions?"

"That's about it."

"What a mess."

"No kidding."

"Someone could be using this boy to divert suspicion."

"Tyrell and I considered Uncle Nabil. But it seems unlikely that he'd throw his own nephew to the wolves."

"Same with the father or mother."

Alexa nearly choked on the sip of tea she'd taken. "Eshan or Zahraa? I never even considered that they would be involved."

"That's one of the things I admire about you. Despite some of the awful experiences you've had, you still see the best in the new people you meet. But what do you really know about the parents?"

"They had to go through pretty rigorous vetting to get approved for refugee status."

"So did Uncle Nabil, right?"

"You're right. I shouldn't accuse the guy of terrorism just because he rubs me the wrong way."

Reese sighed. "This is up to the cops, not us. But my money is still on some right-wing militia group. I can see some fundamentalist yee-haw getting his kicks by having his son plant a hot gun in the refugee kid's gym bag. Of course, I realize that my past work on those groups makes me see militia behind every bush."

Alexa said, "I guess there's one good thing. The focus on Bassam should end any lingering suspicions the FBI might have about you. That, and the fact that you were on the other side of the country during the last murder. Their Al-Shabaab theory never did make much sense."

Reese's voice was subdued. "I'm glad to be off the list of suspects. But at the expense of a seventeen-year-old kid? That sucks. I have to believe there's another explanation."

# CHAPTER TWENTY-EIGHT

As always, Melinda was first to hear it on the news. While completing all her assignments on time, she still managed to keep abreast of both news and gossip. She caught Alexa between meetings with the latest.

"They're saying on the news that the cops arrested a teenage boy, a refugee, and he might be a person of interest in the ISIS murders."

"What? It's on the news? Information about juveniles is supposed to be confidential."

"They haven't given out the kid's name," Melinda replied. "But, how many teenage refugees are in this area? Not many; especially Muslims. I mean, that family that Tyrell Jenkins had in here a month ago was the first one I knew about . . ." Melinda's eyes grew big as she noticed the distraught expression on Alexa's face.

"OMG. Not that little boy with the broken arm. He couldn't be a killer."

Alexa gave a reluctant reply. "Didn't I just say that most juvenile proceedings are confidential?"

Melinda ignored her boss and continued. "No, it wouldn't be the little boy. It would be the older one; the kid with a chip on his shoulder. But murder? A terrorist?" She frowned. "They seemed like such a nice family."

Alexa drew her assistant into the office. "Look, Melinda. I can't talk about this case since I don't represent the accused, so I can neither confirm nor deny your assumptions here. But, please don't share your conclusions with anyone. The Qassims were here on a very different matter. And remember, all of our client cases are confidential."

Abashed, Melinda agreed. "I'd never do that, Alexa. I just got a little carried away."

"No problem. It's hard not to get overzealous about something this big happening right here in Carlisle." Alexa smiled. "Just one more thing: The police have never confirmed anything about ISIS."

"Tell that to the crowd down on the square. There's going to be an anti-terrorist rally at noon. I heard the kid is going to have a hearing this afternoon."

In her shock that this information had also leaked, Alexa didn't hear the phone ring until Melinda slid by her to pick it up.

"Tyrell Jenkins." With a knowing expression, Melinda passed the phone to Alexa and walked out the door.

"What a disaster. Have you seen the news?" Tyrell wailed as soon as Alexa said hello.

"Heard about it. Bassam's name isn't out there yet, right?"

"Just a matter of time, the way this is going. I blame the Carlisle Police. Where else could this be coming from?"

"Half the high school probably knows about the arrest," Alexa countered.

Tyrell sighed. "You're probably right. Anyway, the hearing for Bassam is in the courthouse at twelve thirty. Can you make it?"

"Yes. I'll be there."

Eshan and Zahraa were both distraught when the juvenile court judge found probable cause in Bassam's case and decided to keep him in detention. The assistant district attorney argued that Bassam's refugee status made him a flight risk. Although neither she, the Juvenile Probation officer, nor the judge mentioned the FBI, Alexa was pretty sure the potential murder charge was the unspoken subtext of the ADA's additional claim—that Bassam was a threat to public safety.

Debra Winslow made a strong argument for Bassam to be released until the adjudication hearing. Alexa appreciated the passion in her voice when she addressed the court. But, the judge erred on the side of caution. Alexa wasn't surprised by the outcome. On paper, the case against Bassam looked strong.

The bailiffs led a pale Bassam out of the room. Shaking, he threw a frantic look toward his parents as he stumbled out, prompting Winslow to pat him on the shoulder and whisper a few words in his ear. She then huddled outside the courtroom with the boy's parents.

Standing a few yards away, Tyrell slumped his shoulders. "I'm bummed," he told Alexa. "When I left Child Welfare, I never expected to spend time in juvenile court again. I hoped she would release Bassam into his parents' custody until the disposition hearing."

"That was generous of you to offer to take responsibility, as an alternative to the parents."

"Judge Crawford knows me. I thought she might go for it."

"She might have in a run-of-the-mill case. But, before she stepped into the courtroom today, I imagine she got the word that this could morph into a much bigger case. She didn't want to be the judge who allowed a possible terrorist juvenile delinquent responsible for three murders to skip town."

"You're probably right." Tyrell shrugged. "Moving Bassam out of detention was a long shot. Especially with the cops still figuring out if the gun is connected to these murders."

"Did you see the crowds outside? I know a lot of these folks are just plain scared. Losing it over the idea of terrorists here in Cumberland County."

"Winslow arranged for Eshan and Zahraa to enter through a rear door, so we avoided the worst of it. I'm hoping we can slip out the same way."

Alexa suppressed a flash of annoyance when Winslow walked over and said, "I have another hearing in fifteen minutes. Can you escort Eshan and Zahraa to their car, please? We discussed next steps. The coming few days will be trying, but we're just going to have to wait. Wait for the disposition hearing. Wait for the ballistics results on the pistol. Wait for the FBI to decide if they have grounds to prosecute."

She looked at the parents. "I'll be in touch tomorrow."

Zahraa dabbed at her eyes with a tissue. Eshan nodded.

Tyrell led the way out of the courtroom and to the elevators. "Let's try to slip out that back door."

Their attempt to avoid the crowds fell apart quickly. When the elevator door opened, they were confronted with bright lights from a bank of television cameras. Alexa recoiled as at least twenty reporters shouted questions.

"Is your son, Bassam, a terrorist?"

"Did you come to the United States to kill Americans?"

"Mrs. Qassim, how did your son get a gun?"

Alexa threw her hand up to shield her eyes from the phalanx of bright lights. "How the hell did they get inside the courthouse?" she muttered and followed Tyrell as he herded the faltering Qassims past the media.

The group took a few steps toward the hall that led to the back entrance, a wall of reporters with microphones following them. But a courthouse guard blocked the way.

"No. You can't bring that crowd back here."

Tyrell pleaded. "Just let us bring these people through. Debra Winslow got permission for us to use the rear entrance."

"I don't know nothing about that. All public has to use the front entrance."

Tyrell leaned toward the guard. "Motherfu—"

Alexa pulled him back and glanced at the guard's badge. She shook with fury. "Are you new here, Mr. Hewitt? Attorneys and their clients are supposed to have access to the rear door. I'll be speaking to your supervisor about this tomorrow."

"How do I even know you're an attorney? You look like a filthy terrorist-lover to me. My son spent years fighting these ragheads."

Alexa grabbed Tyrell's arm just before he punched the guard. "This guy's an asshole, but that won't help. It's the last thing we want on camera."

Tyrell exhaled audibly. "You're right." He calmly turned toward the Qassims. "Eshan, Zahraa. Keep your heads down. We're going to have to leave by the front entrance. There's a big crowd out there. But we'll make it. Once we get down the front steps, follow me to the left."

"Maybe you should deal with the press," Alexa suggested to Tyrell. "Just say that no one will be making a statement at this time. I'll text someone to pick us up in the alley. Maria?"

Tyrell nodded and held up his hand to the press. "Please. No one will be making a statement at this time. I would remind you all, however, that juvenile proceedings and the names of juveniles are confidential. That includes printing or broadcasting information that would identify the juvenile's name—such as those of the parents."

The press quieted at Tyrell's words, then groaned. When the four moved forward, however, the media parted to allow them to walk through the throng. Although the reporters continued to shout questions, Alexa was pleased to see some of the television reporters motion to their cameramen to cut the film.

Even Alexa hadn't expected the size of the crowd out front. She slowed in dismay as they emerged from the courthouse door. The noise of the protestors hit her like a blast, and she glanced toward Eshan and Zahraa in concern. What looked like upwards of a thousand people blocked the square, the crossroads of the two main thoroughfares through town. Their group shuffled forward, then paused for a moment at the top of the courthouse steps. When the crowd caught sight of Bassam's parents, a roar went up like the sound of an angry beast.

Tyrell turned to two Carlisle Police officers who were positioned by the doors. "Can you help us get through this?"

"Why didn't you leave by the back?" one asked.

"The guard on duty wouldn't let us through."

"Asshole rent-a-cop," the other policeman muttered. The two policemen started down the steps.

"Follow us and stay close," the second cop instructed.

"Thank you, Officers," Alexa remarked. She took a quick glance at the Qassims. They looked to be in shock but followed Tyrell's guidance as he steered them through the crowd.

As the cops parted a path through the mass of bodies, Alexa expected the people to make way like the reporters had. Instead, the presence of the Qassims seemed to enrage many in the crowd, who pushed forward, howling and screaming. Alexa wanted to grab them by their collars and yell back, ask them why they were so angry. Did they really think that these two people and their teenage son were a threat?

"Ragheads!"

"Terrorist!"

"ISIS!"

"We don't want your kind!"

"Muslims, go home!"

The insults came fast and furious, but the police fended off the most aggressive hecklers.

Alexa and Tyrell received their own share of verbal abuse. "Muslim-lover" and "Jihadi scum" were two of the most frequent. She shrugged off the insults but was outraged that this mass hysteria was coming from a community that she'd grown up in and loved.

She was surprised, too, at the diversity of the crowd. She saw a lot of camouflage, Harley Davidson jackets, and MAGA hats. But there were also women, young and old, who looked like soccer moms and bridge players. She thought she saw one of the tellers at her bank. And the guy who delivered pizza to the office sometimes. He'd come back from Afghanistan with a head wound that impaired his speech and more. She almost didn't recognize the snarling face of her mother's old friend, Helen. Apparently, fear was a powerful uniting force.

As they continued to push through the crowd, anger and heat from the mass of people crackled like kindling. Alexa picked up her pace as she felt the warmth on her face, imagining that, at any moment, the crowd could erupt into a blaze the police would be unable to control.

Although it seemed to take an hour, the group reached the edge of the crowd in just a few minutes. Alexa was thrilled to see Tyrell's second-in-command, Maria, parked in her SUV at the corner of the courthouse building on Liberty Avenue. She and Tyrell helped the Qassims into the vehicle as the crowd rushed forward. The two policemen held people at bay as Maria backed down the small street and sped away.

Two blocks down, Alexa said, "Drop me off here. I need to get back to the office."

Tyrell gripped her arms. "You OK, girl?"

"I've been better. I'm more pissed than anything." Alexa looked at the Qassims in the back seat. "I am sorry. You're seeing the worst of America. The worst of Cumberland County. It might be irrational, but people are afraid. And they do crazy things when they're afraid."

"Believe me, Alexa," Zahraa spoke in a shaky voice. "We know fear. We know what frightened and desperate people can do. Eshan and I can deal with this anger and abuse. Our only concern is Bassam. He is innocent. I know he is. But we have little confidence in the police and the courts, even in this land of freedom."

Tyrell said, "We'll go back to the RESIST offices and talk this through. Thanks, Alexa. I'll be touch."

Alexa slipped out the door. As she walked the few blocks to her office, she passed people leaving the demonstration, some carrying vile protest signs. No one gave her a second glance. A lesson in the bizarre behavior of crowds.

She was discouraged by the dreadful behavior of her neighbors and fellow citizens. Despite what she'd said to the Qassims about fear, she had higher expectations for the good people of Cumberland County. But, here they were, losing their shit at the first hint of danger. And, really, nothing in the information released by the police even indicated any threat against the general population.

Alexa ducked into the law office through the back door. "Melinda. I don't want to be disturbed. No visitors. No phone calls."

Alexa marched to the couch in the corner of her office and collapsed onto the seat. Minutes later, she stretched out and fell asleep from sheer emotional exhaustion.

# CHAPTER TWENTY-NINE

*October 16, 1859*

Your horse is white, your garment is bright. You look like a
man of war.
> —*"Bound for Canaan," a Negro spiritual*

*Elijah's heart jolted at the loud clank of metal on metal behind
him. He was terrified to be on this road below the Mason-Dixon Line.
Back in the South he'd worked so hard to flee.*

*Clank. There it was again. He turned to look at the bed of the
wagon, but in the light of the half-moon he could see only the faint
outlines of a blanket-covered mound. Beneath the blanket lay a stash
of pikes for the slaves, who they expected to join the rebellion, and
a supply of Sharp's rifles. The men called them Beecher's Bibles.
He hoped that no one was on the road to alert the authorities that
Brown's band of raiders was coming.*

*Ahead of and behind him, a group of eighteen men spread out
along the Maryland road, making their way toward the Virginia
town of Harpers Ferry. Several more men had stayed back at the
farmhouse near Sharpsburg. They would bring wagonloads of
supplies to a schoolhouse on the outskirts of Harpers Ferry after the
larger band secured the town. Elijah's job was to stay outside the
town and keep his two draft horses quiet; then bring these rifles and
pikes into town after the main force had seized the armory.*

*Like an avenging angel, John Brown rode at the head of the
line, cloaked in black with his white hair and beard flowing in the*

wind. Elijah was awestruck at the righteous energy of the man who carried this group of white abolitionists, free Negroes, and runaway slaves into danger. To foment a slave rebellion. Admiring Brown's zeal for the cause made Elijah ashamed of his fears about returning to the South. But, he couldn't shake his terror about the danger of this raid.

As they approached town, small groups of riders peeled off toward their assigned tasks. Although Elijah didn't have the full details of the plan, he knew from listening to the briefing and from Coleman's chatter that some would cut telegraph wires, and some would take outlying families hostage so they couldn't raise an alarm. At some point, the larger group would move to seize the armory.

Elijah jerked out of his daze when Mr. Brown rode up and down the line. "We'll group at those trees ahead." Elijah steered his wagon into a gap among the trees as planned. Someone from the group had scouted out the woods weeks ago, as a place to stash the wagon until it was needed. Elijah looked around the dark grove of trees and at the small stream that trickled through its midst. He'd be spending at least the next hour here, watching over the wagon and draft horses. He wouldn't know how much concealment the small woods offered until dawn broke in a few hours, but he was anxious about waiting here on his own.

For a few minutes, the grove was alive with activity. Men filling up on food, watering their horses in the stream, and claiming one of the Beecher's Bibles for the fight ahead. The commotion came to an abrupt halt when Mr. Brown held up a hand, bowed his head, and led the group of men in prayer.

The prayer was like no prayer Elijah had heard on the plantation. Mr. Brown's words sounded more like a battle cry.

"God has chosen us to be warriors in the fight to wipe the abomination of slavery from the land. Holiness does not consist in mystic speculations, enthusiastic fervors, or uncommanded austerities; it consists in thinking as God thinks and willing as God wills. God wills action. And we are his instruments of that action. Lord, we do your will in raising up the slaves and rallying them to thy standard. Hebrews 9:22 says, 'Without the shedding of blood there is no remission of sin.' This group assembled before you, God, has taken on your holy cause and will spill whatever blood necessary to erase the vile sin of slavery. In thy name, Amen."

Brown's prayer electrified the men, who murmured their amens and sprang onto their horses.

"*Stay here until we send back men to retrieve the wagon. Don't stray, even if you hear gunfire. That's to be expected,*" Brown instructed Elijah.

"*Yes, sir.*" Elijah trembled in the presence of the man, who seemed to crackle with righteous fervor. The boy hadn't really wanted to be part of this, but, weak in the knees in the presence of this crusader, he couldn't say no to Brown. He wondered how many of the other men felt the same way.

Just before the group rode out, Coleman guided his horse to where Elijah stood. "*Son, I'm proud of all you done in getting north with me. And in joining in this cause. A man has real purpose when he accepts God's plan.*"

"*Travel safe, Coleman,*" Elijah whispered on the verge of tears. He was frightened for his friend and overwhelmed by having sole responsibility for the wagon. But, he could see how excited Coleman was to take part in the raid, so he bit back his tears and waved. "*See you soon.*"

By midday, Elijah was frantic. This copse of trees overlooked the town of Harpers Ferry at a distance. He could see the gleam of the Potomac and Shenandoah Rivers and the shapes of houses but couldn't make out any activity in the town. In the early morning, he'd heard scattered gunfire. Two whistles signaled a train arriving in town, and, after the crackle of more shooting, the sound of the train moving on down the track. After a brief period of silence, there had been yet more shooting; some of it from the hills near town; some from in the town itself.

Elijah quieted and fed the horses. He paced back and forth by the stream. From time to time, he crept forward to the edge of the woods to look for traffic on the road. As the day wore on past noon, he became even more worried. The plan had been to take the armory and the guns before dawn. Someone from the group should have come long ago to get the wagon. The other wagon bound for the schoolhouse was to take another road; he had no idea if they'd delivered those supplies or not.

Almost dozing in the midday warmth, Elijah leaned against a wagon wheel and studied a late-season spider in its web. The large spiral web, stretched between the branches of a small tree, wafted in the breeze. A big fly that had been buzzing near the horses flew too close and got tangled in the web. Elijah watched in fascination as the spider scurried forward and began wrapping strands of silk around the helpless fly; spinning, spinning, until he'd trapped the fly completely. Then, Elijah swallowed hard. If he didn't take care, he could become a fly in a patroller's web. Without the protection of Mr. Brown, he was vulnerable out here, all alone.

Anxious, Elijah rose and took another look at the road. Still empty. As he gnawed on a johnnycake, he heard another spate of shooting. This time, it went on for almost an hour. Elijah knew there was something very, very wrong.

Should he go back to the farmhouse in Maryland? Even though it was only about an hour's ride, he hesitated to drive the wagon back in broad daylight. The sight of a young Negro boy alone might attract attention. Would his forged papers of freedom hold up back here in Virginia?

Every time he thought of running, he remembered Coleman, who might be trapped somewhere in the town. And he also feared the wrath of Mr. Brown. Perhaps the raid had run into a delay, and riders from their band would show up any moment. What would happen if they found him gone? He admired Mr. Brown, but he'd seen the man's temper, and it wasn't something he wanted to face.

In late afternoon, Elijah again made his way to the edge of the woods. Sporadic gunfire continued below, so he hid in the shadow of the trees. The first thing he noticed was a flock of blackbirds circling in the distance above Harpers Ferry. Not much more than specks at this distance, the birds seemed to glide on the currents, rarely flapping their wings. Then, Elijah looked below the birds, at the town.

"Lord Almighty," he exclaimed aloud as his knees buckled. Riders dressed in dark blue filled the bridge over the Potomac and extended beyond the bend leading to the river. At this distance, Elijah couldn't make out much detail, but a rider at the head of the group carried what looked like a flag. This was a military force of some kind. He stifled a sob as his worst fears were confirmed. Mr. Brown's raid on Harpers Ferry looked to be doomed. And Coleman was in mortal danger.

Frantic with grief, Elijah waited until dark and headed back to the farmhouse in Sharpsburg. Perhaps the three men who were to supply the schoolhouse would still be there. But when he arrived, the log house was empty. Inside, things were tossed about as if someone had ransacked the place. But they hadn't taken the food. With a constant ear tuned for intruders, Elijah gathered up provisions in a rucksack. Then, he stabled the draft horses and made sure they had grain and water. Imagining that soldiers might show up at any moment, Elijah crept upstairs to the loft. Next to the blankets where

Coleman had slept, he found the man's small tinderbox and slipped it into his pocket, whimpering with fear and sadness. He didn't want Coleman's prized possession to fall into a stranger's hands. Scrambling down the ladder, Elijah took one last look around the farmhouse and fled out the door into the night.

Heading north on foot, Elijah decided he'd be safe on the roads during the night but needed to avoid them by day. The route toward Hagerstown gleamed in the light of the half-moon. Elijah's shoulders shook with grief as he thought of the moon only two nights hence and what promise it seemed to hold for the Brown party's mission. And now, the raid had almost certainly failed. Even worse, the men could be dead. Coleman could be dead.

As Elijah contemplated that awful thought, he realized how dependent he'd grown on the older man. He'd even adopted as his own, Coleman's dream of living as a free man in Massachusetts or New York State. With tears in his eyes, Elijah placed one foot in front of the other in the bitter night and fought an urge to collapse in the middle of the road and wail.

As the moon dropped in the sky and the night deepened, he looked to the big dipper, the drinking gourd, and thought about Coleman using those stars from the song to guide them to Pennsylvania. Elijah's hand grasped the tinderbox in his pocket, and he took a deep breath of resolve. Coleman wouldn't want him to be captured and dragged back to the plantation. Despite his devotion to John Brown, Coleman had been unhappy to learn that the abolitionist had recruited Elijah for this raid, no matter how small his part. In fact, Coleman had once drawn a map in the dirt to show him the way from Chambersburg to the farm in Sharpsburg. At the time, Elijah thought that the map was just part of Coleman's general enthusiasm about all aspects of the raid. Now, he wondered if Coleman might not have been preparing him for the worst. For exactly what had happened.

"If you're gone, Coleman, I'll live free for the both of us," Elijah pronounced into the stillness of the night. Squaring his shoulders, he picked up his pace and headed north to Pennsylvania.

# CHAPTER THIRTY

"YOU, MOOSLIM-LOVING bitch. If you don't love America, go live with them damn jihadis."

Alexa deleted the phone message. What a way to start the day.

"Terrorist. You should be ashamed."

Delete.

"Traitor—"

Delete.

"Bi—"

Alexa started deleting the minute she got the caller's drift. Delete. Delete. Delete. She almost erased a valid message before she recognized Melissa's voice.

"Hey. You're famous, girl. Maybe not in a good way. You're all over TV and the newspapers. Did that Bassam kid really murder people? Tyrell must be really freaked. Oh, I almost forgot why I called. I won't be at yoga. Have to do some Christmas shopping since I haven't started yet."

Alexa smiled at the sound of her friend's voice. Then, she sighed and ran through the rest of the messages: More of the same vile, anti-Muslim crap. She deleted them all.

When the messages had started pouring in over the weekend, Alexa and Reese had quickly learned to stop answering the phone. At first, perhaps because of Reese's supportive presence, she'd laughed off the outpouring of anonymous hate—all spurred by a five-minute walk with the Qassims through the crowd at the courthouse.

But, she hadn't been able to fool Reese. "Don't be a martyr, woman. That crap would get to anyone," he'd said before pulling her into a big hug.

"Thanks; that helps." Alexa sighed. "It's amazing, the things total strangers say over the phone."

Reese replied in a wry tone. "Yeah, you'd think people with such strong feelings would at least have enough conviction to identify themselves. But most of them are cowards who only have enough courage to scream in the midst of a big crowd or in an anonymous phone call."

"I know you went through something similar with that false rape charge. Now I have a better appreciation for what you had to endure." Alexa nodded. "'Cowards' sounds right. That would go with the panic over these three murders. Totally out of proportion to the danger that any single individual in this county might be in. I don't get it."

Reese's tone was amused. "I'm sure you don't. You're one of the strongest people I know, Alexa. Fear isn't something you spend a lot of time considering."

"I've been afraid more times than I can count."

"But, when you're afraid, you act. You don't dwell on it. You just power ahead. There are a lot of people in the world who tremble at the slightest hint of danger and succumb to feelings of powerlessness. Those are the types who pretend they're brave by lashing out by phone, on social media, or whatever."

Alexa giggled. "What wisdom you speak, Yoda."

Reese folded his arms in front of his chest. "Speak truth, I will."

Her mood lifting, Alexa cracked up. "I'm not sure if that's Yoda or Tonto. Let's bundle up and go for a walk. Get away from these calls."

After breakfast on Monday morning, Alexa stood on the deck, wearing a down jacket and hat over her work clothes. Overnight, the forest had turned into a winter wonderland. The few inches of wet snow that had fallen during the evening hours clung to the bare branches of the oaks and beech trees. The towering evergreens in the pine grove wore a frosting of white on every bough. As the ringing of her landline echoed from inside the house, Alexa addressed the mastiff sitting quietly by her side. "I guess switching my number to unlisted didn't make that much of a difference. I'm still listed in the last phonebook. At least they don't have my cell phone number. I'm glad I got that signal booster so I can use the cell phone up here."

Scout whined and licked Alexa's hand. "I agree. It is a crappy situation. But, people will lose interest me in soon enough. Imagine what the Qassims are going through."

Scout took off and frolicked in the open space in front of the cabin, shoveling his nose into the snow. When the cell phone in Alexa's pocket rang, the mastiff dropped onto his back, kicking his legs into the air.

"Hello." As she answered the call, Alexa stifled her laughter at the dog's antics.

"I wish my morning was going as well as yours," Tyrell grumbled.

"I'm watching Scout play in the snow. What a goofball," Alexa replied. "Scout. Not you. What's wrong?"

"Every time I start to trust in the Man, I get it shoved right back in my face. I don't know why I even try."

"Something with the cops?"

"First of all, we had to move the Qassims over the weekend. Luckily, RESIST had a house ready and furnished out in Dickinson Township for our next family. They're delayed until at least February. Some glitch with the paperwork."

"Why'd you have to move the Qassims?"

"The mob. The mob found their house and demonstrated out front for hours on Saturday. The cops tried to break up the crowd, but they kept coming back. When I talked to them about protection, they balked. Pretty rich when the information about Bassam's arrest and his name could have come from the police."

"Or someone at the school. Or a student in Bassam's gym class."

"But only the cops knew about the hearing. Have you been getting the hate calls? They've been pouring into RESIST."

"Yeah. Don't call me on my home phone. I'm not answering it right now."

"I figured as much when you didn't pick up just now. That was me calling right before I tried you on your cell." Tyrell sighed. "People can be horrid. I thought I'd been exposed to the worst with our sex-trafficking work. But now, this. Who knew ordinary people from Cumberland County could be so vicious?" Tyrell's lament hardened into anger. "But, the worst happened first thing this morning."

Alexa knew what was coming.

"Debra Winslow called. The FBI got the results of the ballistics tests. The gun in Bassam's bag matched three bullets. One recovered at each of the murder sites. And the gun in his bag was loaded—except for three missing bullets."

"So, we're right about a pistol being used to shoot each victim in the eye?"

"Looks like it. But, seriously. Alexa. Can you see Bassam doing something like that?"

Alexa's reply was careful. "Not the Bassam I know. But the kid has seen a lot in his short life. He has a temper. He spent some important formative years in a refugee camp and could have been radicalized. I don't really know him that well. And even though you've spent more time with the family, you don't know him that well either."

Tyrell's tone turned defiant. "No, Alexa. I'm not going to let you do this. I believe Bassam is innocent, and some kid at school framed him. Reese's theory. An adult in some right-wing militia group got a kid to put the gun in Bassam's gym bag."

"I want to believe you're right. I do. But you need to consider how it looks to the FBI." Alexa shivered as Scout trotted up onto the deck. "Hold on a minute. I'm going inside."

In the house, Alexa hit the speaker button on the cell to continue the conversation while she shed her coat. "What does Winslow say about the FBI's case? As far as we know, they only have the gun, even with the ballistics match. Seems like they'd need more to bring charges. Can they place him at any of the three sites? Bassam doesn't drive, does he? How could he get to these remote crime scenes, especially the one in West Virginia?"

"Winslow says they think he's part of a larger group. And that the FBI's going to try to get him to give up the other players. But I can't wrap my head around that theory either. The Qassims arrived in late June. When was the guy killed in Harpers Ferry? July?"

"Toward the end of August."

"Still. That would mean this kid drops into Cumberland County from the other side of the world, reeling from the adjustment to a new country, home, and language. Yet, he manages to hook up with an Islamic terrorist group, that's unknown to authorities, and participate in one of their executions less than two months later. I should ask Winslow about Bassam's alibis."

"I agree it's a stretch. Unless a family member or a friend recruited him. All the things you just reeled off about Bassam's new life—those could make him vulnerable; open to recruitment. But we can speculate until the cows come home. The important issue is whether the FBI has any evidence of this."

"Winslow says they've got him cold on the gun possession charge. The serial numbers are gone; so, no way for her to follow an ownership trail and argue it couldn't be his. She'll fight tooth and nail, but she expects him to be adjudicated delinquent. The FBI has time to investigate while the kid's stuck somewhere in residential placement."

Alexa glanced at the time. "Tyrell, I have to get to work. I have a meeting, and the roads might be icy. I'll talk to you tonight after yoga."

"Maybe tomorrow. I promised the Qassims I'd spend the evening with them. They are distraught and having serious doubts about their decision to emigrate to America."

"OK. I'll catch you later."

# CHAPTER THIRTY-ONE

AFTER YOGA CLASS, Haley didn't even wait for Ariel to deliver the drinks before she laid into Alexa at the Om Café that evening. "What were you thinking, getting your picture plastered all over the news? With terrorists? And Tyrell too."

Alexa stole a glance at Sloane, who looked taken aback. Unclear whether their new friend was reacting to Haley's outrage or Alexa's bad taste in hitting the news, Alexa replied, "Haley, I wasn't angling for news coverage. Tyrell and I were just supporting the Qassims."

"Their boy's the terrorist?"

"My God, Haley. You have a journalism degree. Learn the facts. Don't spout off mob hysteria. Doesn't the Chamber pay you to know what's actually going on?" Alexa's temper rose.

Sloane jumped into the tension. "We're talking about Bassam Qassim, I take it?"

"At this point, why hide it?" Alexa conceded. "He's been charged with a gun-related offense in juvenile court. His name is supposed to be protected. The official media has mostly played by the rules. Although they ran those photos of Tyrell, the Qassims, and me. But, Bassam's name is all over social media."

"The boy's done quite well in Taekwondo. Seemed like the discipline was giving him a real focus for his energy and anger." Sloane shrugged. "Perhaps I was mistaken."

"You know this kid too?" Haley gasped in horror.

"Yes. I was unhappy to see him arrested and at the center of all this publicity."

"All these killings." Haley threw up her hands. "Everyone knows that they're linked to terrorism. That this kid is involved. Blair says that's what happens when we let refugees from those countries into the United States. And why Cumberland County? I adore Tyrell, but RESIST should have just stuck to helping sex-trafficking victims."

Exasperated, Alexa rejoined, "Haley. As far as I know, the police have not confirmed any connection between these homicides and terrorism. Bassam hasn't been charged with anything beyond a gun-related crime. I get it that a lot of locals are caught in the grip of mass hysteria. Believe me, most of them have left rabid messages on my answering machine. But maybe you'd be more effective at PR for the Chamber if you downplayed the terrorism angle. Unless and until the police disclose that it actually exists."

"Alexa. Sometimes you can be such a . . ." Haley paused to search for a word, then sputtered, "lawyer."

Both Alexa and Sloane broke into laughter. Finally, Haley joined in.

Alexa turned to Sloane. "With your time in the Middle East, I'd think you've had to live with terrorism. We've had some right-wing militia activity in this area, but nobody seems to label their violence as terrorism. Maybe because the militias spend most of their time training for some phantom crisis, usually based on a wild conspiracy theory. Only a few militia incidents have spilled over into actual violence. This fear of 'ISIS,'" Alexa used her fingers to make air quotes around the word, "is a whole new ballgame."

Haley downed the last of her tea and laid money on the table. "Sorry to run, ladies. Blair has one of those calls to Tokyo again tonight. I promised to be home in time to bathe Charlotte." She patted Alexa on the cheek as she left. "Next time you plan to be in the news, wear something brighter. Maybe blue or fuchsia."

As Haley disappeared out the front door, Sloane shook her head. "Wow."

"I try to cut Haley some slack. You met her husband. Blair is Mr. Conservative, a financial guy. Straight as an arrow. And she hangs out all day with all those business types down at the Chamber of Commerce. She is what she is. But, we've been friends forever. At her core, Haley's a good person."

"I like her well enough. But she seems very different from you and Melissa. A little uptight."

"Maybe." Alexa laughed. "To be fair, Haley's not the only person freaking out over the threat of terrorism. You should have seen the crowd at the courthouse for Bassam's hearing."

Sloane sipped her coffee. "You're correct. I have seen the impact of terrorism in the Middle East. I lived in what Haley calls 'those countries.' Egypt during my teenage and college years. Then,

I served the State Department in Tunisia and Morocco. Perhaps not the places that grab headlines here in the United States. But none of those countries have escaped unscathed. And the violence in places like Lebanon, Yemen, Iraq, Israel, Iran—much more immediate when you live in the region.

"The concept of terrorism also becomes more complicated when you live in its midst." Sloane leaned forward, and her voice rose. "Religious and tribal disputes go back not decades but hundreds of years. Is an uprising against the government, like in the Arab Spring, a justified revolution against systematic oppression or a group of radicals trying to disrupt a lawful government? Is fighting an invading foreign power, like Russia or the United States, that intervenes in your country's civil or religious war, an act of terrorism or patriotism?"

Alexa could tell that this issue was something Sloane felt strongly about. Of course, her experience and worldview were so different. She'd lived what Alexa only knew as headlines in the newspaper. Alexa responded carefully. "I don't pretend to have knowledge of all those complexities, other than the little I've read in the news."

Sloane nodded. "Now that I'm back in the States, I've found that most Americans know neither the big picture nor the details. Mostly, you're fed soundbites by both the government and the media. Even veterans who've fought in the Middle East often have the most cursory knowledge of why they were there."

"I'm probably better informed than most civilians." Alexa gave a rueful laugh. "And that's sort of sad, given my meager understanding."

"You don't need to know all the details to keep an open mind. You seem like a thoughtful person. One who makes connections."

Alexa shrugged her shoulders.

Sloane smiled. "Your guy, Reese. He told me that he lives in Harpers Ferry. I went there to see the site of John Brown's raid. He's a perfect American example of the question: Terrorist or hero?"

"Good point." Alexa nodded. "Some people say he was an anarchist for trying to foment a slave uprising and killing US soldiers in the process. Others credit him with bringing attention to the Abolitionist movement and jump-starting the Civil War; thus, freeing the slaves."

"Exactly. John Brown's always been one of my heroes. Not because of the violence. But because of his courtroom speech. And because he had the vision to make real change years before the rest of the North, even Lincoln, got on board."

Alexa weighed her next words but decided to proceed. "Your husband died fighting in Iraq. Is that correct?"

As Sloane nodded her head, Alexa continued. "Do you believe he knew what he was fighting for? Here in the States there was a lot of debate about the weapons of mass destruction, whether we were really justified in going into that war."

"My husband was a dedicated soldier. He very much believed in his mission. And I don't think he died in vain. He was a hero."

"You must miss him." Alexa's tone was sympathetic. Sloane's grief was palpable.

"Every day. Even after all this time," Sloane replied, wiping away a single tear.

After a moment of silence, Alexa tried to lighten the mood. "Melissa missed class tonight to do her Christmas shopping. Hard to believe it's just over a week till Christmas. This is the holiday when my mother goes a little crazy with decorations and a big meal. But, I'm actually looking forward to the distraction."

"Yes," Sloane came out of her reverie. "She invited me to an open house. But I'm going to be tied up with friends over the holidays. Honestly," she confided, "Christmas is not a holiday that I embrace since my husband died. Growing up, my father always found us some sort of tree to decorate. In most of his postings, we could get a pine tree. He came up with some fairly offbeat substitutes during our years in Egypt; mostly potted palms. But, it was never much about the religious holiday. It was more a time of celebration.

"Like I said, I'm still grieving for my husband. Some say it's been long enough. But, grief is a highly individual process. These days, step by step, I'm moving closer to finding things to celebrate. Christmas isn't on that list yet. I've already conveyed my regrets to your mother."

Sloane rose. "Alexa, I'm glad we had this time to talk. You've been very welcoming to me, a complete stranger. I appreciate your friendship." As she walked away, Sloane called over her shoulder. "Have a wonderful holiday."

Alone at the table, Alexa noticed that the entire café was empty. "Ariel, I'm sorry. You're trying to close, and we were just sitting here, gabbing away."

Ariel slipped into a seat at the table. "No problem. That one." She nodded toward the door. "It's clear she needs a friend who can help lift some of her sorrow. I didn't want to disturb your conversation. Gave me a chance to get a head start on the morning setup."

"You're always so observant. It's amazing how you develop such insight about your customers from such limited interaction."

"Sloane comes in here from time to time on her own. And once for lunch with a man and a woman; they looked a bit like ninjas. Wouldn't want to meet either of them in a dark alley."

Alexa smiled at Ariel's apt description of her Krav Maga instructors, Lev and KC.

"But this woman, Sloane, always looks alone, even when she's with a group. She's been touched by tragedy, right?"

"Yes. She lost her husband in Iraq."

"And so young. I hope the yoga and your friendship helps."

"Me too." Alexa grabbed her coat and jumped up. "I'll get out of here and let you go home, Ariel. Have a wonderful holiday if I don't see you before Christmas."

"You too."

Alexa took careful steps as she made her way across the icy parking lot to the Land Rover. Except for Ariel's Volkswagen Bug in the far corner, the lot was empty. Alexa backed out of her parking space, shifted into first gear, then switched on the headlights. Her lights caught a pickup parked across the street. Alexa drove to the exit, preparing for a left turn out of the parking lot. She jumped in surprise when the truck came alive, headlights glaring. She lowered her high beams. For a brief moment, she flashed back to the monster truck that had menaced her weeks ago at the Qassim house. But this was a standard-sized pickup, unremarkable except for several white splotches along the side of the vehicle.

Alexa wrinkled her nose at the decrepit-looking truck. Was that bird dirt?

She hesitated at the exit, waiting for the truck to proceed. And waiting. Exasperated, she edged into the street just as the pickup rumbled away from the curb in a cloud of blue smoke. Alexa braked in disgust. They were the only two vehicles on this stretch of road. It was almost as if he'd been waiting to cut her off.

Almost reflexively, she looked at his license plate. Her recent experience with the monster truck had made her a little leery of erratic pickup truck drivers. 54KX . . . Alexa couldn't make out the remaining numbers as the faster truck sped away from her. Under her breath, she repeated the letter-number combination to herself.

After the rocket start, the noisy truck had to slam on its brakes at the stop sign less than half a block away. Alexa smiled in perverse pleasure when she saw the truck's back wheels slide a bit on a patch of black ice. What was it with these people who thought driving a truck entitled you to act like a jerk?

Alexa followed the truck down the dark street but soon lost sight of it. Keeping her speed well below the limit on the icy road, she drove on, preoccupied with thoughts of Sloane. She agreed with Ariel that the woman seemed lonely, but Alexa had caught a puzzling vibe in their discussion of Christmas. Could Sloane be more deeply troubled than her new friends imagined? Her grief over her husband's death seemed profound and raw, yet years had passed since he'd been killed.

Perhaps there was something more. Sloane had used an odd, detached tone when she spoke about her father, even when talking about happy times. She'd apparently been quite young when her mother died. That had to have impacted her childhood. Then to be widowed so young.

On Hanover Street, Alexa glanced in her rearview mirror as she hit the turn signal for Walnut Bottom Road. A pickup truck pulled from a parking space a few car lengths behind her. When the traffic light turned red, the truck rumbled up behind her, stopping just a few feet from her bumper.

"Can't be the pickup from the parking lot," Alexa said aloud. But, when she turned right, the truck followed her. And on the turn, she saw splotches of white on the front fender.

Tensing, Alexa sped through the yellow light at the I-81 entrance, and the pickup followed, catching the red. "What the hell?" Alexa's mood veered between scared and pissed. The last thing she wanted was for this guy to follow her the whole way home. Her immediate thought: Was this some anti-Muslim nut who'd somehow tracked her down? None of the others had gone any further than leaving nasty messages on her answering machine.

Without signaling, Alexa made an abrupt turn into the crowded McDonalds. The pickup kept on going. Exhaling her tension in a long breath, Alexa decided to give this guy ample time to clear the area. She was sure it was the same truck as the one at Om Café, but how would he know that she'd be driving down Hanover Street? Maybe she'd overreacted and this guy was some lousy driver who happened to be going in her direction. Still, to let more time pass, she steered toward the drive-through line to order an iced tea she didn't really want.

Iced tea in the cup holder, Alexa guided the Land Rover toward the exit. Beep. Beep. Beep. Alexa looked toward the honking on her left and felt the first real tremor of fear. A pickup truck sat at an angle across four parking spaces that paralleled the exit lane. The driver, who had honked to get Alexa's attention, opened his window. He was wearing a ski mask over his head. Only his furious eyes and angry mouth were visible as he shouted at Alexa.

"Muslim lover. You'll find out what happens to bitches who kiss up to terrorists."

Alexa could hear his taunt even through the closed window of the Land Rover. She wanted to jump out of the car and confront this nut. She was so tired of the abuse. And now it had escalated from phone calls to personal confrontation. But caution stopped her. Someone this rabid could be packing a gun. She noted that the color of the truck was dark blue with a white cap over the bed. She recalled the bit of the license plate she'd seen: 54KX.

With a quick glance to the left, Alexa gunned her engine and pulled out onto Walnut Bottom Road. Even if he followed, a barrier prevented him from just pulling onto the road from where he was parked. The driver would have to circle the McDonalds to exit.

Alexa hung a quick right at the next traffic signal and sped down winding Alexander Spring Road. Behind her, the truck had emerged from McDonalds and was gaining ground. She flew past the hospital, glancing in the rearview mirror as the truck gained on her. Slowing just enough to make the turn, Alexa whipped into Commerce Avenue and drove into the state police barracks parking lot. She fumbled in her purse for her phone, thinking she could get a photo of this jerk's license plate.

The pickup slowed and then accelerated, disappearing down the dark road. In just minutes, he could drive onto the interstate or one of several other highways and roads. He'd left too fast for any photos.

Slumping in her seat, Alexa took a moment to regain her calm. Then, she slid out of the vehicle and stalked into the station to report the incident to the state police.

# CHAPTER THIRTY-TWO

REESE AND ALEXA snuggled on the couch two days after Christmas. "I love the tree. Because it's our tree." Alexa sighed with contentment. "This might be the best Christmas ever. Even cooking Christmas dinner here for Mom and Dad was fun."

"I missed seeing my parents a little. But I didn't make it home when I was working in Kenya either. And I just saw them at Thanksgiving. It will be fun to spend New Year's Eve with them."

"You sure they're OK with Scout coming along?"

"Yes, they'll love having a dog around. I think I told you about some of our dogs when I was a kid."

"You told me about Blackie and Hershey the very first day we met. Made me laugh even though I was reeling from a terrible experience. I think I fell for you that day. It just took me a while to figure it out."

Reese replied with mock sternness. "And I'm certainly glad you did." His tone softened. "Even though it's taken us a couple of rounds to get to such a good place."

Reese sat up and looked at Alexa. "That reminds me. I never breathed a word to my parents about finding that body, being questioned by the FBI, any of it. After what I put them through years ago with the faux rape charges that girl brought against me, they didn't need any more worries."

"Hope they didn't see my face plastered all over news."

"That was all local, right? Western Pennsylvania is in a different media market."

Alexa kissed Reese and smiled. "Believe me, I'm happy to spend a few days with no mention of refugees, ISIS, terrorism, or murder."

"OK, OK. We're on the same page." Reese's broad smile vanished. "At your parents' extravaganza before Christmas, I pulled Jim aside and told him about that guy who harassed you. He still has contacts with the state police unit that monitors militia groups. He's heard of one or two new white supremacist groups that are active; they're calling themselves alt-right now, you know. Some of them participated in that rally in Charlottesville, Virginia. He's going to ask around, see if any of these groups have a particular hard-on for refugees or Muslims. Might help identify this asshat who stalked you."

Touched by his effort to protect her, Alexa smiled. "A long shot. But worth a try. Even though I haven't seen the guy again, the experience has me a little jumpy. I'm always looking at pickup trucks as if they're going to turn and follow me. It's getting a little out of control. The other morning, I almost called 911 when a pickup pulled into the law firm lot next to me. Then Vanessa jumps out. She was driving her boyfriend's truck because her car was in the garage."

Reese rubbed her back. "I can tell you to chill, not to treat every truck as a threat. But, I think it's going to take some time. You had a couple of real scares."

"You're right, but I feel ridiculous. I bet one in three households in Cumberland County owns a pickup. And I know that most of them are lovely people who don't chase women and shout anti-Muslim crap."

Reese gave her a sympathetic smile. "I still think whole Bassam Qassim thing smacks of a militia setup. I'd love to know if the FBI has any other evidence trails they're following on those murders."

"They haven't leveled any additional charges against Bassam in relation to all that; even though the gun was a ballistics match. Could be that the FBI is just taking its time. I know they like to be methodical. But it might mean something more."

"What about Uncle Nabil?"

"I've had no contact with the Qassims since the hearing—I don't want to get jammed up with the bar because of the whole conflict thing. Tyrell says that the family is still distraught. And that Nabil has been very supportive. He credits him with keeping the family from falling apart. Maybe I misjudged him." Alexa paused. "Or maybe he feels guilty for sending his nephew to kid-jail for a crime *he* committed."

Reese shook his head. "The situation is far from funny. I'm convinced that right-wing radicals are behind the murders. You think Uncle Nabil is a closet terrorist. The only thing we agree upon: Bassam is probably taking the fall for someone else. The kid must be out of his mind with anger and confusion."

# CHAPTER THIRTY-THREE

CLASS ENDED EARLY Thursday evening for individual Krav Maga progress updates; Lev and KC took time every few months to speak with each student and deliver an assessment. When Lev sat down on the mat across from Alexa, she and Barb were the last two left in the room. KC led Barb to another corner.

"KC and I believe that you've improved quite a bit," Lev said. "You're throwing yourself into the up-thrusts. You're very good at finding an angle of attack in the knife exercises. We both believe you're ready—you have the competence—to continue into the next level of training. Our concern is your lack of aggression; your mental preparedness." Lev's expression was solemn. "Krav Maga can teach you valuable self-defense skills. But, this is not a technique for those who approach it in a tentative way. If you engage an assailant, you need to be ready to kick his ass until you have an avenue to escape. Your thoughts?"

Alexa shrugged. "Your criticism is valid. I've learned a lot in these classes. The physical exercise is great. I'm really toned. And I believe I've improved a lot. I'm finally getting the hang of the moves. But my heart's not really in it. Most of the time, I feel like I'm pretending to be a hard-ass. I've been seriously considering dropping out. Not going on to the next level."

"As I recall from our original intake discussion, you've been confronted with," Lev tilted his head as if trying to remember, "more than one situation where you've been in danger? And that's why you turned to Krav Maga. To strengthen your capacity to fight back. To defend yourself and defeat an opponent."

"You're right. I had to shoot a man who was trying to kill me. And there have been a few other incidents." Alexa twisted her hands. "I seem to end up in trouble more often than most. At least twice, my attacker far outclassed me in height and weight.

"It's the attitude of aggression that I'm really wrestling with. Maybe I'd get in that zone if confronted with a real threat. But, it's hard for me to summon that level of combativeness in class. I also wonder: Will Krav Maga give me a false sense of security?"

Lev smiled. "I see that it would be good idea for us to do a refresher with the entire class on the purpose of Krav Maga for defense. Look. You have the physical capacity to move into the next series. And to improve your skill level. You'll have to decide whether the psychological aspects of Krav Maga are something you're comfortable with."

"Thanks for being honest, Lev. I'll think about all this and let you know." Alexa looked up to see that Barb had left the room, and several teens in Taekwondo gear had drifted in.

Lev stood and gave Alexa a hand to pull her to her feet. "On to the next class. Quite a difference from your group. Keeping twenty teenagers on track is a real challenge."

"Where's your assistant, the young guy? I noticed he hasn't been here lately."

"No, we're looking for someone else to help out. Keith was arrested for DUI a few weeks before Christmas. Then, he just disappeared. We suspect he skipped town and probably the state. I was disappointed, both with the DUI and the choice to run rather than face the consequences. KC and I both thought that young man embodied the Krav Maga discipline. I guess we were wrong."

"Too bad," Alexa murmured as she slipped away to the locker room.

Damn. She was even less sure that tackling a higher level of Krav Maga was the right thing to do. Discipline. Mental preparedness. Psychological readiness. The way Lev talked, it was more like committing to a long-term relationship than the brief flirtation she'd imagined. Look at Sloane. She'd been doing Krav Maga for years and had turned it into a way of life with Courage.

Alexa resolved then and there that she'd stick with class through the end of this level in January. Then, that was end of Krav Maga. The flirtation had lasted for six months, long enough to know that she and the martial arts just didn't click. She was so over Krav Maga.

Skipping to the Land Rover, Alexa felt like a huge weight had been lifted. She'd joked to Graham about the Krav Maga decision being a burden but hadn't realized just how much it had been bothering her. She tossed her gym bag into the back seat and stopped to take in the sky. It was a clear, crisp night with just a sliver of moon. A great night for the hot tub when she got home.

Alexa put the vehicle into gear just as a group of preteen kids and parents spilled into the crowded parking lot. She waited a moment until she saw a clear path forward and exited toward home.

As she drove, Alexa remembered with a grimace that she hadn't scanned the parking lot for pickups. There had been no further incidents like the one after yoga. Her entire holiday vacation had been serene. But, just when she'd started to feel safe, the local newspaper included the demonstrations at the courthouse in their year-in-review issue. Alexa had been pissed to see the photo of her, Tyrell, and the Qassims headlining the brief article. Since she'd been back to work on Tuesday, Alexa had the feeling that someone was watching her. But she'd seen no one.

As Alexa castigated herself for not being more careful, she laughed aloud. "A parking lot full of parents and kids, and you're looking for stalkers to pop out of the trash cans or something." She took two cleansing breaths and chanted, "Serenity now, serenity now," before breaking into giggles. When she sat down to meditate, Reese would hum this phrase in the background; his lame idea of a joke.

Right after Alexa turned onto North Dickinson School Road, far behind her, headlights slashed through the night. Cresting the dark hill, she slowed to navigate broken asphalt in the middle of the deserted, narrow road. Then the road spooled into a long curve. From behind, the other vehicle's headlights descended the hill at a pretty fast clip.

Must be a local, she figured. She'd only discovered this shortcut recently and still took its twists and turns at a cautious speed.

As Alexa veered left onto a tiny road, a large, dark bird shot out of the woods ahead with a sharp cry. The wide swath of bright headlights from her vehicle and the one behind silhouetted the bird's flight against rising ground fog.

Kew. Kew.

"A night heron?" Alexa marveled aloud as she identified the squat body and long, pointed beak. It was rare to see one. Something must have startled it from a roost near the stream. Maybe a fox. As she neared the creek, the ground fog thickened. Alexa slowed on her approach to the narrow bridge and underpass ahead.

As she drove onto the single-lane bridge, several things happened at once. The vehicle following her picked up speed. In an instant, it had narrowed the gap and rode just off her back fender. Alarmed, Alexa looked in the rearview mirror and recoiled at the merciless reflection of its headlights. Another truck. From the height of its lights, a big truck.

She gritted her teeth and turned her focus back to the road ahead, startled by movement in the mist beyond the windshield. She blinked several times, trying to clear spots in her eyes from the headlight glare. Then, she gasped and jammed on the brakes. In the swirling fog, a throng of people dressed in dark clothes held a white sign unfurled across the road, blocking the entrance of the underpass.

Heart pounding, Alexa knew she was in trouble. The Land Rover was blocked from both the front and the rear. And the small creek that wound on either side of the road was too deep for the vehicle to cross, at least in the dark.

"TERRORIST BITCHES MUST DIE." As the words on the banner hit home, she grabbed her phone and pressed Emergency. No tone. No cell coverage. She was in a dead zone. Alexa began to laugh hysterically. A dead zone.

She snapped back into trembling silence when, like wraiths, two more lines of people materialized from the woods on either side of the Rover. Now she was hemmed in on all sides.

Frantic, she locked the passenger door. The rest were already secure.

Trying to stave off panic, Alexa thought about weapons. She rummaged beneath her seat and pulled out a bottle of Windex. Wedging the spray bottle next to her on the seat, she lifted the long-handled ice scraper from the door pocket.

Why weren't these people worried that she might have a gun?

As the group swarmed closer to the vehicle, she saw that many of them gripped nasty-looking long rifles or assault weapons in their hands. The rest had rifles slung over their shoulders. Even if she'd had a pistol, these people had overwhelming firepower.

Tap. Tap.

Alexa jumped at the knock on her window. While she'd been focused on the larger group, a man had walked right up to her driver's side door. Unlike the rest of his companions, he was dressed in a white winter parka and snow pants. A white balaclava covered most of his face. The little skin that showed was dark with paint or charcoal. In the glow of the headlights from the truck behind, his eyes burned like black holes. Alexa shrank from the man. He looked like a living skeleton.

The man knocked at the window again.

Keeping her hand low, Alexa found the phone on the console and hit Emergency again. No tone, but the flash of light had caught the skeleton's attention.

He raised the barrel of the gun toward the window. "Put that down," he shouted. "Roll down the window. We won't hurt you."

Right, thought Alexa. The Terrorist Bitches Must Die sign is just for effect, right? She knew she couldn't trust a word he said. Instead, she was going to have to rely on this beast of a Land Rover to escape. But how?

The big truck still had her wedged in from the rear. If she went forward through the people holding the sign, she'd have to run them over to get to the narrow underpass. If she veered right, off-road, she'd plunge into the winding creek then run into the steep hill that supported the elevated train track. But there was a rusted gate ahead to the left. Maybe there was a lane through the woods on the other side. If she could smash through, maybe she could circle back into the fields she'd just passed. That's what the night heron had done when these people had disturbed his rest.

Her Defender had been built for African safaris and other impossible terrain; maybe it could make it. A long shot, but better than sitting here, waiting to die. Alexa tensed, looking for her chance.

The man outside her window knocked again. This time, his companions mimicked him by pounding on the Land Rover. Bam. Bam. Bam. Bam.

Bam. Bam. Bam. Bam. More people joined in.

Alexa flinched at each thump as the crowd hammered on the fenders, the sides, the hood, and the back door of the vehicle.

Bam. Bam. Bam. Bam.

The steady rhythm of the pounding frightened Alexa even more than the presence of all these guns. Her heart fluttered against her chest at the sound of each blow hitting metal. Losing it, she bit her knuckle to keep from screaming.

Then, she made the connection. This was like the pounding on the bulging door in that old movie, *The Haunting*. The thumping on the Land Rover had pushed that terror button from her childhood. But this time, she knew who was doing the pounding. A group of scary assholes in camouflage, hiding behind masks.

Identifying the root of her fear gave Alexa enough distance from what was happening to collect her wits. She had to be prepared for an opening.

Outside, the skeleton man shouted a command, and the pounding stopped.

In the ominous silence, he stepped back to the vehicle, holding the stock of his rifle as if poised to shatter the window.

Alexa took a quick glance at the crowd to the left. Although they'd stopped pounding with their fists, many were still clustered near the vehicle. Near the gate, they'd left a gap in their line. She decided to go for it.

"Open now or I'll break it," the skeleton commanded.

Exaggerating the expression of terror on her face, Alexa wound the window down a few inches. "What do you people want with me? I think you have the wrong person."

Skeleton Man emitted a bleak chortle, which Alexa took as his rusty attempt at a laugh. "Girlie, we ain't got the wrong person. You're Alexa Williams, ain't you? Fancy lawyer from Jew York City who consorts with dirty A-rabs and Moslems. Satan worshipers who defile clean white women. Your mama must be ashamed to have spawned a clueless libtard snowflake like you."

"I might say the same about your mama. Does she know you harass women dressed up like Frosty the Snowman?" Alexa's voice trembled.

"They said you had a mouth on you." Skeleton Man chortled again. Then his voice took on a dangerous edge. "But I'm tired of playing, girlie. We ain't going to kill you. We just want to educate you on how a good Christian woman should behave." He slid the barrel of his rifle into the window opening and tapped the glass. "Roll this window down. Now."

"Please don't hurt me," Alexa wailed, playing up her very real fear. Keeping her hands low, she picked up the Windex and transferred it to her left hand. Then, she rolled down the window, one slow turn of the handle at a time. As the final inches of glass slid into the door, Alexa tensed. She noticed that the crowd had drawn even closer to the car during the conversation.

The skeleton cackled. "That's right, girlie. Now get ready to slide on over; we're going to drive somewhere for those lessons I talked about. My friends here want to meet you too."

He slung his rifle over his shoulder and leaned forward to raise the lock on the door. Gritting her teeth, Alexa shot her right hand out of the window and hooked her hand over the neck of the man's coat, just above the zipper. And yanked. Hard. A Krav Maga yank. His forehead hit the top of the door with a solid thunk. As his head rebounded, Alexa thrust the Windex bottle out the window and sprayed his face and eyes.

Running on pure adrenalin, Alexa barely registered his curses or the commotion among the crowd nearest to their leader. Instead, she dropped the Windex, slammed the Land Rover into first gear and shot forward with an immediate up-shift to second.

The crowd surged toward the car, and Alexa heard a few gunshots. But she kept going, preparing to take a hard left into the woods, hoping to find a clear path that skirted the stream. Chances were that the vehicle might crash or bog down in swamp beside the road. If it did, perhaps she could ditch the Rover and slip away in the darkness.

Just as she braced for the turn, Alexa noticed that the people holding the banner across the road were fading into the woods. Then, she saw the underpass brighten as a set of headlights hit the far wall. Alexa changed plans and shot forward into the underpass, laying her hand on the car horn as a warning. With only inches to spare, she rocketed past the front fender of a small SUV.

Fighting her instinct to flee, Alexa skidded to a halt and yelled through her open window, "Go back. Go back."

The frightened twenty-something man slid down his window. "What, lady? You nearly hit me."

"Go back. There are men with guns," Alexa gasped.

Automatic gunfire crackled, and a divot of concrete from the underpass ricocheted into the guy's SUV. His eyes widened in fear.

Alexa figured he'd gotten the message and threw the Rover in gear. At the stop sign ahead of her, Alexa took a quick glance to the left and rolled right through, tires screaming. Behind her, the SUV had backed up and was hard on her heels.

Still trembling, Alexa drove the few miles to the King's Gap General store. It was under new ownership and stayed open till nine o'clock now. She looked at the time on her phone; not even eight o'clock. Trying out her shaky voice as she turned into the store parking lot, she said, "It seems like hours since I left Courage. Courage?" Alexa broke into hysterical laughter, struck by the absurdity.

I could have used more courage a few minutes ago, she thought. Who the fuck were those assholes?

When Alexa opened the door, she realized that she'd never closed the window. Biting her lip, she wound the handle until the glass was in place. The winding motion bothered her right hand. As if detached from her body, Alexa wondered whether she'd sprained her wrist when she'd grabbed Skeleton Man. She slid from the Land Rover onto the ground but had to grip the door handle for support when her legs buckled.

Alexa knew that she looked a mess as she stumbled into the store.

"Are you all right, honey? You're pale as a sheet. Did something happen?" the older woman behind the counter asked.

"Please call 911. I've been attacked."

A burly man in a flannel shirt and baseball cap caught Alexa as she swayed again. "Thank you. The heat in here made me a bit faint." She pointed to the woodstove burning in the corner.

"Honey, I called 911. Is someone after you?" The woman took a baseball bat out from beneath the counter.

"I don't think so. Another car came, and they ran." Alexa sank into the chair that a second customer offered and closed her eyes.

"Don't worry, honey. The police are on their way."

# CHAPTER THIRTY-FOUR

"YOU SHOULD TAKE today off. Stay in bed." Reese rolled over and placed an arm across Alexa's torso when she turned off the alarm.

"I have a full day."

"Which Melinda could easily rearrange. Any court appearances?"

Alexa squinted at her phone calendar. "Nope. All client meetings. And a planning meeting for that anti-fracking coalition I work with." She gave her boyfriend a gentle poke. "You're the one who should stay in bed. It was after three o'clock in the morning when you got here." She squiggled closer. "Thank you for coming. I was pretty freaked out."

Reese gave her a long kiss. "Me too." His expression turned stormy. "If they'd been successful in dragging you off, who the fuck knows what could have happened."

"I think we both know I'm lucky."

"And brave. Woman, you have balls of steel."

"Really? The only compliments for bravery are sexist?" Alexa sat up and shook her head in dismay.

"Good point. It's like lions. The females are the ones who do the hunting, raise the cubs, and fight off most threats to the pride. Most of the time, the males come in after a kill and bully the females to get their share of the spoils. They spend the day marking their territory and get into scraps with other males from time to time to maintain their dominance of the pride. Yet the Kenyan saying, 'You have the heart of a lion,' is always shown with a photo or drawing of a male."

"We really don't need a contest for which is the bravest sex. In any species. Last night, I was terrified. I didn't feel brave at all."

"But you acted. You weren't frozen by fear. I'll amend my statement. You have a heart as fierce and true as a lioness."

Alexa giggled and pushed up off the bed. Her right wrist throbbed from the pressure. Definitely a slight sprain or strain. In the shower, Alexa closed her eyes, and her heart began to pound. For a moment, she was back in her vehicle with the Skeleton Man reaching through the open window. She shivered in the warm water and shook away the thought.

When Alexa walked back into the bedroom, Reese was fast asleep. She smiled and slipped into a sweatshirt and jeans. Gesturing to Scout, she whispered. "Come on, we'll let him rest." She closed the door behind the dog and padded downstairs in her bare feet.

Scout raced outside for his morning romp. Another cold but clear morning. Rubbing her sore wrist, Alexa took a second look at the day's calendar and came to a conclusion. She would stay home today. She and Reese had planned a quiet weekend. Why not start a day early?

She called and left a message for Melinda to clear her schedule. Said she wasn't feeling well. Then, she gritted her teeth and called Graham at home.

Kate picked up the phone. "Sure, he's here. Just about to head out for the gym. Are you OK?"

"Yes. But there was a bit of an incident last night. Some extremist group targeted me. Stopped me on the way home from Krav Maga. I escaped; called the police. They didn't hurt me. But I thought I'd loop Graham in."

"Oh my heavens. Let me grab Graham. I'm glad you're OK, Lexie."

Alexa caught an undertone in her sister-in-law's words: bewilderment at the scrapes Alexa managed to get into. Kate had never in her quiet life been confronted with a dangerous situation. Sometimes, Alexa envied her.

Graham's deep voice came on the phone. "What happened? Kate says there was an incident? Were you injured?"

"My wrist hurts a little from grabbing one of the guys who stopped me. Otherwise, I'm OK. But I think I'm going to rest today—I'll be back to work on Monday."

"Were you assaulted? Where did this happen?"

"On North Dickinson School Road, almost to Pine Road. It's a shortcut I take from my evening classes at Courage." Alexa paused to reflect. "Used to take."

She filled her brother in on the entire incident and the hours she'd spent with the state police afterward.

"All this just came out of the blue?" Graham asked in a puzzled voice. "Why did they target you? Why now? Are we representing someone that has ties to this possible white supremacist group?"

"Not what I'd call ties. You know about the pro bono work I did for RESIST with the Qassim family?"

"Yeah, the ones that got your photo plastered all over the news during the terrorist scare. That was over a month ago, wasn't it? I thought that whole issue was quiet."

Alexa sighed. "I didn't want to worry you or the parents. So, I downplayed the reaction to that. I was swamped for weeks with vicious, vicious calls. And before Christmas, a man in a pickup truck followed me. He shouted some anti-Muslim slurs. I reported it to the state police but had little identifying information. Didn't get the entire license plate number. I mean, how many pickups are there in this area?

"I don't really know what triggered this thing last night. Maybe the *Sentinel* article at New Year's where they re-ran that photo of me and Tyrell with the Qassims. Maybe it had been in the works a while. One of the creepiest parts of the whole thing—other than being scared out of my mind the entire time—was that they seemed to know a lot about me. That I'd lived in New York. That I take classes at Courage. The way I drive home from the studio."

"They could have Googled your work history, but the rest . . . yeah. Be careful. Is Reese there?"

"Yes. I called him not long after the whole thing happened. He arrived late last night."

"Is there anything I can do?"

Alexa asked in a hopeful tone, "Maybe you could let Mom and Dad know what happened? I'll talk to them later, but it might soften the angst if they heard it from you first."

"Sure. I'll call them when I get to the office. They won't hear it on the news or anything?"

"I don't think so. And I doubt that the state police would put out a press release or anything—unless they're looking for citizen help in identifying these jerks. I got the impression that they have a few known white supremacist groups that they plan to question as a first step. Of course, there were a few people at the King's Gap Store when I stumbled in there for help. You never know whether one of those folks might call in a news tip. But, I didn't really give them much information other than I'd been attacked."

"OK. Get some rest. Isn't this world-famous Winter Ball next weekend? Mom will want all the Williams women to turn out in full force. You better be ship-shape."

"Now you're mixing your metaphors. It's time to go." Alexa's joking tone became somber. "Thanks, Graham. It's nice to have a big brother to lean on in times of trouble."

"No prob. I just wish you had fewer times of trouble."

After she hung up, Alexa called Scout into the house and filled his food bowl. She threw a few logs in the woodstove before she crawled onto the couch, pulled a furry throw to her chin, and fell back to sleep.

Late Saturday morning, Mom and Dad showed up at the cabin, unannounced, with a huge pot of chili, still warm from the stove. With an abashed look on his face, Dad said, "Sorry to just drop in like this, but we're worried. Graham says you're fine. But we needed to see for ourselves."

Mom slipped her coat off. "I'm not sorry at all. I needed to see you, Lexie. What a horrible experience. In case you wanted to invite us to stay for lunch, we brought chili."

Scout pranced around the dining room, happy to see the pair. Reese looked at Alexa with a grin, then turned to her parents. "Hey, how would the two of you like to stay for lunch? I think we plan to have chili." Chuckling, he took the pot from Norris and carried it to the kitchen stove.

"Very low heat, dear. Just enough to keep it warm," Susan shouted.

Alexa hugged both her parents. "I'm glad to see you. After our conversation yesterday afternoon, I'm not surprised you're here."

Her father said, "We're your parents. And half the year we're in Italy, so we need to provide extra support when we're here in Carlisle."

"Logical," Reese commented.

"I adore this young man," Susan said with a pat to his arm.

Alexa started toward the living room. "Let's sit in here until we're ready to eat."

"Anything more from the police?" Dad asked when they were settled around the wood stove.

"No, I checked with Trooper Cannon. Remember him from when Mom was shot?"

Both parents nodded.

"He said they're rousting all their contacts in the militia world. Strange word, 'rousting.' And they have interviewed several known white supremacists. I don't think I could identify any of the people from that night. It was dark. They were bundled tight and wearing masks or face coverings. I might be able to recognize the leader, the one I thought of as Skeleton Man, from his voice."

"Skeleton Man?" Her mother shivered.

"He dressed in white and had his face painted black. He's the only one who spoke to me."

Reese said, "The state police have a unit that specializes in crimes committed by militias. When I was at Michaux, I worked with some of those guys. They keep a pretty comprehensive database on the groups they've identified. But some groups dissolve. New ones form."

"Interesting tidbit." Alexa sat forward. "One way the police investigate now is to comb through these guys' social media accounts. Twitter, Facebook, Reddit, Instagram, something called the Dark Web. They're looking to see if they can find any chatter about that night. Or the phrase on the banner they carried."

"Phrase?" Mom asked.

"Just typical white supremacist bullshit." Alexa regretted mentioning the banner. Her parents would be appalled to hear that this group threatened to kill her. Suspecting that she could have been harmed was way different from knowing about a very real threat of death.

Just before her parents left, her mother touched on the upcoming Winter Ball. "I hope your wrist is healed by Friday, dear."

"I'm sure it will be, Mom. It feels much better today. At this rate, I'll make yoga on Tuesday. You have the decorating covered? I hadn't planned to come over to the Heritage Center early. Especially since I skipped work yesterday."

"No, no. We have all the help we need." Mom beamed. "I'm excited about this event. All the tickets are sold. It should be outstanding."

Not long after Alexa's parents left, Agent Carter called. He wanted to come out to the cabin and talk.

"So much for a weekend of peace and quiet." Reese dropped the book he was reading. "This place may be remote, but it's a revolving door today."

"He said 'we' would be coming out. I hope that doesn't include Agent Fox."

"That would put a damper on the day." Reese frowned.

When Carter showed up an hour later, he had an eager young agent in tow. Alexa's eyes hurt when she looked at the shine on his black wingtips. Carter wore polished but more sensible oxfords with soles for walking.

"This is Agent Purcell. He's working with me on the terrorism case. He's a data and research expert."

When Alexa led them to the living room, Reese stood. "Hello, I'm Reese Michaels. I can go upstairs if you need to speak to Alexa alone."

Alexa said, "I'd prefer that he stay."

Carter said, "Reese. Good afternoon. You may have heard me introduce Special Agent Purcell. I have no problem if you stay. In fact, I heard through the grapevine that you'd suggested looking into this angle awhile ago."

"Angle?" Alexa motioned for the agents to sit.

"We had been looking at the possibility that right-wing militia, white supremacist, or neo-Nazi groups could be responsible for the three so-called terrorist murders. The classification of these groups has become pretty fluid. But, as you know, the Counterterrorism Unit honed in on the idea of an outside Islamic group or a homegrown group of jihadis.

"When we got a report about the assault on Thursday night, Alexa, the Harrisburg office decided to take another look at the right-wing militia angle. I think the state police are proceeding based on the assumption that the publicity you received in conjunction with the arrest of Bassam Qassim made you a target for one of these groups. I understand that there were previous threatening phone calls and harassment. A reasonable lead for the state police to pursue.

"But, we're looking at a different angle." Carter looked at Reese. "I understand that you and your forest ranger friend, Jim Kline, had discussed this. He talked to a contact at the state police who spoke to Purcell here in our office. It's a question of motive. What if this group's motive in targeting you, Alexa, was related to the terrorist murders? To the fact that you found body number two? That you may have knowledge that could link this group to the murders?"

Reese snapped his fingers. "From the first day, I thought a right-wing hate group could be responsible. But, I have a bias here. In my old forest ranger job, I investigated militias who were using the State forests for training exercises."

"Why now?" Alexa asked. "We found that body in October, almost three months ago. And why just me? Neither Tyrell nor Reese has run into any harassment. Well, Tyrell did get some nasty phone traffic, but that went to RESIST."

"I don't know. Maybe you're a more visible public figure. Maybe because you're a woman, and they consider you more vulnerable. Maybe because only your name leaked out. This case has been less than airtight, with all the levels of law enforcement and ancillary support involved."

Purcell asked, "Can you walk us through exactly what happened? At this incident and the earlier one that involved a single individual in a pickup truck?"

Alexa recounted both incidents to the agents, even though it was a repeat of her interviews with the state police. In her detailed accounts, she even mentioned the monster truck from the night vandals had defaced the Qassim home.

Purcell looked at Carter. "All these incidents fall into the recent playbook for at least two groups that we're keeping an eye on. The last incident is more elaborate than what we've seen so far. And the man in white," he addressed Alexa. "You dubbed him 'Skeleton Man.'"

"Mainly because his face was smeared with charcoal or some sort of black face paint. His coat and pants were white," Alexa explained.

"One of these groups calls itself Blizzardwaffen. Real shining examples of Aryan purity. But they've really hit it out of the park with the name." Purcell's tone dripped with sarcasm. "The Nazi reference with *'waffen.'* And 'blizzard' packs a double whammy with both a reference to white power and a forceful storm. In the online chatter, I've seen one of their leaders referred to as the Snowman. Could be the same guy. Could be a total coincidence."

"Let's look into it," Carter said. He smiled at Alexa. "Thanks for your time. We want to look at all the angles. That's it for now."

Reese tilted his head with a puzzled look. "Question. I understand that you have to pursue all potential leads. Like whether I was involved with Al-Shabaab." His tone took on a bitter edge.

Carter looked uncomfortable. "Like you say, we have to track down everything until we're satisfied."

"It makes sense to look at the white supremacist angle. In my experience, most of these guys are dumb as dirt, but a few of them are pretty sophisticated. They might get a real kick out of killing people and pinning the murders on Islamic terrorists. But you already have Bassam Qassim in custody, caught red-handed with at least one of the murder weapons."

Alexa nodded. "I've stayed away from the Qassim case, as you requested. So, I know little about what's happening—other than the kid has been placed in a residential facility. The way it looked before Christmas, you were going to bring more serious charges, maybe even multiple murder counts against him. Or what, deport him back to Syria?"

"The white supremacist angle and the Bassam-is-part-of-a-refugee-terrorist-cell theory—or whatever your working assumption was—don't seem to jibe," Reese observed, steepling his fingers.

Alexa knew he was chafing at the bit to add, "To state the obvious." She flashed him an appreciative smile for showing restraint.

"Turns out that the kid alibied out for all three of the murders. Some of the primary verification came from family, who aren't solid witnesses. Especially when it comes to major crimes. But secondary sources verified most of the timeline for the kid's whereabouts. Can't divulge much more. We haven't formally eliminated him as a person of interest. Like you say: He had the gun. And it was definitely involved in the three murders."

"From the start, Bassam said he was framed," Alexa exclaimed.

"Trouble is, they all say that," Carter countered.

Reese and Purcell nodded in agreement.

Purcell looked at Carter, as if seeking permission, then said, "Under the white supremacist theory, someone at school could have planted the gun on the Qassim kid. A parent might have directed their son or daughter to drop the gun in his gym bag. Heck, some of those groups recruit teenagers and younger to their organizations. Who better to frame than the new Muslim kid? If nothing else, it worked as a distraction."

Reese shot an "I told you so" glance at Alexa. This theory mirrored the thoughts he'd had all along.

Alexa reacted to the legal implications. "If he was framed, Bassam should be released and his delinquency adjudication reversed. The kid's a victim. Miscarriage of justice."

Carter held up his hand. "You're getting out ahead of things. Number one. We haven't verified this white supremacist possibility or even begun to build a case. Number two; we're well aware that we need to take certain actions regarding Bassam Qassim. Those should play out over the next week or two."

"Frankly, the kid might be better off in juvenile placement if the Blizzardwaffen or another group learns that we're zeroing in on them for the murders. At least he's safe there." Purcell's voice was somber. "These groups are like a den of rattlers. You don't want to be nearby when someone pokes them with a stick."

"That goes for you too, Alexa. I understand the state police are doing drive-bys out on the main road. For now, you need to be very cautious. Stick to main roads. Set your security alarm. Don't walk alone. Maybe these people only wanted to put the fear of God into you. But maybe they'll be back again." Carter rose from his seat to leave.

Alexa's shoulders sagged. The FBI agent had voiced her biggest fear: that, whatever the reason, these scary people were not finished with their attempts to 'educate' her.

When the agents left, Alexa quipped, "I guess that rules out the hot tub for tonight."

Reese was not amused. "He's right. You shouldn't be alone. Monday, when you're at work, I'll drive home and pick up all my work materials. I'll be back by the time you're home, and I'll stay until this blows over."

"Don't you have to go into the Trust offices? You can't disrupt everything for me."

"Not a big deal. We're doing a final review of the expanded report this week, which is mostly reading and editing. And the rest I can do by phone."

"Don't forget to bring your tux."

"Of course. Hard to believe I actually own a tux. But, with all these Trust events, it's cheaper than renting."

"Michaels. Reese Michaels," Alexa said, mimicking the phrasing of James Bond's introduction.

"Right. Reese Michaels, international man of mystery."

"That's not James Bond. That's Austin Powers." Alexa's voice softened. "You're much more the James Bond type, as far as I'm concerned." With a suggestive look, she pulled him down onto the couch, ignoring the twinge in her wrist.

# CHAPTER THIRTY-FIVE

BY TUESDAY, ALEXA'S wrist was all but healed, and she was chafing at the necessity of looking over her shoulder every few minutes. She called Reese at the cabin. "I really need to go to yoga. For my mental health. I'll just spend a few minutes afterwards with the gang at the Om Café. And I'll make sure that someone walks me to my car. Tyrell, if he's there tonight."

Reese replied in a bemused tone, "I knew it wouldn't last for long."

"What?"

"The shock; the panic. I'm not saying you aren't still exercising caution. But I figured you'd drift back into your routine soon."

"You're right. I'm not going to cower in the corner somewhere. But it's wonderful that you're staying at the cabin. I'd be pretty jumpy if I was alone there at night."

"Gotta go. I have a phone meeting in about five minutes. I'll see you when you get home," Reese signed off.

Isabella focused the yoga session on twists and deep breathing, almost as if she knew Alexa needed a meditative practice. When a yoga session really clicked, Alexa became so focused that she drifted into the stillness of the moment. Tonight was one of those nights as intruding thoughts of angry messages, Skeleton Man, and even the joy that was Reese all fell away and she reached a meditative state.

Alexa was still floating when she and her friends headed to the Om Café after class.

On the short walk to the café, Sloane said, "Tonight's session was so relaxing. I'm glad I discovered yoga. It gives me a rare sense of peace."

Alexa smiled. "Yes. Yoga can be wonderful. It's almost the polar opposite of Krav Maga. I wasn't sure you'd get into it."

"Opposite in some ways. The same in others. Both disciplines require you to be totally in the moment. Both require physical skill and flexibility." Sloane smiled and lowered her voice. "I'll confess, I wasn't sure I was going to like yoga. Like you say, it didn't seem to be my thing. But when Haley suggested it, I thought why not?"

As Sloane preceded her through the door to Om, Alexa felt a twinge of sympathy for the woman. She was an accomplished businesswoman, a good companion. But it was hard to figure out what it would take for Sloane to drain the moat that surrounded her castle of loneliness.

Inside, the minute they ordered, Melissa announced, "Jim and I have set a date."

Haley caught on first and chirped, "I love weddings. When?"

"June twenty-first."

Tyrell smiled. "Congratulations. So, you're going the traditional June bride route?"

Melissa looked taken aback. "June bride? No. It's the Summer Solstice. What better day to celebrate our marriage than the longest day of the year? We'll have it in the evening since it's a weekday."

"Wonderful." Alexa clasped Melissa's hand. "I'll be there."

Sloane was more reserved. "I wish you much happiness, Melissa."

Alexa remembered the private conversation she'd had with Sloane before the holidays. Melissa's good news must have awakened memories of Sloane's own marriage, cut short at first bloom.

"Is everyone psyched about the Winter Ball?" Haley hooted, stepping on Melissa's news.

Tyrell, who was seated next to her, rubbed his ear. "Damn, girl. You gonna bust my eardrum. This is the Om Café, not the Gingerbread Man. That shriek just wiped out the chill I had on from yoga."

Haley ignored him. "I have Winter Ball fever. I went down to King of Prussia on Saturday and got a new dress. It's a vision. All silvery and shimmery." She whispered, "I didn't tell Blair how much it cost. What are you all wearing?"

"A penguin suit," Tyrell answered in a sulky voice.

"Sorry, I meant the ladies," Haley said.

"Sexist," Tyrell muttered.

"I'm not sure," Melissa laughed, ignoring Tyrell. "You know I go with my mood. I'll pull something out of my closet on Friday afternoon."

Alexa smiled. "Melissa. Remember the Chanel that the Townes family gave me?" She turned to Tyrell. "It belonged to Cecily, in her debutante days, before she went into the convent. So it's vintage. This is the first chance I'll have to wear it."

"Sweet." Melissa bounced in her chair.

Alexa stifled a smile at Haley, whose face had fallen at the word 'Chanel' but perked up again when she heard that it was vintage. Haley was more of a brand-new-is-better type of girl.

Sloane looked glum. Alexa wondered if the holidays had been hard on her. Except for their brief exchange earlier, Sloane's thoughts seemed somewhere else tonight.

Haley either hadn't noticed or didn't care. "Sloane, what about you?"

Sloane gave her a blank look.

"Your dress. Do you have one picked out for the ball?" Haley asked again.

"Oh. I'm in Melissa's camp. I have a few possibilities in mind. When I worked for State overseas, attending cocktail parties and official dinners was part of the job. Most of those dresses have been collecting dust in the back of my closet. So, I have quite a few choices. You're right; I better get on that since the event is Friday."

Alexa downed the last of her chai. "Tyrell, can you walk me to my car?"

Tyrell looked surprised, then replied in a smooth tone, "Does Reese know that you're inviting hot men into the parking lot?"

She laughed. "Yeah, he does. I promised him I wouldn't walk to the car alone."

Melissa leaned forward. "What's going on? There's more to this story."

Alexa told them about the group of people who had accosted her along the road last Thursday night, downplaying the danger. She also mentioned the earlier incident when the guy in the pickup followed her from the Om Café.

"From here?" Haley squealed.

"Why? Is this something to do with your law practice? A case?" Melissa crossed her arms. "We're still not getting the whole story," she echoed her earlier statement.

Alexa glanced at Tyrell. "Probably just some more of the blowback from those protests about Bassam Qassim's arrest. And the rumors about terrorism. Since Tyrell and I were on the news with the Qassim family, I've been getting a lot of crank calls."

Tyrell looked dismayed. "I never meant to put you in danger when I asked for legal advice for the Qassims. We got similar calls at RESIST, but they tapered off before Christmas. I had no idea you had all this going on."

"Reese is spending this week at the cabin. The police told me to be extra careful for the next week or so."

"Do they know who these people are?" Haley asked. "I didn't see anything about it in the news."

"I don't think any news outlets picked it up—which is fine with me."

Sloane had been stirring her coffee in a desultory way. She raised her pale blue eyes to look at Alexa. "I still feel bad about Bassam. The boy loved Taekwondo. I'm glad you're unharmed."

Alexa shot Sloane a wicked grin. "You'll be glad to know that I used what I'll call a modified Krav Maga move on one of the guys who stopped me. I was fresh from class. And he made the mistake of leaning through the open window."

"Wait. Are you saying that one of these people followed you from Courage?" Sloane sat up.

"The parking lot was crowded. He could have been sitting there waiting for me to leave. He could have been somewhere nearby. I don't know."

"Maybe we should consider better lighting or a camera for the parking lot. It never occurred to me that I would need that level of security in a small town like Carlisle."

Haley leapt in. "Very good idea. The Chamber advises all its members to go the extra mile when it comes to safety and security of customers."

At that, Alexa rose. "See you all on Friday at the social event of the season. I think that's what my mom's calling it these days."

"I'm looking forward to it." The rancor in Sloane's tone seemed at odds with her words.

"See you," Haley said.

"Take care." Melissa waved.

"Congratulations," Alexa said again. "We'll talk."

"I'll be back in a moment. Don't touch that muffin," Tyrell cautioned as he stood.

On the way to the parking lot, Alexa whispered. "What's with Sloane tonight?"

"Not sure. Could be Haley rubbed her the wrong way. Sometimes that woman doesn't know when to quit. But Sloane's been offish for the past few weeks. If I knew her better, I'd recommend some grief counseling."

"Always the social worker. But sometimes you can't fix everyone's problems. They have to figure it out on their own."

"Don't I know it." Tyrell stood by the Land Rover until Alexa buckled her seat belt. "Stay on the main roads." He laughed. "Oh, right. There are no main roads out in the boonies where you live. You get my drift though." He closed the driver's door.

As Alexa pulled out of the parking lot, she could see Tyrell still standing there, watching. She instructed her phone to call Reese and waited for him to pick up. "Hey. I'm just leaving Om. Should be home in twenty minutes."

"Got it. Dinner's in the oven."

"Another bonus of having you work from the cabin. I'm so lucky." Alexa ended the call and drove home.

# CHAPTER THIRTY-SIX

*November and December 1859*

Keep your hand on that plow and hold on.
                    —*"Hold On," a Negro spiritual*

*"Sit in the back and stay quiet," Deacon McClure whispered to Elijah as they entered the courthouse in Charles Town, Virginia. They'd left Chambersburg long before dawn to make it in time for the proceedings.*

*Nervous, Elijah watched the deacon make his way through the crowd to shake hands with a well-dressed man, standing by a row of benches. That must be Mr. Branford, a Virginian who the deacon did business with, thought Elijah; Branford had arranged a seat for the deacon at this explosive trial.*

*Elijah found a place against the back wall and wedged onto the narrow bench. He was taking a chance coming back to Virginia yet again, even though the deacon could vouch for his papers that declared him a free man and a clerk in the lumber business. But, Elijah owed it to the fallen Coleman to attend the trial of his hero and commander, John Brown.*

*From the daily reports that had filled the newspapers and dominated the conversation in Chambersburg, Elijah knew the trial had been contentious. The deacon had told him, "I'm afraid Mr. Brown doesn't have much of a chance. Judge, jury, and local public opinion are united against him and the other five men who survived the raid. Virginia folk didn't take kindly to an abolitionist* attacking one of their towns, killing their citizens, and trying to raise an insurrection of slaves. They think of Mr. Brown as the barbaric murderer of Pottawatomie, Kansas."

Elijah had swallowed hard at the deacon's words. 'Barbaric murderer'? He'd always been a little scared of the towering Mr. Brown, especially when the imposing man burned bright with the fire of God. But if he was a madman and his cause a fool's errand, had Coleman died in vain? Elijah shook his head. He couldn't accept that.

Late yesterday, the deacon's pessimism about the trial had been borne out by news telegraphed to Chambersburg. After a trial lasting more than a week, the jury had deliberated less than an hour and found Mr. Brown guilty of treason, murder, and inciting a slave insurrection.

Today, Mr. Brown would be sentenced. Deacon McClure had suggested that he and Elijah make this trip to support Mr. Brown with their presence. Elijah could see that the deacon felt wretched in the aftermath of the raid. The man had lost weight. Late at night, he paced the courtyard outside Elijah's window. He'd heard Mrs. McClure call the deacon's state of despair a "moral dilemma." The deacon had supported Mr. Brown with help and money. He'd been in favor of the idea of the raid and a slave rebellion. But he was also afraid that his role in the plan might be discovered, and that he would be arrested.

Elijah was mourning Coleman. And he felt sad that Mr. Brown's raid had failed. He would have liked to see all the slaves in the South rise up against the masters and escape bondage. Then he could have gone home to bring Mama and his sisters away from the plantation. But his conscience was clear. He kept to his assigned role in the raid until it was obvious it was a bust. Then, he'd managed to find his way back to Chambersburg, walking for three days and dodging army patrols along the way.

A rapping sound from the front caught Elijah's attention, and a voice cried, "All rise." A solemn-faced man in a black robe took a seat behind a high table. The deacon had said Mr. Brown would be sentenced first thing. Confused, Elijah didn't understand why another one of the raiders, Edwin Coppock, was brought into the courtroom.

Then, he heard a man nearby whisper, "They're going to try Coppock first."

For several hours, important-looking men gave long speeches and questioned a series of people. A lot of it went over Elijah's head, but most of the speakers seemed hell-bent on making Coppock out to be as bad as the devil himself. Although they never said it, some of the men seemed afraid. He finally figured out that they feared what could have happened: that Coppock and Brown could have prevailed, and the slaves could have risen against their masters.

Elijah connected with the deacon at an early afternoon break and ate a little of the food they'd brought. Not long after they returned to the courtroom, a man rose and declared, "We the jury find Edwin Coppock guilty of all counts."

Then, there was rustling through the crowd as a group of men carried in a man on a stretcher. When the prone man turned his head, Elijah recognized Mr. Brown. He'd heard that Mr. Brown had been injured and could see cuts and bruises on his forehead.

Elijah tried to pay attention as a man spoke about dismissing judgment. It seemed the man was speaking on behalf of Mr. Brown. Although Elijah didn't know exactly what this meant, his heart dropped when the judge said, "Motion denied," and a buzz swept through the courtroom.

Then, the clerk turned to the cot and asked, "Mr. Brown. Do wish to say anything before sentence is pronounced?"

Elijah held his breath as Mr. Brown arose, looking tentative, and said in a halting voice, "I have, may it please the court, a few words to say." Then, Mr. Brown drew himself tall and spoke in a clear voice. "In the first place, I deny everything but what I have all along admitted: the design on my part to free slaves." He continued for several minutes about his past actions in Missouri and commented on the trial itself.

Elijah noticed that the entire courtroom was hanging onto Brown's every word as he continued. "Had I so interfered in behalf of the rich, the powerful, the intelligent, the so-called great, or in behalf of any of their friends, either father, mother, brother, sister, wife, or children, or any of that class, and suffered and sacrificed what I have in this interference, it would have been all right; and every man in this court would have deemed it an act worthy of reward rather than punishment.

"This court acknowledges, as I suppose, the validity of the law of God. I see a book kissed here, which I suppose to be the Bible, or at least the New Testament, that teaches me that all things whatsoever I would that men should do to me, I should do even so to them. It teaches me, further, to 'remember them that are in bonds, as bound with them.' I endeavor to act up to that instruction. I say, I am yet too young to understand that God is any respecter of persons. I believe that to have interfered as I have done, as I have always freely admitted I have done, in behalf of His despised poor, was not *wrong, but right. Now, if it is deemed necessary that I should forfeit my life for the furtherance of the ends of justice, and mingle my blood further with the blood of my children and with the blood of millions in this slave country whose rights are disregarded by wicked, cruel, and unjust enactments, I submit; so let it be done!"*

*Mr. Brown spoke for a few minutes more, but Elijah could barely process the words. He was thinking of Coleman, who had given his life to try to end slavery, and that he must have died proud that he was doing something so important.*

*Elijah concentrated again on Mr. Brown when he heard him say, "Now I have done." For a few minutes, the old man stood there with a bleak look in his eyes that soon gave way to the burning fervor that Elijah recognized.*

*The courtroom broke into a loud hubbub until the judge banged his hammer. When the noise quieted, the judge said, "John Brown, I sentence you to hang by the neck until dead. May God rest your soul."*

*Most of the people in the courtroom cheered while Elijah sat silent. Although the deacon had prepared him for this verdict, to hear it said stunned him to his core. John Brown was a force of nature. It seemed impossible that such a man could die, although he knew all men were mortal. Even white men had to pay for their crimes, and Brown and the rest of his raiders had killed people.*

*But, Elijah understood that, to the judge and jury and most of the spectators here, Brown's bigger crime had been to imagine that slaves could be freed, that colored men should have the same rights as white men. Looking at the celebration all around him, Elijah was seized by the sudden fear that someone would look at him and know he was an escaped slave. That they'd take him back to the plantation. He slipped out the back door and headed straight to Deacon McClure's wagon.*

*Elijah and Deacon McClure drove in silence until they had traveled well beyond Charles Town. Then, the deacon pulled off the road next to a grove of trees. Elijah was glad for the protection the small woods offered from the biting November wind. The deacon handed him a sack with some food and lifted a jug of water to the seat between them.*

*"Are you all right, sir?" Elijah asked. The deacon had been deathly pale since they'd walked out of the courthouse.*

*"I knew it likely that he would—they all would—hang. But hearing it like that was hard. I know even some in the abolitionist camp think*

*old Brown goes too far. That violence ain't the answer to cruelty and oppression. Especially the Quakers preach that we ain't true to God's will if we engage in bloodshed, no matter how mighty the cause. And I have to admit that sometimes Brown burns with a righteousness that seems to border on madness. But it's madness for a holy cause."*

*The deacon pointed to several huge black birds with scaly red heads, perched on the bare branches of a nearby tree. "Look yonder, Elijah. Most people recoil from those scavengers. But, I believe turkey vultures are God's way of teaching us about equality. A vulture will rip off the flesh of a dead man, no matter if his skin is white or black. And, beneath that skin, our bones look just the same. God made our outside look different, but the vulture reveals God's message: that on the inside, we're all the same. John Brown is like those birds; willing to strip off the skin to get at the core of God's truth."*

*The deacon jiggled the reins and the horses trotted back to the road. At the noise, the vultures scattered, ascending into the clouds. He whispered, as if to himself, "I never thought they'd kill anybody on this raid."*

*Elijah replied, "But they had a lot of guns."*

*"I guess I was living in a fool's world of books and the beauty of the word of God. I should have known the Virginians would fight back. I should have known that a slave uprising would mean bloodshed."*

*"Deacon, Mrs. McClure wouldn't want you to get yourself in such a state," Elijah said in a calming tone.*

*"You're right. We can be glad you made it back from the raid, even though Coleman fell. Mrs. McClure and I have a proposition for you. I like your work at the sawmill, and Mrs. McClure likes having you around the house to help with chores. We were hoping you'd bide with us a while in Chambersburg. You and Coleman had planned to head north. And we can send you north through the network, if that's your wish. But we'd be pleased to have you make your home with us until you're ready to move on."*

*Elijah was stunned. For a moment, he was silent as he absorbed the invitation. He had worried about traveling alone to Massachusetts, which would be a frightening and unfamiliar place without Coleman by his side. He ventured a shy smile. "Thank you. I be quite partial to Chambersburg, and you have been so kind to me. Yes. Yes, I'll stay."*

*The deacon patted Elijah's arm. "Excellent. There is a risk. Although we've had no trouble with the law or the patrollers, we could be rousted. You could get swept up and returned south. But your papers are good. The men who prepare those papers for us have people in free Negro communities who will vouch for their truth. And you've lived here without incident for almost four months. People in the town know you by sight."*

*"I'm much obliged, Deacon. I want to stay."*

As Elijah settled deeper into the routines of his new home, the aftermath of the Harpers Ferry incident swirled throughout the country. Mrs. McClure was helping him improve his vocabulary skills by reading newspapers. And the past month's articles had been filled with competing opinions on John Brown's failed raid.

Details of Brown's new constitution were found in the Sharpsburg farmhouse, and his plan to free slaves far into the South emerged. Coupled with Brown's use of force, most in the South railed against Brown and cursed his ideas as more dangerous than Nat Turner. The most extreme used Brown's raid as an argument for secession from the Union.

Among northern abolitionists, opinions diverged. Prominent voices like Henry David Thoreau and Ralph Waldo Emerson hailed Brown as a visionary who had done what was necessary to end slavery. Others like Nathaniel Hawthorne decried Brown's extremism and worried that it would lead to war.

Moderate politicians like Abraham Lincoln of Illinois, who was running for the Senate, admired Brown's goals but warned that his tactics were flawed.

Elijah read these articles and discussed them with Deacon and Mrs. McClure, but his attention was focused more on exploring his new town and settling into his job. One afternoon, he skidded into the kitchen after work. "Sorry I'm a few minutes late, ma'am."

Mrs. McClure smiled. "You're just in time. We have guests arriving tomorrow; seven is what the deacon was told to expect. Can you go freshen the bedding with straw? Make sure there are candles. And then come back here and help me sort through the store of clothes we can offer them."

When Elijah returned from his tasks, Deacon and Mrs. McClure were seated together at the table. He was holding his wife's hand, and her eyes were wet with tears."

The deacon looked up when Elijah entered. "We've had bad news. You may as well hear it too. John Brown was hanged yesterday. A great man has fallen."

Elijah felt like he'd been punched in the gut. Grief for Coleman came back in a rush and deepened his reaction to Brown's death. He whispered, "I'm sorry to hear of it. What about the others?" He thought of the other men who'd been captured, most of them not much older than himself.

"They only have a few days longer." The deacon looked back at Mrs. McClure, whose weeping had intensified.

He continued. "The newspapers report that Brown sent a last note by one of his guards. I'll read it to you. 'I, John Brown, am now quite certain that the crimes of this guilty land will never be purged away but with blood. I had, as I now think vainly, flattered myself that without very much bloodshed it might be done.'"

Through barely suppressed tears, Elijah contemplated Mr. Brown's words, then said, "A white man who is willing to die to end the slavery of colored men. That be something to admire. Word will get out and slaves on the plantations will praise John Brown's name."

Mrs. McClure managed a sad smile. "I imagine they will. And Mr. Brown will be standing before the God he so loved in life."

The next afternoon, Elijah helped Mrs. McClure get a new group of escaped slaves settled into the secret room in the barn. He served them food and tended to their cuts and bruises. Even below ground, the early December chill penetrated the crawl space; he fetched another blanket for each of their guests.

"Is we in Canaan yet?" one thin young man asked.

"No. But you're in the North; above the Mason-Dixon Line. We still have patrollers in Pennsylvania, so you're not safe yet. But, each day, the network will move you farther north. By Christmas, you'll be beyond the patrollers' reach."

"Praise the Lord," an older woman whispered.

As he always did, Elijah scanned the faces to see if he recognized any of these travelers. He continued to hope that, someday, a runaway from his old plantation or one nearby would appear. And he would be able to ask about his mother and sisters. But he knew no one from this group. He asked, "How far have you traveled?"

"A long distance."

"We traveled on a river and then walked from full moon to new moon."

"A man and a woman took us in their cart."

As the chorus of voices shared their stories, Elijah reached into his pocket and touched Coleman's tinderbox. He thought of Coleman and Mama with a wistful longing then rose to his feet and said, "The journey is long and hard, but it's worth it. Praise the Lord who guided us to freedom."

# CHAPTER THIRTY-SEVEN

ALEXA'S DAY HAD been crazy busy, with a court appearance in the morning and back-to-back meetings all afternoon. At three-thirty, Alexa escorted her last client to the door, surprised to see Melinda still at her desk.

"I thought you were going to leave at three?"

"I wanted to finish these letters. Have a clean desk for Monday."

"Nope. They can wait. Go home; get glamorous for the ball. I'm going to take a catnap on the couch before I get dressed. Reese said he'd pick me up at five-thirty."

Melinda powered down her computer and gathered her things. "You're right. George refused a clip-on tie with his tux rental; wanted the real thing. So, I need extra time to help him get that tied right." She threw on her coat. "I'll look for you. I'm excited. So glad the firm decided to sponsor a table."

After Melinda raced toward the exit, Alexa locked her door and set her phone alarm for a twenty-minute nap. She stretched out on the couch, snuggled under a warm throw, and went right to sleep.

The twenty minutes ended much too quickly. Alexa knew she'd catch her second wind before the ball, but she wished that the committee had scheduled it for a Saturday. Her mother had explained something about availability of the Heritage Center and another War College event.

Her gown had been hanging in the coat closet all day. Thanks to one of the original partners in the law firm who had liked to run at lunchtime, each partner's office had a small bathroom. Before she went in for a shower, Alexa took the rest of her evening attire, makeup, and a towel out of a large leather tote. She'd packed the bag yesterday morning, knowing that she had to leave early for court today.

"Oh, no," Alexa moaned aloud. "No shoes."

She ran to the phone and dialed Reese, hoping he was still at the cabin.

"Hi. You caught me on the way out the door. Do you want me to pick you up at the front door or in the parking lot?"

"I have a fashion emergency," Alexa cried. "I don't have my shoes."

"Are they here? Describe them and I'll go upstairs and find them. Problem solved."

"You can bring me the black pair in a clear box on the top shelf. They have red soles. Only pair of Louboutins that I have left."

"Lou Bartons?" Reese sounded confused.

"Black. You'll know you have the right ones from the red soles. But they're not the ones I wanted to wear. I wanted to wear the black velvet Manolo Blahniks with the crystal buckle. They're perfect for the Chanel dress. I know exactly what happened. I packed two bags yesterday morning, one for Krav Maga; one for today. I stuck the shoes in the gym bag by mistake. I put them in my locker at Courage during class and forgot them. What an idiot."

"You're sure they're not in the gym bag? I could check."

"No. I dumped the whole thing out after I got home last night. Didn't think about the missing shoes.

"New plan," Alexa said. "Why don't we do this? I'm going to run over there now. The shoes should still be in the locker. I'll text you the phone number for access to the back gate of the Heritage Center and I'll just meet you there."

Alexa fretted on the drive across town to Courage. She hoped no one had stolen her prized Manolo Blahniks bought just before she left New York City. They were practically brand new. She skidded to a stop in the parking lot and jumped out of the Land Rover.

Alexa raced down the hall to the locker room, but the locker was empty. No shoes. She checked several lockers on either side of the one she'd used, just to make sure. Distressed, Alexa stepped back out into the corridor where she ran into KC.

"Aren't you supposed to be at that fancy ball with Sloane?" KC asked.

"Yes, but I left my shoes here last evening. Long story."

"Black party shoes with a fancy crystal thing on them? They should be in the Lost and Found."

"Where's that?" Alexa brightened.

"Down by the main office." KC gestured for Alexa to follow her back toward the entrance. When they reached a small office, KC picked up a box from the floor and pawed through the contents. "Nope. Not in here."

Alexa leaned over her shoulder to look at the collection of sweatshirts, hair bands, and a single sneaker. She sighed in disappointment.

KC dropped the box to the floor. "Maybe Sloane put the shoes in her office. She said something about the shoes being expensive. She was sure the owner would claim them."

She opened a door down the hall. "You can go in and check. I have to get back to class. Turn off the light and close the door when you leave. If the shoes aren't there, check with Sloane next week."

"Thanks, KC."

"No problem. Nice makeup, by the way. But I hope you're wearing something a little more elegant than sweats to go with those fancy shoes." She laughed at her own joke as she rushed back down the hall.

Alexa flipped the light switch and stepped into a small office that housed a desk and two chairs. A bookcase filled the back wall, and, there, on one of the shelves, were the prize shoes nestled beside a stack of T-shirts. As Alexa moved toward them, she noticed how bare the office was. No photos. No personal items except for martial arts trophies. The books on the shelves seemed to focus on Krav Maga and Taekwondo.

When Alexa slid the shoes from the shelf, she knocked a Courage T-shirt to the floor. She dropped to her knees to retrieve the shirt. It had tumbled under the well of the desk and lay next to a small roll of Persian carpet. Alexa snagged the shirt and placed it back on the pile of tees, neatly folded. When she turned to leave the office, Alexa saw that Sloane had, in fact, made a minimal attempt at office décor: Two framed prints that looked like those standard inspirational posters on teamwork or success. On closer inspection, Alexa could see that these were more unusual in their choice of quotes. One said: "Set your life on fire. Seek those who fan your flames."

Rumi, right? She'd had a roommate at Columbia who was a total Rumi disciple, and these lines seemed familiar. Maybe because her roommate, Faith, had a habit of flying too close to those flames before crashing and burning.

Alexa couldn't place the origin of the quote on the second poster. While familiar, it wasn't very inspirational: "I am quite certain that the crimes of this guilty nation shall never be purged away but with blood."

On her way out of the office, shoes in hand, Alexa reflected that she had a lot to learn about her new friend. Sloane was a complex and moody woman. Had she always been so intense and driven? Or was her husband's untimely death behind the zeal that drove her to perfection at Krav Maga and making Courage a success?

Grinning at her foray into amateur psychology, Alexa shook her head. Maybe you should stick to a few gentle suggestions on interior design, she thought. Like some more upbeat prints. Even those crap motivational ones would be better than Sloane's choices. Remembering the carpet sample under the desk, Alexa brightened. A carpet would improve the ambience.

As she drove the dark road to the Heritage Center, Alexa giggled at KC's parting remarks about her outfit. Her plan was to slip into a small room near the back door and don the dress and shoes. She envisioned the picture she'd presented to KC and laughed again. Perfectly made-up face, baggy sweats, L.L. Bean duck boots, and a full-length fur coat. Alexa had picked up this faux fur, in a dark brown called "Soft Seal," during her days in the big city. This one had been a particularly off-the-wall purchase when she'd gone to a fashion show with several of her girlfriends. Alexa broke into giggles again. Now that she thought about her outfit, she realized that the buttoned-up KC had actually been quite restrained in her comments.

The Heritage Center was blazing with lights as Alexa drove by. Like all the planning committee members, she had parking privileges in the back of the center. At the far edge of the property, she turned left into the back-entrance road. She coasted up to the closed gate and dialed the security office on the phone. Waiting for someone to answer, she wrinkled her nose at the smell of skunk. On the far side of the gate, the remains of a small carcass rested on the road. It had been ravaged by vultures or other scavengers that had left nothing but some scraps of fur and the pungent odor. Odd, because it was still too cold for small critters like skunks and opossums to emerge from their dens.

"Hello. Can I have your name, please?"

"Alexa Williams."

After a pause, the man on the other end of the line said, "All right. You're on our list. Drive on in."

Since she hadn't helped with the setup earlier in the day, this was Alexa's first trip down the lane that skirted the back of the Heritage Center complex. There were a few lights, but the road seemed dark compared to the floodlit parking lot out front. She kept her speed slow, aided by a series of speed bumps. When she reached the far end of the drive, Alexa noted the building entrance and searched for a parking space. All the spaces were full.

Alexa spied a sliver of asphalt on the far side of the last car in the lot. She couldn't deal with toting her dress a half-mile. Hoping that they didn't give out parking tickets, she backed the Land Rover into the snow next to that last car. Its left tires touched the asphalt; that had to count for something, right?

Behind the car was a natural hedgerow. Whatever was beyond, probably the War College golf course, was swallowed up by darkness. Alexa sat in the dark car and sent Reese a text. "Just parking. I'll be inside soon."

She gathered her phone, her evening purse, and the precious Manolo Blahniks into a small tote. She'd have to walk around to the back door to retrieve her dress, which meant trudging through some snow. She giggled. It was good that she was still wearing those duck boots that had given KC such a kick.

Just as Alexa reached for the door handle, she caught a flash of movement out of the corner of her eye. She stopped and peered through the windshield, trying to pinpoint what she'd seen. To her right, the outdoor exhibits for the Heritage Center dotted the landscape along the Army Heritage Trail. The path, which wound in a loop at least a mile long, featured historical artifacts of war: re-creations of GI barracks from World War II and cabins from the Civil War; an assortment of helicopters, tanks, and other armaments representing America's various conflicts. The motion that Alexa had seen was out near the WWI fortifications that depicted how the soldiers in that war had dug deep trenches at the battlefront.

There. She saw it again. A man? No, two men, dressed in white, passed by a tank that sat on the ridge. The white gear made Alexa immediately think of Skeleton Man, or as Agent Purcell had called him, the Snowman. Would the Blizzardwaffen disrupt a ball raising money for refugee programs?

Alexa's hand went to her phone, but she hesitated. These people could just as easily be part of the Heritage Center security team. She should check it out before calling it in. Her mother would kill her if she triggered some sort of incident and it turned out to be the good guys. But what if it was the Blizzardwaffen? She had to know.

# CHAPTER THIRTY-EIGHT

ALEXA HIT A switch to deactivate the door light and slipped out the driver's side. She circled behind the Land Rover, keeping to the shadows. Then, still in shadow, she darted past two small maintenance buildings and across a few yards of open field to the cluster of replica World War II barracks. Almost a foot of yesterday's snowfall covered the ground, muffling Alexa's footsteps as she ran. She was surprised to feel a warmer breeze on her cheeks, as if the temperature had risen.

The cluster of buildings sat in a rough square. She ran to the back of the closest building and stopped to listen. Although she knew that ball guests were pouring into the Heritage Center, the main entrance was far away; so distant that, out here, everything was silent and still. She couldn't even hear traffic from the nearby interstate.

Alexa walked to the left corner of the wood-and-tarpaper barracks. A light by the back door of the Heritage Center bathed the side of the barracks in a weak glow. Her dark fur coat and black sweatpants helped her blend into the shadows, but Alexa worried that her silhouette would be visible against the white snow even in this dim light.

She took a deep breath and rushed along the outside wall, feeling like a moth in a spotlight. She emerged into the makeshift courtyard in the center of the buildings. As she'd hoped, the barracks on the left blocked the light, plunging this central area into dark shadow. It took Alexa a few moments to regain her night vision. In the process, she stumbled over a rough patch of ground but regained her balance.

Breathing hard, more from fright than exertion, she crept to the back wall of the biggest building. She recalled from a walk here with Courtney and Jamie that this was a replica of a typical World War II repair center. This building sat on a straight line of sight to the ridge above the World War I trenches where she'd seen the suspicious movement. The trenches were maybe sixty feet away.

Alexa skirted the back of the structure, tiptoeing to the right, keeping to the dark side. She edged around the corner and found an entry door. She tugged on the door handle, but as expected, the building was locked. Moving forward, she hugged the tarpaper wall as she crept to the front corner. Looking out toward the trenches, her shoulders slumped.

Damn. The ground where she stood was much lower than the ridge and its guardian tank where she'd seen the men in white. The rise impeded Alexa's view of the fortifications behind the ridge. Even worse, a light ground fog was now hovering over the open field, giving everything out there an impressionist feel. Discouraged, Alexa decided to stop skulking around in the cold, like some sort of junior G-man. Reese was probably waiting inside, wondering why she was late.

Besides, would the Blizzardwaffen group really try to disrupt such a large gathering, knowing the entire Army War College, with its garrison of soldiers, was only minutes away? A protest or some act of disruption against refugees and the people who supported them might grab some satisfying headlines. But it could also get many of their members thrown in jail.

Abandoning her Keystone Kops spy mission, Alexa elected to call the Heritage Center security number. She could simply ask if there were guards out on the trail as part of tonight's security protocol. That's what she should have done right off the bat. Shielding the phone light with her coat, Alexa tapped in her pin and found the number she'd used at the gate. Ready to hit redial, she paused. More movement. There was something going on near the trenches.

Rising onto her tiptoes, Alexa was able to get a clearer view. A figure in white ran along the misty ridge and then abruptly slipped down the backside into the trenches. Her mouth turned dry when she processed what he'd been holding in his right hand, silhouetted against the white of his clothing: A long black gun. An assault rifle.

"Oh my God," she gulped as her thoughts flew to the night the white supremacist group had stopped her along the creek. They had all been heavily armed and dangerous. What if this was the militia group, and they had a much darker intent than simple protest?

Alexa hit Call as she rose, making a swift retreat to the back of the mess hall. She rushed back around the corner, pulling up short at the sight of a ghostly figure in white standing in the middle of the dark courtyard.

"Hello? Hello? This is Security."

As the voice on Alexa's phone answered, the figure in white said in a muffled voice, "I don't think so."

Alexa took off, racing toward the back barracks, coat flapping. Her feet slipped on the icy snow as she screamed into the phone. "Help, men with guns on the Heritage Trail. Help."

In a few swift strides, the man overtook Alexa and knocked the phone from her hand with a sharp jab to her bent elbow. The phone went flying into the snow several feet away.

Alexa kept running, hoping to circle around the barracks and make it to the back door of the main hall. But the big man stopped her short as his arm looped around her torso like a steel band. He placed his other hand in the center of her back and dragged her back into the courtyard. This guy was incredibly strong, but Alexa struggled against his grip. She tried the move she'd learned in Krav Maga, tucking her chin and pressing a shoulder against his chest. But, he had created a space between them that made it impossible. She resorted to twisting and kicking, even though her feet couldn't touch the ground. The minute they were back in the shadowy courtyard, he loosened his hold and came to an abrupt stop. She rocked onto her feet and tried to regain her balance, still imprisoned in the circle of his arm.

"I'm not going to hurt you," the muffled voice said.

"How can I believe you?" Alexa didn't trust him at all but thought it was better to try to engage the guy.

"Settle down. But don't turn around. I don't want you to see my face." The man spoke in a soft, soothing tone. His one arm still held her trapped against his body.

Alexa obeyed, waiting for an opening. Another chance to flee. She hoped against hope that the dispatcher in Security had been able to hear her plea for help. Alexa blanched and swayed on her feet when she heard a whispery rustle. She'd learned that sound of metal on nylon in Krav Maga, and it always signaled a weapon; the kind that could kill you in silence like a knife or a garrote. She understood that he didn't want to use a gun and give away his position.

She tensed her body and flinched when the man slid his hand to rest loosely on one arm. "You can turn around now."

Instead, Alexa slipped right out of her bulky fur coat and bolted through the rising mist. Toward the light. Toward the Heritage Center.

"Bitch." It took a moment for the man to toss the coat to the ground before he raced after Alexa. His footsteps pounded through the snow behind her. Alexa knew that the big man had the edge over her with his longer stride. He grabbed at her sweatshirt. He was closing in. Taking a huge chance, she whirled to face her oncoming pursuer. Using a basic Krav Maga move, she launched a kick into his groin and prepared to chop a hand against his head when he doubled over. But her boot slipped on the nylon of his snow pants, blunting the impact of her kick.

Alexa's move caught the man off-guard for a moment. He dropped the knife he was holding into the snow.

When man bent to retrieve the knife, Alexa turned and kept running. But he caught up in just a few steps. Feeling him closing in, Alexa turned to confront him. Stay fierce. Wasn't that what Lev and KC had taught her?

When Alexa moved in close and threw a series of punches at his face, the big man parried her attack with a swift chop to her arm, shocking Alexa to the core. A Krav Maga expert? What were the odds?

The two battled through a series of parries and counter offenses, but this man had the advantage of both strength and skill against Alexa. She was tiring. Her only play was to draw him out into the light and hope someone would come to help. With each exchange, Alexa slid a few steps toward the parking lot.

"I don't have time for this shit." The man in white seized Alexa and threw her backwards several yards.

She hit the ground hard and rolled into a gully, glad for the cushion of snow. Alexa willed her body to scramble away, but she couldn't breathe. She couldn't move. Her relentless attacker stalked down the slope toward her. He dropped to his knees beside her, gripping a knife in his hand.

Alexa gagged at the acrid smell of the man's sweat. A drop hit her face, and Alexa gasped out a muffled scream. Desperate, she rocked her body, trying to escape.

Images of Reese, Scout, and her parents flashed through Alexa's mind. She couldn't give up. She took a deep breath of the misty air and rolled onto her side. Freezing snow burned her exposed waist. Alexa rose to her knees.

But the man grabbed her shoulder and flipped her back to the ground. He straddled her body, pinning her down. Above his mask, Alexa could see the wild look in his dark eyes.

"You interfered in the mission. An eye for an eye," he whispered and raised to his knees. His knife plunged toward her chest.

"No," Alexa screamed. She grabbed his descending arm with both her hands and brought her knee upward. She heard an "oomph" as her knee grazed his groin. Then he recovered and leaned forward. Alexa pushed against his lower arm with all the strength she had. But the knife came closer. Closer.

A bright light hit Alexa's eyes. She ignored it and continued to grip the man's forearm with both hands. Gasping, her arms started to shake. Then, the knife pulled back. The man straightened. Alexa heard voices shouting.

"Back off and raise your hands."

"Leave her alone. We won't hesitate to shoot."

The man rolled off Alexa's legs. She scrambled onto her hands and knees, then leapt to her feet and staggered away, wheezing. She ducked at a succession of sharp bangs until she identified the sounds as the slamming of car doors.

Her assailant jumped to his feet and fled toward the darkened courtyard. A group of uniformed people with weapons swept by, hot on his heels.

"He has a gun back there," she croaked and ran toward the vehicles. The SUVs had been left running, their headlights illuminating the World War II complex. Alexa opened one of the SUV doors and took cover behind it. Across the open field, toward the World War I trenches, she heard the crackle of gunfire. Venturing out from behind the door's protection, she could see another group vehicles, their lights trained on the fortifications. The high-wattage lights cut right through the mist and illuminated a line of men in white walking with their hands in the air. Several armed soldiers shepherded them toward the vehicles.

A single shot rang out near the barracks in front of Alexa, and she darted back behind the door. As she stood in suspense, waiting to find out what had happened, cold hit Alexa like a block of ice. She hugged her body to stop a sudden bout of shivering.

A few seconds later, four people in uniform returned. One of them walked behind Alexa's attacker, holding a gun at the ready. The man in white had his arms cuffed behind his back and walked with a limp. He kept his head down, never glancing at Alexa, as one man steered him toward the other SUV. Two of her rescuers drove the prisoner away as one of them, a woman, approached Alexa. The fourth stood a few yards away, speaking on a walkie-talkie.

"We've got an ambulance on the way. Are you hurt?" The woman looked at Alexa with concern.

"Just c-c-cold. My coat is somewhere over there, by the barracks. My phone too. I dropped that mid-call."

The woman opened the back of the SUV and took out a blanket that she wrapped around Alexa's shoulders. "The medics will have a space blanket to warm you up. We'll look for your coat in a few minutes. Why don't you sit?" The woman nodded toward the back seat.

Alexa perched on the edge of the seat, her legs still outside the car. Her shivers were subsiding, but she pulled the blanket tighter.

The man with the walkie-talkie joined the woman and said, "It's over. There were seven of these guys out there, all heavily armed. Looks like they were going to attack this charity event. The one we took down must have been scouting the perimeter. The captain's sent a team to go over every inch of the trail. The tracks in the snow indicate they came over the fence from that storage rental place at the far end." He ended with a questioning nod toward Alexa.

The woman shook her head.

When they walked over to Alexa, the woman spoke. "I'm Officer Guerin. This is Sergeant Sternberg. Are you the one that called this in?"

"Yes. I can't thank you enough. I fought him off for a while, but he overpowered me." Alexa's voice caught as she continued. "Another few seconds and it would have been too late. He was going to stab me."

"What's your name? Did he grab you from the parking lot?"

Alexa explained what had happened, starting with the glimpse of a figure in white across the field to those final frightening seconds that could have been her last. Just as she finished, an ambulance drove into the lot, sirens screaming.

As the two guards walked Alexa over to the EMTs, the sergeant said, "I believe you prevented a tragedy here tonight. What you did is remarkable. But, why didn't you call us before you went out there on your own?"

Alexa slowed her pace. "I thought they might be security, your team. Things have been jumpy enough around here regarding refugees. Guests were entering out front at the time. My mother—the event organizer—would have killed me if I'd triggered a false alarm that drove all those guests away. She's been planning this night for months."

Just as they reached the ambulance, Reese came dashing out of the back door of the Heritage Center.

"Alexa. What's wrong? Are you hurt?" He grabbed her face between his hands.

He looked at the EMTs. "Are you treating her? Was there an accident?"

"I'm OK. There was a situation with some intruders. One of them grabbed me, but security here came to the rescue. I'll tell you more about it in a few minutes. The medics want to check me out."

The two EMTs took over, wrapping Alexa in a shiny space blanket and examining her for concussion or other wounds. Reese hovered over them until they'd finished the examination. Then, he drifted over to the two in uniform. Alexa assumed he was grilling them to get a more complete picture of what had happened.

The brunette with kind eyes removed her gloves and said, "You seem fine. No signs of concussion."

Her partner, a gangly young guy who looked just out of college, added, "You were headed toward hypothermia, but we raised your body heat just in time."

"Climb in. We'll take you to the ER to be checked out more thoroughly. For sure, you're going to discover some bruises tomorrow. You might be pretty stiff."

Alexa looked at Reese, who caught her gaze and rushed back over. "No ER," she told the EMTs. Then, to Reese, "How much of this ball have I missed?"

"Are you sure about this? I think everyone would understand if you punted and we just went home?" Reese said, holding her close.

"It's the social event of the season." Alexa was surprised she could still manage tongue-in-cheek after the evening's madness.

With a bemused smile Reese gave in. He kissed her forehead. "They had just begun to serve the salad when I left. The speechifying hadn't even started."

"OK then." Alexa looked at the EMTs. "Just one question. Are my hair and makeup totally ruined?"

The brunette patted her shoulder. "I'd do a little repair work if I was you." She looked at her partner. "I think the patient is refusing further treatment. Let's roll. When I get home, I'm going to tell Jillie that tonight Mommy treated Cinderella on her way to the ball."

Alexa said to Reese, "I have to get my dress and shoes out of the Rover. And that bag with my makeup."

"Shoes? You found them?"

"They were at Courage."

Seeing Alexa on her feet again, the officers approached. Officer Guerin held Alexa's fur coat in her hand. "Looks fine. Maybe a little damp."

"We found the phone too." Sternberg passed it to Alexa. "Might be frozen from sitting in the snow. Give it until tomorrow; sometimes they work after they thaw and dry out."

"Like me. I'm warm now." Alexa smiled. "Thank you. I forgot to tell you one important item: Contact Special Agent Carter. He's with the FBI in the Harrisburg office. He's been investigating a white supremacist group called Blizzardwaffen in relation to several mid-state crimes. I can't say for sure, but these guys tonight, they could be part of that group."

Reese advised, "Don't underestimate them. If the men you arrested are part of Blizzardwaffen, they may have been involved in those three so-called terrorist murders."

"Thanks for the heads up. We'll follow up when we return to headquarters. Someone is going to want to interview you about this in the morning."

Alexa clasped each guard's hand. "You saved my life tonight. Thank you so much. Words can't express my gratitude."

Reese scowled as they headed toward the Land Rover. "This was a bigger deal than you're telling me, right?"

Alexa wrapped her arms around him in a swift, hard hug. "It was. But let's have a good time with what's left of the evening. I'll tell you everything tomorrow. OK?"

"Everything," Reese insisted. "On our way home, not tomorrow."

# CHAPTER THIRTY-NINE

REESE GUIDED ALEXA to their table just as the senator from Connecticut finished speaking. When her mother threw a questioning look their way, Alexa mouthed "sorry" and raised her hands in a gesture of penitence. Susan nodded in acknowledgement before she turned back to her mistress of ceremonies duties, thanking the senator and segueing into the introduction of Tyrell, the next speaker.

"You missed the salad," Melissa whispered when they sat down. "Flag the waiter for a drink. Where have you been?"

"Tell you later," Alexa promised and grabbed a roll from the basket in front of her place setting. She was nauseated and starving at the same time.

Tyrell managed to make his remarks appreciative, charming, and, best of all, brief. As he was speaking, Alexa looked around the packed ballroom. Her parents sat up front with the commanding officer of the War College, Major General Roger Perez, and his wife, Anna, an honorary co-chair. The Al-Badris and the Finleys rounded out that table. She spotted Graham and Kate across the room with Melinda and the rest of the law firm group. When she saw that the three adult Qassims were seated at one of the RESIST tables, Alexa's eyes grew moist.

As the crowd gave Tyrell a standing ovation, Alexa leaned toward Reese. "Look. Eshan, Zahraa, and Nabil Qassim are here. What courage to come out tonight—after all the terrible publicity over Bassam's arrest."

Everyone took their seats, and the waitstaff flitted through the room, serving dinner. Alexa felt like she was viewing everything through a haze. The bright ballroom made her slightly queasy. The twinkling crystals reminded her of the struggle for her life in the glittering snow. She could have died.

Alexa couldn't stop looking at Reese. She'd nearly lost him. Well, he'd nearly lost her. Same thing. The life together that she'd been longing for, cut short. Alexa was so grateful to the men and women who'd rescued her.

"What are we having?" Blair peered at a nearby table that had already been served.

"Seriously, honey?" Haley shook her head. "Chicken. It's always chicken at these events."

"I hear the food is good," Jim offered. "One of the other park rangers was here for a wedding a few months back." He grinned. "Said the chicken was outstanding."

Alexa tried to focus. She looked across the table at Sloane, then turned to include Melissa. "You two did a spectacular job with the decorating. This place looks like a winter fairyland." She waved her hand toward the ceiling. "The crystals are just beautiful. When I lugged that sample case all over town then out to your house, Sloane, I didn't quite get this vision that Melissa talked about. But, wow." Alexa had to look away because the crystals still made her woozy.

Melissa interrupted, "And I told you about the giant gift boxes that Sloane hustled from a set designer friend. Sweet, right?"

"They are. Did your friend make them just for tonight?" Alexa asked Sloane. The collection of silvery boxes stood in each corner of the room and in front of the podium. They ranged from two-to-four feet high and one-to-three feet square. Each was topped with a huge, crystal-encrusted bow. More crystals, more snow.

"No. He's a friend of the family. Designs sets for Broadway and regional theatre. I'd seen these in a production he worked on, an over-the-top revival of *Holiday Inn*. Remember the old movie with Bing Crosby?"

Everyone at the table nodded.

"The revival never made it to Broadway, but Nils had squirreled away these boxes. When I asked to borrow them, he said, "Of course, darling, my creations will knock them dead. Broadway comes to Carlisle."

Melissa leaned forward. "The boxes almost didn't make it in time. The delivery truck got caught in traffic on I-90." She turned to Sloane. "I'm grateful that your volunteers from Courage were able to set them up at the last minute."

"Seriously, last minute," Sloane said. "The band was warming up when they arrived."

Everybody laughed except the man seated next to Sloane. He shifted in his seat as if uncomfortable with the story. When he tugged at his shirt collar, Alexa decided that maybe he was just uncomfortable in a tux.

She was trying to place the guy when Sloane said, "I'm sorry, Alexa. I didn't introduce you to Boone. You two may have met at Courage already?"

"That's why you look familiar." Alexa smiled. "You're in one of the super-advanced classes, right? Way out of my league."

"It just takes practice. And more practice," the man replied in a deep Southern drawl.

Alexa bit her tongue, thinking that even if she practiced for years, she wouldn't have been able to fight off the man in white who had just attacked her. She wondered if she'd been right about some of these white supremacists taking classes from Courage. That night at Sloane's house, that monster pickup truck. Could its driver have been the one that harassed her and possibly the Qassims?

Reese took Alexa's hand and gave her a questioning look.

"I'm OK," she mouthed but continued to clutch his hand.

As if Melissa could read her thoughts, she asked in a demanding voice, "So, why were you late? It better be good." Her best friend looked like a sophisticated gypsy in a multi-colored velvet gown. Typical Melissa.

Not about to alarm her friends about the attack that had been averted, Alexa shot Reese a glance. "A combination of work and a shoe emergency." She looked across the table. "Sloane, I left my shoes at Courage after Thursday night's class but didn't realize it until late this afternoon. KC helped me find them. Thanks."

"At Courage?" Sloane gave her a preoccupied smile. "I knew the owner would come looking for them. Great shoes."

"Part of my New York City wardrobe."

The server interrupted the conversation, offering extra dinner rolls to Melissa and Jim. When he circled to Reese and Alexa, both waved away his offer.

After he moved to the other side of the table, Reese leaned close to Alexa and murmured, "You're going to keep the armed posse outside a secret?"

"Just for tonight. Why send people into a tizzy about something that was stopped before anyone was put in danger?"

Reese kissed Alexa's ear, and for a fleeting moment, he brought his forehead to hers. "Except you. You look at little out of it. Sure you don't want to leave?"

"I'm fine," Alexa lied.

"You two are so adorable together," Haley tittered as Reese and Alexa broke apart. "Alexa, you look lovely. When you said vintage Chanel, I envisioned some sort of flapper costume with fringe and beads. But the dress is lovely. All that black lace in tiers is stunning in its simplicity."

Blair groused, "Even I know that Chanel is one of those fancy French designers. Haley always watches the movie stars walk the red carpet at these awards shows." He turned to Haley. "Not in our budget, sweetheart. Not now. Probably never."

"Not in mine either," Alexa said. "This dress was a gift."

Melissa jumped in and enthused, "Did you see Haley's beautiful dress? Perfect for tonight. She looks like a crystalline snowflake."

"You do look lovely. Can't wait to see the whole thing." Alexa smiled at Haley.

In a swirl of shimmering silver chiffon, her friend jumped up from her seat and did a pirouette next to the table. When they all applauded, Haley did a curtsey and returned to her chair.

After the servers cleared the main course, Susan Williams walked back to the podium. The dais was raised about two feet so that the entire ballroom could see the speakers. Alexa's table was in the first row, to the left of the dignitaries' table. On the other side, the RESIST tables filled out the remainder of the front row.

Susan tapped the microphone until the room quieted. "Over dessert, we'll turn to the last few items on our scheduled program. That should leave plenty of time for dancing or putting in your final bid on the silent auction items."

When the polite laughter ended, Susan said, "This wonderful evening did not come together on its own. A crew of dedicated people volunteered countless hours of their time to make it a success. I'd like to thank all of them." She launched into a detailed list of committee members and their functions, finally wrapping up with a word of appreciation to the commanding officer of the Army War College.

"And I would be remiss if I didn't acknowledge the fine work that Tyrell Jenkins, executive director of RESIST, has done in expanding their organization's services to sponsor refugees. If not for RESIST, the Carlisle area would not have the opportunity to provide a safe haven for refugees who are fleeing war, oppression, and other hardships. Nor would our community be enriched by the diversity and depth of experience these refugees bring with them.

"Now, let me welcome Deidre Townes, whose late aunt, Cecily Townes, was the founder of RESIST. Cecily made the wise decision to headquarter RESIST here in Carlisle and kept it here even as it grew into a renowned international organization. Deidre, who is interning at RESIST, will introduce our next speaker."

Deidre made her way to the mic, guiding a man wearing a white shirt and charcoal pants. When he hesitated at the top of the steps, she spoke a few words into his ear and directed him to a place by the podium.

As the young woman began her introduction of Samuel Motombo, a refugee from the Democratic Republic of the Congo, Alexa leaned back in her seat. The fuzzy feeling she'd had was gone. But, the fight with the man in white had taken more out of her than she'd admitted to Reese. Under the table, she rubbed her wrist. The tussle had aggravated the sprain from last week's encounter with Skeleton Man.

Although the entire room seemed engrossed, Alexa tuned out the refugee's nervous speech. She closed her eyes for a moment and took a deep breath to regroup. When she looked up, Alexa noticed that the seat next to Sloane was empty. The ghost of a smile flitted across her face; Boone must have decided to skip the speech too. Probably for a bathroom or smoke break.

The scrape of a chair across the room caught Alexa's attention. She looked toward the sound and saw Boone exit through the rear ballroom door—the one that led to the back parking lot. She assumed that he'd figure out it was the wrong exit soon enough.

Sloane hadn't noticed her date's mistake. She was typing into her cell phone with an intense look on her face. Her lips were pursed, pale blue eyes almost silver with concentration. Or maybe it was just the light.

The crowd broke into applause, signaling that Samuel Motombo had finished his remarks. Alexa scanned the room for Boone. Maybe he'd found another way to the men's room. Or maybe he really had been jonesing for a cigarette and couldn't wait till the program ended. Either way, not her problem.

Wondering whether this guy was just a plus-one for the ball or whether he and Sloane had a romantic relationship, Alexa studied her friend across the table. Everyone thought, as a grieving widow, Sloane wasn't ready for romance. But maybe they had it wrong. Maybe Sloane had been involved with this guy along. Either way, she wasn't too concerned with her missing date. Sloane was still fiddling with her cell phone.

"We are going to end our formal program tonight with something very special. The focus of the Winter Ball has been supporting RESIST's refugee resettlement efforts. But the event has also demonstrated the close working relationship between the US Army War College and the Carlisle area community. So, when one of the War College's current International Fellows came to me with a proposal for this evening's program, it seemed a wonderful way to demonstrate that partnership."

Only half-listening to her mother, Alexa's thoughts continued to drift, her gaze still on Sloane. Then, it hit her out of the blue. The quote in Sloane's office about the nation's crimes only being purged with blood. That was from John Brown, the abolitionist. The night she and Sloane had the heart-to-heart talk at the Om Café, Sloane had mentioned Brown as someone she'd admired. She'd said he had the vision to make real change. Still, a strange quote to frame on your wall.

As Alexa heard her mother's tone change, she knew that Susan about to introduce the next speaker. She snapped out of her reverie, jarred by the sudden realization that there was something very odd about Sloane's fixation on her phone. Alexa sat up straight and glanced around the table. Everyone was focused on Susan's remarks. Melissa and Jim even had their chairs turned toward the stage so they could see the speakers. Alexa looked around the room for Boone, who still hadn't returned to his seat.

Something was off here, but Alexa couldn't put her finger on what made her so uneasy about Sloane and her mystery date. She looked back toward Sloane, who had put the phone on the table and was sitting upright and alert. Her face was pale against the jet-black shantung silk of her mandarin collar. Her unusual dress, which had the look of a caftan, rippled in a dark, flowing cascade over her rigid body.

Susan said in a warm voice, "General Salim Al-Badri of the Iraqi Central Command will provide the specifics. General Al-Badri."

# CHAPTER FORTY

WHEN HER MOTHER spoke Al-Badri's name, Sloane jerked her head up, and, with a triumphant smile, turned to look at the podium. Her posture reminded Alexa of the leopards she'd seen in Africa as they crouched in anticipation, ready to leap on their unsuspecting prey.

General Al-Badri thanked Susan, the War College, and offered effusive praise to RESIST and the Carlisle community before he explained his main purpose. "During the gravest days of what you here in America call the Iraq War, my country relied heavily on our brothers and sisters in the United States Armed Forces. We will be eternally grateful for the assistance you gave us in restoring Iraq to the fine democracy it is today. Tonight, I want to express my personal gratitude to a particular officer in the United States Army, your own Colonel Dean Finley."

Alexa jumped as the general leaned too close to the microphone, filling the room with a manic screech. Al-Badri moved his head back, tapped the mic, and then plowed ahead. "Without the intervention and bravery of Colonel Finley's company, neither I nor several other members of the Iraqi high command would be alive today. Although many of the details are classified, our group came under fire in a targeted attack led by Kaamil El Sayed, a young Al-Qaeda leader, who was lionized by his followers. They called him *Al-Shaer*, the Poet, for his eloquence.

"There came a point in the surprise attack when Kaamil El Sayed and his fighters had us pinned down. We had lost many men already, both Iraqis and Americans. That's when several units under the leadership of Colonel Dean Finley intervened. They pushed back the assault, eliminating most of the Al-Qaeda attackers. The rest retreated in the confusion of battle. Kaamil El Sayed was one of those killed. Neutralizing this pivotal Al-Qaeda leader was a blow to the terrorists, which went far beyond the loss of an individual fighter."

The general was a compelling speaker—even though his glowing remarks about the current state of his country seemed a tad optimistic. When he launched into the combat story, which she'd heard before, Alexa stole another look at Sloane, who seemed riveted by Al-Badri's remarks.

When Al-Badri got to the part about the Al-Qaeda deaths, Alexa was shocked to see a tear slide down Sloane's cheek. Had her husband been one of the American casualties in this battle? Or perhaps the very thought of a battle in Iraq dredged up painful memories of his death. Either way, the tightly coiled leopard had disappeared as Sloane slumped in her chair.

Al-Badri continued. "The Iraqi government has tasked me with a very special honor tonight. Colonel Finley and General Perez, could you both come forward?"

The beaming commandant of the War College ushered a reluctant-looking Dean Finley up to the podium. Then the general announced with a flourish, "On behalf of the Iraqi government, I am pleased to recognize the brave officer who demonstrated exemplary leadership in his command of the company who saved us that day. And who performed a service to the Iraqi people in eliminating Kaamil El Sayed, a terrorist scourge upon our land.

"We are awarding Colonel Dean Finley with the newly created Friends of Iraq Medal, for both his heroic action in combat and his years of friendship to our nation through his multiple tours of duty in Iraq during the perilous transition of our country's government."

The colonel gave a quick glance to his commanding officer, who nodded and clapped him on the back.

Al-Badri placed a case on the podium and opened it.

Focused on the drama playing out among the men, Alexa was shocked to see Sloane push back her chair and race toward the stage. She slowed to take a glance toward the back of the room, then bounded up the stairs toward the three military men. In her hand, Sloane clutched her cell phone, her thumb on the screen.

A murmur of confusion swept across the room as the audience tried to figure out what was happening. Susan started to rise from her chair, but Norris pulled her back down.

Reese leaned toward Alexa. "What's going on here? She looks furious. Like some avenging djinn from *1001 Arabian Nights*."

Alexa shook her head, glued to the scene unfolding on the stage. The three men stopped short when Sloane dashed up to the podium. The general and the commandant both had puzzled but indulgent looks on their faces. Dean Finley was staring at the phone in Sloane's hand with an expression of horror.

Sloane screamed at the trio, "What animals. How can you celebrate the deaths of untold numbers of people by giving the chief executioner a medal? How can you dishonor my husband and his soldiers? Did their deaths come so cheap that they can be justified with a tawdry piece of metal and a dollar's worth of red and black ribbon?" Cheeks wet with tears, Sloane snatched the medal from its case and held it high.

The three men exchanged glances. The commandant edged toward Sloane as if he planned to physically subdue her. Two men in army uniforms, pistols drawn, ran into each side of the room, but Major General Perez motioned for them to stop. They halted at either edge of the stage, guns still drawn.

Sloane thrust her cell phone into the air and screamed at the commandant. "Back off or I will press this button now. I am prepared to die here. Are you?" She looked out into the room at the sound of scraping chairs. "Sit. I want all of you to hear this. Or I will press the button."

Alexa turned cold at Sloane's words. Could this tormented woman really be a suicide bomber? She reached for Reese's hand under the table as she wondered how big an area would be destroyed by whatever bomb the woman had strapped beneath her loose caftan. Their table and her parents' table were no more than fifteen feet back from the stage. At least Graham and Kate were in the back of the room with the law firm.

"Easy now, Ms. Chapin," Dean Finley spoke in a calming voice. "Clearly, you have something important to say about your husband's death. No need to press any buttons. I'm listening. Everyone here is listening."

"You should be listening," Sloane sneered. "America has killed thousands of people around the world with its so-called military interventions. Innocent civilians. Fathers, mothers, children, just trying to live their lives. And when the people who America attacks fight back to preserve their way of life, their very survival, they're branded terrorists. My husband was a kind, gentle man. A man of faith. A professor of literature who thought the words of the poets could solve the world's problems.

"Until America invaded Iraq and threw the region into turmoil. Then, he knew he had to fight. We had just been married, in secret, because my father thought I was too young to make such a commitment. And, even after all his years in the Middle East, he was reluctant to have me marry a foreigner, an Egyptian.

"Despite our bliss as newlyweds," a wistful smile flashed across Sloane's face as she paused, "my new husband had no choice but to heed the call of Islam, to join his brothers in arms. And so, my poet husband committed himself to jihad and became the man you killed, Colonel Finley. Kaamil El Sayed. And now, this fat Iraqi pig who you saved from my husband's sword wants to give you a medal for it."

Alexa's pulse raced higher with each new word Sloane spoke. She tried to ignore the cries of fear and muffled sobs that reverberated through the room. She could see Reese and Jim drawing diagrams on the tablecloth as if they were planning to storm the stage. The thought of Reese rushing toward a bomb that rested in the hands of an unstable woman terrified her.

"You know, it's sheer luck that I have the two of you here together. My original plan was to strike at the War College. Then I met the two of you, and my heart leapt with joy. Now I could carry out my husband's mission on the two men most responsible for his death. Allah is kind."

She turned to the commandant, her words dripping with disdain. "And to punish the Army War College that trains Americans to march out and destroy other nations in the name of democracy and freedom? That's an additional blessing. John Brown said it best: 'I am quite certain that the crimes of this guilty nation shall never be purged away but with blood.'"

Sloane brought her hand with the cell phone closer to her body and seemed poised to hit Send. She shouted, "An eye for an eye. Allahu Akbar."

Women screamed. People scrambled toward the exits in terror.

Sloane yelled at the crowd, "Stop! There is no escape. These beautiful white crystal boxes are filled with explosives. And outside each exit there is a man with a gun. They are with me in waging jihad and cannot wait to enter Paradise." With fury in her eyes, she held the cell phone aloft as a warning.

The runners stopped short. Others abandoned the doors. Those who had tried to flee returned to their seats. Several women slid to the floor where they stood.

During those few moments of pandemonium, Alexa put most of the pieces together. She could see from the look on Reese's face that he had too. And it wasn't good. But Sloane and Alexa had established a fragile connection. Perhaps she could get through.

She whispered to Reese, "Run. When you can. Get everyone out."

He looked at her with a stricken expression.

Alexa shot to her feet. "Sloane, you're wrong. All those men you're expecting were arrested hours ago. Security discovered them out in the trail area and hauled them away. And Security put extra people on the back door. I noticed Boone never came back. If his role was to open the doors to let the others in the building, he was probably arrested the minute he stepped outside." She softened her tone. "Sloane, please don't do this. You've made your point. You've honored your husband. But don't kill all these people." Behind her, Alexa could hear rustling as people took a chance and headed toward the doors.

On the stage, the three military men were fanning out, looking for an opening to rush Sloane.

Sloane warned the three men off with a shake of the cell phone then took a few steps toward Alexa with a sigh. "Thank you for your friendship, Alexa. I'm sorry that you're here tonight. I always knew that my recruits were unreliable, even with their past military experience. Several of them showed a lack of discipline in Krav Maga. I had to discharge three of them who waivered on their commitment to our jihad.

"That's why I decided to be the one to detonate the explosives." Sloane looked out at the people who were escaping. "Looks like I should take care of that now."

Just as Sloane turned back toward the podium, Nabil Qassim walked to the edge of the stage. He was dressed in a flowing robe and a skullcap. "My child," he addressed Sloane. "I am an imam. May I give you a blessing before you send us to Paradise? I have been ready for many long years to enter Jannah. I would like to read you a passage from the Koran before we face the angel of death." He reached into his pocket and withdrew a small book.

"Yes, Imam. I would be grateful," Sloane replied in a small, surprised voice.

As Nabil mounted the steps to the stage, Reese and Jim guided Melissa, Haley, and Blair from the room. Reese came back for Susan and Norris Williams and the others at their table. Jill Finley looked at her husband on the stage and brought her fingers to her mouth in a kiss. He jerked his head toward the door, urging her to leave.

The commandant's wife and Noora Al-Badri both balked at leaving, but Jim and Reese pushed them toward the door. Across the room, Tyrell and Maria were ushering Deidre and the refugees from the room. As Eshan and Zahraa hurried out, Eshan cast a last look over his shoulder at his brother, who had reached Sloane. Pistols held high, the two soldiers edged closer to the center of the stage, as if weighing their opportunity to take Sloane out with a bullet.

Believing she could do nothing more to stop Sloane, Alexa started backing away from the table. When she saw Reese return to the room, she hastened toward the man she loved, knowing that Sloane could hit that button at any moment.

Behind her, Nabil began reciting something in Arabic in a singsong voice. Both Sloane and General Al-Badri joined in, as if reciting a prayer. Then Nabil said in English, "Child, you have suffered with the death of your husband. But an eye for an eye is not the only path. The Prophet always chose forgiveness, even for grievous wrongs. The Koran says 'Let them forgive and overlook: do you not wish that God should forgive you? For God is Oft-Forgiving, Most Merciful.'"

Sloane burst into tears. "But I can't. I owe Kaamil retribution." Even as she protested, her shoulders slumped, and she sank toward the floor. As Sloane's grip on the cell phone loosened, Nabil snatched it from her hand and slipped it to Dean Finley. The soldiers rushed forward and covered Sloane with their guns. Other uniformed men streamed in the door and hustled Finley, Al-Badri, Perez, and Nabil from the stage. Another man holding a dog on a leash strode into the room and onto the stage.

At the ballroom door, Alexa wobbled, legs trembling from a delayed reaction to the danger. She looked back as Reese reached out to steady her.

Alexa's last image of Sloane was of a woman destroyed, her elegant features wracked with grief as she lay collapsed on the floor in an inky pool of black silk. Cast aside in the confusion, the gold medal glinted at her feet. On full alert, a German shepherd sat by her side, signaling to his handler that Sloane was wearing a bomb.

# EPILOGUE

"I BROUGHT THE drone along in case you want to fly it again after lunch," Tyrell announced.

"No way." Reese groaned. "After what happened last time?"

"I know how it works now, man. And what are the odds of finding another body?"

Alexa carried the quiche Lorraine from the counter to the table. "You're seriously asking that? With my track record?"

Tyrell conceded. "You're right. Why tempt fate?"

Reese asked him, "When do you leave for India?"

"Thursday. I'll be there for a month, visiting all the RESIST operations. I decided to do the Africa and Thailand sites this summer. I had to get approval from the FBI to leave the country. I'm not sure why. They've interviewed me seems like a hundred times. And I hear none of this might even come to trial. They expect Sloane to plead guilty. The rest of her crew might plead out too."

"What about her buddy, Boone?" Alexa asked.

"Didn't you hear? He was AWOL from the Marines. He's already been returned to them for court-martial."

Alexa grimaced. "Sloane preyed on all those vulnerable vets. Agent Carter told me that she swept these guys up from homeless shelters; posed as a war widow who wanted to help them get back on their feet. She put them up in a dorm on that big farm she had. After they'd recuperated from life on the streets, most of them got warehouse jobs. From day one, she started to indoctrinate them. Most of them were already nursing grudges against the military."

Reese snorted, "Or dealing with PTSD or were effed-up to begin with."

"My Krav Maga teachers, KC and Lev, knew that Sloane was spending time in Philadelphia and Washington, helping out at homeless shelters. They admired the work she was doing. They even knew about the dorm at the farm. But they just thought Sloane was passionate about helping veterans. KC even told me that she worried about Sloane and had warned her to be careful with these guys. Some of them were volatile."

"At least three of them developed a conscience and tried to get out. Like that poor brother we found dead last October. Damn, that seems so long ago."

"I keep asking myself." With a contemplative look in her eye, Alexa let her fork dangle in midair. "Why didn't I realize that Sloane was someone who'd slipped off the rails? I liked her. Yes, she seemed troubled. Maybe a little intense. But a terrorist?"

"Hell, we're all asking ourselves that same question," Tyrell huffed. "I knew that girl had some unresolved issues. But not the kind that she'd deal with by blowing up hundreds of innocent people."

Reese chopped his hands into a T. "Timeout here, you two. I only met the woman a couple of times. But it's not like Sloane stormed around town slinging an AK-47 over her shoulder and waving an Al-Qaeda flag. That woman-of-mystery vibe she had going was great camouflage; how could anyone have known what she was hiding? She played on everyone's sympathies with the war widow story."

Tyrell snorted. "Yeah. She conveniently forgot to mention that the husband played quarterback for Al-Qaeda. We all thought he was Team USA."

Reese continued, "Plus, keep in mind—Sloane's act was so convincing, partly because she didn't think of herself as a terrorist. You heard her; she believed that she was a hero."

Alexa nodded her head. "You're right. She idolized John Brown. She's on the same side as Henry David Thoreau and others who credited him as a great man—one whose actions and martyrdom precipitated the Civil War to free the slaves. I think she fancied herself a modern-day abolitionist whose cause was to end Western oppression of Iraqis and others in the Middle East."

Tyrell turned social worker. "Sloane is no more hero than some of those screwed-up kids I dealt with in juvie. Her mother died when she was young. She idolized her father, but he was absent much of the time. Raised by staff. Meets this romantic firebrand in college. And it was all downhill from there."

"Maybe. But, this woman had determination, skill, and a mighty powerful hatred driving her," Reese countered. "No doubt about the screwed-up part."

"She never actually pressed that button," Alexa reminded them. The part of her that had been drawn to Sloane still had trouble accepting that her new friend had almost succeeded at mass murder. One that would have killed Alexa and everyone she loved.

Reese pushed his empty plate away. "When you announced there were no guns waiting in the halls—that's when Sloane lost it. She was so engrossed with you, and then Nabil, I don't think she noticed everyone racing for the exits."

"Didn't notice or just gave up? We'll probably never know."

Scout stirred from his place on the floor and sat up at the sound of plates clanking. "No, buddy. You're not getting any quiche."

"But it has bacon," Reese spoke for the mastiff.

"Nope." Alexa stood firm as she rose to clear the dishes.

Reese scratched the dog's huge head and whispered, "I tried, big guy. I tried."

Tyrell asked, "Can I help wash dishes or something?"

"I have this covered. Do you want another cup of coffee?"

Reese and Tyrell sat at the counter, sipping coffee and watching Alexa put plates in the dishwasher.

"You mentioned Nabil. I have to own my bad on that guy." Tyrell scowled. "I had him pegged as some rabble-rouser, secret ISIS sympathizer. My God, Alexa. You and I even thought he might have planted that gun on his own nephew. Instead, he's a religious guy and one fearless dude. The way he walked up on stage then whisked that phone out of Sloane's hand. That's Superman stuff."

"You're right. What a shocker. We all thought he was sketchy. Clearly, we were wrong." Alexa closed the dishwasher and joined them at the counter with a cup of tea.

"Eshan told me that, in Syria, Nabil was an imam who devoted his life to studying the Koran. When the conflict hit their city, he started helping at Médecins san Frontières with his brother. Nabil fled the country and hoped to come to America. But he knew that writing 'imam' on a refugee application would probably kill his chances. So, he said his occupation was hospital orderly.

"I guess that's why he acted standoffish. Conservative rules about women. A religious thing. It's a tough lesson on not being so quick to stereotype people. A wakeup call to find that I'm guilty of what I'm quick to call others out on," Alexa mused. She felt terrible that she'd misjudged Nabil. She still didn't like the guy but owed him such a debt of gratitude. With his selfless bravery, he'd saved their lives.

"An unexpected benefit of Sloane's attempted bombing—there's been a real outpouring of sympathy for the refugees. Especially the Qassims, after their ordeal with Bassam and all the other harassment. Ali has had no more problems in school. Zahraa says he's made new friends and is doing well."

"And the older boy?" Reese asked.

Tyrell smiled. "The wheels of justice grind exceedingly slow, isn't that what they say? But Bassam was released from the placement on Wednesday. His juvenile record's been expunged."

"Duh," Alexa scoffed. "The kid didn't do anything. He didn't kill anyone. He wasn't a terrorist recruit. One of Sloane's minions planted that gun when he was taking Taekwondo."

Tyrell frowned. "I thought she was being kind when she offered Bassam free lessons. Now I wonder if she planned to frame the kid right from the start."

Reese shook his head. "That's cold. Frame a refugee kid for murder to divert suspicion. Of course, this is the same woman who almost killed a ballroom full of innocent people."

Alexa took a sip of tea, then replied in a pensive tone, "I think planting the gun on Bassam was a spur of the moment, Hail Mary play—a shiny object that would occupy everyone's attention. That third guy that they killed, the one who taught at Courage and got a DUI. Agent Carter thinks Sloane was worried that he had revealed something to the police while in custody."

Reese walked around the counter to refill his coffee cup. "You guys were wrong about Nabil. I struck out on my pet theory about the militia. They had nothing to do with Sloane's Looney Tunes scheme."

"Maybe not, but Skeleton Man and the group that stopped me on that back road—the Blizzardwaffen—they were behind the pumpkin blitzkrieg on the Qassim house too. And their members harassed me twice in their pickup trucks. So, you weren't completely wrong."

"Damn, what a fucked-up world we live in." Tyrell shook his head in disgust. "We have one group of people playing Al-Qaeda, trying to blow up anyone who harms Muslims. We have another group who idolizes the Nazis, threatening anyone who helps Muslims. And over in the Middle East, one type of Muslims is fighting another type of Muslims. Meanwhile, the military's invading and blowing shit up over oil or whatever the fuck suits our current national interest."

Alexa said, "Maybe all we can do is try to straighten out one little piece of the chaos at a time. That's what you're doing with the RESIST sex-trafficking and refugee projects. That's what Reese is doing with saving big cats in Africa. That's what I'll be doing when I testify against Skeleton Man at his trial." Alexa giggled. "Did I tell you that his real name is Chester Fields?"

Tyrell grinned. "His mama must have been a heavy smoker."

"People call him Chess, but that's a lot less scary than Skeleton Man."

Reese put his hand over Alexa's, and she cradled it in her own. Alexa realized that he knew she was using humor to put that terrifying night behind her. They'd both had trouble sleeping these past few weeks.

Looking at his watch, Tyrell said, "Thanks for brunch, but I have to book. I have to finish packing this afternoon. My mama is insisting I spend the entire day with her tomorrow."

Alexa hugged Tyrell. "Safe journeys."

Reese shook his hand. "I'm jealous. Temperatures in India will be in the eighties all month, right? Scout, let's walk Tyrell to his car."

Later that evening, Reese and Alexa sat together on the big leather couch; the woodstove was roaring to ward off the single-digit temperatures outside. Scout draped his huge body over their feet.

Alexa had felt unsettled ever since Tyrell's visit but couldn't put her finger on the cause. "I'm going to miss Tyrell. Yoga nights are going to be a little lonely. No Tyrell." She grimaced. "No Sloane. And it's possible that Blair may never let Haley leave the house for the rest of her life. He was even more freaked out by the bomb incident than she was. And he really went bonkers when he found out that Haley was the one who brought Sloane into our circle of friends and told her about the medal award ceremony at the ball."

"Your parents will be heading back to Umbria soon too," Reese said. "I know that your father would be happy to go now, even though it's still cold over there. He told me that your mom feels responsible for the Winter Ball turning into a disaster and wants to stay until Noora Al-Badri has settled down a bit. The woman's lived in a country that's been at war for decades. It's kind of hard to believe that she's so traumatized by what happened at the ball."

"Well, her husband was one of Sloane's main targets. And maybe she's lived a protected-enough life that she never experienced direct danger before that night."

"Maybe. But look at Jill Finley. I doubt that she's ever been in the line of fire, and she came through it just fine."

"Maybe I'll talk to Mom and tell her that Dad needs to get back to Umbria. That might get her to leave sooner. But I'll miss them both."

"How about we take a trip to visit them in the spring? I've never been to Italy. Staying in an Italian villa sounds like a marvelous experience." Reese flung his hand out in a dramatic gesture. "Unless I have to wear my tux."

Alexa gave him a soft punch on the arm. "No tuxes. You know it's more like a farmhouse, right? Still, it's very charming." Her mood brightened to hear Reese making plans for the future. For their future.

He turned to face Alexa and spoke in a hesitant voice, "I've been thinking. I've been staying here almost full time. And the big cat project is moving into a new phase. Now that the report's all but done, the Trust wants me to head up implementation of the conservation project. That includes bringing a lot of conservation agencies together, which will be a combination of phone meetings and traveling around the country. I don't need to be based near Washington."

"Why don't you move in here?" Alexa cried.

Reese grinned. "You didn't let me finish." He paused. "I was wondering if I could move in here."

"Yes. That would be wonderful." Alexa kissed Reese. "We're still taking this one step at a time, right? This is a pretty big step."

"But it feels right, doesn't it?"

"Anytime we're together, it feels right." Alexa's smile faltered. "But Africa is always looming out there. I know you might want to return some day."

"Yes, I miss Africa. And certainly, one day, I will return for a few weeks or even longer. Maybe you'll go too. But, for now, I plan to stay here—where my heart is."

"That works for me." Alexa wrapped her arms around Reese and sighed with contentment.

With a loud woof, Scout jumped up and tried to wedge his huge head between them.

"See?" Alexa laughed. "Scout agrees. Welcome home."

# AFTERWORD

*Dead of Winter* is a work of fiction, and its characters are drawn from my imagination. Any resemblance to actual people, organizations, or companies is purely coincidental. The only exceptions are public or historical figures, such as those who played a role in John Brown's raid on Harpers Ferry.

The US Army War College, its International Fellows program, and the US Army Heritage and Education Center do exist and provide an important educational service to our nation and its allies. It's also true that there is considerable interaction between these institutions and the local Carlisle community. However, the characters, events, and other aspects of this story that relate to the War College and USAHEC are entirely fictional.

John Brown's raid on Harpers Ferry did happen. Even today, its impact on the Civil War and slavery remains a controversial topic in American history. But, the houses where Brown stayed in Chambersburg, PA, and near Sharpsburg, MD, remain standing, as does the site of the raid in Harpers Ferry, WV, now preserved as part of a National Historical Park.

Some of the passages in the historical story are drawn from speeches made by John Brown and by Frederick Douglass. The famous courtroom speech by Brown is quoted verbatim.

To tell Elijah's story, I drew from a number of historical resources. Some of the most sobering were the first-person narratives from freed slaves collected by the Federal Writers Project in the 1930s.

The quotes that introduce each chapter of Elijah's story are from Negro spirituals that were sung on plantations before the Civil War. Many of them are still popular and sung more widely today.

# ACKNOWLEDGMENTS

Often, a story can spring from the most mundane of events. The germ of the idea for *Dead of Winter* came to me as I was sitting in an ophthalmologist's chair, watching an aerial video scroll over a computer screen. Dr. Drew Stoken told me that it was a drone video and talked briefly about the technology. Watching that video led me to wonder: What if the drone had filmed a dead body? And, that was the start of *Dead of Winter*.

Of course, there was much work to be done after that initial concept, and many people who helped along the way. I want to acknowledge the key people who were kind enough to assist me with *Dead of Winter*.

First, thanks to my husband, Mike, who supports my writing in so many ways. He reads my early drafts, gives me sound advice, and copes gracefully with all the hours I spend writing.

I also want to thank the Knowlton/Kuehn clan, who give me feedback on manuscripts, offer moral support, and more. This group includes my son, Josh; daughter-in-law, Laura; Steve, Pam, Dave, Nancy, and the late Todd Knowlton; and Denny and Coe Kuehn.

Cumberland County Judge Thomas Placey and Judicial Law Clerk Bryan Bartosik-Velez were invaluable in teaching me about the juvenile court system in Pennsylvania. Cumberland County Chief Juvenile Probation Officer Samuel Miller provided additional information about Juvenile Probation's role in the juvenile justice process. It's clear that these professionals are committed to helping kids in the juvenile system get their lives back on track as quickly as possible.

Thanks, as always, to Pennsylvania State Trooper Jessica Williams for her help in getting the state police lingo right. And, to my new friend, Henriette Evans, who was kind enough to translate the phrases that appear in Arabic throughout the book.

I also want to thank the Franklin County Historical Society for preserving the John Brown House in Chambersburg and keeping tales of the Underground Railroad in Southcentral Pennsylvania alive. Thanks to Christopher Ryan and his crew from ACE Drone Services in Carlisle, PA, who helped educate me about drones, including a hands-on demonstration at a Professional Photographers of Pennsylvania meeting.

I owe a big debt of gratitude to Val Muller, a fellow author and teacher, who gave me insightful feedback on *Dead of Winter* in its final stages.

I also want to thank the crew at Sunbury Press: Publisher Lawrence Knorr, who continues to support the Alexa Williams series; Jennifer Cappello, whose amazing editing helps enhance each book and brings continuity to the series; Crystal Devine, who is adept at the technical aspect of production; and Riaan Willems, who designed a compelling cover for the book. And, I can't forget my marketing team, Adrian Stouffer and Kim Lehman, who help me place each new Alexa Williams book in the public eye.

Thanks to all of these generous people who have helped me make *Dead of Winter* more accurate. If I've misinterpreted any information, the fault is purely mine.

Finally, I want to thank all my readers. Your continuing interest in the Alexa Williams series is gratifying and inspires me to keep writing. I would like to ask my readers to help spread the word about my novels by leaving a brief review of *Dead of Winter* and my other Alexa Williams books on Amazon, Goodreads, Barnes and Noble, Indie Bound, or Sunbury Press. And, of course, tell your friends. Thank you.

# ABOUT THE AUTHOR

**Sherry Knowlton**, award-winning author of the Alexa Williams suspense novels, *Dead of Autumn, Dead of Summer, Dead of Spring,* and *Dead of Winter*, developed a lifelong passion for books as a child. She was that kid who would sneak a flashlight to bed at night so she could read beneath the covers. All the local librarians knew her by name.

She spent much of her early career in state government, working primarily with social and human services programs, including services for abused children, rape crisis, domestic violence, and family planning. In the 1990s, she served as the Deputy Secretary for Medical Assistance in the Commonwealth of Pennsylvania. The latter part of Sherry's career focused on the field of Medicaid managed care. Now retired from executive positions in the health insurance industry, Sherry runs her own health care consulting business.

Sherry and her husband, Mike, began their journey together in the days of peace and music when they traversed the country in a hippie van. Running out of money several months into the trip, Sherry waitressed the night shift at a cowboy hangout in Jackson Hole, Wyoming, and Mike washed dishes in a bakery. Undeterred, they embraced the travel experience and continue to explore far-flung places around the globe.

Sherry lives in the mountains of Southcentral Pennsylvania, where the Alexa Williams suspense series is set. She has a BA in English and psychology from Dickinson College in Carlisle, PA.

www.sherryknowlton.com